Seventh Hall Chronicles

Seventh Hall

Ode to the Survivors

Bastion of the Deep

Eric Kercher

FROM THE AUTHOR

There are days when we all need an escape from a terrible job, a terrible day, or a terrible life.

Join my newsletter and get an escape from the real world, stories, and lore designed to entertain and delight.

You'll also get *Stories from the Deep*, an exclusive, unpublished anthology chock full of extra epilogues, short stories, and lore from the Patmos Sea Fantasy Adventure Series.

Join now at erickercher.com.

Enjoy the book.

-Eric Kercher

SEVENTH HALL

SURVIVING THE FIRST YEAR

ERIC KERCHER

1

JUDGEMENT

Deep in the damp, rat infested cell Dorian waited for his sentence to be carried out. He didn't know how long he had waited, but when the footsteps came, he knew it was time.

Light from the torch burned eyes used to pitch black. Rough hands dragged him to his feet, cold iron slammed around his arms and legs. It was painful, but he didn't give them the satisfaction of crying out. Dorian's eyes adjusted to the light, but it still hurt.

"It's your day Dorian," Yurgo, the jailer, said. His crooked teeth gleamed yellow. Dorian followed out of the cold cell that smelled like filth, and into the corridor to be flanked by guards. Dorian was surprised to see their golden armor. *King's men.* Without a word, they slipped into formation, their chain mail clinking and echoing in the dungeon.

"He should be clean for his audience," Yurgo said to the head guard. Dorian didn't recognize him.

"Move out." The dwarf had a commanding voice and stood a full head taller than the others. A chain across his left shoulder, golden, meant he was a dwarven commander. The escorts moved, jerking the chain that bound his feet and hands.

Dorian walked, his legs creaking from the years of neglect. Smoke from the torch filled his eyes and nose, stinging them and making his eyes water. It chased away his own stench. They left the dungeon and started up the stairs.

Within a few feet he was breathing heavily, his muscles burning from the effort, but the guards didn't slow. In step they led him from his prison beneath the city and up the winding corridors and stairs to the dungeon entrance.

The guards on duty scrambled to attention when they passed. Dorian stole a glance, they were gaping at him. He wondered what he looked like. *Doesn't matter what I look like when I die, I'll still be dead.*

They took a right, marching up the back alleys and into the main tunnel. When they got to the shaft and entered the elevator, the commander surprised Dorian.

"Up," he said. The dwarf running the elevator nodded and turned the lever. The elevator pulled them up, its old wooden frame creaking on the tight rope. He expected to go down, to the execution chambers. There was still hope.

His escorts got off at the surface, exiting the main entrance to the mines. He thought the torch was bad, but it was daylight out. Dorian had to be pulled along, covering his eyes that still burned even though they were closed. The sun penetrated his eyelids.

They went down the main street, smells and sounds he hadn't heard in years assaulting him. There were crowds here, yelling and laughing. Many were talking about him, pointing out how wretched he looked, wondering when he was to be killed. He ignored them.

Instead, he breathed in the first taste of fresh air and savored it. Even though it was mixed with the unpleasant smells of the city, it was pure delight. Pulled through the streets, he blindly followed his escort, jerked in the right direction if he strayed.

Then, they were back inside, giant doors closing shut behind him with a boom. His heart sank. When his eyes adjusted to the bright, but not burning, light, his fears were confirmed.

King Lightaxe was seated on his throne, the room empty except for a few advisers behind him. Dorian's guard pulled him forward to a respectful distance and pushed him down onto the red carpet, bowing themselves.

"The prisoner, as you commanded," the commander said, his booming voice swallowed by the size of the room. Dorian felt the soft carpet on his fingers, and his knees. He looked down. His clothes were tattered rags, brown and stained by years in his cell.

"Dismissed." The adviser to the King's right waved the men away. Two guards hauled him to his feet and unchained him. For a second he thought about running, until his wobbling and weak legs convinced him otherwise.

"Dorian Ironstrike, what have you to say for your crimes?" It was the adviser again, his slicked back hair and smug look. Dorian narrowed his eyes and stayed silent. "You will speak when you are told."

Dorian opened his mouth and coughed. He wasn't even sure he could speak after all this time.

"Speak, dwarf." The advisor's eyes were blazing, black as night but filled with fury. The King held up a hand. The adviser's eyes flashed, but he shrank back. "Since you refuse to speak you will listen.

"The King, in his great mercy and wisdom, has decided to spare your life and commute your sentence." Dorian was confused, then almost took a step back. His head swam as he recalled the last few seconds. *Did he just say...?* "However," the adviser continued, refocusing his attention, "this act depends on your...cooperation."

Dorian closed his jaw. King Lightaxe had aged, gray fleck were streaking the regal brown hair and beard. From his expression Dorian could tell this was no joke. They weren't going to whisk him away and cut off his head after this, what he rightfully deserved.

"You are to lead an expedition into the Tremble Mountains. You will delve deep and find the ore we suspect is hidden there, and you will bring it up from below." Dorian shut his mouth, he hadn't realized it was hanging open. What he cared about was buried here, deep under Zirad. What use was metal to him?

King Lightaxe was watching him, his eyes filled with all the strength he remembered. The adviser had gone silent. Dorian realized they were waiting for him to respond.

"I— " his voice cracked, "I don't have a choice, do I?" Someone gasped. King Lightaxe leaned back, all eyes on him, then he chuckled.

"No, you do not." It was the same voice that had sentenced him, the same voice that had made him a promise. One he hadn't kept. Anger flared up in Dorian, but he smothered it. There would be time, later.

"Your children will be waiting for your return. In three years, they will be released to you, if you are successful." The adviser was smiling too, a wicked smile, and Dorian's heart fluttered. How could have he forgotten them? The adviser swept his hand away, and the guards returned, shackling Dorian again. "Prepare well, you leave in one week."

He gasped, his body tensed from the shock of the water. Its icy remains dripped down his wet hair and onto his body. Dorian shivered from the cold, but the other dwarves didn't give him time to recover.

"Pick it up." A guard tossed a bar of soap on the ground, and Dorian reached down to grab it. Another pushed him, and he fell. Laughter rang out, hard and mean, but he reminded himself that there would be a day for revenge, but it wouldn't be today.

Dorian pushed back up, clutching the soap with shivering fingers, and washed himself. Layers of grime and dirt peeled off him, and they dumped him again in water and made him do it all over. After the third time the guards were about to do it again when something stopped them.

"That's enough," a voice growled from behind him. Dorian recognized it and turned. "Finish it now and begone." A guard stepped forward, something gleaming in his hand. Shears. Dorian backed away, but firm hands held him fast.

They were quick and made it painful, pulling on his beard and hair. It fell in clumps to the floor, chunks of wet, brown hair piled up until it was gone. Another guard shaved him, cutting what was left, and Dorian held still out of fear he might cut him. Finrail Goldenhammer watched until they were finished, meeting his gaze.

There was nothing but coldness in his eyes, and Dorian realized his old friend was gone, replaced by a general. When the guards finished, Finrail dismissed them. They saluted and marched off as one, snickering over their shoulders at him.

Cool air played across Dorian's chin and scalp, and he reached up to feel it. Smooth, empty. His beard gone, his head shorn. Finrail didn't speak until the door shut behind him, then he glanced around the room to make sure they were gone.

"Dorian." Finrail's voice cracked, and his cold eyes melted to sorrow and joy. Arms outstretched, he embraced him in a hug. "I'm sorry for what's happened to you."

The sudden change took him by surprise, but then his emotions poured back. He returned the hug, but then the memories made him draw back. "What's happened to me? You're sorry?" Dorian coughed, still not used to talking.

Finrail's eyes crinkled, and he frowned. "I should have been there." Dorian couldn't look at him, he was too angry. "I spoke with the King. He won't say it but he bears the burden of her death, that's why he's spared you."

"To be used as fodder in his quest for wealth and power."

"You don't know." Finrail took a deep breath. "You've been...gone too long. What you go to do is important, not just to the King. To us, to all of us here." Dorian refused to look him in the eye. Even after all these years, it was too soon.

"I wasn't sure how you'd respond. Here, take this with you." He offered an object covered in brown cloth. Dorian thought about it, but his curiosity got the better of him and he tugged at the corner.

Bright steel gleamed in the firelight of the torches, sliding down the double cutting edges and caressing the dark oak of the haft. Dorian drew back. "I can't."

"It's yours."

"I swore long ago I would never use it." Fear and anger fought inside him. "Put it away." Finrail wrapped it back up, returning it to an unassuming, plain package.

"Where you go, you may need it. At least take it, it may be of some use to you someday." When he didn't respond, Finrail set it by the trunk that was to be his possessions. "Will you say anything to me?"

"What is there to say?" Years had driven a wedge between them, time lost that could never be recovered. His life was over, their friendship was over too.

"Goodbye Dorian, may the earth lead you to peace."

Dorian nodded stiffly, and Finrail gave him one last look before he too departed through the door.

Long after Finrail left Dorian stared at the axe, thinking.

Something scurried down the tunnel, disturbing the silence. It had the smell of food and the heat of life in it. Delicious, precious life. Hunger stabbed at it, throbbed inside it, but it didn't move. Many days of its life had taught it patience.

The sounds faded farther down the tunnel, but then they changed. The animal could sense it.

It didn't move. The animal waited too. It was close, but too far to be sure of a good kill.

Eventually, the animal was satisfied and moved, sniffing and scurrying forward. But it couldn't see what was waiting in the dark until it was too late.

The animal was trapped now, gone too far down the tunnel. It moved then, following the vibrations in the dark to find its prey. It didn't bother to save it for later, it was hungry now.

Jaws bit into the warm animal. Juicy, warm, throbbing. It was delicious.

But small.

Soon the animal was empty, a devoured husk of what it once was.

And the hunger was still there.

Stabbing, throbbing, dulled.

But still there.

It moved then, deeper into its hunting ground. Things traveled in the dark maze of tunnels down here. Bigger things, more satisfying things. Things filled with life that begged to be drained.

In the dark it would hunt to satisfy its hunger, yearning for the day when juicy, fat things would come to it. Until then, it would go to them and devour them.

2

STORM OF RAGE

The afternoon sun beat down on them, the warmth overcoming the chill from the wind. Dorian looked back down the valley to see where the others were.

Lumdir Delvenwright and Barileth Steeleyes struggled to bring the cart up. It was overloaded, and the two young goats that pulled it strained against the grade of the mountain.

Dorian went back down and helped to push the wagon without a word, straining with the weight. It rattled and clanked, bumping and jostling over the rocking outcroppings and uneven terrain.

The rest followed, carrying the supplies they had to take off the cart to get it this far. Kimec and Yudoline Roundhammer carried a box with pots and pans, Yander Helmsplitter struggled with a bundle of tools, and Skover Porkbarrel brought up the rear with two bags draped over his round belly.

"Might'n we stop for a moment?" Skover said, wheezing from the exertion and covered in glistening sweat. Kimec and Yudoline didn't wait for a response, but set the box down and collapsed in the grass.

Breathing heavily, Dorian let them rest and pulled out the map. They had turned southeast after crossing the headwaters of the Zazinargzig, and the foothills of the Tremble Mountains had fought them every step of the way.

Squinting in the harsh daylight, Dorian surveyed the valley below. Sparse oaks and ash dotted the side of the mountain, huge boulders of granite poking up between the dense layers of grass and foliage below them.

The peak was still hundreds of feet up, maybe more, and the mountains would give them shelter from the harsh southern winds of winter. The sun was sinking to the horizon, with less than an hour to sunset.

"We're here," Dorian said.

"Here? As in finished?" Skover asked, perking up. Dorian nodded.

"About time," Barileth said, taking refuge in the shade of the cart. A goat nuzzled beneath him, searching for the grass to eat, and he shifted.

Dorian had to agree with him. They were told the journey would take two weeks at most. That was three and a half weeks ago, time they didn't have. He folded the map back up and put it into his pocket.

"Blasted rivers," Kimec said. "If we didn't have to go around them so far, we would have been here earlier. Dorian wasn't sure what to think of them all yet, even after three weeks with them. They were soft, though, too used to city life.

"I'll go get some water," Yudoline said, getting a bucket from the cart. She wandered off toward the brook they followed up the mountain while Kimec got up to inspect the nearest tree.

He looked up at its bare branches, small buds of green just beginning to show. Then, he walked around it and up to it to feel its bark. "It's small, but a few of these would do." The trunk was only as round as he was.

"I'll get some firewood," Yander said. "I used to do it when I was younger, I would wander out to the forest and pretend the sticks were swords." He chuckled, but his smile faded when no one else laughed. "...I'll go get them."

Lumdir was unstrapping the tent poles, and Dorian went to help him. While each of the others was performing their assigned tasks, Dorian oversaw the making of the camp.

The tents went up first, poles holding up sheets of canvass that doubled as a covering for their supplies while they were traveling. There were two, with enough room to just hold them all, and with Lumdir, Doria, and Barileth helping, they went up fast.

Skover had started a fire by the time they were done, setting a pot to boil the water Yudoline had carried. They each took some of the cold water remaining in the bucket. It washed away the dust from Dorian's throat and hit his stomach like a slug of ice.

"I found a big stash of sticks farther in the forest," Yander said. He had made a big stack of them beside the fire. "By the beard, it's beautiful up here." The clouds were colorful with the setting sun, something Dorian had missed before.

"Better if we were safely underground," muttered Lumdir. "What I'd give for a solid roof of rock over my head right now."

"Soon enough," Barileth said. "We'll dig deep and fast and be beneath the mountain before you know it." Yander was backing the cart up under the biggest tent. Dorian preferred they unload everything tonight, but he didn't say anything.

"What's it like, starting an expedition? I've heard stories before, of course, but never from anyone who has been there." Yander watched Lumdir as he unhooked the goats and tied them up to graze.

"Like any other, I suppose. I've never done it," Lumdir said. Yander looked at Barileth.

"Me either."

Yander scrunched up his face. "But I thought…" he paused. "Has anyone been on an expedition before?" The other dwarves said no, but Dorian didn't answer. He tied the tent tight to the stakes he drove in the ground on the west side.

"Mr. Ironstrike?" Yander asked, tentative. The other dwarves stopped what they were doing. Dorian felt their eyes on him. He straightened and checked the sky. The clouds had disappeared, the first few stars of twilight shining. Dorian leveled his stare at Yander, who wilted under it. "Never mind, I'll go get some more sticks for the fire."

With his departure the other dwarves sprung back into action. Skover stirred his soup vigorously, splashing some into the fire. It hissed and he yelped, a comic sight, but no one laughed. They were too preoccupied looking busy.

It was fine by Dorian. The less they knew of him, the better. He wasn't interested in their lives, even though he was forced to listen to them on the journey. He wasn't sure how the next three years would go.

While the others finished setting up the camp Dorian walked the perimeter of the camp. He was looking for more than if everything was in place.

He kneeled in the fading light, surveying the small tracks in the ground. *Rabbit.* Satisfied, he continued his round. When he finished Skover was dishing out the soup. He took his and retreated into the dark while the others sat on makeshift chairs of sticks or the ground.

"Ah, it's good to be in one place again," Yudoline said, sitting beside her husband. "Isn't it Kimec?"

"Hmm?" He looked up from his bowl of soup. "Yes, dearie."

"So many trees too," Yander said. "I've never seen so many, other than the forests we passed through. They had quite a few too, although those seemed to be bigger and less…"

"Sickly looking?" Skover offered.

"I was thinking thin."

"They'll do for our purposes," Kimec said. "They've got a lot of life in them. Good, solid wood that will last."

"Bah, throw the wood on the fire. Metal is what we're after, and metal is what we'll get." Barileth's face was animated by the flames, his braided beard dripping some of his meal. "We'll pull it up by the boatload, ship it down the river by barge until they can't get enough."

"What kind of metal do you think?" Yander asked.

"Gold, silver, steel. All of it, I imagine." Dorian almost snorted at his ignorance, but kept silent. He chewed the pork in his soup, letting the salty broth wash down the remains. It hurt his teeth, far harder than the thin gruel he had lived on for years.

"Gold? Real gold? We'd be rich beyond our wildest dreams." Dorian almost pitied Yander, with the faraway look he knew so well. So many dwarves he had been with through the years had worn it too, almost all of them disappointed. So wealth is what he's after.

"Gold isn't so easy to find," Lumdir said. "It likes to hide in the rock. You have to coax it out little by little."

"How would you know?" Barileth asked. Lumdir drew back and hunched his shoulders.

"I had a cousin once that mined it up north. Told me about it."

"A cousin! Hear that everyone, he has a cousin that knows everything there is to know."

"Oh, knock off it," Skover said, grabbing the ladle and stirring the pot again. "Have some more soup, there's more here." He helped himself while Lumdir glared at Barileth, who glared right back.

"I'll be glad to get underground again. The feeling of open sky has me feeling off," Yudoline said, changing the subject. All the dwarves agreed on it, dispelling the air of bad blood between Lumdir and Barileth.

Dorian finished his meal while the others kept talking and stretched his legs. The wind had picked up from the east, sending the trees into a shiver that creaked their branches.

He smelled the air and looked up into the sky. Clouds were rolling in. The unmistakable scent was thick. Rain was on the way.

The torrent hit and it was fast and furious. Lightning flashed and thunder rumbled. Water filled the air, filled his nose and splashed on him. Dorian sat away from the others huddled around the tent pole and trying to sleep.

They were failing. The storm was too much. Each flash of thunder brought a yelp from the mass, either Yudoline or Yander, he couldn't tell which. The booming thunder rolled over them seconds later, or less.

The mention of family brought back memories of Dorian's own. His brother and sisters, his mother and father. And, as usual, when he thought about them, his own thoughts turned inevitably to his wife and children.

Soft caresses in the morning, gentle kisses at night. The sound of her voice as she hummed baking bread, kneading the dough with firm hands. He hunched over, rocking back and forth and wishing they would go away.

The promise he made when he left that day, even though she begged him to stay. A bad feeling, she said. He had dismissed it with a laugh and went anyway. The waves of sadness and anger rolled over him like the rain rolled onto the tent.

Something snapped somewhere, but he was too busy trying to run from the ghosts of his past to care. The years hadn't made these memories any easier. He couldn't get their wedding day out of his mind.

Other than the birth of his children it had been the happiest day of his life. *Ruby, Xanther.* He almost moaned out and clutched his stomach, hard as a rock. Where were they now? Were they safe?

"Your children will await the completion of your task, kept here at Zirad in comfort until the mine can support them." The greasy smile of that dwarf, he wanted to reach back in time and throttle him.

But Lightaxe was reasonable, wasn't he? *You remember the last promise he made to you, don't you?* Anger bubbled up, replacing the sadness. The night stretched on and the storm grew stronger. So did Dorian's anger.

If he could leave now, find out where they were he could rescue them. But even as he thought it, he knew it was impossible. They would be hidden, kept far from his home. *They might not be in the city at all.*

The thought chilled him more than the icy rain. *I'll have his head if he does anything.* It was an empty threat, and he knew it.

No, he was stuck. He would either see this mission through to success or fail and never see his children again. There was no running, he had no allies or safe places to run to. There was no fighting, he wasn't strong enough on his own.

That left finishing the path that was laid before him, for good or for bad. Finally, the storm died out in the early hours of the morning. Dorian sat in a puddle, dripping water and shivering.

"I will finish this and see my children again, if it's the last thing I do," he whispered to himself. "I'll make this mine produce in three years and build a fortress like no one has ever seen."

3

REMEMBRANCE

Sunlight revealed the effects of the storm. Dorian, tired, cold, and wet, was the first up and the first to see.

The tent that covered their goods had collapsed in the night, exposing the front half of the cart. The sound of him moving boxes off the top woke the others.

"By the beard, what happened?" Yander asked, rubbing his eyes. Dorian dumped out a bucket of rainwater. The barrels of pork underneath looked to be intact.

"What a terrible night," Yudoline said. "I thought I was going to drown."

"I've got to get out of these clothes." Barileth tore off his wet shirt and wrung it out, a splash of water falling on the ground.

"Nothing dry to replace them with, I'm afraid." Kimec held up his spare shirts. They dripped water they were so water logged.

Lumdir joined Dorian at the cart and together they pulled the tent off. It protested, holding onto the wood of the sides of the cart. Yudoline gasped, and Dorian saw why.

The tent pole had fallen on the side of the cart, smashing into a barrel of rockbread. The dull gray foodstuff spilled out over the cart. It had been packed in tight, with no place to go.

"Not my seeds," she said, and hurried over. Reaching over the side she plucked out a small keg and turned it over in her hand and opened it. After the inspection, she sighed. "Safe and sound. Sticks and stones that gave me a fright."

"Ruined." Lumdir held up a piece of rockbread. It slumped and crumbled in his hand. He threw it to the ground in disgust and it slapped against the grass, wet and thick. It smelled soggy, the deep yeasty smell musty. "The whole barrel."

They wrestled it out of the cart, at least three times the weight it should have been. When they tipped it over water spilled out in a flow, pooling beneath the cart. It wrapped around the wheels and flowed down the mountain in rivulets.

"Get the rest out," Dorian said. Without a word they emptied the cart one piece at a time. The over packed cart creaked and groaned as it was unloaded, each box, barrel, or individual item carefully laid on rocks or among the wet grass.

The seven of them stood around the wreckage. "The tools got wet too," Yander held up a hoe. Its handle was broken and small tendrils of red covered the iron head.

"I could fix the handles, but this..." Kimec fingered the blade. Bits of red flaked off, falling to the ground. "We'd need a smith, and a proper one too. I don't have the skill for that." None of the other dwarves seemed to either.

All they had to survive the next year was around them. Two barrels of rock bread ruined. Almost all the handles of the tools were broken, except the axe and the pickaxes, and even they were starting to rust.

"How are we going to survive?" Yudoline asked. "With the rockbread gone?"

"We'll survive, we have more food in the cart." Barileth was pulling loaves out one by one and tossing them aside. Each splattered to the earth, waterlogged. He took a bite of one, made a face, and then spit it out. "No sense in keeping them though."

"I hate to see good food go to waste." Skover watched him mournfully, clutching his belly.

"The goats are fine, and the chickens." Lumdir held up the coop. The chickens looked small, soaked by the rain. "Could probably use a good soaking anyway." The goats had taken refuge in the dwarves' tent and were happily eating the rockbread.

"Who put up the tent?" Barileth asked. The dwarves ceased their activity and all eyes swiveled to him.

"What do you mean? We all put up the tent." Lumdir crossed his arms and narrowed his eyes. The old dwarf may have been getting on in years, but his muscles still had a vitality to them.

"Not all of us."

"I made dinner, it wasn't me," Skover said nervously. He drummed his fingers on his stomach and his eyes searched for an escape route.

"And I went to get water," Yudoline said.

"I suppose I helped with the tent. I've been helping with the tent for a few days now," Yander said. "I can't remember what I did exactly. If I hammered stakes this time, or if I helped put the center pole up. Sometimes I've done that, even though I have trouble with— "

"Enough of your yammering." Barileth cast a hard eye on Yander, then squinted. "I remember you doing something last night, what was it?" He stroked his beard, and none of the other dwarves said anything.

Dorian watched, not saying a word. While the others had secured their belongings, making sure their personal chests weren't wet, he had rearranged his. The axe that Finrail gave him was shifted to the bottom, beneath the spare changes of clothes, his documents, and a coat.

He didn't intend to pick it up ever again. Dorian thought long and hard and the first chance he got he was going to bury it. No good could come of using it again.

Tension in the air broke his memory, bringing him back to the present. Dorian wondered if the King's men had given them the usual goods or padded it. With this group the more he had, the better.

Barileth tugged on his beard suddenly. "That's right, you did something with the cart. You broke the tent pole, must have backed up right into it, I think."

"N-n-no, I didn't do that. I remember backing it up nice and slow, stopping just before the pole. Lefty and Righty, that's the names I've given the goats as to them always being tied up to the cart on each side, stopped right when I gave the command. I know they wouldn't go farther." Yander was backing up as he talked, Barileth advancing on him.

"You'll meet my Lefty and Righty for what you've done." Barileth held up his hand and curled them into threatening fists.

"Wait now," Lumdir said. "The boy wasn't the only one working last night. I recall you hammering in the stakes on this side. I think you didn't do what you were supposed to."

Barileth paused, and turned back. Lumdir's own arms were tense and rippled with muscle, showing the strength he had after years of hard labor.

"And who packed the cart?" Kimec asked.

"You stay out of this." Barileth leveled his glare at him.

"You packed the cart," Yudoline said, raising herself up to her full height. "If you would have put the barrel on the bottom we wouldn't have had this problem."

"We would have and you know it. That rain was too powerful to not ruin things."

"Let me make breakfast, we can talk about it after everyone's had a good meal," Skover said, trying to diffuse the situation. *It won't work, not with everyone tired and wet.*

"You would want to eat, wouldn't you?" Barileth turned his steely gaze to Skover. Dorian had seen this play out before, but never this early. "Always stuffing your fat face."

"Now, that's uncalled for." Skover frowned and took a step back.

"What's called for is a reckoning," Barileth said.

"And you're the dwarf to give it out?" Yudoline wagged a finger at him. "No sense giving out what you can't take."

"Tame your wife, before I do."

"Rock and earth." Kimec's eyes flashed. "Don't you dare talk about my wife that way. The way I see it you're the one who lost us the rockbread, and you'll be the one to pay for it."

"I'll pay for nothing."

"You'll take back what you said." Kimec's hand found the axe, and he hefted it, holding it across his chest at the ready. Barileth's eyes opened wider, then he turned back to Yander.

"The tent was your fault, and now we're out of food and tools."

"I really don't think I did anything wrong, I'm sure of it. The goats are so responsive and wouldn't ever do anything bad."

"Leave him be," Lumdir said, bristling.

"Or what? You'll gang up on me with the tree cutter and the cook?" Barileth shot him another glare. "Last week you told me how much you hated his cooking and now you want him on your side?"

"You don't like my cooking?" Skover looked more wounded at that than the insult earlier. "But my ma taught me from when I was young. It's all her recipes."

Lumdir looked nervous. "That's not exactly what I said, more of a paraphrase." He ran a hand through his beard. "Look, I think I need some more time to learn to…to get used to it, that's all."

"It's the salt, you use too much of it," Yudoline said. "I thought you knew."

"The salt? I barely sprinkle it in at all." Skover sat down hard on a rock, looking dazed. Yudoline patted him on the back, trying to console him as the others argued on.

"I'm sure it was all a big misunderstanding." Yander was waving his arms overhead for some reason, and sweating profusely. His forehead looked clammy and pale.

"We've had enough of your yammering," Barileth said.

"And we've had more than enough of yours. How about instead of throwing accusations around you learn to keep your own tongue." Kimec took a threatening step forward, and Barileth looked around for his own weapon. He found it, picking up the broken scythe.

Still debating on how badly he needed them, Dorian saw that intervention would soon be needed. Even listening to them was making him tired, and they were losing daylight.

"Put down the weapons," Yudoline said. Barileth and Kimec were staring at each other. "Someone do something!"

"We might need to knock some sense into this dwarf," Lumdir said, picking up a hammer.

"Come try it and they'll be plenty of food left for the rest of us once you're in the ground," Barileth said.

"You're on the wrong side of everything dwarf," Kimec growled.

"Except I'm the only soldier here." Kimec paused, casting an uneasy glance at Lumdir.

Dorian had enough. He walked, straight through the knot of them, over where the supplies laid. It was there, lying on the ground, and he stopped in front of it. Yander was talking to him, and maybe a few of the others. They could bicker and fight for all he cared. Maybe they might kill each other, maybe they wouldn't. That's no business of mine.

He hesitated. The pickaxe was new, never had felt earth before. The shaft was white, some sort of oak, with an iron head now riddled with rust. He knew it would come off as he worked though.

Dorian reached out, his too-thin fingers touched the handle and he shivered. *How long has it been? Too long.* He closed his fingers around it and lifted it with a firm grasp.

Then he added his other arm and closed his eyes, feeling the weight of the head. The other dwarves had gone silent, he assumed they were watching him now. It was well weighted, not too top heavy, and would have a good swing to it.

The sun caressed him, playing over his face as the wind blew across his clean head. Dorian snapped his eyes open and held the pickaxe to his chest. Almost reverently he walked over to the side of the mountain, a site he had chosen before they had even finished the journey.

He stopped on the side of the mountain, a small bump. This would be the entrance, for better or for worse. Dorian took a deep breath, and swung the pickaxe over his head.

For a moment he held it there, feeling the eagerness of it. It wanted to surge forward, meet the ground and break it. A flutter of a smile flashed across his face, and he let it fall.

The pick sunk deep in the earth.

4

COMPANION

Damp earth. Dorian breathed in the smell and let it linger. He drew back the pickaxe, dragging it through the grass to break up the sod. He pulled the pickaxe out and swung it again. It went deeper, catching in the dirt.

Again he broke the sod and pulled a pile of dirt out of a small hole he had made. Then he swung again, and again. It felt good in his hands, the new handle rubbing some. He kept going.

The hole grew, and so did the pile of dirt, mud, and grass that came out of it. Soon it was big enough to hold him, then deep enough for him to enter. He stopped and turned.

The others surrounded him, quiet. Dorian dropped the pickaxe and rubbed the dirt on his fingers off, letting it fall back to where it came. *This is what I've missed for all these years.*

"What do we need to do?" Yander was the first to speak up, which surprised him. The sun had dried out most of their clothes, and they looked to him.

"We retreat into the earth, make our home here." Dorian pointed over his shoulder with his thumb. Yander smiled, the others looked less gloomy than they had. "Who can shape rock?"

"That'll be me," Lumdir said.

"Good. Break up the surface rock and build me supports. We have a mine to dig. After breakfast, of course." Skover brightened.

"I'll go get it started." He hurried back to the supplies. There was no wood dry enough to start a fire, so Dorian knew they would be eating a cold meal.

"And I'll work on the rock," Lumdir said, gathering his tools and heading for the closest exposed rock. It looked like granite, gray flecked with bits of black. It would do well for them.

Dorian was about to go back to digging, but four dwarves watched him expectantly. "What?"

"I'm not sure what to do," Yander said. The others had the same confused look. *If I do this, there's no turning back.* He didn't see anyone else to do it though. Dorian sighed, feeling the burden fall on him again.

Kimec was easy. "Start felling trees. Clear out a hundred yard circle around the entrance. Barileth, you help him." Kimec frowned, but nodded. Barileth was impassive.

"Gather whatever food you can and dry it in the sun," he told Yudoline. "Berries, fruits, roots. Whatever you can find. Plant your seeds above the entrance, and make sure the goats can't get to it."

"What about me?" Yander asked.

"Breakfast," Skover yelled. Dorian was hungry, and he wasn't sure how long his body would last without the energy. The other dwarves hurried over and Dorian placed his pickaxe on the ground and followed.

"Wood's too wet to start a fire, but the other barrel of rockbread was perfectly fine and goes well with cheese." Skover handed out plates with a thick slice of rockbread on it and a thick pad of butter. "I'd like it better toasted, but oh well. We work with what we have." He was carving big slices of cheese off a wheel to each of them.

The food was nourishing, and they were too busy eating to say anything. Dorian preferred the silence anyway and sat a few feet back from them under the shade of an oak.

The cheese was soft, the bread hard. Just the way he liked it. The goat butter soaked into the crevices of the bread, but his mind wandered. What secrets were buried beneath them?

Gems, metal ore, something more? He closed his eyes in memory of his previous expeditions. Striking that rock, breaking open the vein and finding untold treasure. That was all behind him now.

He finished and stood up, brushing the crumbs off his stiff pants. He almost wished for his prison rags, they were so much easier to move around in than these new leather clothes.

The others were chatting. "Back to work," Dorian said. They finished whatever food they had left and scattered. Skover was left to clean up, and Yander.

"Help forage for food when you're done," Dorian told Skover.

"What about me?" Yander asked again. The young dwarf looked like a wounded cave pup. Something stirred in Dorian's heart. Yander had been staring at the pickaxe for a while now.

"Get a shovel." Yander's face broke out with a huge smile.

"Thank you, thank you. I know I'll be a big help in the mine, you can count on me."

"Don't make me regret this."

"Oh, I won't. I'll do whatever you ask and learn as much as I can." The dwarf's eye gleamed as he talked, and Dorian started to wonder if it was a good idea to take him. There were a thousand things he knew had to happen, but getting below ground took precedence over all of them.

"Bring a bucket too." Dorian turned and left without seeing if his order was followed, heading back to the dwarf shaped hole in the ground. Off to the right, near a makeshift quarry of above ground rock, Lumdir was chiseling away at the cleft.

The dwarf was skilled at his work. In the few minutes Dorian had talked to Skover and Yander he had managed to cleave off a piece of the exposed stone. Now he was working it, the steady ring of his hammer and chisel on the stone a constant drumbeat.

He might be able to keep up with us. Dorian grabbed the pickaxe and mounted the small dirt pile he made. He surveyed the hole, gaged its roundness. Yander was waiting by his side with the shovel and bucket.

Dorian pointed a few feet to the right of the opening. "Dirt there." Yander nodded.

"Got it, dirt goes there." Dorian retreated into the hole. "All the dirt or just some of it?" Dorian ignored the question and started to dig, matching the steady pace of Lumdir. "Mr. Ironstrike?" Yander's voice echoed in the hole.

The ground was wet from the rain and when it shifted uncomfortably Dorian stopped. He eyed the top of his hole, just as a crumbled of dirt fell away and landed beside his feet.

Right now it was big enough for one dwarf, and just barely one. He came back out, took a look at the size of stone Lumdir was cutting, and made a mark in the side of the mountain.

"What's that for?" Yander had found a shovel and was scooping dirt into a bucket. Dorian was glad he hadn't had to tell him where to find it, or walk him over and put it in his hands.

"Support." Dorian scratched out a rough outline and started chopping, cutting away more sod.

"Support? Why do we need support over there? I always thought the support was going to go on the top."

"It is." Dorian worked his pickaxe along the side. Large chunks of wet mud fell off the wall and he pulled them out of his way back to

Yander. He turned back, the dwarf was still staring, shovel in the dirt. "Dirt isn't going to move itself."

Yander scrambled, shoveling a load and hurrying off with it. *This is going to take a while.* While Yander worked Dorian walked over to Lumdir's makeshift quarry. Farther off an axe was chopping a tree, joining the ringing of the stonework.

One square column was done already, laying in a blanket of chips. He was hard at work at another, chipping away with his chisel. Lumdir took off rough sections, smoothing it to a general flat.

"This will do," Dorian said, running his hand along the rough surface of the granite. Nothing like the fluted columns of the Hearthome, but this was to be a working mine not a palace. Dorian looked to the work in progress.

"Twenty, maybe twenty-five a day. I could do less if you want more." Lumdir paused and wiped his sweaty forehead. "The sun makes it harder." Dorian nodded.

"That will do. It will give us a supply to take from." From down the slope a tree cracked, then crashed to the ground. The sounds of industry were back, and they sounded good.

It had been a long time since he heard them. Dorian grimaced, then called Barileth over. They each took an end of the column and pulled it off the ground.

Dorian's back protested, but he powered through it and they walked the heavy stone over to the opening.

"How deep are you going?" Barileth asked. Yander had moved most of the tailings away, giving them enough room to set the stone down.

"Deep."

"We're going to have the deepest mine, aren't we?" Yander walked up with his empty bucket. "I can't wait to get in and mine the ore. I'm sure we'll fine tons of it, more than we can carry."

"Go get the other column when Lumdir is done," Dorian said.

"I'll go back for the wood." Barileth shot Yander an unpleasant look, then left. Yander talked as he scooped dirt, about the mine and digging and how excited he was, but that he was also nervous about it too.

Dorian returned to his work, checking his dimensions. His carving had been shallow, so he deepened it, but the width had been close enough. He carved a spot above it for the lintel while Yander had gone to empty his bucket again, giving him a moment of peace.

"Take that end," Dorian said. Yander smiled and dropped his shovel, grabbing the stone.

"Thanks for letting me help with this. The first real construction of the mine, isn't it?"

"Lift it in."

"Ready. Oof, that is heavy. Bring it around? All right, I'm moving my end. What do I do now?" They set one end in place.

"Push it up." Yander strained, and Dorian joined him. Together they wrestled it into place, set into a shallow hole Dorian had dug for it. It stood on its own, resting against the wall of the cave.

"That was heavy, how many more do we have to go?" Dorian didn't want to tell him, that was the first of hundreds, so he kept it to himself. "Back to moving dirt right?" Dorian grunted and worked to inspect the column, making sure it was set.

Yander wandered off, talking as he went. The dwarf couldn't stop talking. After years of silence, it was getting unbearable for Dorian.

He prepped the other side, but Yander came back.

"That's for the other side, right? Then we'll put in the top. How do you suppose we'll get it up there? I'm sure there's a way to do it and you'll show us."

Dorian took his chances in the cave, going deeper to get away, but Yander followed him.

"I thought you wanted to make sure everything was supported before you started working in here?"

"Don't you have dirt to move?" Dorian asked, a hint of exasperation in his voice.

"I moved it all. It was a lot of work, that bucket was small and I had to run a little bit to make it." Yander went on about how much work it was, and the more he talked the more annoyed Dorian got.

He talked until Lumdir finished the other column, then talked all through them moving it and setting into position. He talked while Dorian adjusted the position, making it take twice as long as it needed to.

Dorian had to listen to him as he carved out a place for the lintel in the mud, more than a little falling right on his face.

"You have some mud on your face Mr. Ironstrike. I think it fell on you just now." Dorian had to suppress his anger now.

"You can stop talking now," Dorian said, scraping the mud off his face and throwing it on the ground with a wet plop.

"Stop talking, got it. I won't say anything more, you can believe that. I'll be quiet as a mouse, even quieter since they squeak a lot and you can hear--"

"Keep talking," Dorian growled, "and I'll cut out that tongue."

5

TEETH

Yander wilted under Dorian's gaze, and then he looked hurt. Finally, though, he was quiet. Dorian turned back to his own work, but a pang of guilt troubled him.

Did I have to be so harsh? The boy doesn't know what I'm capable of. He thought about if he could hurt him, and wasn't sure, and that hurt him even more. What kind of dwarf have I become?

He stopped and waited until the supports were done. Yander was quiet, and avoided his gaze, as they carried it over.

"We'll lift it into place," Dorian said, answering the question in Yander's eyes. "Just like we used to do." He knew it would fit, he had carved the opening over-sized, but since this lintel was longer it was significantly heavier than the sides.

"Up on your end, put it in. That's it." The stone was diagonal now, resting on top of the left support. "Pull this one up." Together they hauled it, which left him breathless, and shoved it into place. It ground to a halt halfway in.

"Go get the mallet." Dorian sucked in the fresh mountain air, glad it was cool. The sun was high in the sky, it had to be past noon. He wiped the sweat off his forehead.

30

As Yander hurried back with the mallet Dorian thought about how much work they had to do. There were caves to cut out, mineshafts to dig, food to raise. Every day that went by was one less day they had to survive.

The others were oblivious. They had never been in the same situations he had. For good or for bad their lives depended on him.

"Got the mallet, what do we do with it?"

"This." Dorian took it from his hands and slammed it onto the lintel, putting as much force behind it as he could muster. It hit home with a satisfying thwack, the handle shivering in his hands. The stone shifted, going back a few inches into the earth and sending a cascade of dirt behind it.

He had hoped it would have seated it with one blow, and eyed the mallet. It was still fine. Years ago that would have been all it would take. A few more blows seated it in place.

"I see, can I try it next time?"

"Yes," Dorian said, huffing.

"Lunch," called Skover from the campsite. Dorian and Yander were the last to arrive. Skover and Yudoline had done a better job, rearranging the supplies into various piles that were now securely under the tent now tied to the trees.

A few feet away from tents they had fashioned a makeshift kitchen, including a work table made from a slab of wood Kimec must have just finished making. Water boiled in a pot, steam mixing with the smoke of smaller branches in the fire.

Skover dished out fried pork and more of the rock bread, and they all ate quickly. Someone had scavenged fresh blackberries from farther down the slope. Dorian ate his on a fresh pile of firewood and logs were stacked neatly outside the kitchen.

The others talked to each other, about their tasks and the valley. When he was done Dorian walked back to them. A hush fell when he entered the circle. He turned his attention to Kimec, still holding a fork.

"Can you build a wheelbarrow?"

Kimec scrunched up his face and thought about it. "Should be able to yes."

"Start work on that and finish it as soon as you can. Simpler the better."

"Right away." Kimec stood up, then looked around, still holding the fork.

"Barileth, keep chopping trees. We'll need a lot." Barileth nodded. Lumdir already had his work. That left Yudoline and Skover.

"Foraging for me, I've got it." Skover wiped his hands off and collected the utensils. Kimec was relieved of his fork and went to his work.

"Where can I plant my seeds? I'll need sun." Yudoline was clutching her keg of seeds. Dorian thought about it, above the entrance would be more advantageous for collection, but would be harder to take care of.

"Upslope, about fifty feet."

"What seeds do you have?" Yander asked.

"Hops for ale, carrots and potatoes to eat. They showed me how to plant them before we left." Her eyes sparkled as she talked. Dorian was glad to see her enthusiasm, but that meant she was an amateur at best. He wanted to ask her what she had grown before, but was afraid of the answer.

"Potatoes, that will be a real treat," Yander said.

"Come on." Dorian left Yudoline to the farming and went back tot he digging. Lumdir had worked a few supports ahead, giving him time to think about the direction.

He decided to dig straight back, a hundred feet at least. That would give them room for growth later, and a place to defend if need be. He got to work, keeping up a steady pace and eating into the side of the mountain.

After a few feet he stopped and cut out room for the supports. With Yander's help he set another triangle of support just like the entrance. It was more difficult to set the top support, since it had to scrape away the top of the ceiling, but with enough malleting they were able to set it in place.

"How many more to go?" Yander asked, then paled. "I'm sorry, I didn't mean to. I just have a bad habit of talking too much when I get nervous and you make me nervous."

Inwardly Dorian chuckled. He never thought himself the kind to make others nervous, just a simple dwarf. "Every few feet, until we hit rock. Then we can space them out more."

"Ah, I see." Yander took a bucket of dirt out, then came back to get more. Dorian was out pacing him, filling the tunnel up. "How far in are we going?" He kept shoveling.

"A hundred feet, or more." Yander hurried out with the bucket, almost running. Dorian paused to take a break and let the young dwarf catch up. He leaned on the pickaxe, feeling the pounding of his heart.

"Is it hard?" Yander came back for another bucket, which was woefully undersized for the task at hand.

"What?"

"Using that."

Dorian chuckled. "No, it isn't hard using it. It's hard doing it all day."

"Do you mind if I try? I've wanted to ever since I was little."

"Use a pickaxe?" Dorian stared at him.

"Be a miner, I mean. I ended up as a clerk because I could read." Yander's black eyes glittered in the light from the tunnel entrance.

"Take a turn." Dorian offered the handle to Yander, who approached nervously. He reached out with trembling hands and took the pickaxe, but almost dropped it.

"Sorry."

"Just swing it." Dorian moved out of the way. Yander lifted it up and swung it, embedding it into the wall. He grinned and pulled away the earth, which tumbled to his feet.

Yander attacked the wall with gusto, over and over again. "I like it, I think I'm getting the hang of it too." Dorian stood back and watched him. He had a knack of the trade, the way he swung the pickaxe was as natural as a dwarf could be.

Dorian let Yander tire himself out, he had left a trail of dirt in his path that gave the tunnel an earthy smell. Yander sighed and gave back the pickaxe.

"When we have a wheelbarrow we'll need to mine faster than we can remove it," Dorian said. "We have another pickaxe."

Yander smiled and went back to shoveling dirt into his bucket as Dorian returned to digging. He paused with it full in his hand. "You wouldn't cut my tongue out...would you?"

Dorian kept digging. "A dwarf will do more than you think, when the right time comes."

They finished three supports before Skover called them out to dinner. Dorian and Yander were the last to arrive. Dorian washed some of the dirt off his hands with spring water someone had brought up.

Dinner was more stew, and again Dorian collected his and withdrew while the others sat around the cook fire.

"I got to mine today," Yander said, chest puffed out.

"Good for you," Yudoline smiled at him and patted his shoulder. She sounded sincere.

"One step closer to the gold," Barileth said.

"Surely gold isn't the only reason you're on this expedition?" Yander asked.

"No, I have other reasons. We all know where the army was headed, and I had no desire to get killed in another senseless war." Barileth slurped the rest of his stew up loudly. "If there was a chance of death, I'd rather have a shot at riches to go along with it."

"I had to get away from the paperwork," Yander said. "Always writing, and always in too little light."

"So you abandoned your family to come out here, eh?" Barileth asked.

"No, I didn't abandon them. They'll come when I send for them. Besides, mother and father are fine at home and I've no other family to speak of."

"We had family," Yudoline said softly. "The memory of it...we couldn't continue on in Zirad." Kimec reached out and pulled her into a hug.

"I'm sorry to hear that." Barileth sounded sincere, a touch of sadness in his own voice. Dorian wasn't expecting that. Maybe the wind and hard work had done some good to him.

"No matter, we're here now for a better life." Yudoline wiped her eyes. "What about you Lumdir? What brought you with us?"

"There was no room for me in the Guild, and my apprenticeship was up."

"You didn't pass the test?" Yander asked. Lumdir stirred, agitated.

"No." The light of day faded into blackness. "I'll show them though. I'll become the best stonemason the world has ever seen."

"You'll have plenty of practice here," Barileth said. The dwarves laughed, breaking the solemn mood. Yander looked over to Dorian, but before he could ask him anything Dorian waked away from the fire.

The night was clear, and he didn't smell rain. Dorian grabbed his bedroll and laid it out among the stars. He kicked off his boots and slipped into bed. A rock jabbed at his back, so he fumbled around in the dark until he found it and threw it away.

His body ached, and he was exhausted. It didn't take long for Dorian to fall asleep.

The dogs barking woke him up. It was still dark. The moon had set so it was even darker than when he had gone to sleep.

"What's that?" Skover sounded alarmed. Dorian listened again, then he heard it too. The sound of chewing, and yipping. Other, unfamiliar barks.

Dorian scrambled out of bed, groping for his boots until he found them and put them on. The fire was banked, its glowing red coals in the distance, and he grabbed a torch and rushed over, tripping to thrust it into the fire.

While he waited for it to catch he listened. The sounds were coming from his right, and dwarves were talking and making noise in the tent to his left.

"What's happening?"

"Where's my boots?"

"Ouch, that's my foot!"

"Get out of my way then."

The torch flamed up, blinding him momentarily, but he had seen what was making the noise. Dorian yanked the torch out and advanced.

Eyes and teeth gleamed in the darkness, reflecting the fire, then they disappeared, scattering. Dorian yelled at them, chasing them away. They barked back but left.

Their own dogs were still barking, tied up for the night. *This wouldn't have happened if they had been free, but then they might be dead.* Dorian made sure they were gone before he returned.

The other dwarves were standing around the fire, tired looking but wide eyed.

"Wild dogs," Dorian said, then he surveyed what they had done. His heart sank, and he frowned.

"What happened?" Yudoline asked. "What did they do?"

He picked up the remains. "They've broken into the pork and have almost eaten the whole barrel."

6

STRIKING ROCK

"Are you sure they weren't wolves?" Yander asked, all sleep gone from his wide eyes.

"We'll set a watch from now on. Each one takes a turn," Dorian said. The meat was spoiled or eaten, which meant they were down to one barrel. It could have been worse, but another loss of food was troubling. "I'll take the first watch, everyone else go back to sleep."

"But what if they come back?" Yudoline asked, clutching Kimec's arm.

"We'll see them then. Tomorrow Kimec will make us spears. It will be enough to take down and kill any wild animal that threatens us." Dorian gave them a hard stare until they wilted and turned back. One by one they left him and went back to the tent. He snuffed out the torch and sat down next to the fire, staring into the glowing coals.

They would have to move faster and dig out a space for supplies. There was so much to do, and so little time to do it. His arms and legs were like weights, and his back hurt. As much as he wanted to go back to sleep, an image of being devoured by wild dogs kept him up.

He stared into the dancing embers long into the night.

"Come up on the right side." Dorian waited until Yander got the rough-looking wheelbarrow into position and took a swing at the wall. Dirt slipped down, falling into it mostly. It had been invaluable, and he was glad he thought to ask for one.

"I'll take it out." The pile outside their mine entrance was getting bigger, fed by their continuous advancement into the side of the mountain. Dorian had stopped shorter than he wanted to go, about fifty feet into the mountain, but he hoped it would be enough.

While Yander took out the load he rested on the pickaxe handle, flexing his hands. Strength was returning to them, the blisters turning to callouses and fading. Down the tunnel he heard the wheelbarrow slam into something. *I've got to get that entrance widened.*

That could come later though. Breath caught, he went back to work breaking up clumps of earth that slid down to the floor. The farther they went in the richer the earth, now it was almost heady with the smell each time he broke into it. Soon he had filled the floor again, advancing at least a foot.

A squeaking wheel announce the arrival of Yander. "That's finished, I'll start on the next load."

"Hold off on it, I'll take it." Dorian dropped his pickaxe and took up the shovel.

"Really? You don't want to be here while I'm digging?"

"You know how now. Like we talked about, ten more feet that direction and twenty that way."

"I've got it, I'll be going so fast you'll never keep up with me. With all the moving dirt I've gotten much stronger." Yander grabbed the pickaxe and went to work, talking as he swung. "This is a lot harder than the dirt back at the entrance."

Dorian took Yander's job, shoveling loads of dirt onto the growing mound outside. He paused after a few wheelbarrow load, squinting against the late afternoon sun.

Kimec had built a rough fence around the food to protect it from wild animals. It wasn't pretty, but it would do the job. Lumdir was still hard at work, adding to a long line of supports growing faster than they could take them.

Yudoline was tending to the garden with Skover, which had its own thicket fences. Some plants had sprouted already from the earth. A fresh gust of wind brought the sound of Barileth chopping wood farther down the slope, and Kimec was hard at work chopping the bark off a trunk dragged from down below.

There was still enough time in the year, if the garden held up. They could bring in a harvest to last, even with the losses. *Would it be enough to last though?*

It would have to, they didn't have any other choice. Now was the most dangerous time for the expedition, the better they worked the more likely they were to survive.

Dorian sniffed. There was something strange in the air, but he couldn't place it. That's when he noticed the goats bleating, high pitched and panicked. *What's wrong with them.*

They had tied them to a stake near the tents, giving them enough pasture for them to graze for the day until they were needed to pull logs back into camp. They were pulling at the ropes hard.

A chill went down his spine, and he shivered. Quickly, he scanned the valley in the direction opposite where the goats were pulling.

Then, he saw it.

His breath caught in his throat, and he gripped the shovel, thankful of the smooth wood of the handle. For a second he wished it was an axe, but pushed the thought away with a growl.

"To camp!" he bellowed. "Get any weapon you can." The steady ring of Lumdir's chisel went silent. Kimec, surrounded by wood chips, took up his axe and looked to Dorian.

He didn't wait for the others, there wasn't enough time, but rushed down the mountain, breathing hard. He knew what the stench was now, the smell of death walking. But how?

It shuffled along, one leg torn off and covered in wounds. Above the sound of wind rushing by and his heartbeat in his ears he wasn't sure it was making a noise.

Dorian spared a moment to glance back. Yudoline was fleeing the other direction, and Skover was frozen in place, jaw hanging open. Lumdir was right behind him, but going slow. He didn't look sure of himself and clutched his hammer close.

But when he looked back he saw Barileth charging up the slope, a wooden stick sharpened to a point in his hand. He was laughing maniacally, not a hint of fear about him.

"Stay back," Dorian warned, but Barileth's laugh turned into a battle cry. His short legs were pumping, and the distance between the dwarf and the abomination closed is seconds.

They collided with a sickening thwack, the spear slipping into the rotten flesh with ease. It caught on something and propelled the dog backward. Barileth kept screaming until the spear stopped him on the tree behind.

The dog tried to fight back, jaws snapping with green slime and sharp teeth. Barileth sprang back, narrowly avoiding a bite. Dorian got there in a few seconds and swung the shovel with all his might.

Drawing back, the dog almost avoided the attack, but the shovel clipped its head and took off its nose, sailing halfway to the next tree before it hit the ground.

"Kill it," Dorian said.

"With what?" Barileth asked, eyes bright and gleaming. Dorian's eyes fell on the axe in Kimec's hand, who was approaching fast. The dog struggled against the makeshift spear, and it creaked and groaned ominously.

Dorian didn't wait, he shifted his grip and swung again. The shovel met flesh, but the dog didn't seem to be affected. He hit it again and again, but other than a dent the foul beast was unfazed.

"Earth and steel." Dorian tried a harder blow, with no effect. "Take off its head." Kimec doubled over, gasping, offering his axe to Dorian. "No, there's no time."

Kimec stared at him, hand outstretched.

"Give me that," Barileth said. In one movement he swept up the axe and brought it down on the dog's neck, cutting it off in one blow. The head rolled to the ground, still snapping, until its red eyes lost the unearthly glow.

"What is it?" Kimec asked when he caught his breath.

"Foul magic." Barileth kicked the head away and tested the spear. It was stuck tight.

"We burn it, far from the camp." The mottled, bloody fur would give up a terrible stench, even though the evil enchantment was gone.

"But what is it?"

"It used to be a dog, you can see that," Barileth said. He sighed. "Didn't put up much of a fight though."

"You stabbed it with a spear." Kimec stared at Barileth. "What do you mean it didn't put up much of a fight?" Barileth shrugged. Kimec shook his head.

The others were coming now that the danger was over. Lumdir held his hammer in front of him as a ward. "I'm not sure we should be here anymore."

"Come on," Dorian said, grabbing the spear. With Barileth they pulled it free, and the corpse slid to the ground. "Take care of this." Dorian walked back where it came.

"You can't leave us now," Skover said, almost shaking with fear. "What if there are more out there like this?"

"Pray there aren't," Dorian said. The others were talking and arguing behind him, but he ignored them. The trail was easy to follow, drips of blood and vile liquid leading north east.

His heart was heavy as he walked, not wanting to believe it. Less than a week since the dogs attacked the camp, and now this. Across the valley the trial turned east.

After less than half an hour he came to the end of it, and his shoulders pricked and his hair stood on end. Dorian rubbed his chin, the rough stubble comforting.

In a stand of tall grass between the trees was a strange device. A trap with a spike, it glowed an unnatural purple color and was etched in strange markings. Some of them Dorian knew.

While he considered his options he searched around, finding no other traps. He knew what kind of trap brought back the dead, and how powerful the necromancer was that created it.

He stood over it for a time. It was probably disarmed now, but perhaps it could be activated again. The camp would be in danger of another attack. But if he destroyed it the person who built it would know.

And would wonder. That person might be curious as to who was around in the remote mountains and conduct a search. That person might find them, and put them in even more danger.

Dorian left it as it was after carefully memorizing the runes. When he returned to the camp the others crowded around.

"Did you find anything?" Yander asked, tugging on his beard.

"The trail ended, I can't be sure but we're safe for now."

"What if it comes back?" Yudoline asked. Dorian peered over at the pile of ashes far down the slope.

"It won't." There wouldn't be enough former life left to manipulate after that. He started back for the mine.

"Where are you going?" Skover clutched at his tunic.

"Back to the mine. We all have work to do." The coolness of the dark enveloped him, and he was glad to be back in the earth.

They hit it two days later, when most of the kitchen was finished. Dorian's pickaxe rang on it, and a satisfying tremor went up the handle to his hands.

"Stone."

"What?" Yander asked, perking up. Dorian scraped away the earth from around it, revealing a gray granite flecked with black and white.

"Beautiful," Dorian said, but then he frowned. "This will slow us down." He glanced at the room they had dug. It would do, for now. It might be smaller than he would have liked.

"This means we're getting into the mountain now, doesn't it?" Yander didn't give him time to respond, but sighed and continued. "Just behind the rock there'll be gems and ore and riches."

Dorian snorted. "Not that easy. We have a lot more work to do before we get to those, unless we get lucky."

"But we'll be lucky, the King said there would be ore here, the King's Seers said it was here." Dorian shrugged. "We will, won't we?"

"How lucky have we been so far?" Yander looked like he deflated with the question, all the excitement gone. "Mining's hard work, riches don't fall into you lap."

"How much work do you think we'll have to do?"

Dorian swung the pickaxe back over his head, bringing it down on the stone and chipping a chunk away. It rolled on the ground.

"We might never find any."

7

LEARNING

"Tomorrow we move the food in," Dorian said. He stood back, examining their handiwork. The rock had been strong, but yielded to their pickaxes. Now they had a finished room, the north end with a carved fireplace.

They had some luck, the chimney had been closer to the surface than he first expected.

"What's after this?" Yander asked. He had progressed faster than Dorian expected, took to finding the natural cracks in the rock like he could sense them.

"We need a place to sleep." They had gone west for the kitchens, they would go east to carve out a wing for sleeping and production. "The farms can wait until that's done. We can live off the aboveground crops and plant the underground ones later."

"How do you know so much about this stuff?" Dorian raised an eyebrow, and Yander held up his hands. "Right, never mind. You've been doing this a long time I think, and with a whole bunch of dwarves. You've probably seen more than I'll ever see."

"Go get the food." Yander grabbed the wheelbarrow and took the final load for the night back out. The others were gathering for the evening meal, and the sun was almost at the horizon. They would have to work fast.

"Dinner will have to wait. We need to move in the supplies, starting with the food."

Skover stopped stirring his soup. "Right now?"

"Now." Dorian went over to the makeshift gate and opened it. He waved Yander over and started loading the wheelbarrow up with boxes. "Roll in the barrels."

The others grumbled, under their breath, but put down their bowls and spoons to help. In a line the dwarves worked, carrying and moving everything they could into the mine.

Skover directed them when they were inside, stacking everything up on the far side of the room across from the hearth. They left enough room for a counter and space for Kimec to build shelves for the cooking supplies.

An hour later all the food was inside, and some of the other supplies too. They took their places around the campfire and ate while Dorian sat alone, thinking.

When he finished he brought back his bowl and walked into the circle. The conversation died off, and they stared at him. He waited until he knew they were uncomfortable to speak.

"Things have changed. We need to too. From now on I'll be giving you tasks in the morning, more than you can probably manage but you'll have to. You can take all day to do them, but they need to be finished before the next day."

"The next day? What if we don't get them done?" Yudoline asked. Yander squirmed on his stump, and Dorian looked each in the eye.

"They'll be done before I give out the next tasks. I don't care how long you have to stay up to finish them." It was silence, oppressively so. The fire cracked and spit.

"That's ridiculous," Barileth said. Dorian knew the others thought the same.

"Nonetheless, its what we must do." Their feelings wouldn't come between him and his children. He would do what needed to be done. "Yander and I will start on the dormitory tomorrow and try to move us in as fast as we can. We won't go as fast now that we hit rock, but we'll do our best."

Dorian left without looking back, knowing there was something else he could say to make it easier, but didn't know what it was. *I'm not an expedition leader and I never wanted to be.*

It was going to be a long three years.

"Kimec, build shelves for the kitchens. Lumdir, we need the supports but we'll need a table too. Barileth, go hunting and catch something to eat, at least a stone's worth." Barileth tightened his lips. "Yudoline and Skover keep working on the farm and forage a basket of edible plants each. Does anyone have anything to say?"

For a second he thought Barileth was going to say something, but he shoveled his mouth full of food instead. His jaw worked fast, and Dorian knew he was biting more than his food. Hearing no objections Dorian got up and went back to the mine.

Quick footsteps behind him meant Yander was following. He was going to have to teach him more, if they were going to be successful at this. That's why when they reached the end of the entrance tunnel he stopped and turned around.

"From now on you'll need to pull more weight." Dorian crossed his arms in front of him, and Yander nodded and swallowed. Dorian squinted at him, assessing. Yander fidgeted.

Finally, Dorian reached back behind him and passed the pick-axe to Yander. At first he stared at it, just looking at the tool in Dorian's hands.

"Are you going to take it or make me hold it?"

"No, no. Of course, I—I just don't know what to say or do."

"Take the pickaxe." With trembling hands Yander reached out and took the pickaxe, turning it over in his hand.

"Did Kimec do this? The last time I saw it the handle was broken."

"He did." Yander ran his hand down the smooth handle. A chill went through Dorian, remembering what it was like when he was new. He smothered the feeling though. *I don't deserve it, not after what I've done.* "It's beautiful."

"You're going to get to know it, so start now." Yander smiled, then took his first swing at the wall, crumbling the dirt to start the tunnel to their new home. He started in with a passion, and Dorian let him go, staying back and loading up the wheelbarrow instead.

They took turns, switching off to dig. Dorian grew stronger now, aching less at the end of the day when they were finished. Strength was growing in his arms atrophied by a long imprisonment, muscle was clinging to them. His body felt old still, and when he couldn't get to sleep at night he wondered how long it would take to shed the last vestiges of the dungeon.

Three days later they finished the tunnel to the depth Dorian felt satisfied with, then they turned deeper into the mountain.

"This will do fine, just enough room." Dorian surveyed the beginnings of the dormitory they had dug out. Approximately twenty feet left enough room to fit their belongings, and more, and would give them a place to expand.

The room was only a few feet wide, they had dug opposite to each other. "How long will it take to dig?" Yander asked, picking up his pickaxe and rubbing the handle with his hands.

"If it's just earth, a week at most." Dorian swung his own pickaxe and felt it sink into the earth.

Then, it struck rock.

"Blast." Dorian dug out around it, exposing the rock face. "Shallower than the other side, I thought we might have enough room to get in the beds at least." Kimec was working on them now, they didn't look too good, but it would be better than sleeping on the ground.

"Rock will take longer to dig out, won't it? That means we'll be sleeping outside longer, right? I don't like sleeping outside in the tent, it's too open and makes me feel weird, I'd rather be inside, hugged by the earth." Yander paused, pickaxe still working on his side. "The others aren't going to like this, will they?"

"No." Dorian swung and broke off a chuck of rock with a satisfying thud.

"What's that?" Barileth squinted against the sun, staring up the slope. Dorian turned from his meal, and, like the others, tried to see what Barileth saw.

"What is what? I don't see anything," Yander said.

"Are you going to finish that?" Skover reached over to Barileth's plate to take the sausage. Immediately, Barileth snatched it away.

"Yes I'm eating this." Dorian saw it too.

Something was moving on the ridge, a shadow of a figure against the sun and sky. Instinctively his hand reached for the axe handle, then Dorian felt ashamed. "Be ready."

Barileth wolfed down his meal while the others dropped theirs and went for the spears. Crude and carved from wood, they were better than nothing. They joined Dorian, standing together a few feet apart like he had taught.

The figure crested the ridge, then came down the mountain.

"A dwarf," Yander said. "It's a dwarf."

"Way out here?" Barileth asked. "Why would they be here?" Dorian wondered the same thing, but then hit upon the reason.

"We don't know if he's friend or foe," Dorian warned. The others shifted their grips on their spears. Dorian still hadn't picked up his, but it was leaning against the tree he had been eating under. He hoped he wouldn't need it.

The dwarf waved at them, then happily tromped along toward them. The voice at the back of Dorian's head told him something wasn't quite right, but the dwarf's smiling face seemed sincere and happy to see them.

"Hullo," he called out, cupping his hands around his mouth. The wind took some of the word away.

"Hullo," Yander answered. Dorian looked at him, and the others gave him a glare. He wilted under their gaze. "Sorry."

"Friend, or foe. Name yourself," Dorian said when the dwarf was close enough to hear them.

"Friend, and a grateful friend I am to see you. Dovig is my name, Dovig Bonebraid." He doffed his hat and gave a small bow, then came forward. "Are you the expedition?"

"Yes, from Zirad," Yander said. "We've been here almost two months."

"That long, already?" Dovig's eyes twinkled as he laughed. "My, I lose track of time so easily sometimes. It's a pleasure to meet you..."

"I'm Yander Helmsplitter." He extended a hand, which Dovig took and shook heartily. *That dwarf needs to learn a lesson.* There was something about the stranger that was keeping Dorian on edge. The other's introduced themselves, following Yander's lead. Dorian did the same, but refused to shake the dwarf's hand.

"It's been a long road, do you mind sparing some food and drink for a weary traveler?" Dovig was eying the campfire and the remains of lunch.

"Certainly, plenty to go around," Skover said. Dorian frowned, he wasn't sure there was, but the damage was done and Dovig was making a beeline for the food. He sloughed off the pack with a clank and took a seat.

"I wasn't sure I would find you, being so turned around and all." Dovig watched Skover get another sausage and stick it over the fire to warm. He took a plate as Yander offered him some rockbread. The others joined him around the fire, and Dorian walked over too. "Thank you kindly. That wind can really cut through the cloak, can't it?"

"It gets bitter up here at night," Yander said. "The cold makes me shiver under my blanket sometimes." Dovig devoured the bread, finishing before the sausage had cooked.

"But the fresh air," Dovig said, patting his stomach and sighing. "Makes me weep to feel it in my lungs."

"You still haven't told us why you're here." Dorian crossed his arms and scowled. It had been a long time since he had been around other dwarves, but it had finally come to him why Dovig didn't seem right.

Dorian thought he saw something flash across Dovig's face, but it was too quick to be sure. He leaned back against the cart as Skover put the piping hot sausage still sizzling on his plate.

"Easy enough, I'm your liaison from King Lightaxe. You might say I'm here to make your life a little easier." Dovig blew away the steam coming from his meal, relaxed and in his element.

"I'll call your bluff Mr. Bonebraid. You can't possibly be who you say you are, because you're too early for a liaison." Everyone tensed up and turned to Dovig to see what he would say.

8

EMISSARY

"They sent me early, something about the expedition not being prepared to weather the winter." Dovig took another bite of sausage, chewed it, and swallowed. He looked Dorian in the eye. "I've been told they don't expect you to survive without...help."

Dorian's ears almost turned red from the embarrassment he felt. Then he started thinking. *Who would have told him that, and why. Maybe he really is the liaison.*

"We have had some unfortunate accidents with our food supply," Yander said. Again, Dorian wished he would keep his mouth shut and learn to not volunteer information. He would have to have a talk with him about that later.

"It's a good thing I came early then. I can arrange everything, don't you worry a thing. How much do you have left?" Dovig stopped chewing and looked around in the silence. "Don't tell me, you don't even know how much food you have?"

"I don't know," Skover murmured.

"That's a problem, who's the leader?" All the dwarves eyes turned on Dorian, who was feeling even more foolish now. He crossed his arms, but felt like crawling into the hole to escape. "You do have an account of all the food, don't you?" There was a small prick of condescension in his voice.

"We've been busy trying to survive," Dorian said. Dovig held up his arms, now finished with his meal.

"I understand, I've been out here to other expeditions before. You aren't the first stop I've made and you won't be the last. Let me help you, share in your trials for a while. I'll teach you what I know and in return you feed and care for me for a few weeks, at most. I'll be out of your beards in no time."

Dorian was hard pressed to find a reason to say no. It had been years since he had been in the world, let alone survive it. The small tickle he was feeling was probably because he had forgotten too much. It would be foolish to turn away the King's representative by itself, let alone when there was knowledge that could be passed.

"Fine, you can stay."

"Great." Dovig clapped his hands together and smiled. "Where's the ale?"

Slowly, methodically. Dorian brought the pickaxe down against the rock, sparks flying from the strike. It gave off the wonderful smell of burning iron, and the smell of progress through the earth. Again, and again.

Chips and rock rained in showers, collecting on the floor like mounds to advancement. They would be cleared away, but for now it was only Dorian and the rock.

"Did I tell you about what happened last night? I had the most wonderful dream-" *And Yander, who could ever forget him.*

"Mr. Ironstrike," said Skover from behind him, jerking him out of his flow.

"Huh?" Dorian turned, breathing from the exertion. Dirt and rock dust mixed with the sweat in his skin, giving him that wonderful gritty feeling he had missed for so long.

"Sorry to disturb you, but I finished counting the food like we talked about. You know, how Dovig told us to do it." Dorian frowned at that memory, but Skover went on. "We had extra provisions before we left, plenty to last through the year until we could be re-supplied or establish our own food industry..."

"But?" Dorian asked when enough time passed he knew Skover wouldn't continue.

"We will run out by mid-autumn with what we have now, assuming we don't eat the goats and chickens." Dorian's throat constricted, and he wheezed. *That was far worse than I thought.*

"That bad, are you sure?"

"I've gone over it three times." Skover rung his hands, his lips stretched tight beneath his beard. Dorian rubbed his face.

"How are we going to survive?" Yander asked, crestfallen.

"We have the crops."

"That's including the crops in the number. It gets worse if we don't count them," Skover said.

"By the beard! What are we going to do?"

Dorian struck his pickaxe in the ground viciously. It stuck in the tailings as he walked off and back out the tunnel. "We do what we always do, get the others and adapt. Skover, round up anyone you see and let them know we need to meet at the fire."

His thoughts churned as he walked out of the mine and back into the morning sun. Less than two days after Dovig had arrived, another mouth to feed. *He did remind me what to do.* Dorian had never been good with the books, someone else had always taken care of that. Again he cursed his luck to be on this expedition in the first place.

Ruby, Xanther. I have to remember them. He called out to Lumdir, Barileth, and Kimec. They stopped their tasks as Skover collected Yudoline from the farm.

"What's going on?" Barileth demanded.

"When everyone gets here." Dorian noticed Dovig resting beneath the cart, who perked up and opened one eye. *He already knows.*

"What are we doing when everyone gets here?" Kimec asked, still holding his spokeshave. Dorian didn't answer, but waited for the others to arrive. It didn't take long, even though Kimec was looking at him funny.

"Now that we're assembled we can talk about a problem. Skover?"

"It's the food. I've counted and we don't have enough to make it through the winter. Unless we get more from somewhere." Skover rung his hands together as he talked, his face scrunched up.

"That can't be right, we had so much when we left. It was supposed to be more than enough," Yudoline said. She was frowning, and holding a hand over her chest.

"You seem to forget what's happened. The bread ruined because of him." Barileth pointed a finger at Yander, whose eyes opened wide, "And the rest taken by wild animals."

"I didn't do it," Yander protested. "I've already said that."

"You probably left the meat out too, didn't you?" Barileth glowered at Yander, who gaped at him.

"I haven't touched the meat."

"That isn't fair, you know that," Skover said. Barileth rounded on him.

"Then it must have been you. Let me guess, you didn't seal the barrel and left it thinking it would be fine in the morning? That it would be too much work?" Skover flushed at the accusation, his mouth working but no sound coming out.

"Why are you so angry?" Kimec asked.

"Why am I angry? Why aren't you?" Barileth pointed at Yudoline. "If not for the stupid actions of a few dwarves around here your wife would have enough to eat this winter and we wouldn't have to starve to death.

You all may be fine dying, but I came here to live and get rich doing it. There's no way I'm going to let anyone else stand in my way if I can help it." Kimec had stepped in front of his wife, his grip was tight on the ax. Tension was thick, and even Dovig wasn't pretending to be asleep anymore.

"You leave my wife out of this." Kimec advanced a step, but Barileth didn't back down. Instead, he drew himself up and cracked his knuckles.

"I'm willing to fight you, and I'll let you keep that little toy of yours if you want."

"That's enough," Dorian said quietly in the oppressive silence. The others turned toward him. "What's done is done."

"That's all you have to say?" Barileth asked. "Some expedition leader you turned out to be." He turned his back and started to walk away.

"Stay here, or be known for the coward you are." Barileth froze, then turned around. "We can bicker and fight like children, or we can come up with a plan that will keep us alive." Dorian looked around at each of them. Barileth's eyes glowed with hatred, but he didn't care.

"I can collect more plants," Yudoline said. Dorian nodded.

"That would help, but I'm afraid that won't work. Look around, how many plants that we can eat do you see?" The side of the mountain was not heavily forested, and there were few bushes. Dorian knew they were forced to go farther each day to forage. Quick forage was running out already and summer hadn't even started.

"What will work?" Yander asked.

"We'll have to plant more crops."

"We've already planted everything," Skover said, confused.

"Not aboveground, under. Yander and I will concentrate on mining out the farm caves, and Barileth can help move earth. We'll be able to make enough to keep us alive." He wondered who would be the first to catch on.

"That means we have to sleep out here then," Lumdir said. Dorian nodded. "Is there enough room to move anything underground?"

"The rest of the supplies, maybe. No beds, no chests." Kimec looked over at his creation half finished, another bed put together hastily. That made six of them finished, with no where to put them.

"Another two weeks out here?" Yudoline asked, frowning. "Isn't there some way we can move in?"

"I'm afraid not. The corridors are too small and the rock slowed us down too much. We'll finish as fast as we can. I don't think we can finish in two weeks either."

"The dwarf speaks sense," Dovig said. "But remember you have me you can count on." He had rolled out from under the cart at some point. "I'll leave here in a few days and come back with as much help as I can muster."

"So we'll have enough then without the caves?" Yudoline asked. Dovig shook his head.

"Don't count on us. You need to be self sufficient, no telling when a random snowstorm blocks us in or a flash flood takes out the supplies cart. Think of it as something extra, a treat. I'll bring the best from back home you can afford."

"Afford, what do you mean?" Yander asked.

"You didn't expect this to be free, did you?" Dovig drew back in shock. "Once the expedition is funded, you're on your own. He knows that, he's got the money."

"You didn't tell us about this," Barileth said.

Dorian shrugged. "I didn't think it was needed. They call it seed money, not enough to survive on. Once it's gone, it's gone."

"That's a relief." Yudoline sighed, Kimec back at her side. "It will mean harder days and nights, but nothing so bad that can...kill us." Dorian looked at her, innocent of everything he had seen. *If only you knew what was out here, you would think differently.*

"Does anyone have an objection?" Dorian wanted this to be over before any of them could come up with any ideas. "Good, then it's settled."

He gave out more instructions to each of them, changed from the morning, and they scattered back to their work. The sounds of industry returned to the valley. The ringing hammer, the steady blows of the axe, even the distant, muffled strike of the pickaxe in the mine.

"Well done," Dovig said when they were alone. "That could have turned out much uglier." His smile was generous, but there was still something that didn't sit right with Dorian. He didn't respond. "If you need any help, let me know. I'll be around, inspecting for the King."

"How is the King?" Dorian asked.

"Oh, as good as can be expected these days. He isn't in the best of health you know." Dorian tightened his lips. He expected him to say the King was doing well, if he knew what he wasn't talking about. *Maybe I'm just seeing things that aren't there.*

"I'll let you get back to your mining, I need to see how much you've extracted from the quarry." Dovig sauntered off with his hands in his pockets, whistling a strange tune. Dorian watched him for a minute, counting the columns and peering over Lumdir's work, then turned and went back into the mine.

As he crossed the threshold back into the cool damp of the earth he sighed. The others wouldn't be happy until they were sleeping beneath the mountain. *I'll finish these caves in two weeks.*

9

HOPS

Dirt rained down as they slid another support into place.

"Steady now." Dorian watched it for signs of collapse. "Let go." It wobbled just enough to be visible, then settled.

"How much more are you digging out?" Lumdir asked. Dorian looked down at what they had excavated. Twenty feet by twenty feet, not enough to keep them alive.

"Double, at least."

"The earth is soft here, it's really easy to dig through. The hardest part is getting it out, now that the corridor is so far away it takes a long time," Yander said, digging into the exposed dirt. "But we're making it go by fast with all the work we're doing, and all the work we've got to go seems light by comparison."

"I'll leave you to it then," Lumdir said, wiping off his hands. They bade him goodbye and returned to their work. The steady rhythm of the pickaxes marked their progress, with Barileth coming to fill up the wheelbarrow and cart it away.

He wasn't happy and glared at Dorian every time he came back. He could feel his eyes on his back, but it couldn't be helped. They worked on in silence until an unusual sound reached his ears. Yander heard it too and stopped.

"Is that wood?" he asked. Dorian nodded. It was the sound of wood on dirt, and a barrel rounded the corner, followed by Skover and Yudoline.

"How is the digging?" Yudoline asked. Skover stopped the barrel in the middle of the room, put it upright with a groan, and leaned up against it heaving. Yudoline was carrying a box and set it down beside him.

"We're going fast, and I'm getting better." Dorian had to admit to himself that Yander was right. He swung his pickaxe with better precision, and tired less. Yander's arms were growing stout from the work, no longer a skinny little dwarf. "That must be the seeds, you're planting aren't you?"

Yudoline patted the sack. "Hops up top and cave berries down here. Soon we'll have a harvest of each and ale and wine will follow right behind." She sighed, a wistful look growing in her eyes. "To taste it, drink deep of something we coaxed from the ground. It's going to be a special day."

"And I'll be happy again to not be drinking water." Skover had recovered, mopping his glistening forehead with his shirt sleeve. Beads of sweat still rolled down his head. "Where can we plant the golden moss?" Dorian thought about it for a moment.

"Over near the entrance, work your way along the sides of the room. Give us enough time and we'll make room for you."

"Are you really going to make ale?" Yander asked.

"Oh, yes. As soon as I can too." Their kegs were still full, but with what the group was going through it wouldn't last that long. Early autumn at the best. Dorian returned to his work as Barileth came back with the wheelbarrow, emptied of earth. "They taught me before we left."

"How was it, making the ale I mean?" Yander asked.

"Ale?" Barileth perked up, the glare replaced with wide-eyed excitement.

"I didn't make any yet, but I think I've got the hang of it." Yudoline pulled out a handful of seeds from the sack she carried. "I'll put the cave berries over here, they need more room to grow."

"Oh," Yander said. "What about wine, was that easy to do?"

"I think so, I'll know for sure once these berries grow." She patted the sack again, then leaned down into the dirt to dig a hole. One by one she dropped four seeds into the earth and covered them back with a layer of the damp, brown dirt.

Dorian wondered how she knew how to make ale and wine without having done it before. He was realizing they didn't send the most proficient dwarves with him. Lumdir was a solid rocksmith, and Kimec knew his way around wood even if he stumbled here and there. But for survival skills? They all seemed to be lacking.

"I didn't know you can make alcohol." Barileth dropped the wheelbarrow and started filling it. "How long do you think it will be until it's ready?"

"A month, at most." Dorian had to suppress a snort, and it threw his aim off. The pickaxe dug into the wall, but took less than he intended.

"Help me with this lid, won't you Barileth?" Skover asked.

"Fine." Together they tried to open the lid, but kept fumbling over each other. Finally Barileth had had enough. "Just hold it." Barileth ended up doing most of the work, prying open the barrel top to reveal the light glow of the golden moss, from which it took its name.

Dorian and Yander stopped to watch them take a handful from the barrel. Skover nestled it in the earth, leaving enough room for each patch to grow out. The hand sized moss starter would spread into each other eventually, leaving a heavy carpet of moss to be harvested.

"Only a few months and we'll have fresh rock bread again." Skover sighed as he worked, knees in the dirt and big belly hanging over his previous plantings. "I can smell it baking now." He breathed in and Dorian smelled it too. Pungent, unlike anything else. A mixture between wheat bread and mushrooms.

It brought back memories. His children first, golden and happy memories that floated through his mind like clouds. Then memories of his wife, which turned the clouds into a thunderstorm that he quickly pushed out of his mind.

"That does sound good. So good my mouth is watering thinking of it." Yander swallowed. "How long until lunch?" The others laughed, and Dorian cracked a smile.

"Let me finish a row and I'll go start it," Skover said.

They returned to work, a momentary reminder of home leaving something else to be desired. Dorian sensed it in the others, but there was nothing he could do to help. *Keep mining. We'll make our own home.*

"A hundred statues, lined up in a row. Each one covered with precious jewels and covered in gold and silver inlay, it's a sight to see." Dovig sighed and leaned back, then took a sip of his cup. He frowned and peered inside. Yander was quick to refill it. "You're a good one Yander."

Yander blushed. "Thanks, Dovig."

"When I get back to the King, I'll beg him for more than what I think you can get. A new pickaxe for you." Dovig tousled Yander's hair and brought out a smile in the young dwarf. "New kegs for you, Yudoline, and a new plane and axe for Kimec of course. Lumdir will have a strong, stout set of steel chisels, and Barileth a battleaxe worthy of you to bear."

He's too charming by far. Dorian sat outside the campfire circle, watching the edge of the mountain for movement. He kept a close eye on Dovig too.

"There's one dwarf I can't seem to pin down though. What would Dorian Ironstrike want, what is his deepest desire?" Dorian felt the eyes on him, but he calmly continued to scan. "Our illustrious expedition leader is secretive and keeps to himself." Dorian met eyes with Dovig. He was searching for a reaction.

The two stared at each other, no emotion revealed in Dorian's eyes, or at least none he hoped. "And what are your secrets?" Dorian asked.

"Secrets? I'm an open book." Dovig spread his arms out and smiled, but it ended before his eyes. Was he a spy for the King? "You'll get your wish, I'm afraid. Tomorrow I depart, before it gets too warm." A round of protests went up around the campfire. Dovig held up his hand and broke the eye contact.

"Don't you remember the supplies you need? As much as I'd love to stay here there are my duties to attend to. Entrust me with your gold and I'll make sure you are well taken care of."

"Kimec, first watch," Dorian said. The dwarves broke up, saying their good nights to Dovig and preparing to retire for the night. With the increased workload they looked tired, they would be woken before dawn and given their tasks. Always more than they could handle.

Curiously, Skover skirted the edge of the campfire toward Dorian, who leveled a stare at him. "What is it?"

"Well," Skover hesitated. Yudoline was still there cleaning up with Kimec. "Yudoline and I were talking about the crops. How are we going to water them?" Dorian sat back, thinking.

"What's wrong with the bucket?" Kimec was preparing for his watch and helping his wife with the fire.

"We use it for milking the goats. We need more."

"Kimec, can you make one?"

"What, a bucket?" Kimec scratched his head and stroked his beard. "I've never made one before but I can't imagine them being that hard to make."

"That will go on the list tomorrow."

"I'll start tonight."

"No, watch only." The words came out harsher than he intended, but they were gone.

"In the morning then," Kimec mumbled.

"Thank you. I wasn't sure how you would respond." Skover looked relieved. *Do I frighten him that much? What about all the rest?* Dorian nodded. He settled in for the night as the camp quieted down, troubled by the day. He thought about his children until he drifted off to sleep.

The hop plants climbed up the stick, winding its way around. Yudoline touched it, feeling the rough leaf, and breathed in the fresh air of the morning. A gentle breeze blew from the east, bringing along the late blooms of wildflowers down in the open patches where the trees didn't grow.

A few more months would bring the harvest in, giving her enough time in the fall to make the ale. With the thought came a hint of nervousness, and a wide swash of excitement. Something about turning a plant into a beverage that dwarves would enjoy always captivated her, but she had never had the chance to do it until now.

"Looks like he's almost off," Skover said, arms in the dirt, pulling weeds from the farming patch. A trail of unwanted plants were strewn behind him, littered on the ground. They were already wilting.

"Less than two months and he'll be back. Fresh kegs, can you imagine?" Yudoline poured water from the pot onto the base of the plants, watching the ground suck it up greedily. It left the dust damp and black, and she moved on to the next ones.

"And a new frying pan, big enough to cook half a pig." Skover licked his lips. Down in the camp Dorian was seeing Dovig off, who picked up his pack, now laden with provisions from their own dwindling stock.

Yudoline followed his gaze, but she was more worried about Kimec. He was in his makeshift workshop, staring at a piece of wood. "He'd better come back quickly." Kimec looked troubled, he was chewing on a shaving and pacing around. "The summer rains will melt the snow and raise the rivers, making it even harder to get here."

Dorian brought out a small, brown bag from his coat and weighed it in his hand. Dovig was smiling and held out his hand, but Dorian pulled it back. Skover wondered what he was doing, but after a time Dorian relented and handed the bag over.

He wouldn't let go and leaned in close to Dovig to say something. It was brief, and the two dwarves parted, the money changing hands. Dovig pocketed the bag and waved to each of them, then he turned north and started down the mountain. His jaunty whistle floated back along the wind, drifting along the valley.

A sudden thought took Skover with his hand still around a weed. Yudoline continued watering and hummed to herself. Skover tensed up and sat back on his heels.

"Yudoline." Skover straightened, bushy eyebrows drawn down. He hesitated. "What if he doesn't make it back?"

10

The Past

It was finished. Kimec stood back, a newly crafted bucket on the plank across two sections of logs that was his workbench. He wiped the sweat from his brow and wondered how it would work.

The trouble was the sides, they weren't straight like boxes were. It had taken him hours to realize that, and many logs split. Now, however, the sides of the bucket sloped up like they were supposed to and clenched the bottom tight.

"Only thing left is to try it." Kimec took it gingerly by the squeaky handle and went down the mountain to the stream. It gurgled and sang as he approached, welcoming him to stop and sink down by the damp earth and drink of its sweet water.

He did, stooping down to cup a handful of water that slid down his dry throat easily. It was fine, did the trick, but ale would have been better. They were rationing it now, until they could make their own, and he wasn't happy about it. No one else was either, except Dorian. He never knew what the dwarf was thinking, he was always closed up and distant.

Kimec knew he was delaying the inevitable and forced himself to bring the bucket over the edge of the water. Looking away he dropped it with a quick splash, then peeked to see it fill up. When he pulled it out a few trails of water streamed out the sides at the gaps. His heart dropped, he would have to make another attempt.

But soon the streams slowed to a trickle and, surprisingly, the bucket held. The sides were dripping with the cold water, but half of the water was still in the bucket. He grinned, then had an epiphany.

He could do the same thing, only larger. Excitement was growing deep inside him, and a strange giddiness he hadn't felt in years flowed through his body. Kimec was going to make a barrel.

The big, plump hop berry resisted her pull, and Yudoline had to hold the vine back with the other hand to get it off. Slightly crushed by the picking, it gave off a wonderful scent and richness. She hummed as she worked, an old tune her mother taught her as a child.

Only a few berries were ready to be picked, but by the time she finished her apron was half filled. The rest of the harvest would come later and leave her plenty of hops to work with.

"How much did you get?" Skover asked, busy at work cutting up meat for another stew. Water was bubbling merrily in the pot on the campfire, the steam mixing with the smoke.

Smiling, Yudoline showed him her bounty. "Enough to make a small batch." Skover returned the smile.

"I can almost taste it now." He licked his lips and sighed. "Fresh ale would be a good change, but wine would be better."

"That will come soon enough." The cave berries were growing nicely, and were easier to water since Kimec had finished his part. He was talking about making barrels now, excited about it too. She hadn't seen the light in his eyes when he talked about it for a long time.

Taking the other pot she went down to the stream and filled it, taking her time walking through the forest to enjoy the coolness of the shade. The stream greeted her with its babbling and the return trip was faster. The water weighed down the pot.

With the water on the fire to boil she took the hops and crushed them like she was taught, using a makeshift pestle and mortar Kimec had hastily carved out. The aroma was heavenly, and she was almost sad to put it in the once roiling water, but she did like she was told and in they went.

She and Skover talked as she worked, sharing in the frustrations of the day and the vision of tomorrow. To the pork in the stew Skover added dried carrots from their journey and a small tuber he had foraged from farther down in the valley, both cut up in slices.

The green leaves played and spun in the water through the bubbles, and she stirred it from time to time to break up clumps that developed. When it was done, she dumped the water into a smaller keg, letting the settled hops not spill over, and reapplied the top.

Less than three hours later the process was finished, and she sat back on the bench to rest, glowing in the accomplishment of it. Now the mash would work, turning the water into ale.

The stew would be ready soon, the other dwarves were winding down their jobs from the day. Lumdir put up his hammer and Dorian, Barileth, and Yander emerged from the gloom of the mine.

Yudoline smiled to herself as Kimec joined her bench with a kiss on the cheek. In less than two weeks they would have their first taste of ale.

"What did you do? Before I mean," Yander said. Dorian considered his question. They were almost finished with the farm caves, with extra work into the night, and throughout that time Yander had talked.

They were nearing the end of the farm cave, at least as much as they needed for now, and were finishing up smaller side caves that the animals would go into. Dorian stopped and leaned on his pickaxe to rest.

"A little of this, some of that." A pause. Yander continued to work.

"What was your first mine like?" That was a question Dorian wasn't prepared for, and it set him back.

His first mine. Dark, deep. Riddled with passages that snaked through the feldspar and chert. The smell of coal dust and smoke, the taste of dirt and ash.

"Why do you ask?" Feelings coursed through him, ones he hadn't remembered in his small, dark cell. He didn't want to feel them, he wanted to do what he had started out to do all those years ago.

Yander shrugged, then shoveled his pile into the second wheelbarrow Kimec made. "I was curious. The way you hold your pickaxe, the look on your face when you're mining. You love it, don't you?"

"I suppose I do."

"I love it too. When my pickaxe sinks into the earth or shatters the stone, when it rains down chips on me that get in my beard and clothes." Yander stopped and sighed. "The thought of striking gold, or precious gems, or a vein of iron ore. Sometimes it keeps me awake at night thinking about it."

Dorian had to admit the young dwarf had grown on him, even if he still talked too much. The light in his eyes, the fire in his talk. He remembered another young dwarf like that and had to turn away.

"When do we get to explore the mountain? Dig deeper?"

"Soon."

"How far down will we go? And what will we find?" Dorian was trying to recover from a moment of longing and didn't respond. Instead, he went back to work, methodically expanding the room, cutting down the dirt, and digging into the earth.

Yander got the message and joined him as Barileth came back into the cave with a pile of sticks on his wheelbarrow and Kimec in tow.

"I finished the fences you asked for, but I wasn't sure about the gates so I've brought rope to finish them," Kimec said, holding out a coil.

"What about the beds?" Dorian asked as they unloaded the fencing.

"Finished, except one. Harder to make than I thought at first, but I've gotten the hang of it now."

"You can almost sleep on the last one he made," Barileth said. "Doesn't wobble like the rest of them. Kimec's eyebrows descended. They started on the fencing, driving sections of them into the dirt and anchoring them to each other with the rope.

"I can fix that."

"A few more days and we'll be able to move them in, won't we?" Yander asked. The other dwarves stared at Dorian. He knew what they were thinking, had heard them around the camp when they didn't think he was listening.

"To be in out of the view of the sky would be good. I'll sleep more securely," Barileth said, and the others nodded their agreement.

"Weeks, at the earliest. Even if you get better Yander." He was crestfallen, playing with the handle of his pickaxe.

"Weeks? We have to sleep outside for weeks?" Barileth's eyes closed to slits, and his breathing increased. *Better to tell them the worst-case scenario.*

"I don't like it any more than you do." Which was true. Sleeping beneath a tent was better than his old cell, but not by much. It got too cold for him at night, and the blanket he used would only wear out and get thinner. The Throne didn't splurge for the best equipment. "We'll finish this today and move back to the rock tomorrow."

"Can you work faster?" Kimec asked, hope in his voice. Dorian shook his head.

"The mountain is good, solid granite. It doesn't yield easily, which works against us right now. In the future, though, it will help." They finished the last fence section and tied up the gates on rope hinges. The first one wobbled.

"The future can go and and bury itself," Barileth grumbled, seizing the handles of the wheelbarrow and spinning it around in his anger. Still grumbling he wheeled it away and out the cavern. They finished the remaining gates in silence.

Three stalls were ready for the goats and chickens. Kimec had built troughs for the goats and was almost done with a nesting place for the chickens, as Dorian directed. Soon they would bring them in and let the chickens forage.

The goats, however, would have to remain in their stalls or they would eat the crops. Skover would have to take them outside to graze until they could get a steady source of fodder growing for them.

"Keep working on the spears and make a few shafts in case we strike metal." Kimec nodded, slapped the dirt off his hands, and followed Barileth out of the farm cave.

"They're asking me when we'll finish the dormitory," Yander said when the others were out of earshot. Dorian went back to work, burying his pickaxe at the back of the stall they would use for the goats. It wouldn't hurt to give them some more room. "What do I tell them?"

"Nothing more than I've said." The others would grow impatient, but they would have to wait. "They can move into the corridors if they'd like, no beds though. They'll have to sleep on the ground."

"That will be cramped, and uncomfortable."

"Uncomfortable inside, uncomfortable outside." His pickaxe flowed in a steady rhythm, dirt was piling up. "I won't have them getting in the way."

Yander joined him, shoveling the dirt into the wheelbarrow. Barileth came back, swapped wheelbarrows, and went to dump it. They worked through the evening until at last Barileth told them dinner was ready.

It was stew again.

"How long until we can move in?" Yudoline asked. Dorian spooned a mouthful of the stew and chewed. *Was everyone going to ask tonight?*

"Few weeks."

"Oh." Her eyes dropped, and her shoulders slumped. Another mouthful.

"Maybe more." Her shoulders slumped more. Lumdir looked deflated too, and Skover was disappointed.

"Is there anyway to speed that up?" Skover stirred his bowl, eyes down in it. Another prick, more irritation in Dorian. *How weak is this group?*

"Would you like to dig yourself? We've only got two pickaxes but Kimec can sharpen a stick for you." Skover turned red, but didn't say anymore. Kimec frowned at his name being mentioned.

"It's been almost two months, he didn't mean anything by it," Yudoline said. Somehow her defense made his anger worse.

"I'll give you the same option I gave Yander. You can move in each night and sleep with the goats." He raised one finger before any of them could say anything else. "But if you get in our way, I will mine through you."

11

MUSHROOMS

"That's it, more than enough room to fit everyone." Dorian's back ached. The granite was harder than he thought, and trying to save chunks big enough for Lumdir to work with had slowed them, but not by much.

"It's still small, we'll have to pack in the beds tight." Yander wiped off his forehead, smearing a trail of gray rock dust across it. "On second thought, I'd rather sleep right next to each other inside than spend another night outside. Those summer rains have been unpredictable and I get wet sometimes since it comes in the side of the tent." Dorian grunted.

"Go tell the others." Yander broke out in a smile and ran off. Dorian worked on the final piles of rock, shoveling as much into the wheelbarrow as he could. Barileth was hunting this morning, so they had to haul their own debris away. The mound outside was growing.

They would come quickly, drop everything they were doing. He was right. Less than a few minutes later they were thundering down the corridor to see.

"This is it?" Yudoline asked. "I thought it would be...bigger."

"Temporary," Dorian grunted.

"We'll carve out individual rooms for each dwarf, or dwarf family," Yander added. "But we have enough room for the rest of our supplies and the beds until we can get deeper in the mine."

"What are we waiting around here for?" Barileth asked. For a second the others grinned at each other, then they headed for the exit.

Together the dwarves moved in, two dwarves per bed. Each personal chest went in after that, then the remaining supplies. By the time they were done beds, boxes, and barrels packed the dormitory from wall to wall.

"That is a sight for sore eyes indeed," Barileth said. He was the happiest Dorian had ever seen him.

"And it means it's time to tear down the tents." Lumdir shifted the last barrel into place, which they would have to move around to get farther into the dormitory. *Storage would be next, and then a place to eat underground.* Dorian made a mental note to start Lumdir making tables and chairs.

Barileth tested his bed and rocked on it. "Doesn't wobble."

"I told you I'd fix them." Kimec didn't look pleased at the comment.

"Good job."

Yudoline clapped her hands together, startling most of the dwarves. "Oh, we almost forgot the surprise." She shared a look with Skover. Barileth sat up.

"Well, what is it?" Yander asked.

"Mushrooms, fresh mushrooms." Skover beamed. "They must have grown in the rains. I've planned a meal, just like my mother made back home."

"And the ale should be ready too," Yudoline added. Anticipation glowed in the other dwarves eyes, lit up by the torchlight. Barileth smacked his lips.

"Sweet, fresh ale? I can smell it now, pulled straight off the tap. What are we waiting for?"

Excitement was in the air, even though the quarters would be more cramped than they would like. Dorian stood up and stretched. "Then tonight, we feast."

The tents were torn down and packed away, the area prepared for the meal. The logs and rough planks they were eating on had been replaced by a simple table made of oak with round stools cut from granite.

Skover and Yudoline worked deep in the kitchens of the mines, toiling away as the others finished the various tasks left to them. Dorian pondered sleeping outside tonight too, but reconsidered it. Being in the enveloping embrace of the earth was an allure too strong to resist, even though it meant being in close quarters with the others.

He would move in tonight with them.

Kimec emerged from the mine entrance rolling a small keg.

"That's it, isn't it?" Barileth asked, coming up beside him, mug in hand. Kimec held out a hand to fend him off.

"Not yet, Yudoline will do the honors. Help me with this." They lifted it onto a stump next to the table, and it sat in readiness like a squat sentry in the evening light. A proud reminder of what could be, if they worked hard enough.

They milled about, waiting. The others traded small talk while Dorian stood back, considering where to mine next. It would have to be the start of the great hall, somewhere to dine out of the sun and weather. Too often they had to take meals under the cover of the tent.

Finally, Skover emerged carrying a big, steaming bowl. It gave off a smell so wonderful it made his mouth water. Everyone converged on the table, taking their seats.

"It's ready." Skover gingerly put it on the table. Yudoline joined him with another platter heaped with pork. "Stewed mushrooms and potatoes in gravy, a family secret recipe." The table buzzed.

"Break out the ale, would you?" Yudoline shot Barileth a stern look. "Please?" he added hastily. Her frown disappeared with his admission, turning into a bright, beaming smile.

"I'll warn you, this is only the first batch. There will be more to come so don't be greedy." Kimec stood next to it, tap and hammer in hand. She took them while he removed the plug in the taphole. Hands trembling, she inserted the tap and gave it a light hammer.

On the third blow she slipped, but after a deep breath she recovered. With more force, she hit it, sending it home on the fifth blow. They tilted the keg up and she took the offered mug from Barileth. She held it beneath the tap and hesitated.

"Go on," Barileth said, breaking the silent ceremony. "Oh, don't cry now, don't be sad."

"I'm not sad," Yudoline said. Kimec wiped small tears from her cheek. "I'm just so happy. After all our work, and the time we've spent together. I — " she sniffed. "Never mind, I'll get on with it."

She turned the tap, a stream of amber brown liquid splashing into the mug. It foamed a little and trickled to a stop, filled to the brim. Barileth took it with eager hands and tried to take a sip.

"Hold on, not yet." Forced to wait, Barileth stared at the mug. Other mugs were passed around until even Dorian had his share.

"To the expedition," Kimec said solemnly, raising his mug in the air.

"The expedition," the others repeated, raising their own to match. Dorian lowered his mug and breathed deep of the ale. It smelled...off. Barileth spewed his out of his mouth, coughing.

"What's wrong?" Yudoline's eyebrows raised, her mouth forming a surprised o. Barileth recovered.

"Wrong, nothing's wrong."

"I knew it," Yudoline said. She took a sip of her own mug, then spit it back in. "It's horrible!"

Dorian had to see for himself. The ale was weak and tinged with a rotten taste, completely undrinkable. Something had gone wrong in the making.

Kimec was trying to comfort his distraught wife, the others disposed of their mugs where she couldn't see. Dorian casually poured his out behind a clump of grass where it wouldn't run into the makeshift dining hall.

"It wasn't all that bad," Barileth said. He had courageously taken a few more sips of his before ridding himself of it. "And next time will turn out better."

"I forgot to drain it, I remember now." Yudoline's few tears had dried up, but she still clung to Kimec who patted her. Skover sat down beside her and took her hand.

"The cave berries are growing now, in a few months we'll have enough to make two kegs of wine." Her frown turned into a small smile at Skover.

"You're right, sticks and stones I had forgotten. Look at me blubbering like a school dwarf." She sat up straight and pushed back her shoulders. "With enough time and space we'll be over-flowing with wine, as dark purple as anything in Zirad."

"That's the spirit," Lumdir said, lifting the gloomy haze from the group. "And we still have a feast to enjoy, with enough ale from our stocks. No sense in wasting a good time."

The kegs were quickly exchanged, the bad batch never to be seen again, and fresh mugs were poured. The foam bubbled and overflowed the mugs, thick heads of it that splashed as they were passed around.

"Come, sit with us Dorian," Lumdir said when everyone had a mug and a plate. They left him a seat at the end, with enough room to respect his privacy. Dorian didn't know what to think. The closer he got to these dwarves, the more he would care about them. And if he cared too much he might not be able to make the hard decisions.

There was something unnatural about, and danger lurked in the wilds around them. But it would be nice to relax for once. To break bread and toast with his fellow dwarves once again. *How long had it been?*

Dorian cleared his throat and nodded. He took the offered seat, along with his plate, and waited until everyone else had filled their plate. Taking his food, he sat back and waited to eat.

When Dorian took his food, the others started eating.

"Wonderful," Lumdir said, and tore off another piece of the still steaming pork. Dorian tried his. The mushrooms and potatoes were cooked perfectly, the potatoes were soft, and the mushrooms weren't soggy. The thick gravy added a layer of flavor and spice to the earthy mushrooms that complemented it.

The pork was juicy and not too salty. It fell apart and was a delight to eat.

"Mmm," Skover sighed, taking another spoonful of potatoes and mushrooms. "Just like my mother made. Brings back memories of my younger days. I was skinny back then." He patted his belly. Dorian took a swig of his ale. It was old, but still good. "And my, how I would get into trouble. One time, I made off with the dining table and chairs. Wanted to host a lunch for my friends. Did I get a talking to then!"

"You, misbehave? I can't believe it," Yudoline said.

"It's true. I was a handful in my younger years. My mother put up with a lot."

"To mothers, may they be ever blessed," Lumdir said, raising his mug.

"To mothers," the others said in unison, then took a drink.

"My mother encouraged me to go," Yander said. "She said it would be good for me, make me stronger. To be honest, I think she just wanted more peace and quiet around the house." Laughter rang out, and red flushed above his beard. Dorian couldn't help but smile. "I miss her cooking too, and how steady she and my father are."

"We all left loved ones at home," Kimec said, patting him on the back.

"And some enemies too." Barileth took a swig from his mug. "That's one thing I won't miss. That, and all the dwarves crammed into too tight a space. Cave, house, it didn't matter. Couldn't walk down the street without bumping into someone."

"Not to mention the humans and elves. They can stay far away from us, and I'll enjoy it," Lumdir said, and the others murmured agreement. "Too many foreigners for my taste."

"But the markets were always full of new and interesting things. Too expensive to buy, but exciting to look at," Yudoline said.

"When we're done here, you'll have all the coin you desire to buy it too," Barileth added.

"What do you miss the most, Lumdir?" Yander asked. He scratched his beard in thought.

"Sweetbreads in the morning, before going to work. So hot and fresh, and the way they tore apart down the middle. Stick a pat of butter in it and it would run down my fingers a moment later." Dorian's mouth watered, even though he had his fill of food. "What about you Dorian, what was your life like before the expedition?"

Dorian sat back. Memories of his dark, cramped cell, the trial, the conviction rushed back to him. He didn't realize he was scowling until he saw the looks on their faces.

"That's none of your business," he growled, the peace of the evening shattered. "And no one else ask again."

12

SONG OF THE EARTH

Assignments the next morning were tense, but Dorian ignored it and gave them out without emotion in his voice.

"Yander, you're with me today."

"What are we doing?"

"We're going into the mountain, down. See what she holds." Against his better judgment, Dorian was excited. Yander, who had looked muted before, cheered up. *Was his emotion spreading?* He tried to remember to keep it in check. There was no guarantee they would find anything, no use getting worked up about it.

With the young dwarf chattering about what they could find they entered the cave and went to the far end of the entrance tunnel. Dorian started cutting into the earth and expecting to strike rock soon.

By lunch they had. Their progress slowed again, but not as much as it had a few weeks ago. They were faster. Rock was pulled out of the mine faster than Lumdir could turn it into furniture. The rough stools they sat on turned into carved chairs, replaced one by one.

A few days later they had gone far enough in Dorian was comfortable digging down. The entrance was barely visible, a bright light coming down the dark tunnel. They had only found granite.

"Down we go." Dorian turned his pickaxe on the floor, smashing into it and sending shards flying. "We'll make a mineshaft here, and carve stairs as we go. Careful not to cut off too much rock."

He showed Yander how to shape the rock, digging down enough to make a comfortable step for the average dwarf. After digging a few out, Dorian got out of his stepped hole.

"You'll make the next one. Careful now, cut it out before you strike." Yander cleft a line.

"Like this?"

"Longer, and cut between here." Dorian pointed to a section between the line that needed to be closer. "Now, give it a go." Yander did fine, chipping an edge of the stair but leaving enough to be usable.

The next few were easier for him, and he got the hang of it. Dorian let him work, taking out the rocks left over from their mining. By dinnertime they were down to the level below, cutting back and leaving a larger carve out in the center.

"We'll cut the stairs now and leave the shaft for later. It will be easier to handle once we have enough material to make the elevator." They had plenty of rope, unless they had to use it for something else. The machinery would have to wait until they had the metal to forge them.

"It's an actual mine now, isn't it?" Yander's eyes glowed under the rock dust and dirt covering his face. Dorian nodded. "My first mine, I can't believe it's happening. All the gems we'll find, and all the ore too! Oh, I can't wait."

"You'll have to, we've got dinner to eat." Yander's excitement was infectious, spreading to Dorian. He touched the wall, the rough, cool stone beneath his hand. It was good to be back underground.

Almost wishing he didn't have to, Dorian joined Yander in the entering the hot, early summer evening for dinner. There was a long way to go, but it was looking more possible by the day.

The steady hum of the mining kept them busy, although Dorian changed tactics. They split up, one carving out a mineshaft and the other to a dining room. Dorian took most of the dining room, sure to leave plenty of support around the columns that would dominate the room. For now it was rough, but later it would turn into something majestic and worthy of a dwarven mine.

While he was cutting out the corner of the room, Dorian heard Yander shouting from deeper in the mine. Stopping his mining, Dorian leaned back and wiped sweat from his forehead. *What is he up to now?*

"Dorian, look," Yander said, bursting through the entryway. Hand outstretched in front of him, he was raising it high into the air in, a smile plastered across his grimy face. "I found it in the rock, just brought down my pickaxe and it was there."

He dropped it into Dorian's hand, but he couldn't see it clearly in the gloom. It was hard and rough, and Dorian held it up to the light of a nearby torch while Yander continued.

"It's got to be something good, I just know it. And I was the first to find something! I can't tell you how excited I am." It glittered in the light, and an icy hand squeezed on Dorian's heart.

"Good," he mumbled.

"What is it? I was thinking garnet, but I'm not too familiar with gems that have just come from the earth."

"No, ruby." Dorian handed it back, arm outstretched, while he looked away. *Where was she right now? Was she even alive?*

"Ruby! This will fetch a pretty price back home, I'm sure we can use it to buy more supplies. What a glorious day to be alive and underground."

"Good work." Dorian grabbed a shovel, pressing a hand against his beating chest. He shoveled rock into his wheelbarrow. "I've got to take this load out. I'll be right back." Wheelbarrow half empty, he left Yander to gaze in wonder at his find.

Dorian almost broke into a run, then forced himself to walk. At the entrance he collapsed against the support, closing his eyes and letting the cool breeze blow over him. His breathing was ragged and shallow.

The day she was born. Holding her in his arms and seeing her smile. Twirling her around the room and listening to her laugh, high and filled with excitement. *Get a hold of yourself. You're no use like this.* His heart ached to see her and his son, and yearned for his dead wife.

"Everything all right?" Yudoline called up. Dorian's eyes snapped open. She stopped laying out carrots to dry down at their outdoor dining hall. *Too far away to see me.* He thought about what he should say, then settled on the truth.

"Found something, we'll bring it out tonight." With a deep breath, he pushed his wheelbarrow out into the sun and dumped it on the pile. He still had more to teach Yander, and after his recovery time, knew he could handle it.

Yander was still grinning when he came back, gripping the rough ruby.

"Show me where you found it."

"I almost forgot, come one and follow me." Yander led the way. "I thought about going down a side tunnel, like you talked about, but thought you wanted to tell me where to dig first so I didn't. This was while I was carving out the stairs, can you believe that?"

Dorian could believe it, especially when he was standing over the hole where it had come from.

"Here?" he asked.

"Yes." Yander crouched down to grab his pickaxe.

"Did you sense anything when you were close to it?"

"Sense anything?" Yander frowned. "What do you mean?"

"In the rock. Were you listening to it?"

"No, I'm not understanding what you're saying." Dorian crouched down next to him. He clasped his hand around Yander's, forcing him to grip the ruby tighter.

"Listen to the rock, hear what it's saying. Close your eyes." Yander complied, after giving him a puzzled look. "Now, concentrate on what's in you hand." Yander screwed his eyes closed tighter. "Don't force it." He relaxed.

Dorian also closed his eyes, trying to remember what it was like. He let go of Yander's hands and put them on the ground, spreading his fingers wide apart to feel as much as possible. "There is life in the rock, if you listen closely. You spend enough time with it and it will sing to you, tell you where the ore and gems are."

"I don't hear it."

"Concentrate." The rock was cool under his fingers, but when he breathed deep he could feel it himself. The vibration of life tickled his fingers and spread up his arm.

"I...think I feel something."

"Don't feel, just listen." How long had it been since he had done this? In his cell he was surrounded by rock, but it was cold and lifeless. He had almost forgotten what it felt like. He had forgotten himself.

There. He sensed it beneath him, just under the surface. Dorian took the pickaxe. "Feel this." Yander opened his eyes and put his hand where Dorian was pointing. He licked his lips.

"There's more, isn't there?" Dorian smiled, then lifted the pickaxe and brought it down in one swift blow.

It was perfect. The rock cracked, revealing two more gems hidden beneath it. He carved them out and handed them to Yander.

"Beautiful, aren't they? Let's take them to the others."

"Bring your end up." The tables just fit through the tunnel, if they wrestled it the right way, but the last one was giving them trouble. Dorian puffed and pushed up on his side, wishing it wasn't taking so long. The table shifted, then popped free.

Dorian and Yander fell backward, caught off guard, and Yander squawked. He landed hard on his back, and the table hit him in the stomach.

Air knocked out of him, Dorian struggled to breathe.

"Are you all right?" Lumdir asked as he and Barileth pulled off the heavy table.

"A bit bruised, but that's it," Yander said, rubbing his back. Dorian recovered his breath, breathing in the sweet, stale air of the mine. He managed a nod. When he had recovered, they continued, finally pulling the table into the completed dining hall.

"Are you sure you can't expand it some now?" Barileth asked, putting the final chair in place. Two rock tables, newly crafted by Lumdir last week, fit well together side by side between two columns of the hall. Torches lit the room temporarily until they could get a more permanent light source in place.

"Not if we want our industry up and running. Leaving the craft dwarves outside isn't going to work." Dorian's left arm stung from where the table had hit it on the way down, and he rubbed the spot to try and help it go away.

"And we have the mine. We can't do everything at once." Yander brushed off the table, then put his weight on it to move it. It didn't shift.

"Everything is so small, that's all I'm saying. Not enough room to sleep, not enough room to eat, no room to work." Dorian knew Barileth was saying what the others were thinking, but there wasn't enough time. Summer was already half gone, and winter would be here before they knew it.

"The apartments will be right after the workshop. Yander has learned a lot and is a much better miner, and we've gotten faster." Yander perked up at the praise, and belatedly Dorian worried it might have been too much. "And we still need defenses. A wall, at the least."

"That will take time." Barileth crossed his arms and leaned back against the column. "I expect I'll be building it?" Dorian nodded.

"Lumdir has plenty of rock left over for it. We'll lay out what we need now, modest defenses, and grow when we need to."

"Why do we need a wall?" Yander asked. "The entrance door can keep the dogs out, can't it?" The other dwarves exchanged glances. Dorian tried to remember being so innocent and naïve. He had to have been at some point, but he couldn't remember it.

"Dogs are the least of our worries," Barileth said. "Goblins, trolls, bandits. Take your pick, any of them would love to come and take what we have, and leave us dead after."

"Goblins? Around here?" Yander was aghast at the suggestion.

"Oh yes. A nice, plump expedition like ours?" Barileth smiled a crooked smile, and in the torchlight it disfigured his face. "With food and supplies we have we'd be an easy target. Mount a quick raid, slaughter all the dwarves, and take what you want."

"You're scaring him," Lumdir said quietly.

"Good, better scared and alive than ignorant and dead."

"No," Dorian said firmly, "as long as I draw breath I'm not going to let that happen."

13

Mineshaft

The humid air was thick with the smell of moss and cave berries. Occasional drips punctuated the stillness of the farm cave.

"This will be a good crop."

"If everything continues as it has," Skover said. Yudoline nodded.

"Yes, if it does." Dorian was taking a break from mining, letting Yander continue carving out a workshop area near the dormitory. The golden moss was creeping together, less dirt on the cave floor than there used to be.

It was a welcome sight. At any time they could harvest it, at the risk of it growing slower, but knowing they had it was comforting. The cave berries had already sprung branches from their twisted trunks, reaching out and casting shadows in the torchlight.

"Keep tending them. Having too much is always a problem I'll take."

"It's much easier to water them with the bucket. Kimec is going to make us another when he finds time, although he's been caught up trying to make a barrel." Yudoline frowned.

"What is it?" Skover asked.

"Nothing." Dorian kept a close eye on her, but she recovered from the odd change and a smile returned to her lips. "A few more months and we'll have berries to harvest."

"And wine after that." Skover clapped his hands. "It will be a good day. We'll have to celebrate."

"Don't get ahead of yourself," Dorian warned.

"You're right. Dovig should be back soon though, with more supplies," Skover said.

"Enough to keep us fed until next year and then some." The torch sputtered as Dorian turned and walked by. "Back to work now." He left them to their work and returned to his.

Listening to the steady beat of Yander's pickaxe, he was caught away as he walked back. They needed metal, which meant they needed ore. So far they hadn't found anything other than the rubies and a few semi-precious gemstones. They wouldn't be worth much in barter, and were far less than what the King would expect.

Competing priorities had slowed them, made him work where he didn't want to be. Other expeditions hadn't been like this. Those were established with strong dwarves in command, willing to squash dissent and focus on survival with a singular mindset. Even the few expeditions he had led before the incident were better managed.

Granted, he had more resources and skilled dwarves to take with him. His captivity had dulled his senses, taken the edge off his vision and it was starting to show. They should have been dug in by now, moved in and working like smooth machinery.

Instead, they were plodding along, vulnerable and slow. If he didn't change his approach, they might find themselves sharing the same fate other expeditions had. He didn't want that for him, and he didn't want that for the others.

"How'd it go?" Yander asked as he walked in. Work had progressed, the room was wide enough now. It would fit all of Lumdir's and Kimec's tools and then some, when they lengthened it.

"Crops are growing. We'll have enough for a feast at the end of winter." Yander sighed.

"I was hoping you would say that. I've been scared to look, in case they weren't."

"Once we expand this enough to house the workshop, we'll move back into the mine." Dorian joined him, cutting into the freshly exposed earth. They were working back out from the mountain and would have plenty of dirt to extract. It would go fast though.

He puzzled through how they were going to set up a foundry, and was still thinking about it that night when he went to bed.

"Right there." Barileth drove in the final anchor, spitting out the rock dust that showered down on him. Yander held out the rope, and he threaded it through the pulley. They had a makeshift elevator now, only a large bucket Kimec made instead of a platform.

Dorian and Kimec took up the slack as Barileth came back down from his makeshift platform suspended over the mineshaft. He and Yander pulled it back in. Finally, after pulling about a hundred feet of rope through, the line went taught. With more effort the bucket swung into the air.

"Swing it out. Hold steady." Barileth pushed it out over the shaft. "Let it down, careful now," Dorian said. Yander joined them, allowing gravity to pull the rope from their hands. The bucket went, and a clatter announced its arrival on the ground below.

"Good." Dorian tied off the rope to a makeshift cleat in the wall he carved. The others were smiling.

"This will save my back and my legs," Barileth said.

"I can't wait. Not having to climb all those stairs with rocks on my back will be a relief." Yander rubbed his back and grimaced. Dorian had to agree with them, it was better now that they had it in place, although that was their only pulley. *We need to find ore.*

"If you need me I'll be in the workshop," Kimec said, waving and retreating back down the tunnel. Lumdir was in his section of the workshop still, hammering away at another block of stone. *At least we won't run out of that.*

"Hunting?" Barileth asked. Dorian nodded. "I'm off then."

"Back to the mine?" Yander asked.

"Back to the mine." Dorian made a mental note to have Lumdir carve some rock gears. With the right system they could lower dwarves in the bucket, it was big enough to hold just one.

The days went by slowly, agonizing. Dorian and Yander carved down into the mountain. Through granite and shale layers they cut, taking time to explore the layers. Every so often Dorian would stop them, feel the rock, and they would cut a tunnel to see if they could find a vein of ore.

They didn't.

"A few gems, that's all we've found," Yander said two weeks later as Dorian stopped him on their latest tunnel branch.

"Patience." If the mountain held treasure it would give it up, eventually.

"I'm trying to be patient, I am." Yander gripped the handle tightly. "It's just the same thing every day. Rock, rock, and more rock." He slammed his pickaxe into the wall, spraying himself with shards. He cried out in anger, a short yell that echoed back through the tunnel and up the mineshaft.

Dorian was young once, and he tried to remember what it felt like. His time was growing shorter too, every minute they had here was one less in his life. It was worse for Yander, he knew that, but he couldn't force him to be patient.

"What do we do?" Yander asked.

"We dig."

So they dug deeper, carving down stairs until they stretched the rope of their pulley, then they tied another rope to it and sent it down farther. The days blended into each other. They woke up, ate, mined, ate, mined, ate, went to sleep, and repeated it again the next day.

Days went by, the dwarves wondered what the miners were doing. Dorian heard them talking went they thought he wasn't listening, heard the whispers. It was beginning to grate on him. They wanted apartments, a larger dining hall, more room. He knew they needed it, but they needed metal more.

He was starting to doubt himself. It had been a long time since he had been on an expedition. Was he wrong and sending them careening toward failure and death?

Dorian was mining with Yander, digging another exploratory tunnel, thinking about it when yelling from the mineshaft stopped him.

"Hold on." Yander stopped, his pickaxe lodged in the wall.

"What is it?" Dorian listened closer, recovering his breath and letting the blood pumping in his ears from mining slow. "They're yelling for you."

"Wonder what this is about," Dorian said. "Bring your pickaxe. We'll see what they want." Yander pulled out his pickaxe, not noticing the rocks sliding down from an opening too black to be rock.

They were yelling his name, Yudoline from the sound of it. The sound echoed down the mineshaft, and he peered up at her from down below.

"What is it?"

"You've got to come up here and see for yourself," she said. With Yander grumbling behind they mounted the steps. Yudoline looked breathless, moving faster than usual. She beckoned to them.

"Come on," she urged. Dorian picked up his pace, wondering what it was. His heart was beating fast again, from the effort of climbing the stairs and the anticipation of what was to come. Butterflies started in his stomach, but he took deep breaths to calm them. "Barileth saw them, while he was hunting."

"Saw who?" Yander asked. They shuffled down the entrance tunnel, heading for the bright light of day.

"We don't know." They burst out of the mine and into the sunlight. Dorian shielded his eyes from the harsh rays of the sun, then blinked away the afterimage as he tried to acclimate. "Down there." When he could see he followed Yudoline's finger.

Small figures were climbing the mountain, still far down at the base where the stream emptied out. They were visible through the trees, glimpses of movement and brown between openings in the canopy.

They weren't goblins, he would have recognized their jerky, unstable walk from this far, and they were too small to be humans or elves.

"dwarves?" he guessed.

"That's what Barileth thinks too," Yudoline said, her eyes brimming with excitement. "Do you think it's Dovig?"

"Could be." He hadn't seen a cart or oxen, no pack animals at all. "Alert everyone else, it's time to prepare." Dorian tested the door, making sure the heavy granite would shut tight. Lumdir had cut a lock for the inside as he requested, if it came to it they would lock up inside.

It didn't mean they would survive though. The others trickled out as the figures processed closer. Barileth came out of the forest.

"Dwarves all right," he said, crossbow slung across his back. He was getting better with it.

"Could you tell if they were hostile?"

"No idea."

"Get the spears." Dorian hefted his pickaxe. It would do for a weapon in a pinch. "Hide them behind the door just in case." Yander scrambled back into the mine and emerged a few minutes, red-cheeked and breathing heavily.

The seven of them waited in a line, the summer sun beating down on them. It was well past lunchtime, but Dorian's appetite was forgotten. He had a sinking feeling inside.

Through the trees the dwarves trekked. They carried chests and boxes on their back, slung across their shoulders. Their clothes were ragged and threadbare. The newcomers saw them and altered their course.

"Well met," the lead dwarf said, doffing his hat and wiping sweat from his glistening forehead. They drew up a respectful distance from Dorian and the founders.

Dorian didn't respond but waited for the five dwarves, two female and three male to draw to a stop. They all doffed their packs, setting them on the grass. The younger of the two females sat down in the shade of a tree.

"Is this Seventh Hall?" the lead dwarf said, after being met with silence.

"Who asks?" Dorian asked, arms crossed. They held the high ground.

"Apologies, I should have introduced myself earlier. I'm Daruik Icebrewer and this is my wife Noreck and daughter Emelda."

"Narfac Twilightfury," said a shorter, stout dwarf.

"Kragnak Grimforge," said the last dwarf. He was thin and gangly by dwarf standards. They didn't look like fighters and didn't seem to have any weapons. That only left one question.

"Well met," Dorian said, then introduced himself and the others. "Why are you here?"

Daruik's eyes opened wide. "I thought you knew, we were told word was sent ahead of us. They've predicted a harsh winter and told us to leave earlier."

"We've had no word of anything," Barileth growled. The newcomers drew back at his tone.

Wringing his hat in his hands Daruik said. "We're migrants, we've come to live here."

14

MIGRANTS

Exhausted and dusty, the pitiable band of migrants stood awaiting their fate. *A migrant wave? This early?*

"Come again?" Barileth asked. Five more mouths to feed through the year. Five more people to keep alive.

"We've come to stay." Narfac drew himself up. "We were made promises, one of them that we would have a place."

"There's no place for you here," Barileth said, a note of warning in his tone.

"We don't mean to inconvenience you," Daruik held Narfac back with a hand. "Work is what we mean to barter with. We'll pull our weight."

"How much food did you bring?" Dorian asked quietly. Glances were exchanged. *They didn't even bring enough for them.* Silence reigned.

"We ran out yesterday and were hoping you had enough," Noreck finally said, a hint of a quiver in her voice. Skover drew in a sharp breath.

"Dorian, a word," he said. Some of the tension had fled, but the air was still tense. Dorian turned away from the migrants and motioned

Skover over to whisper in his ear. "We barely have enough food for ourselves, I don't think we can feed them."

"Yander, will you get our visitors something cool to drink?" Dorian asked. So little time, so few supplies. Turning back to the migrants he appraised them. "What were your professions?"

They listed them. Beekeeper, wax worker, wax worker, wood burner, smith.

"Well, not a full smith exactly," Kragnak hedged. "I didn't pass the guild test." So failed smith, then. Yander was back, passing around a bucket of water and mugs.

"Rest here, we'll be back," Dorian said. The migrants sat to rest beneath the trees while the rest of the dwarves retreated to the mine.

"We can't have them stay," Barileth said. "Send them back."

"You can't do that, they'll die!" Yudoline said.

"Not our problem, unless you want to keep them and have them all die here."

"Barileth has a point," Dorian said, and Barileth smiled smugly. "Unfortunately we don't have a choice." The smile was wiped off his mouth.

"What?"

"Expedition rules. We must accept all living migrants, no matter the state of the expedition." Barileth gaped at him.

"We don't have a choice?" Lumdir asked. Dorian shook his head. Most expeditions needed the labor, but this wasn't the only time more bodies would be a drag on a mine.

"Which means we should welcome them." Yudoline turned and opened the door.

"Except they have no place to stay. Where are we going to put them?" Kimec asked.

"They'll stay outside for now, or they can live in our exploratory tunnels. How long will it take to build them beds?"

"A week or two, faster if I rush it."

"Put a premium on it. The good news is that when we find ore we'll have a smith to work it." Barileth said some rather colorful words in relation to their predicament, and Dorian told him to keep it to himself.

"Come on in, we'll get you something to eat." Smiles broke out on the migrant's dirty faces, and they scrambled to their feet. They shook hands with the founders and rushed into the tunnel as soon as they could.

After a late meal huddled around tables too small for all of them Dorian broke the bad news.

"No room to sleep?"

"You can take the outside, the tunnels, or the kitchen." Dorian was still working on how the mine would be able to support itself. The golden moss might be ready to split, but they would need more farm caves to grow it.

Narfac looked like he was about to say something, but Daruik jumped in. "We'll be happy to sleep wherever we can. Like we said earlier, we mean to earn our keep."

"You can start by telling me more about your skills."

"I've been a beekeeper ever since I can remember, even as a young dwarfling. Father kept them too and he would bring me along. I've kept a few hives on our journey, it might be late in the season to establish them but I'll do my best." Honey. Not particularly useful to them right now.

Daruik must have seen the look in his eye, because he hastily continued. "Honey isn't the only thing they produce. A good hive will have plenty of wax for candles and crafts, and it can even be shaped for casting certain metals." He pulled out a small box that buzzed. "These are cave bees, they'll help grow crops too. What kinds do you have planted?"

"Cave berries, and golden moss," Yudoline said.

"Ah, cave berries are good. That will make their honey sweet. Don't worry about hives, I can make some if you have some spare rock sitting around." Yander snorted at that.

"Have as much as you want," Lumdir said. "We've got too much already."

"What about the smith, can you do anything else?" Kragnak shook his head. Dorian shifted his attention to Narfac. "If we don't have much wood to burn what else can you do?"

"First aid, and anything to do with fire. I imagine I'd be able to run your smelter." Dorian perked up.

"Did you say smelter? What about making one?"

"You don't have a smelter?" Narfac asked, leaning back against the wall and thinking. "I suppose I could help build one if I had to. Can't say I'd like it much, but if that's what I had to do I could make it work."

They went through the supplies they brought. Bees, wax-working tools, extra wicks for candles. A well-used hammer from Kragnak, and that was about all that was useful. They weren't as useless as he first expected, but they still were far from being the best migrants he had encountered.

"Get some rest tonight, we'll start with assignments first thing in the morning." Dorian got up, stretched his legs, and headed back to the dormitory to sleep. Barileth caught up to him in the tunnel.

"Dorian, a word in private if I may." He looked behind him to make sure the other dwarves were well out of earshot. Dorian obliged, turning to face him. "These migrants, they don't show up this early, do they?"

"No." Dorian didn't see the use in concealing the truth.

"Why would that be? Is there something that you know about this expedition that the rest of us don't?" There were no torches in this section of the corridor, and it was almost pitch black. Even with his eyes adjusted Dorian couldn't make out Barileth's face. There was a lot he knew that the others didn't, but what good would knowing do for them?

"Nothing comes to mind." Barileth stepped forward, reached up and grabbed his arm. His grip was strong.

"Are you sure?" Dorian looked down at his arm. He felt each individual finger.

"Get your hand off me." A second longer of the pressure, then it was gone. "I'll forget this. Once and only once. I've killed better dwarves than you and I wouldn't hesitate."

"That's not what I meant--"

"I'm sure it isn't. Now, if you don't mind I have a lot to think about and sleep on." Dorian turned and walked away, an icy grip on his heart. Some of his anger had come through when he didn't want it. He couldn't do it again. Not knowing what he knew now.

A means to an end. Once I'm through these next few years life will change. I'll see her again, I know it. He cast off his boots and took off his dirt laced clothes, setting them on the chest at the foot of his bed.

There was still too much to do, and now they would have to change strategies once again. Food supply, a problem he thought was solved, now was an even bigger problem. The others trickled in, taking their beds to sleep, but Dorian was the last to fall asleep.

He laid in the dark, listening to the raucous snoring of Skover, until he drifted into a fitful, nightmare laced sleep.

"The whole way?"

"Starting over there, yes." Narfac gaped at him, and the others were less than pleased too. The track Dorian had made in the dirt earlier this morning was a long arc, cutting a wide swath of the mountain and even enclosing some trees.

It was large, even Dorian had to conceded that, but would leave plenty of room for defenses and expansion later.

"How much rock are we going to need for it?" Kragnak was eying the pile of rocks to the left of the mine. It was a large mountain, bigger than the tailings of earth next to it.

"We'll see how much you use when you get done."

"I've never built a wall before," Kragnak said, wilting.

"It's easy. Take a rock." Dorian picked up a chunk. "Set it in place. Pick up another." He stacked another rock on top of his first, matching the faces until they were close enough to mate. "Repeat until it's high enough and long enough to keep out bad things."

They would need more rock, of that he was sure, but what they had already removed from the mine would be more than enough to keep them working for a few weeks, maybe even a few months.

That would give him breathing room, time to dig out more of the farm caves and plant more crops, until he could figure out what to do with them. This was the best plan he could come up with.

It would also bolster the mine's defenses, something Dorian suspected they would need. Harden them against would be attackers, and deter anything looking for an easy target. If they had to work with the migrants, they might as well put them to use.

"Simple enough." Narfac tested a rock next to him, then adjusted his feet to get more leverage and heaved. With some effort he picked it up and staggered the few feet to the cluster Dorian had stacked, letting it drop with a tremor that Dorian felt from feet away.

"I'll get the smaller stones." Kragnak sorted through the stack, rolling away larger chunks of rock, until he got one that was more manageable.

"A wheelbarrow is available, if you need it, but if you don't we'll be using it. Yander is widening the dormitory to make room." The other dwarves followed Narfac's lead, except Emelda who hung back and followed him a short way.

"Mr. Ironstrike." Her voice was thin and soft, and it stopped him. He turned to see her clutching her skirt in her hand with tight fists.

"Yes?" Dorian grunted.

"We aren't wanted, that's clear to see. Should we leave now before we become too much of a burden to you?" She raised her voice, loud enough for the other migrants to hear. Inwardly Dorian cursed the girl, but shifted feet. *How am I supposed to respond?*

They weren't wanted, but they were here. Given a few more months Dorian and the other founders might have had different thoughts on the matter. Like many other things in his life he would have to get used to them staying.

"No, we don't want you to leave."

"Then why do you stick us in tunnels and look down on us? I hear your whispers in the cave, I see the looks the others give." There was anger in her voice.

"Does it look like we have an abundance here? You've been here a night, are we overflowing in treasure and wine?" Dorian advanced a step, and she shuffled back. *Good, let her be afraid. Better afraid than pompous.* "Do you think we're hiding food in our footlockers?"

"No." It was quiet, almost a squeak.

"What does it matter what we think of you?"

"I don't know." He stopped advancing, she stopped retreating.

"I'll tell you what I've told the others. We may not like that we're stuck together here, but we have a job to do. Do yours and we'll get along just fine." The other side of the promise hung in the air, but from the look in her eye she knew what it was.

He softened his tone. "As long as I can help it you'll have food to eat and a place to sleep."

15

HOLES

"Have you talked to her much?"

"Who?" Dorian asked.

"Emelda. What is she like? I wonder if she likes rock bread." Yander was talking as he worked again, and it was irritating Dorian. He thought he was over this, that they had developed a certain rapport. Yander would be quiet, and Dorian would not listen.

"No."

"Well then, do you think she likes granite?"

"I mean no, I haven't talked to her." Dorian brought his pickaxe down harder than he wanted, striking a shower of sparks and shearing off a larger than usual chunk of rock. It tumbled forward and he had to leap out of the way into the dirt.

"Do you think you could?" From the ground, Dorian looked up at Yander flabbergasted.

"Why would I talk to her?"

Throughout the day Yander's attention wandered, focusing on places other than the rock before him. Much of his daydreaming was about Emelda, wondering where she came from, what she was like.

He sighed as he took a break and leaned up against the pickaxe. Even in her tattered clothes she was beautiful from the moment he laid eyes on her. She also happened to be the only available female dwarf, but she put even the girls he knew back home in Zirad to shame.

Dorian wasn't happy with him, correcting him and telling him to pay attention, but it would only last a few minutes before he was off lost in his thoughts again.

He had to talk to her.

The hours seemed to drag on until at last it was dinnertime and Dorian called a stop for the day. They hadn't gotten as far as he liked, and Yander recognized the brewing anger in Dorian. He quietly helped put the beds back into place and joined him in washing up.

Lumdir had finished making more tables, now there were enough for them all to eat on. They had to bring back some of the wood stumps they used for seats, but there would be chairs soon enough. Yander tried to sit next to Emelda at dinner, but her parents took up guard positions next to her.

Instead of talking to her he kept quiet. The meal was subdued, they were rationing the food in case they weren't able to grow or forage any more this year. There wasn't much to go around.

After dinner Yander helped clear the tables, hoping to get some time alone with Emelda, or at least any time at all. His chance came when he was coming back to get another load, she was walking his way.

A knot formed in his stomach, and an odd sensation came over him, almost like he was floating.

"Hello," he said, then paused. He realized he was standing right in her way and she was staring at him. "Oh, here, let me help you with that." Yander reached out to take some of her load, a plate from the top, but when he moved forward he tripped. "Yeargh."

He face planted on the ground, falling off to one side so he wouldn't take her with him. Pain blossomed in his nose, and he sneezed from the dirt that got in it.

"Are you hurt?" Emelda was crouched down next to him.

"Hurt? No, I'm not hurt." Yander was glad for the darkness, it would hide his embarrassment. "I just tripped on something but I'm fine. Sometimes I do trip, but usually I don't fall, unless I can't stop myself."

Emelda let out a suppressed giggle. Hearing it made Yander feel better, and some of his shame receded. He picked himself up and dusted off. "You're funny."

"I try not to be, but sometimes I can't help it." Another giggle, and warmth ran through him. "Here, let me help you with that."

"Thanks."

"We've been out here months now, I still can't believe it sometimes. It felt like yesterday we were leaving with the cart hooked up and all the supplies loaded." They walked back to the kitchen as he talked.

"The journey was long, wasn't it?"

"Oh yes, we had to go around the river and up the mountain. The cart only moved so fast so we had to go slower than we liked. Did you all make the trip on foot?" They reached the kitchen and went to the washtub.

"Yes." She sighed. "It was longer than I've ever walked before, and carrying the supplies too."

"That's right, you had to carry them on your back didn't you? I think it would have been hard for me too, before I mean. Now I think it would be easier."

"What do you mean?" Yander took the dishes from her and dropped them into the wide bucket with a plop. He pushed up his sleeves and reached in.

"Ever since I've been mining things have been easier. I think I'm getting stronger," he confessed. "Not that I was weak before," he added hastily. She giggled as he scrubbed. "Can you get the drying towel? It's right over there."

"Where, here?"

"No, to your left." She searched, then found it. He dipped the plate into a clean tub of water and handed it to her. "Why did you all come here? Life would have been much easier back in Zirad."

Emelda wiped the plate dry on both sides, before doing it again. The second time was slower. "It was mother's idea. Father didn't want to, but she worked on him every day until he gave in. This was the first opportunity that came up, and since it was so early in the season, we decided to take it so that the bees might have a chance to establish a hive when we got here."

"So... here you are. Did you leave...anyone behind?" His heart was thumping, and he tried to sound casual.

"No, everyone we cared about came. I have no brothers or sisters."

"Good." She stopped drying and gave him a funny look. "No, I mean good that you didn't have to leave anyone behind." He wanted to hit himself, but instead he scrubbed harder. Half the dishes were washed and dried.

"What about you?"

"I left my parents. To be honest I think sometimes they might have wanted me gone. My mother found out about the trip and told me."

"You must miss them." He handed her another plate. When she took it their hands grazed. They both looked away hastily. Yander's ears burned, and he knew his face was red. He hoped she didn't notice.

"Yes, when I have time to think about them, which isn't much." He wasn't sure what to do now, should he be careful not to touch her or did she not mind? In his mind he was replaying how it felt, how soft her hand was. Stealing a glimpse he realized her hands were deft and graceful.

"It must be very hard."

"We're doing something good here, and think of all the things to discover!" His excitement came back. "Gems and ores, digging deep into the earth. You have to admit it excites you."

She smiled at him, and it lit up her face. "I'll stick to what I know. We were hoping to keep up with the waxwork, if it goes according to father's plan." Yander took his time with the last cup, not wanting it to end.

"You'll have plenty of work to do, and lots of things to make. I'm excited and hope that we can provide gems for your work too. Did you hear about the rubies we found?"

"Emelda?" She looked around to the sound of her father's voice coming from deeper in the cave.

"In here, father." Emelda stacked the last cup and flicked the towel. She hung it up to dry as Daruik entered.

"Here you are, we're going to bed now. What were you doing?"

"Helping with the dishes." Yander gave a halfhearted wave, feeling uneasy under his gaze.

"Come along now." Daruik ushered her out. She turned as she was swept away.

"Good night Yander."

"Good night," he called to her retreating form. After they were gone, he sat back and wondered.

"Wax working! Can you believe it?"

"I can believe it." Dorian kept swinging, breaking apart the soil. Who would have thought the daughter of a beekeeper would work wax?

"She's got a bracelet she made, and she's promised to show me how to make candles." Yander sighed. The dwarf had become insufferable since the migrants arrival. Dorian contemplated sending him back down the mine again, just so he could get some peace and quiet. Unfortunately, there was too much to do so dropping him down the mineshaft wouldn't turn out well for them. He settled for grunting instead.

"Do you think we'll find more gems soon? I'd like to give some to her. She said she could make wax rings that you can use to cast the real thing. To see that in action."

"Yes, I imagine that would be something. Watch the ceiling."

"What? Oh, thanks." Yander plucked at a chunk of dirt that was falling from above him, it shattered as it hit the ground with a slap.

A few more days in the farm cave would double its size. Double the size would mean double the crops, and enough to feed them all. Things were finally starting to turn around. Once they got the farms working, they could return to the mine.

There they would find ore and gems, the building blocks of his freedom and the return of his children. It was close now.

"Can I dig out their apartment when we get the chance? I'll do it in my free time so I don't have to impact..." As Yander rambled on Dorian felt his eyes glazing over. *If I can survive Yander.*

"Come quick!" Yudoline's panicked voice echoed down the tunnels. She wailed, the otherworldly sound making Dorian tense up. A chill went down his neck to his back.

For a moment his mind went to the axe safely buried at the bottom of his chest. *No, not ever again.* Dorian gripped his pickaxe handle instead, the weight comforting. The others leaped up from the tables and went for the spears.

Dorian was the first out of the room, Barileth close behind. "Where are you?" His voice roared around the cave.

"The farm caves, come quickly!"

His heart thumping in his chest and his lungs burning, Dorian led the charge. Barileth was right on his heels, torches flickering as they ran by. Yudoline was still calling for them, her voice high.

"We're coming," Dorian said, panting from the exertion. He hadn't been as strong as he thought, because he was almost winded when they burst through the opening into the caves.

Yudoline was standing just inside the entrance, and Dorian quickly scanned for danger. Nothing else was moving in the room, just Yudoline clutching herself tight with a pained look on her face.

"What is it?" Barileth asked, and more dwarves poured out, armed with wooden spears and anything else they could get their hands on. There wasn't as much light in the farm caves, which struck Dorian as odd. The glow from the golden moss should have provided ample lighting, but it was just a solitary torch that burned.

With a shiver Yudoline uncoiled one arm from her body. She looked dazed now that help had arrived, and pale. Dorian moved closer in case she fell over. Now that he knew there was nothing else in the cave he was worried about her.

A finger pointed down to the ground. Dorian followed it, a gasp from behind. His breath caught in his throat. *No, it can't be.*

The golden moss was savaged. Chunks of it were rooted up and strewn everywhere. The cave berry bushes were broken, branches fallen and ripped apart. Dorian leaned down and collected one. Bite marks along the edge, ones he recognized.

"Moles." The crops were ruined.

16

UNWELCOME

A new smell. It shifted in the darkness as the stale air of the caves oozed around it. Even though its belly was full this was interesting, exotic. It had a strange smell, like some other beasts that roamed the cavern, but different.

It kept still, waiting and lurking in the dark. There was more than enough within reach to keep it satisfied, but food was always trying to get away from it. A new arrival might be a welcome meal, if it could find it.

For now, it would let its prey come to it, stumbling into the deadly snare unaware. The meat was more tender, more juicy that way.

Settling down, it went back to sleep, but dreamed of a new and exciting feast.

"Most of the crops are destroyed, what are we going to eat?" Barileth tightened his fist and slammed it on the table.

"We didn't come here to starve to death. Surely there must be something that can be done?" Daruik looked just as agitated. For the fourth time in ten minutes Dorian wished he didn't have to have this conversation with them.

"Calm down everyone, we aren't going to starve." Dorian held up his hands to quiet them, calming them to murmurs. "The season is still early, golden moss is tenacious. Wait to see what will happen."

He already knew that it wouldn't come back fast enough to satisfy them. Something else had to be done, but he wasn't sure what it was yet. He needed more time to think.

"The King will save us, remember the liaison. He'll come back with plenty of food, he promised us," Yander said. Murmurs ran through the dwarves, chairs moved against the stone. The smell of breakfast, fried pork, lingered with the smoke of the torches.

"Will they come back again?" Yudoline asked. Kimec held her in his arms, trying to comfort her. She had put so much work into keeping the crops alive, and it was hitting her hard.

"If they do, they'll have a nasty surprise." Barileth cracked a smile. "We could use the meat too." If only it were that easy. The mole hole was obvious when they searched the cave, big too. At least half the size of a dwarf, maybe larger. Adding a deadfall trap to the entrance might net them a catch, but a watch would work better.

"You said the King is sending food?" Daruik asked. The migrants looked less worried now.

"We don't know when they'll come. It's better if we rely on our own food supplies." Dorian rubbed his beard. It was coming in nicely, at least an inch and a half long now. No one questioned it or gave him disapproving looks about it anymore. The migrants would never know.

"I used to fish a little back home, I could try my hand in the river," Kragnak said.

"Good, the rest of you will forage and Barileth will go hunting. With enough effort we'll build up a stock to keep us going until winter starts. After that we'll have to raise what we eat." He didn't want to have to kill any of the goats or chickens, they would need the milk and eggs. "There will be more work again, harder than before."

With a steady gaze he looked each dwarf in the eye. Some of the new arrivals shifted theirs, uncomfortable with his assessing eye. Overall they seemed like they could be counted on though. The other dwarves looked uneasy. They knew what kind of work that meant.

"Starting today." He gave out new assignments, some dwarves to take care of the farm plots, the others to forage for food. Lumdir and Kimec would stop working for the next week, everyone would need to gather as much as they could.

They scattered, Dorian going back to digging out the dormitory. He sent Yander away, and in the peace and quiet he was able to think. He wouldn't rely on the charity of the King to save them, he wasn't sure that there was any where he was concerned.

Dorian knew he was being used, but he'd rather take this assignment in the middle of nowhere than to be back in that cell. At least out here he had a chance. He remembered her face, the touch of her hand. He was going to bring her back.

A week had passed and their food stores were looking better. The valley was almost picked clean of any fruit, vegetable, tuber, or other consumable plant so they had to expand the search to the other side of the mountain and farther from the stronghold.

They traveled in pairs now, for safety, equipped with the wooden spears. Lumdir and Kimec were back to creating supplies for the mine, and some of the migrants were pulled off foraging duty to assist in bringing supplies to them to keep them working.

Yander and Dorian had expanded the dormitory and were finishing up the last of the expansion. A few more feet would give them enough room to move in the migrants, if Kimec could finish the beds. He had two more to do, halfway through the first.

The mining was slower than he hoped. Yander was dragging, bags under his eyes from the long days. They were able to lock the entrance door now, after some modifications by Lumdir, but they still kept a watch on the farms at night.

"Lunch is ready," Skover called down the tunnel. Yander sighed and dropped his pickaxe, dusting off his hands.

"I'll get the others outside," Yander said. Dorian grunted and headed down the tunnel behind him, going straight when Yander turned right at the entrance tunnel. He didn't bother to wash up, he was just going to get dirty and dusty again.

Lumdir and Kimec were already seated. Dorian nodded to them as he took a space.

"How is it going?" he asked.

"Now that I've finished the hives Daruik asked for I've been able to work on the doors." Dorian nodded. They would be scattered through the mine, setting up choke points in the unlikely event something made it through the front.

"You've made how many?"

"Four, so far." That left six to go.

"We can set them tomorrow, two more will be enough. Start the chests after you're done with that." dwarves were trickling in now, and the smell of lunch was wafting in with them. Dorian sniffed. Roasted mole with potatoes.

Barileth caught it during his watch. The deadfall had only stunned it, he had to finish it with a spear. Dorian doubted that any of the others would have had the daring to try the same thing, it was a massive mole and a wonder it fit down the tunnel.

They would have their revenge though, eating the beast that had decimated the crops. Skover brought it in, a chuck of it still steaming on the platter.

"Give it some time to cool. I just took it off the spit." Dorian's mouth watered at the sight of it. They still had some pork, but fresh meat was a welcome sight.

"I'll need more stone today," Lumdir said, eyes focused on the platter. Kragnak and Narfac came in just then. They'll do.

"Narfac, I'm reassigning you to haul stone to Lumdir. Take it from the dormitory after lunch until he has as much as he needs then go back to the wall." Progress was even slower there, less than ten feet of if built.

Not having it was making him nervous, but there were too many other things that needed to be done first.

"A break from hauling stone to haul stone," Narfac muttered. Dorian ignored the comment. Everyone was here so they dug in, passing the meat around.

The room was silent the first few minutes, everyone was focused on eating. Juice flowed from the meat when Dorian took a bite, it was tender and sweet, and he was glad to have Skover. The dwarf knew how to cook his meat he would give him that.

"I was thinking about our mole problem," Barileth said, breaking the silence in conversation.

"What about it?" Doria asked between bites.

"No sense in letting a good opportunity go to waste. I say if they keep coming to us we'll keep eating them." Dorian was inclined to agree with him.

"What did you have in mind?" Kimec asked. Some of the hatred between them had thawed lately. Dorian wasn't sure why, but he hadn't been around to hear all of their conversations.

"Give me enough supplies and I can make a better trap, smash the buggers real good when they come. Not a light tap like what we have."

"You want to put a bigger stone up?" Yander asked.

"No, I want to make a smasher." Barileth gave a nasty grin. "One that will give them a surprise." He made a fist with one hand and smashed it into the other and laughed. Chuckles spread around the table.

"Leave some meat on them please," Skover said, cutting another hunk off the platter and sliding it onto his plate.

"What do you need?" Dorian asked.

Barileth scratched his head and looked up. "A big rock." There was plenty of that around. "Rope, a big handle, and some planks I think."

Dorian looked at Kimec, who nodded. "Make it tonight after you get down with another barrel. Work on it tomorrow Barileth, we'll move tasks around."

Barileth's Hammer, as they were calling it, was less of a hammer and more of a club. Firmly lashed to a thick oak plank, almost half a tree thick, was a stone that must have weighed a hundred pounds or more.

Ropes kept it propped up right above the mole entrance, hanging suspended in the air and ready to fall at any second. The rope was attached by a series of rough wooden pulleys Kimec had carved to a tripwire across the entrance.

Dorian was appraising it, curious how he had managed it in a few days. It was an impressive trap, and he wondered if they could employ it elsewhere.

The only problem was that it needed a lot of room above it to activate. *Maybe if we turned it sideways? It won't fit in the entrance tunnel unless we raise the ceiling and rearrange the supports.* He was still puzzling it out when Yander rushed in.

"Dorian, we have another dwarf visitor. Yudoline saw him coming when she was taking care of the farm." *Another one?* For being out in the middle of nowhere they sure saw a lot of dwarves.

When he emerged the others were huddled near the entrance, wooden spears in hand. Coming up the mountain was one dwarf. As he drew near Dorian felt apprehension.

His clothes were clean, made of good stout hide and cloth. A silk undershirt shimmered as he walked. Other than dust from the trail they were clean and well taken care of. The dwarf's beard was trimmed and neat. This was no migrant, he had a pack but only enough for a journey, the rest was being carried by a pack goat.

"Put away the spears, this one means us no harm," Dorian said. The others milled around as he approached, standing behind Dorian.

"This is Seventh Hall, isn't it?" The dwarf drew up his goat, letting it graze a few feet from the dwarves.

"Yes."

"King Lightaxe sends his regards and bids you good mining. May the earth cover you in fortune." He drew himself up and flourished into a bow.

"King? Another liaison already?" Yander asked. The newcomer gave him a puzzled look.

"Another liaison? What do you mean, I'm the liaison tasked with your care and observation." All the misgivings Dorian had about

Dovig rushed back. His ears started burning, and a flame of anger grew inside him. "I'm Tufolin Caskforge," he said, digging in his pack and pulling out a small gleaming metal disc that flashed in the sun.

Dorian knew what was on it without even needing to see. An axe framed in a sunburst, the King's seal.

"What about Dovig?" Yudoline asked.

"A liar and a thief," Dorian barked. "We've been fooled."

"No, that can't be true." Yudoline clutched at her dress. The flame was a fire of anger now.

"I'm afraid he's right," Tufolin said, "I'm the only liaison from the King to visit here. There hasn't been another."

Red flooded his vision. Dorian clenched his fists and tried to breathe. "If I ever see that dwarf again, I'm going to wring his neck."

17

A WARNING

"I'm sorry to hear about your troubles. Could we move inside?" Tufolin was eying the door. He had to be tired from the journey. Dorian swallowed his anger, letting it simmer and bubble.

"Come in and rest. Skover, can you get something to eat and drink?" While they headed inside Dorian took one last look at the valley. Clouds covered the sky, reflecting the cloud that had descended on their expedition.

There was no help coming. "I'm afraid I'll have to ask everyone else to go back to work." Once again they were left on the edge of a knife, balancing the future with the present. No one grumbled though, the suppressed anger in his voice probably helped.

"I'll ask to see your records, but we can do that after I've refreshed." Tufolin sighed as he eased into the chair in the dining room. Skover brought out a plate of bread, cheese, and cold ham with a mug of ale. "Thank you."

"What word is there in Zirad?" Skover asked, standing as Dorian sat with Tufolin.

"A great deal is happening in the kingdom." Tufolin picked up the bread and sliced off a hunk of cheese and meat. "Enemies are coming for us, and goblin bands have been active raiding villages in the west."

Skover shifted feet. "Where did they hit?"

"Oh, small villages and mines. Gathiz, Stelm, I can't remember the rest. Troops have been mobilized to protect the flank and are garrisoned in the mountains, but they can't find their nests."

"I imagine they can't." Dorian still seethed at the betrayal, imagining having Dovig in his hands, begging for mercy. He knew it wasn't charitable, but he didn't care. If he could only inflict the pain he felt. "And the merchants?"

"On the way. They'll be here by the middle of autumn."

"And we have no funds to barter with." Dorian sat back. Tufolin gave him a sharp, puzzled look.

"Where are your starting funds?" When Dorian didn't answer he connected the dots. "You didn't ask to see proof?" Dorian chewed on his answer as Tufolin chewed on his food. It would do no good to make an enemy of this man. He had the ear of the King, no matter how small or inconsequential their expedition was.

"Like I said, the dwarf was a thief. Stole it from us with cunning and trickery." *Tricks I shouldn't have fallen for.* A large part of his anger was reserved for himself. Dorian had been on too many expeditions. He should have known better.

Tufolin took advantage of the silence and finished his meal, only a hint of disapproval in his looks. He pushed back from the table. "We can start now."

Small and sickly as they were, the cave berry bushes has small, gleaming white berries clustered among their broken branches. Yudoline tested one. It came off easily in her hand, and she examined it, caressing the fruit.

"Skover, it's ready."

"Hmm?" he looked over from watering the moss, bucket still half tipped. "Ah, finally!"

Yudoline couldn't hide the excitement she felt. The berry rolled around between her fingers, its rough flesh giving in just enough to let her know it was ripe. "Help me gather them, and we'll see how much we have."

Not all the cave berries were ready to be picked yet, only about a third of the bush was ripened. The rest would come in a week or so, giving her enough time to work with what she had. The bushes shook as they gave up their fruit, most of them about half their original size. They still hadn't recovered from the mole attack, and she wondered if they ever would.

"Berry picking," Skover sighed. "It reminds me of home. We had a cave berry bush growing right outside our apartments. It was a small, grizzled thing, but it gave us enough fruit to use in pies and dishes."

"Never enough to make wine?"

Skover shook his head. "That we bought from others, or traded. My father was a cook too, in the great kitchens of the King. He fell out of favor, though, when he over salted the main course during a particularly important feast. The others thought it was fine, but the visiting elven princess expressed her displeasure."

"What happened after that?" Yudoline paused, her apron half full of berries.

"He was demoted." Skover held a berry to the torchlight, scrutinizing it too intently. "Never really recovered. He's still cooking, but only for the family now."

"I'm sorry to hear that."

Skover shrugged. "He says cleaning suits his talents now. Chimneys are his specialty. Looks like we got what we can." He stood up faster than he weight would belie and clapped the dirt off his hands. "You go ahead, I'll finish the rest."

"Are you sure?" Skover nodded. Before she left, she gave his shoulder a gentle squeeze. "Your father is a great man and a great cook. I can tell from the passion you have and the way you carry on the tradition.

He gave a sad little smile and turned back to the crops, but she could see the small glimmer of hope in his eyes. All the way back she wondered, and thought.

Back in the kitchens she found the empty vat Kimec had made for this purpose and emptied the cave berries into it. It filled it halfway to the top.

"More than enough for a small cask, I think." She selected one that was emptied, what used to hold the seeds. "This is fitting. Now, how did it go?"

From her lessons she remembered making wine was easier than ale. "First you juice the berries." She grabbed a wooden spatula. "This will do. I'll ask Kimec to make me something better next time."

Carefully she crushed the berries with it. Since it wasn't made for the task it took longer, but with each gentle squish the juice at the bottom of the bucket accumulated. The mound of berries shrunk, and the juice grew, until there wasn't enough left in the berries to squish out.

Yudoline cleaned the small barrel with hot water, like she was told, and then poured in the cave berry juice. It bubble and whispered as it rushed in. Milky white in the fire of the torchlight, it would be transformed.

Now that it was in Yudoline stepped back and thought for a moment. Was there something else she was supposed to do? A distant memory, perhaps of something she missed, nagged at her.

But it didn't come, so she searched around for the plug she had taken out, found it in her apron, and stoppered the cask. Yudoline found a nook where she could cram it in that would be out of the way, moved some boxes to make space, and set it down.

She stepped back, admiring her work. Now all she had to do was wait and pull out the deep red wine that it would turn into in time. Would it bring joy? Happiness? Or would it be spoiled like the ale and bring nothing but disgust to those whose lips it touched?

Stepping back, she paced around the room in a large circle. There was something she forgot, she just couldn't remember it. Or was it something else? If she stayed in the kitchen any longer it would eat her up.

So, she left. As she walked out the door, she cast one last glance back to the keg now nestled under a pile of boxes. Just time, that's all it needed, and it would turn into wine.

She hoped.

The days were a blur for Yander. He spent long hours mining with Dorian, first expanding the dormitory to house everyone, then expanding the workshops to make room for storage and additional work areas.

When he wasn't mining, he was spending as much time with Emelda as he could getting to know her.

They would walk down the corridors of the mine as he pointed out branches and different sections of rock in their exploratory tunnels. She was helping with the crops and they examined them and took walks in the cool evening air, the moon fat and lazy in the sky.

He was thinking about her more every day. Daydreams filled his mind, and Dorian grew frustrated with him. The reminders to pay attention or get back to work multiplied.

"If you don't pay attention, I'll have you swapped with Barileth. You can cart the garbage out of the mines," Dorian said. Yander snapped out of another daydream.

"I'm sorry, I'll be more careful this time." A rock he had dislodged had fallen next to Dorian, it almost landed on his foot. Yander hung his head in shame and couldn't meet Dorian's withering glare.

Footsteps in the corridor between their pickaxe strikes ringing on the rock brought Daruik into the workshop. Lumdir was still working, used to the sound of tools ringing on rock, but Kimec had moved out of the workshop temporarily.

"Good morning," he said. Dorian stopped working and turned to face him, Yander gave him a nod and kept going. Daruik was stone faced and cold, had none of the warmth he usually bore.

"Morning." He wondered what brought him down here, he should have been building the wall with the others. It was growing now that they were focused on it, but they still had a long way to go until it would be secure.

"Can I borrow Yander for a moment?" Yander's head jerked over, and he paused, pickaxe still embedded in the rock. *Interesting*.

"It's about break time anyway. Go ahead Yander."

"Oh...all right..." He tore off a good chunk of stone, looked longingly back at the wall, and put down his pickaxe. The dwarf's hands were trembling, and he looked like he wanted to be anywhere but here.

"Bring him back in one piece," Dorian said as they walked together out of the workshop. Yander looked rigid as he walked out, and Daruik had a storm cloud brewing over him.

"Lovely day for a walk isn't it?" Yander said. It was hard keeping the nervousness out of his voice, it still crept in despite his attempt to hide it. "We've done a lot of digging the past few days and I think we're making progress. At this rate we'll be able to expand the mine and go back to exploration deeper. We haven't found any ore yet, but I think we will soon."

Daruik looked sideways at him. "Hmpfh."

"B-but you've done a lot of work yourself, haven't you? I've seen the hives and the bees." It was hard not to, they were everywhere in the food caves and had even started buzzing about the tunnels leading out of it. Yander often wondered what they were looking for out there.

They were farther down the tunnels, going back deeper into the mountain. Daruik stopped then and looked around. Yander was sweating, and he wiped it off. They were alone.

For some reason Daruik intimidate him, and now, under his stern gaze, he felt even more uncomfortable. "I know what you're doing." Yander blinked. His mind raced.

"What do you mean?" he asked when it came up short.

"I want you to listen to me, and listen well. My father was a bee-keeper, and his father before that. My sister married a beekeeper, and so did my mother." Daruik was almost whispering and Yander had to lean closer to hear. What did any of this have to do with him?

"You'll stay away from Emelda from now on." Yander nodded, then his brain caught up to his ears, and he jerked back.

"What?"

"I've seen you two. In the tunnels, tending the garden. Even taking walks outside." Daruik's words came out short and choppy, held back even. "You've no right to do it."

Yander gaped. "But we're just friends!" He squirmed under the words, not even wanting to believe them as he said it. Daruik took a hold of his shoulder with a dangerously tight grip.

"No miner will ever marry my daughter while I draw breath."

18

CRAFT

Dorian was digging into the side of the wall when Yander shuffled in. He didn't hear him at first, since he was caught up in his work, but when Yander picked up his pickaxe the scrape of it against the stone startled him.

"Yander, why did you do that?" Dorian's heart was pounding. He had jerked back from the shock, and brought his pickaxe up instinctively. Now he lowered it. Yander kicked at a rock.

"Sorry. Didn't mean to frighten you." Yander swung halfheartedly at the rock, and the pickaxe bounced off. It hadn't even made a scratch.

Dorian returned to his work, only he moved off to put some distance between them. A few minutes later Yander materialized by his side and sighed heavily.

"What am I going to do?" he asked. Dorian gave him a sideways glance. The dwarf was clutching his pickaxe and cradling it in his hands. "All because I've chosen, no I've been chosen, to mine?"

A large chunk of rock broke free, falling into the rock dust at Dorian's feet. It kicked it up, and it went into his nose and tickled it. He sneezed out the rough grit and waved the remainder away.

"A lot of work to be done," Dorian said, not stopping to admire his handiwork. They had to remove a few more tons, at least, from this wall to give them enough room to work.

The Icebrewers had brought enough tools with them to do their waxwork when there was wax to be had, but in the meantime they were going to try their hand at stone craft.

"It isn't fair, not that that's what I was intending to do at all. I mean, he had us all wrong." Yander didn't get the hint, he was still standing there moping. "I can't help it if the rock sings to me, calls me. I'm drawn to it, and am I supposed to be punished for that?"

"You'll be punished if you don't help me dig." The sadness in his voice was getting to Dorian. He didn't care what kind of troubles Yander was having, this was a functioning mining expedition. If it had any chance of succeeding he was going to have to pull his weight.

"Oh, I can't pretend to focus at a time like this." Yander slumped down and leaned his head against the wall, moaning. "I'm too young to be denied a chance with a good, solid dwarf. Think of everything we had ahead of us, not that I'm implying I had any idea to do it. But now it's gone, crushed before it even started."

Yander wasn't trying to hide his meaning, but the implied words brought up something else in Dorian. Memories of his own courtship, fraught with its own troubles, and the subsequent marriage. He hit the wall harder, breaking off a big section.

He didn't want to be reminded of her right now. It was distracting him. "Get back to work."

"You have to see how terrible this is for me, and her too." Yander got back up to his feet and started working on the wall beside him, taking off one small chunk for every five of Dorian's. *As long as he keeps quiet I don't mind.*

"Do you even know what it's like, losing someone you care about?" It was like a punch to the gut and stopped Dorian. "To see everything you've ever loved gone in a heartbeat, taken from you?"

He had. He still did. The wound was still fresh, after all these years, and Dorian had to choke it down. The thoughts of her, the dwarf responsible. His botched attempt to make it right.

"That's enough." Dorian's voice was edged, but Yander didn't seem to notice. He kept hammering away at the rock and kept talking.

"What kind of injustice could wound so much? What kind of cruel world do we live int hat--"

"I said that's enough." His voice rang in the stillness of the cave. Lumdir had left, they were alone. Dorian rounded on Yander, who had drawn back. Hurt and rage boiled together and bubbled up, bursting forth. "You don't know what you're talking about and you're a fool."

Yander's eyes had gone wide, his mouth open in shock. Dorian knew he was yelling, but it felt good to him, pushing aside his own hurt. "You had no chance at marriage, any dwarf could see that. And you can't call yourself a miner, you haven't even found a vein of ore. What kind of miner would that make you?"

It was out before he could stop it. Yander's mouth clipped shut, and there was deep pain in his eyes. They were starting to water, but Dorian didn't care. *About time something made him shut up.*

Turning, Yander dropped his pickaxe and fled. A momentary pang of guilt followed in Dorian, but he smothered it. *No time to get soft now.* He returned to his work, the sound of his pickaxe on stone sounding as hollow as he felt.

Yander didn't come back for the rest of the day, and wasn't at dinner that night either. Dorian wondered if he had gone too far. It was too late now though. What was done was done.

"What happened to Yander?" Tufolin asked as they passed the rockbread around. He tore off a chunk as the others glanced around.

"I haven't seen him since lunch," Skover said.

"He went off into the woods," Yudoline said. Dorian glanced at Emelda. She was hunched over her plate, nibbling at her bread. Her hair hung down over her eyes so he couldn't see them.

"He'll be fine, I'm sure." Dorian took a helping of stew, still steaming. It smelled earthy, and it tasted good. Pork, they were running out of it.

"Should we go look for him?" Yudoline asked, brows lowered.

"A grown dwarf can look after himself," Daruik said, spooning up a mouthful of stew. He was next to his daughter and wife. Emelda pushed her bowl away and got up.

Without a word she turned and fled.

"Emelda, where are you going?" Noreck asked. She didn't respond and was gone before anyone else could get up.

"Give her time, my bee. She'll cool off and come back." Daruik hadn't moved and was still eating, but the side of one eye twitched. Noreck looked like she was going to say something else, but clamped her mouth instead, pursing her lips.

An air of discomfort hung in the air, and the dwarves ate without talking for a few minutes. Tufolin was watching him. One more mouth to feed. The pleasure of eating was gone now, cast in a cloud of darkness.

"What have you heard of the outside world?" Tufolin broke the silence, pushing back his plate half eaten.

"Nothing that I believe," Barileth said, eyes drawn into slits.

"I have something to tell you, and it may be hard to hear." He paused for effect. All eyes were on Tufolin. "War with the goblins to the west has continued, and they've grown bold. Raids have struck to the heart of the kingdom, even as far east as Arakzir."

If it was quiet before it was silent now. Only the sound of the torches spitting and flickering could be heard. "That's only a few days travel from here," Dorian said.

"Less, if they travel light."

"So they could be here tonight, they could attack us now?" Yudoline asked.

"I'm afraid so. I was going to mention it earlier, but it didn't seem like the right time." Tufolin smile, bright and cheery under his thick, black beard. "Besides, you already had half a wall. It looks like you're well armed too."

"Some rock and sticks don't make a protected fort," Barileth snapped. "How likely is it they attack?" Dorian was thinking of asking the same question.

"Unlikely. I'd be surprised if they even knew you were around. The location of Seventh Hall has been kept quiet for a reason." Dorian couldn't believe what he said.

"The King knew about this?" Dorian asked.

"Knew is a strong word. There was always a distinct possibility, like there is in any expedition outside of the immediate vicinity of a garrison." Tufolin didn't seem fazed by the looks he was getting, which made Dorian's anger grow hotter.

Instead of speaking he gripped the side of the table, feeling the cold stone under his fingertips. It helped stop him from throttling Tufolin, who really had no say in the matter. He was a representative, that was it. He couldn't make decisions like that.

King Lightaxe did.

Dorian breathed out, forcing himself to calm. Once more the King had betrayed him for his own selfish reasons. The dwarf had no regard for the lives of others. *Eventually, no matter how long it takes, I will make him pay.*

Sounds came back to him, the others were talking over each other. Tufolin was trying to silence them, his hands raised. "-been so good at surviving so far, I really don't think you have a lot to worry about. Be calm."

It wasn't working. They needed weapons and armor, but before they could make them they needed ore. He was so caught up with trying to get enough food for the mine he neglected his duty to protect it.

"That's enough arguing." Dorian raised his voice above the others, and they quieted. "No sense in worrying about it now, we'll keep the doors locked when all the dwarves are in and redoubled the effort to build the wall." He stood and collected his bowl and spoon.

"Get back to work tonight, we'll regroup in the morning."

The sun beat down as Dorian added another rock to the wall, sweating in the evening sun. He spied Tufolin up above the mine in the fields, talking with Yudoline and Skover as they huddled around a plant. What was he doing?

"I'll be back," Dorian said. Kragnak nodded, adding his rock to the growing pile. They still had at least thirty feet of wall left to build, and were running out of rock. Yander was mining out more, but he wasn't sure he could keep up.

"Ah, Dorian, glad you could join us." Tufolin smiled as he approached, and Yudoline gave way for him to join.

"Tufolin has been showing us ways of making the plants grow better," she said.

"Has he now." Dorian wasn't sure what he felt about the dwarf, if it was the bad news he bore or something else. "I didn't realize you had those talents as the King's liaison."

"We all have to start from somewhere. My family were cave farmers and they taught me the trade, just like your family taught you." Dorian locked eyes with him. There wasn't a hint of mockery or judgment in his tone or look, but it threw Dorian off, nonetheless. *He had to know.*

"Did you know our kitchen scraps could be used to help the plants?" Skover asked.

"If you let them rot, they'll feed them," Yudoline added. Dorian shook his head. He wasn't a farmer.

"We've identified a few ways to help coax your crops back to life. Yudoline told me what happened to them, what a terrible shame." The mole hole had gone dormant after the third kill.

"Anything will help," Dorian said at last, after running through different responses.

"And you have some talented craft dwarves here too." Tufolin held up his wrist. A wooden bracelet adorned it, covered in vines and bees. "I'll take a few of their works back with me to the local merchants and see if they'll buy them. If they're good enough they'll send a caravan to barter for more."

Another supposed liaison had promised that, and the memory was still raw. It was good, they were on an expedition to produce riches after all. He just wished he could feel the ore, after two weeks not even a hint of anything.

"And the defenses are coming along too. It looks like a few more days and you won't even need me. You'll have a well-defended fort."

"This expedition will defend itself," Dorian said, casting his gaze back over the wall in progress. "Against any enemy, we will survive."

19

FORGED

Dorian was anxious to get back to mining, but for the next few weeks too much got in the way. With trying to bolster the defenses of the expedition, trying to find enough tasks to keep everyone busy, and starting to carve out a forge there wasn't enough time in the day to get it all done.

Sleep was the first to go. Like the others he was working longer hours, but with most of the work underground it was hard to tell. The days and nights mixed, becoming a blur.

Barileth had come up with several ideas for traps, some of which weren't possible right now, but some were easy to implement. Kimec was kept busy with various spikes, beams, and supports, while Lumdir had to be pulled off his normal stone crafting to make stone gears.

They were dangerously low on rope. Barileth wanted to make more traps, but Dorian had to stop him. There were already two stone hammers, a wall of spikes just inside the door, and a few spike pits outside.

"Just a few more stone hammers and I'll be done." Barileth was standing by three rocks selected for the heads. They were larger than the one he used for the moles.

"Not enough rope, we've gone over that." Dorian was on his way to help with the wall when Barileth caught him. "And Lumdir needs to go back to doors, no more gears for now."

He started to leave the workshop when Barileth caught his arm. Barileth leaned in close, lowering his voice. "You know that wall isn't going to stop a raiding party just as well as I do."

"Maybe not." Barileth let go of his shoulder. He had Dorian's attention now. "But it will discourage an undetermined enemy."

"If they find us they may leave, but they'll smell blood and come back with a bigger force." Barileth was probably right. It made him uncomfortable, agreeing with the disagreeable dwarf.

"What do you propose? We hide the mine?"

"Not possible, you know that. You know what we need to do."

"They aren't ready for that, and we don't have extra dwarves sitting around doing nothing." Barileth crossed his arms.

"Then teach them, at least enough to be dangerous." Dorian ran through the tasks still left if they were to survive. Not enough time.

"You know how to fight, if we take...four of the other dwarves that might give us a fighting shot." Dorian stroked his beard. "Without proper weapons and armor though..."

"Better than being pigs ripe for the slaughter." Barileth left him, going out to hunt. Dorian was left with a nagging feeling, and couldn't shake that image out of his head.

"What do you think?" Kragnak asked. Dorian considered it. A rock represented the anvil, another the forge, and a rough sketch in the sand beside it.

"You're sure this is how it worked?" Dorian was squatted down to get a better look. Steady ringing from Lumdir working filled the workshop. Kimec was shaving bark off a log.

Kragnak scratched his head. The spindly dwarf shifted from foot to foot. *How did this dwarf even lift a hammer?* It didn't look like he had a muscle on him. Dorian leveled his best look his way.

"Well...it's what I can remember." He squatted down to join Dorian, pointing to his scratchings. "The smoke has to go somewhere, so a hole to the surface is obvious, and the fire has to have somewhere to burn." He traced the depression in the stone that would have to be made for the forge.

"The firepot will hold it, and we'll blow air under the fire to get it good and hot." He seemed to know about basic foundry work. Dorian straightened, and Kragnak did too, jerking upright.

"Why did the Guild fail you?" The question caught him off guard, and Kragnak's eyes opened wide, then dropped them to the floor. He seemed to shrink under the memory.

"Couldn't finish my Work," he mumbled, almost too quiet to hear. "I tried for three days, then ran out of time." He got far, almost to the end then. Maybe Kragnak was worth more than he first thought.

"So you know what you're doing then? I mean, you've smelted and forged before?"

"Some," Kragnak mumbled. He shuffled one foot. It didn't inspire confidence. What else could they do though? No one else had any experience building forges.

"Make it bigger than you would need right now, and deeper. We'll use it." Dorian thought Kragnak needed some encouragement. "Work with Lumdir for anything rock related. I'll start the chimney. This will work."

Kragnak nodded after a long pause. This side of the workshop was set aside specifically for the metalwork, it was closer to the surface and the chimneys would be easier to dig.

If they wanted to make Zirad sized furnaces, they would need a bigger exhaust. Dorian thought he had left enough room in the central shaft to go up. They would have to build it, but it could be done. That was far in the future though, they had to survive first.

"Dorian." A voice down the tunnel grabbed his attention.

"Get started right away," he said to Kragnak. Turning he walked to the entrance. "Lumdir, this takes priority over everything else." Lumdir stopped working and nodded.

Noreck was calling for him, and came in the workshop.

"What is it?" he asked, thinking they had seen another intruder. *We really need to get that wall up.* Instead of responding she held up something in her hands.

He squinted, it looked like...grass? Longer than what grew just outside and on most of the mountain, where the trees let it. "Is this supposed to mean something to me?"

Cocking her head to the side, Noreck peered close at him. "Do you mean to tell me you don't know what longleaf grass is?"

"I know what it is." It grew in the valleys around the kingdom of Zirad. A memory stirred in him.

"We can use it." Noreck held it up again, shaking it like it was an offering.

"Of course, rope." Dorian almost kicked himself. It was obvious and he should have thought of it sooner. None grew on the mountainside though, it had slipped his mind. Yet again knowledge he had tucked away in his brain should have been surfaced earlier. It was worrying. "Where did you find it?"

"Down in the valley. Almost a quarter of a day's trek, but there was some forage that I thought would be down there." About a foot and a half long, each grass leaf could be dried and then woven into a thick, tough rope. It wouldn't be the highest quality rope, but anything was better than nothing.

The migrants were full of surprises. He honestly didn't think they would be useful, but now that they were settled in some of their not so useful skills were turning out to be better than he expected. It was almost enough to change his mind about them.

"Can you weave it?" Noreck's smile diminished, then disappeared.

"When I was younger I used to help my mother, but that was a long time ago." Her face scrunched in concentration. "I—I'm not sure."

"Take the cart, tomorrow, and gather up as much as you can by hand. I'll have a few more join you. Do what you can, it isn't that hard to put together." The rope was abundant in the poorer communities back home.

A harvest of a day would yield enough to last them for at least another year. And, if they were lucky, they would trade with the merchants for a wider variety of seeds. Once their food supply was secure, they could start growing it to produce more.

The expedition would be one step closer to self-sustaining, and one step closer to independence.

"Nothing, for another day." Dorian picked up a chunk of rock and hurled it at the wall. It smacked and clattered down the tunnel. "Another wasted day." They weren't quite done yet, but it was right before dinner, which was later, and there wouldn't be much time to dig afterwards.

Yander grunted. The dwarf was sullen since his conversation with Daruik. As far as Dorian knew he was respecting his wishes, staying away from Emelda. Their furtive glances at meals didn't mean things had changed between them.

"I'll meet you at dinner." Feeling frustrated and sad he marched off. *Why am I sad? Yander is a fully grown dwarf, he can fend for himself. I'm not his father.* The thought slipped into his mind, which made him confused. *Where did that come from?*

Dorian shook his head to clear it, climbing the final few steps to the main tunnel. He turned into the workshop just in time to see Kragnack hunched over the new forge. He wasn't sure what was happening at first, but the crackle of flames and the smell of smoke made him realize what was happening.

Small flames burned in the firepot, climbing the sticks of a fire. Slowly Kragnak built it up, feeding it larger sticks until it was blazing happily. Now, with the orange glow reflected on his face, he added a full sized log, then another.

A majority of the smoke wafted back, up the chimney that Dorian had dug out and Kimec and a few others built the flue for.

"We just finished it. I thought we would have time to test it before you found out." Kragnak's cheeks were reddened from the effort of blowing, and maybe a touch of pride. He seemed to take some measure of satisfaction watching his creation work as intended.

The air was clear still, and the fire had been burning for a few minutes. "It looks like you did well, the only question is if she'll melt metal. Kragnak grinned and put a foot on the bellows. Kimec made the paddles and Noreck sewed the bellows from a few rabbits Barileth had taken down and tanned.

He leaned on the bellows, and a whoosh of air blew from them. The fire sputtered and dipped, but then the bellows gave out and it roared to life, leaping up at least a foot above the firepot. Dorian almost felt giddy watching it. As soon as they struck ore it would mean metal for crafting.

Another step closer. If they struck ore. He congratulated Kragnak and Lumdir for the good work, and was in a daze during dinner. It dissipated once the food was gone, and he had to return to the mine.

"Don't be so glum," he said. Yander was dragging his feet, head down as he walked.

"I just don't feel like I used to." Dorian was getting irritated again. The dwarf hadn't talked to him like he used to in a few days now. He didn't know why it bothered him. *First it bothers me that he talks so much, now it bothers me he talks so little.*

"You have your whole life ahead of you. Try to look on the bright side." They were back at the side tunnel. Dorian thought he felt something in the rock here, after going back to their exploratory tunnels. He tried to feel the rock again, but was distracted. After a few seconds he gave up and and started digging.

"Perhaps." Yander struck the rock. He wasn't as enthused about it as he used to be. Dorian let the silence stretch, and he returned to his work, methodically enlarging the side of the tunnel.

He was thinking through all the things that needed to be done, but kept getting distracted by foolish thoughts of Yander and the others. It would be so simple if they weren't here, but he needed them at the same time.

The sound of his pickaxe striking changed, ringing out differently. Something silver gleamed in the light of the torch. "What is it?" Yander asked.

Dorian squinted, then wiped off the side of the wall. There it was, in all its glory. A smile spread across his face, and the rock sung to him. "Metal. We've struck metal."

20

MOLTEN METAL

The warmth of the ore washed over him, and Dorian basked in its reflection. He touched it, feeling that excitement of the first strike once again. It was intoxicating, more mind altering than a night filled with ale.

"We did it," Yander said. Dorian smiled.

"Metal, at last." They worked quickly, and as a team, to break off chunks of rock around it, exposing the vein as it traveled up the wall. It was about three feet tall, and a few inches wide. Dorian broke a chunk free, letting it fall to the ground.

He picked it up and held it to the torchlight. "Tetrahedrite, and a good vein too. This will be enough for a few weapons at least."

"What will it make?"

"Mostly copper, but a little bit of silver too."

"Silver." Yander breathed it out, as if he was feeling the word with his mouth. They were a few floors down below the surface, and far back into the mountain. Dorian had been right to trust his gut on this floor. He wasn't loosing his talents, at least not yet. "We could barter with this, couldn't we?"

"Not as good as gold, but yes." Dorian flipped it end over end in the air. It scattered the light, and he caught it as it came down. "Go get the bucket, we've got some work to do."

While Yander was gone he cut more ore out of the wall. The vein continued deeper, and a small pile of ore gathered. Iron ore would have been better, but copper would do. They could make something out of it for protection. It wouldn't be the best weapons and armor if they had enough, but it would be better than the clothes they wore now.

Exhaustion fled his body, a renewed energy flowing down his limbs. They worked together long into the night until even Yander was faltering. Dorian wiped the sweat off his brow and stopped.

"That's enough for tonight." The pile had grown larger than both of them. *Plenty to melt down tomorrow.* "Everyone else is probably asleep, we'll call it a night." He shook his head, and sweat droplets flew onto the wall. It was hot in the narrow tunnel, since they had been working.

Yander had a satisfied look in his eye and sighed. "It's wonderful, isn't it? I feel like I could dig forever now that we've found something. When Emelda hears--" He stopped. The silence drew out, but before it could become awkward Dorian turned and walked out.

"Sleep first, before anything else." He relished the coolness of the caves. Tonight was a good night.

The fire leaped up, fanned into a brilliant hue of orange, red, and white. Kragnak worked on the bellows, steadily feeding the fire air. It was working, the logs crackled and spit, and coals and ash glowed cherry red in the firepot.

Heat billowed off the fire, radiating out and flushing Dorian's face. It burned away the smell of smoke, which was going straight up and out the chimney.

"It's ready," Kragnak said. They had a stone crucible, with sides as thin as Lumdir could carve them, already filled with broken up rocks of tetrahedrite. Kragnak picked it up and moved it into the fire, which died down since it wasn't being fed air.

The crucible blocked their view of the fire, tamping down on the lighting in the room. Dorian blinked, letting his eyes adjust.

"How long will it take?" Yander asked. Dorian frowned. He should have been mining more of it, but he wanted to be here just as much as Yander did. The dwarf had helped discover it, so he should be able to see the first bar melted.

"Depends on the heat of the fire. This I was good at." Kragnak had taken earth and piled it up in a small mound on the ground. He had made a rectangular depression in the mound, about six inches deep. "If it's hot, it will go fast."

The fire was hot, for it being a wood fire. Color crept up the crucible walls. Yellow at first, then red. The ore started shifting inside, and after a while, melted.

Chunks of ore were reduced to a simmering liquid taking up less than half the crucible. It was a strange concoction, yellow and red with flecks of black. Kragnak skimmed something off the top with a flat stone attached to a haft of wood and dumped it on the ground beside him.

"Aren't you going to use that?" Yander asked.

"Slag. It isn't good for anything. The metal is still in there." There was less black in the liquid now, and it swirled in the crucible. It gave off a strange smell, like sulfur mixed with the smoke. A few more times removing the slag left the molten metal clear and uniform in color.

Kragnak put down his slag remover and picked up one of the only tools he had brought with him: tongs. They were iron and seemed to have enough weight to them. Dorian wasn't sure they would be able to lift the crucible though. Kragnak didn't like it either, but until they had metal that he could shape into a workable tool it was all he had.

Gently Kragnak clipped his tongs onto the side of the crucible. He had to hold them up over his head at a strange angle to get them to work, contorting his small body. It would have been comical had he not had the future of the expedition in his hands. Sweat poured down his face, which was tensed up in concentration.

"Stand back." He lifted the crucible, his muscles straining against the weight. Dorian was glad Kragnak had talked to Lumdir about the size, he would have asked for a bigger one, but with the angle and the tenuous grasp on the side of the crucible smaller was better.

The glowing crucible lifted out of the fire. Tongues lashed out, as if they were trying to take it back, but Kragnak had his grip firm. He swung it over to the mound and tipped it over.

Glorious red liquid fell over the side and splashed into the depression. The earth sizzled and steamed, sending up its white that lingered in the air before it was sucked up the chimney. The metal cooled fast, losing its red and turning to orange. That faded to yellow, then to a silvery gray.

"Great work," Yander said, pounding Kragnak on the back. He gave a tired smile, then put the crucible off to the side to cool. It would be filled again, many times.

"I never thought I'd be doing it again." Kragnak spoke softly, wiping his face off with the sleeve of his shirt. It was stained with sweat from both the heat and stress of the situation.

"You're the only smith we have," Dorian said. Something flickered across Kragnak's face. Dorian knew he wasn't allowed to call himself that, not after being discharged from the Guild. "There's no Guild in this place." Kragnak pursed his lips and turned away.

"We'd like to stay, but we have work to do. Yander, come on." For a second he thought he was going to have to drag the dwarf away, but finally Yander tore himself away from watching the cooling ingot and followed.

Dorian basked in the moment, letting the stress melt from his limbs and forgetting his cares for a moment. They had metal.

The sounds of the other dwarves sleeping filled the air. Yander opened one eye. All the others were mounds in their beds, breathing deeply or snoring. He couldn't see clearly but thought that one bed was empty.

Gingerly he picked up a corner of his blanket and took it all the way off him, to his feet. The cool of the cave spread over his bare feet, and he swung them out over the edge of the bed.

Slowly, heart pounding, he lowered them until they touched the rough, cool of the stone. His flesh tingled and tried to recoil, but he pressed on. A dwarf stirred to his right.

Yander froze. The form moved and shifted. It was Daruik, the last dwarf he wanted to see awake. His heart beat wildly and his throat caught. Without moving a muscle he waited. Time seemed to stretch on.

But Daruik rolled back over. In a few seconds his snores were added to the others, a strange melody that repeated itself. Even though his lungs were bursting, Yander dared not breathe more than a few long, shallow breaths.

There was no time to put on his boots, he grabbed them and snuck to the exit. The door was still open, and he was glad he didn't have to try and open it. It squeaked on the stone hinges.

Out in the hall he could breathe again, and he leaned up against the wall to catch his breath, gulping down the stale air of the caves. The smells of his new home came with it, smoke and earth with a faint hint of sweat from their work.

His heart calmed and his breathing steadied. No one came to follow him, no one tried to stop him. Even so, he tiptoed down the tunnel until he thought he was far enough out of earshot to slip on his boots in the workshops. They had made more progress, expanding it to house everyone who had a craft.

Emelda and her family had set up their workstations too. Scissors, knives, odd shaped tins, and long strings of wax were laid neatly. There wasn't any wax to work with, but the workbench was covered with half finished sections of wood and a neat pile of shavings.

Yander wished he had a skill like that. Maybe Daruik wouldn't dislike him so much if he did. Even the thought of not being able to mine anymore made him sad, and he wasn't sure why. After they had struck the copper ore he longed for the rock even more.

There would be more treasure buried there.

He went through the tunnels until the glow of the farm cave peeked up ahead. He slowed down, a thought struck him. It would be fun to sneak up on her, so he slowed down and stepped lightly. The opening was just up ahead, and he slowly poked his head around it.

"Hello Yander." Emelda was looking right at him while she carved. Red crept up his cheeks and he stepped out of the darkness.

"Good evening."

"Sneaking around in the middle of the night?" She returned to her work and clicked her tongue. "What would they say if they caught you?" He was good and caught, and smiled sheepishly.

"They would say hello." Emelda didn't say anything, but her lip twitched. Yander waited, and then she looked up. Their eyes met, and she smiled and laughed.

"Come on, sit down." He joined her in the empty stool, a thrill running through him to be so close to her.

"Have you had to fend off any wild animals?" A spear leaned up against the support, ready to be snatched up at a moments notice.

"Nothing yet." It was her watch, they took turns, and it wasn't the first time they had stayed awake to talk to each other. Yander had done it first, arranging his watch to follow without getting Daruik involved. They had stayed up far into his watch, almost losing track of time.

They were more careful now.

"I'd hate to run into the moles that made that hole though." She eyed the opening, now covered with a large rock to keep out the pests. Her smile fled, and she shivered. "Who knows what lives down here." He stared into her eyes, absorbing the picture of her face.

Yander thought about what he'd do if something was to ever come out of the depths below. The giant mole might be big, but he wouldn't be scared. *I'd protect her, no matter what happened. If anything comes up, I'm going to protect her.*

21

WEAPONS

"Shouldn't we be digging deeper, finding more ore?" Yander asked. Dorian stopped and looked over at him. Something was off about him.

"No. You look tired." Yander looked away hurriedly. Dorian shook his head.

"I'm just thinking we should get more. Do we really have enough?" His pickaxe clinked against the rock, another section fell to the ground. *Fine, have it your way. It's not as if I care, anyway.*

Dorian was irritated he even thought it, and he let his irritation show in his voice. "We have more copper than we need, for now. The forge takes wood, and it takes time to chop it." Everyone was busy with their tasks, they barely had time to keep up the farm caves and forage for food. Summer was ending already and the forests around them had changed.

Yander mumbled something under his breath.

"What?" Dorian asked.

"Fine." He kept working. Returning to his own work, Dorian let the conversation go. Why get into an argument when he could work in the relative peace and quiet?

They were back in the hall now, carving out larger wings on the side. Dorian insisted they leave large pillars running down the sides of it, and they had taken on an impressive form. They would need scaffolding to excavate above them, but that could be done at a later time.

Now, however, they needed the room. The tables were crammed in together, barely enough room to get the chairs in. The expansion would help with that and give them more space for storage. Not that they needed it, there was barely enough to fill up the space they had.

Always working ahead, thinking of one step forward. But he had forgotten so much, and with they years passing as they did Dorian wondered what he hadn't thought about, what he hadn't considered. He shook the thought away.

At least the liaison was leaving, a few more days. Dorian had to admit he had been more helpful than liaisons in the past. Was that an intentional act by King Lightaxe, or was someone else looking out for him? Or was it pure luck? Somehow, that seemed unlikely. The vast majority he had dealt with would laze about, demand meetings at the most inopportune times, and generally be a drain on the expedition.

"Scatter it around the base and you'll have bigger yields in no time." Tufolin grabbed a handful of the rich, dark stuff and tossed it with a flick of his wrist. It hit just under the cave berry bush, and sent its waves of deep, earthy smell up around it. A lopsided pile pressed up against the scraggly bark.

"On everything?" Skover asked. He didn't seem so sure about it.

"Everything that will grow." Skover rubbed his belly and tightened his lips. "That's all there is to it, if you get it to rot right." Yudoline saw he was going to say something else and stepped in.

"Thank you Tufolin," she said, giving him a wide smile illuminated by the golden moss. It had almost recovered from the attack and the splitting. Now it nearly filled the cave up, pressing around the nearest cave berry bushes. That would be the first to be harvested. "We'll keep it in mind."

"Kitchen scraps and dead things," Skover muttered. Yudoline pulled Tufolin away, thinking it best to avoid a potentially damaging interaction. "Will you walk with me back to the outside plots?"

"Certainly, I'd be honored to join you." She felt better when they were out of the cave and safely in the tunnel. "There is a topic I'd like to broach with you, if you don't mind." They walked side by side, and she cast him a glance.

"What is it?"

"I've heard about your...unfortunate situation." She didn't know what he was talking about, and stared at him. "About the ale." He raised an eyebrow.

"Oh." Yudoline looked down, too ashamed to meet his gaze. "You heard about that?" He put his hand on her shoulder and squeezed.

"When I was younger, not much younger I might add, I tried to learn to juggle." The image of him juggling flashed into her mind, and the silliness of it took away some of the shame. "I see your smile. I know, foolish. But the way the traveling minstrels juggle, keeping their balls and cabbages flying through the air. Something about it pulled at me."

They were at the entrance now and opened the heavy stone door. Light blinded her at first, then her eyes adjusted. "You can't imagine how many balls I dropped. It's a good thing I didn't start with eggs." Yudoline giggled, then they laughed together.

"What does this have to do with me?"

"I didn't really learn until I found a minstrel to teach me. He showed me a trick, now I can keep them flying like any court jester." They climbed the bank to the outside farm plots, and he brought them to the hops. "You should try again, I've got some more information for you."

She stared at him. "You can brew ale too?"

"Brew, no. But my mother used to and I still remember everything she used to do. Can you walk me through what you did?"

She told him. He listened and nodded at the appropriate times. When she finished, she felt better. After holding it in for so long it was good to get it out. "Do you think I did it right?"

"No, and I'll tell you what you did wrong."

"Much bigger than it used to be. How much more do you have to dig out?" Barileth asked.

"Finished, for now." Dorian leaned back, feeling the tenderness in the small of his back. With all the digging they were doing it hadn't been a fun few days.

"You'll be happy about these." He held up a bundle of spears, tipped with sharp copper points that gleamed in the torchlight. Yander gathered up the rest of the tailings from the great hall with the shovel, dumping them into the wheelbarrow with a crash.

"Those are the spears aren't they?" Yander asked.

"What do you think?" Barileth shot Yander a glare, which he ignored.

"Let me see one. It's heavier than I thought it would be. For some reason I didn't think adding that little amount of metal to the front would change it all that much." Yander hefted the shaft, then tossed it in the air. He made a few tentative jabs toward the ceiling.

"Not much danger to anyone else with that I see," Barileth said. Yander turned red and dropped the spear back into the pile.

"Stage some near the entrance, some here. Those on guard duty will check them out in the great hall." Dorian headed for the door. "And Yander, take care of the rest before dinner." While he walked to the workshop he wondered if he should ask Tufolin why he was sent to them.

He was still thinking about it when he walked in, but didn't have an answer to his own question. Instead he went to Lumdir first. "How is it coming along?"

"Most are done, I think I have three more left to do." Ten new stone chests were in a row to the right of his workbench. The one he was working on now had started to hollow out, a block of granite from their mining with what looked like a square hole halfway down.

"Faster than I expected. Good." Kimec was also hard at work, and Dorian went to him next. Stacks of barrel staves were piled under his workbench, and he was hunched over a half finished barrel. "Almost done already?"

Kimec stood up and stretched. "If I can keep working. I'm used to working on a bench and these barrels are taking a toll on my back." Dorian knew what that meant, he would be behind in his assignment.

"How much more time do you need?" Dorian had built in an extra few days. The barrels were going to hold the golden moss harvest, if they had one. Kimec's eyes widened.

"None, I'm almost done. Two or three more to go."

It was Dorian's turn to be surprised. "Where are the others?" he looked around, but they were no where to be seen.

"In the farm cave. Daruik and Skover got them this morning for the harvest."

"Harvest? I didn't think they were ready."

"They are, it seems the trick Tufolin showed them is working already. If you didn't have anything for me next I was planning on making more crates. Noreck and Emelda have been busy and are almost full on the one they have."

How did that get away from him? "Already?"

"It looks like they've gotten faster. Better too, based on what I saw."

"Crates are fine for now." Dorian suppressed his astonishment. "I'll check up on them. Do you need more wood?"

Kimec shook his head. "No, Barileth's kept me in good supply. More than enough to keep going, and the branches have made good fuel for the furnace."

"Good," Dorian said. Kragnak wasn't the best smith, his rough spearheads workable but not great, but he had kept the fire burning. All the ore they found was smelted now and was stacked in piles. It gleamed in the reflection of the flames.

In addition to the copper he had managed to pull off a few bars of silver. They were small, and still dirty, but if push came to shove, they could use them for barter. Or refine them later, if they ever had a jeweler arrive.

But it was the other crafting workbench that caught his attention now. Noreck and Emelda were working and talking to each other. They stopped as he approached.

Dorian didn't know what to say. "Is it dinnertime?" Emelda asked. Dorian shook his head.

"Almost. I've heard you've been busy and I've come to take a look."

"Wood is harder than wax, but once we had some practice it almost cuts the same," Noreck said. They had knives out, and each was working on something. Emelda was carving a line of leaves on a bracelet, and Noreck was carving a small figure of a goat.

"May I?" Dorian took the offered bracelet and examined it closely. Even though they had the light of the furnace it must have been difficult to carve. Nestled among the half carved leaves were bees, with incredible detail. "Beautiful."

Emelda blushed, but her half-hidden smile revealed her pleasure. "Mother taught me well." Noreck gave her a half hug.

"She has deft fingers, and a good eye."

"I can't wait to see what you'll be able to do with wax then." Dorian handed the bracelet back. "Kimec will be making you another crate or two." The crate was almost full, and a quick glance revealed similar bracelet, many figurines, and toys.

He bid them goodbye and went back to his work. For the first time since they arrived he thought they might have a chance. If they could survive the winter and the next few years, that was.

Yander had finished taking the tailings at, and the hall was quiet and empty. It was the biggest room in the caves now. Dorian sat down to think.

He didn't know how long it was when dwarves started coming in. Yudoline at first, followed by Kimec. Then the others came in. Food followed, and drink.

The night was a blur, the food delicious and the ale flowing freely. Dorian relaxed, and let himself enjoy it. There was nothing to do for the rest of the night that couldn't wait until tomorrow.

Something strange happened. It started with a smile, that then turned into a laugh at a joke told. Then, he was having a good time. The first he had remembered since his release from prison. Dorian tasted it and savored it.

There was another first tonight. For the first time since her death, Dorian thought that there was a chance, however small it might be, that he could learn to live without his wife.

22

WATCHER

"Add it after?" Yudoline looked at the small pile of crushed cave berries. They were still white and oozed their juices on the cutting board. It looked black, but she knew it was a trick of the light.

"Right after you boil it. It changes the wort to ale." Vague memories stirred at the instructions that Tufolin had given her. The cave berries, that was new though. "It adds a hint of flavor, but not enough to change it. Otherwise you need a brewer's spoon."

As soon as he told her what he remembered of his mother brewing ale she realized what she had done wrong. She had thrown the wort out when she should have kept it.

She wasn't sure she could do it, but there was the barrel full of ripe hop berries in the corner calling to her. If it worked this time…

"Would you stay and watch me?"

Tufolin considered it. "I have enough time, if you have everything ready now." Yudoline was moving before he could reconsider, swinging the big pot over the fire to boil.

He helped her bring the barrel of hops over, which she crushed in the big mortar that Kimec carved for her. The kitchen filled with the scent of hops, which mixed with the steam from the pot. It was a heady, intoxicating smell.

Into the pot went the crushed hops. The green bubbled and roiled, and when it was long enough, she took it off the fire. She wasn't going to throw it away this time, now she knew how important it was. Instead she dumped the pot into a waiting barrel of water.

It hissed and spat at her, but she left it to roll over the barrel it would make a home in. With Tufolin's help they poured the mixture into the barrel, set on the top, and sealed it.

"Done at last." Yudoline slipped onto the stool to rest. "This time I know it will turn out."

"I'm sure it will be delicious, just like my mother used to make." Yudoline offered Tufolin some cheese and rockbread, which he took. She carved off slices for her as well and they shared it, basking in the warmth and glow of the fire.

"Thank you for your hospitality. I've much to report."

"Are you sure you don't want to stay for a few more days? Storms look like they're brewing," Yudoline said. Tufolin smiled and shook his head.

"No, I've got a long journey ahead of me." He patted his bag, filled with provisions for his journey. "And plenty of food to get me there." The other dwarves were there too, assembled at the mine entrance.

Tufolin walked down the line, shaking hands and exchanging small words with each dwarf in turn. Dorian watched, arms crossed. In addition to the food in his bag were crafts and trinkets, pretty things to attract traveling merchants brave enough to wander out into the wilderness. Would their small things attract them?

Finally only Dorian was left. Tufolin was smiling as he approached, but Dorian didn't drop his hands. Reaching out a hand Tufolin waited. A message from the King, but what kind of message was it? Dorian uncrossed his arms and reached out his hand.

They clasped, both dwarves holding tight. Dorian felt the strength of Tufolin's grasp, who never stopped smiling. "Watch out for them Dorian Ironstrike. You know how much depends on it."

Dorian's eyebrows tightened, but there wasn't a hint of menace in Tufolin's voice. What did he mean by that? Was that another threat to his children?

"I know what waits for me."

"Is it what waits for us all?" Tufolin released his grasp, but Dorian didn't respond. Antagonizing the dwarf wouldn't help their cause, it would only make trouble. "Farewell friends and fellow compatriots. I wish you luck and deep delving."

With his final words Tufolin turned and started his journey. The dwarves watched for a while, but then, one by one, they went back to their assignments. Dorian was the last to go, watching the liaison pick his way through the trees.

When Tufolin had gone he looked over the valley. Summer was hanging on, not letting the cooler days of autumn begin. There were clouds in the sky, dark and ominous. A breeze blew from the north, but it was fickle and barely rustled the leaves in the trees.

Something was off. Dorian didn't know what it was, but he felt it. From the bottom of his feet it crept up to the back of his neck, tickling him. An eagle drifted in lazy circles above him in the sky. Its head craned as it searched for prey below, ready to dive on it in a heartbeat.

Are we being watched by more than birds? He peered into the trees. They had cut back the line of them, giving ample room to see anything that might be coming. The half-finished wall didn't make him feel secure, it wouldn't until it was finished. Even then, it was just stone. Things could climb stone.

Bad things.

"Dorian?" The voice almost startled him, but his subconscious had picked up the footsteps in the entrance tunnel. "Are you coming?" Yander was peering out of the doorway when he turned. It was another reminder of the work that he had to do, the long road left to travel.

"I'll be there in a minute. Go ahead and start without me." After they were done expanding the farm caves they could finish fortifications. The others wanted him to start on the apartments. They all agreed that one level down would be best, close enough to get to their places of work but far enough away to leave them there.

He agreed, but there were more pressing tasks to finish, ones that would keep them alive. Remembering the strange magical trap he told himself that goblins weren't the worst thing that prowled in the wilderness, far from guards and armies.

Dorian gave one last searching look along the valley, but after seeing nothing he went inside.

"Will you go get me some of the rockbread?" Yudoline asked, cracking another egg over the frying pan. She dropped it and it hissed on the heat.

"We're out, where did we keep it?" Skover asked.

"Back behind the kegs." She cracked another egg and added it. Soon the pan was covered in a blanket of white with little yellow yolks spread on top. Suppressing a yawn, she got out a tub of butter that they would use for the bread.

It was almost empty, and she frowned at it. "We'll have to make more." Kimec had made a bigger churn, and it would speed up the process. The goat was still giving milk though, so it would be easy to do.

A loud crash from behind her in the storeroom made her jump. She spun, shrinking back from where the noise came from, heart beating fast.

"Oww," Skover groaned.

"Skover? What happened." Yudoline crossed the room and peered around the corner.

"I thought I could reach it," he said. Skover was lying on his back in a puddle of something, his foot stuck in the top of a keg. It was still rolling, spilling its contents on the ground.

"Sticks and stones! Let's get you up." Together they pulled him to a sitting position, and he felt his back.

"Oh, tender." He paused to assess. "Nothing broken though, I think." Yudoline helped pull the remains of the keg off his leg. When she did, a thought struck her. The keg of ale she made was back here, tucked away a few weeks ago. She had nearly forgotten about it, but something reminded her of it.

Skover sniffed and drew his eyebrows together. Yudoline smelled something too.

"Does it smell like ale?" She asked.

"I was about to ask the same question." He reached down his hand, touched the liquid, and brought his finger to his lips. His tongue darted out and tasted his finger. "Tastes like it too, a little weak though."

Yudoline realized why she smelled ale and Skover tasted it. Sure enough, the keg was the one she had made her batch. Her heart sank as she looked inside. There was barely enough for a mug left. "This was it. My ale."

"You made it? I thought it was something we brought with us."

"No, those are on the other side." She gestured to the opposite nook of the store room, where barrels were stacked on top of each other. All at once she felt like crying, but she held back her tears.

"I was going to say it wasn't too bad." Skover got to his feet, still feeling around for injuries. "Whatever you did this time, it worked."

"Really? You aren't just saying that to make me feel better."

"No." Skover held up his hands in protest. "I mean it. It's a shame its gone." His eyes fell to the floor. "I've ruined it." An icy stab of guilt pierced her heart. All this time Skover had almost hurt himself, and she was worried about ale. What kind of dwarf would think that?

Putting a hand on his shoulder, she comforted him. "Don't think that. It wasn't much good anyway. Tell you what, there's some left. You can have the rest now, get a proper taste of it." A half smile grew on his face, and he nodded.

"I never do anything right."

"Except the growing and the cooking. Don't be too hard on yourself," she said as she went to fetch a mug. When she came back they poured the rest in, Skover lifting the keg and Yudoline holding the mug steady.

It had a weak head of foam that left a trail on Skover's mustache when he took a sip. She waited to see his reaction, dreading it. All she could think about was the horrible faces they made with the last batch. She didn't want it to be the same.

Relief washed over her when he smacked his lips and his eyes lit up. "That's a proper ale. Could use some more time, like I said earlier, but it tastes good."

Yudoline clapped her hands and smiled. "I'm glad." She spun on her heel and marched out the door.

"Where are you going?" Skover asked, reaching out to her.

"To make the next batch," she said over her shoulder.

Another storm was brewing. Dorian watched the clouds in the sky, but behind him was where he was concerned. Deeper in the mine he knew the others were meeting. Tempers were getting short, the dormitory was getting cramped, and no one liked the extra hours building the wall they were forced into.

So he waited for them, out in the open, pickaxe beside him in the dirt. It had been a tough few weeks, but the wall was almost done. The two sides grew from the slope, curling around to finally meet in the middle where a door would go.

Big enough to let in a cart, but small enough to defend. That was the best way to do it, or so experience had taught him. He shivered from the memory of his earlier years, but footsteps behind him caught his attention.

"Dorian, we need to speak with you." Daruik. He expected Barileth to be the leader, but he was skulking at the back. *Interesting.*

"You have my ear." Daruik's face was drawn and tight, and the others looked worried. Dorian picked up his pickaxe, absentmindedly twirling it around in his hands.

"We need a break, and we need places to stay that aren't so close you step on each other getting out of bed." Daruik crossed his arms and looked confident, standing straighter.

"After the defenses are built, we've talked about this."

"No, we can't wait longer. We've been building this wall for months now, and look where it's gotten us. Nowhere. There isn't anything around we need it for." The last part didn't have as much confidence.

"So you want to be torn to shreds?" Dorian asked. "Because that's what will happen if we aren't prepared."

23

A Place to Call Home

"That won't happen. We've got the door to protect us."

"A door?" Dorian stood up. The dwarves took a step back. "You think this flimsy piece of rock is going to protect us? Against what, a bear?" They weren't the only tired ones.

Dorian had done his fill of mining in the middle of the night, getting the traps and carving out rock to use for the wall. Spending hours turning the problems around in his head, figuring out where to put them. He was tired too, and he let it out.

"Did they tell you about the dog?"

"Dog?" Kragnak asked.

"Oh, they neglected to tell you about a dog that came back from the dead." He swung the pickaxe to his shoulder. The migrants looked uneasy, the others ashamed. "There are more dangerous things out there than you know. I've lived it. Barileth has seen it."

Barileth shifted, and his eyes twitched. He sunk farther back. Daruik wasn't straight anymore, and Dorian saw the doubt in his eyes.

"What about the goblins that Tufolin mentioned? Or more thieves like Dovig." Dorian spat the name out. "Should I leave you fools to die out here where no one will help us?" There was nothing but silence.

"We want our own places, that's all," Daruik said after a long pause. "We'll work harder if you dig them for us.

Dorian was tired, and he felt it now. They were almost to winter, half a year gone already and weren't even close to supporting themselves. Only the bounty of the surrounding wilderness kept them alive.

He closed his eyes and dropped the pickaxe. His children, he had to think of his children. And her, there was still a chance, no matter how remote it was. When he opened his eyes the group was still there.

"Yander, get your pickaxe. We'll start now." Dorian had hoped to get back to the mining by now. He walked forward, and they parted without a word.

"What are we starting?" Yander asked as he swung open the mine door.

Dorian looked back over his shoulder. "The apartments."

The first apartment was finished in two days. "That went fast," Yander remarked. Dorian studied the room from the doorway. Had they improved that much?

"Better divide up then, you start on this side, I'll do that." They separated, mining to the markings Dorian had made up after they had finished the hallway tunnel. There was going to be twelve apartments total, six on each side, one level down from the main level.

"Kimec started the chests for us today," Yander said. Dorian grunted, focused on letting the swing of his pickaxe carry him away from his thoughts. "I asked him what they were going to look like, he said they'd be plain but well built. So well built Skover could sit on one and it wouldn't even whimper." Yander laughed.

Something had changed. He was back to his usual self, cheery and talkative. Dorian wasn't sure what to think, other than be annoyed. Although he couldn't keep a small smile from his lips. The dwarf had been too sullen for too long.

He had his suspicions as to why, but couldn't prove anything. While he yammered on, punctuated by the staccato of both their pickaxes, Dorian turned his thoughts to other things.

Lumdir had almost finished the doors they would need to equip the hall. They had twelve dwarves, but since the Icebrewers were sharing a room they would only need eleven finished. They already had the beds, that left Kimec to make them chests and cabinets.

It would be bare, but from the excitement he heard around the meal table they didn't care. He shook his head. *If only they knew what was really important, they'd be less worried about where they slept.*

However, the nature of a dwarf couldn't be changed easily, so he had to do what he could. A mutiny wouldn't help his cause any. Better to pick a fight later and not have to worry about it. He'd heard about expeditions failing because of internal fighting.

Taking a deep breath, he cleared his mind. Dorian shifted his grip on the pickaxe, feeling the smooth wooden handle worn by months of use. The head was balanced perfectly, some red rust showing the signs of its age.

Clink. Clink. Clink. Yander's steady hammer blows and tongue kept up a rhythm. Warmth spread out from the stone. No ore, but friendliness from the earth. It wanted to envelop him, welcome him in.

Should I resist it? Why does it call so longingly? It had accepted the body of his long-dead wife. She slept there, beneath the mountain. His heart ached for her touch, her steady way, her smile. The choices he had made mocked him from his past.

The smell of stone and fire. The taste of dust and ash. He brought up the pickaxe, then let it fall in a graceful arc. It struck the stone, cutting into it and a crack snapped across the face. Just what he thought, a schism to drive his tool deep into.

He shifted the handle, bringing it over slightly. It was enough. The face of the rock parted, cleaved from the mountain to roll off. Lumdir would be able to use it, it was flat and clean.

The sound of it hitting the ground made all his thoughts rush back. The plans, the actions, the tasks. All the things that would need to be done in order to succeed at his task. Too much for today and tomorrow and the next day. Too few hands to accomplish it.

So he mined, kept up his own steady rhythm, and the hours slipped by one by one.

Once again, Yander quietly slipped out of bed, careful not to rouse the sleeping dwarves around him. It was easier now, the dormitory was almost empty except Kragnak, Narfac, and him.

Emelda wasn't on guard duty tonight, it was Barileth's turn now. The dwarf would be alert, so Yander had to stay as far away from him as possible. He snuck through the tunnels, heart pounding.

The mine was asleep, nothing stirred in the dark. After a few feet his eyes adapted to the dark, but he took a torch with him just in case. He might need it where he was going.

At the crossroads he turned left and descended the stairs, wary of falling without a light. Once past the apartment level, which he cast a glance at, he thought about lighting it, but didn't. Emelda was sleeping in there, calm and peaceful. Her father and mother too, and he hoped they were asleep.

Down into the mine he went. Down passed the tunnels that they had dug to explore the mountain. Deeper than the one they had found the ore in, although he thought it might hold what he needed. He paused, but on second thought, he kept going.

What he desired would be deeper. Much deeper. His rock sense was getting stronger since they discovered the copper, the mountain was always talking and he was beginning to hear.

Yander stifled a yawn. If he was quick he could be back in bed in a few hours or less, and maybe less if he was lucky. This wasn't the first time he had been down here on his own. For the last few nights he searched, and it was starting to take its toll. The last few nights he had spent closer to the surface, down the tunnels of exploration. He hadn't found anything.

He moved deeper, trudging down the steps and thinking about what Daruik would say when he presented Emelda with the biggest gem he had ever seen. He would come up to Yander, head hung low, and beg forgiveness. Then, when Yander had graciously granted it, he would shake his hand, look him in the eye, and say he was wrong about him.

Before he knew it the stairs ran out. He was as deep as they had gone. A quick glance up the mineshaft let him know it was dark at the top, the bucket still safely in its nesting place. There was something about being down here by himself that set him on edge and made him pause at the edge of the stairs.

Was that a sound he heard? Yander stopped breathing to hear. Nothing. He told himself he was being silly. This was a dead end, they hadn't found anything down here the first time.

There was only one tunnel here. It had been so long since they had been here, months ago. He couldn't believe it, that was right before Emelda came here. The tunnel was short and stubby and he picked up where they left off, choosing the right side of the tunnel to expand. After lighting the torch, he set it on the ground to illuminate his work area and started.

It was hard to be quiet while digging into rock, but Yander did his best. After a few strikes he would stop and reach his hand to the wall, closing his eyes and feeling it. There had to be more of a trick to it, because he thought he felt something just out of reach.

He decided to dig an hour or two more, maybe less. That would give him enough time to explore. After a few more rounds he didn't think he could feel anything. Disheartened, he turned to the other side of the tunnel.

This time, he felt something. A glimmer, a spot of warmth. It could have been in his mind, but he decided to go ahead, anyway. While he dug, he wondered what the others would think about him being down here.

Dorian would think him foolish, but nothing more. The others wouldn't care, probably. They didn't seem to think much of him, try as hard as he could to make himself useful. Not like Daruik, they didn't look down on him for choosing to be a miner.

They think I'm young and naïve, but I'm not. Yander had put his younger years behind him, he was now on an expedition out into the wilderness in the heart of contested lands. No dwarves trod here, and he was brave to try.

He was making progress, the warmth of the stone was getting stronger. There was something down here hidden beneath the rock. Yander increased his effort, caring less about the sound. Down here the sound couldn't carry far, or so he rationalized.

The pickaxe struck deep in the rock, but instead of resistance, it went forward, surprising him. Yander pulled it back. A small, black hole stared at him from the rock. He stared back.

Excitement shivered through him, and he took another swing. The hole expanded, rock crumbling down and clattering to the ground. He kept going, enlarging it until he could see through it.

Something made him make it bigger, big enough for him to go through, and soon it was. He stopped to catch his breath, he hadn't realized how fast he had been working. Yander's blood pumped, and he felt a touch lightheaded, then scooped up the torch to see.

Blackness gave way to torchlight, which scattered and shot out of the hole. His excitement faded as he looked. It was a cavern, and something smelled foul in the air that came out. Stalactites and stalagmites glistened with faint wetness.

Suddenly Yander didn't want to be there. He backed up, almost tripping over his pickaxe. Something about it felt wrong, and he had done it by himself without asking permission. It wasn't right, and he didn't want to be there anymore.

He fled up the stairs, looking back every few steps, but nothing came out of the darkness. At the top of the stairs he paused to listen. It was silent. He doused his torch and stumbled back through the dark to bed.

Without saying a word he got back into bed, pulling the covers tight over his beard. He couldn't tell the others about it, not now. Yander couldn't bear their harsh words. He would say nothing.

The thing stopped. It had been long since it had traveled this way, but a strange scent wafted through the air.

It remembered.

Something new, something fresh, something delicious.

The past few days had been... disappointing. Hunger was growing inside, fueled by the strange newness that came to it. What would this new thing be? Would there be enough to savor, or would it be small and tiny?

It stalked through the cavern, catching a small creature unaware and devouring it in an instant. The meat was lacking, and its hunger was not satisfied. Something bigger would have to do, and something new.

The scent was like a trail, leading it on into a place it was familiar with, a place it had hunted for a long time. At the end of a tunnel, it knew well there was something different.

Where once only rock had been, a small hole now was. The smell was stronger here, and so enticing. It crouched down, making its body as small as it could, and pulled itself through the opening.

24

DETAILS

The pot bubbled cheerfully, and Yudoline hummed as she stirred it. This would be the one, she knew it. After having done it once she was filled with confidence. Kimec was hard at work making her more barrels, and she would fill them all.

The look on all their faces would be worth it. She pictured Skover as he tasted her ale, the pleasant shock and then the look of pleasure. It would make them all happier, and they needed it too.

In a place like this the small things would make all the difference. That was something she learned from her mother. "Take care of the details, and the rest will follow." She could almost picture her now, ruddy cheeks stirring a pot over the stove.

It was her turn to carry on the tradition. She reflected on her life up until now, how living in Zirad was difficult tin a way, but was nothing compared to everyday life here. Back home she was pampered, and she realized that now.

Food from the market, ale from the inns and way stations along the main roads. Merchants that brought strange and exotic goods from all around the world. Safety. High walls, strong guards. Smelters that ran day and night to boil down and spit out their molten metal from all the ore gathered from the earth.

And their own apartment. She sighed. It was so nice to be back in a private place. Sharing a space with the others had been...diff icult. Even after living with Kimec, who had his own quirks like sleeping with his bare feet sticking out the bottom of the blanket, it wasn't something she wanted to repeat.

The boiling was done, and she cooled the pot, stirring in her crushed cave berries and pouring the concoction into a keg big enough to hold it. She capped it, setting it with a final ring with a wooden mallet that made her heart melt.

"You just take your time," she said, patting the top of it. "We'll be waiting when you're done to enjoy you." With a smile, and one last caress of the rough wood, she returned to her other work, basking in the glow of her success.

"Last one, we'll finish this today." Dorian stretched his arms and eyed the granite rock ahead of him. They had already been working a few hours now finishing the last apartment. It had taken more than a day. Yander was moving slower than normal, and he didn't look right. Dorian paused. "Yander, what's wrong?"

"Huh?" Yander blinked, fixing his eyes on Dorian. "Nothing, nothing's wrong. One more, we'll get it done." He brushed passed Dorian and attacked the wall, carving out the doorway. *Something's off about him.*

Dorian was so preoccupied he didn't realize what he was smelling until his nose had already curled. Yander was pounding away, and shards of rock were flying, but it wasn't the smell of stone dust he recognized. It was something else.

What is it? Where have I smelled that before? Memories were stirring up, and a strange sense of dread, that something else was amiss. He thought he saw a shadow on the wall and turned to the opening.

The torch they were working by flickered and cast its glow into the carved stone corridor that led a short distance to the stairs. It was less than twenty feet to the door opening, and another ten to the stairs.

Light didn't go far enough for him to see, but he peered into the black opening beyond the apartments.

"Dorian, what is it?" Yander had stopped working. Dorian held up his hand to stop him talking and listened. Did he hear something out there, or was it his imagination? The torch fluttered and spat, the only sound in the mine besides the distant working of the craft dwarves up above.

"Must be nothing. Let's get to it." He glanced back over his shoulder, glad he had a strong pickaxe in his hand and wishing it were something else.

Narfac paused, setting down his load of wood in the corridor to take a break. He had been sweating from the strain, and the coolness of the mine helped. After wiping the sweat off his forehead, he leaned it against the side of the wall.

For another time that day he wished he had drawn a different job, other than building the wall. That was the only other thing that he detested more. But Kimec and the Icebrewers needed wood, so someone had to go get it.

Something clicked down the stairs. Narfac's head snapped up and over, banging against the wall in his haste to look busy. He cried out in pain, then quickly tried to collect his load of wood before whoever it was caught him.

When no one came out of the stairs he felt foolish, but then he caught the strange scent wafting in the air. It was...bad. Putrid, rotting, like something had died. They hadn't slaughtered any animals that he knew of.

Then a hiss. Out of the darkness of the stairwell came something that smacked into his logs and pushed him back. It was sticky and wet, and then more of it was coming. Fear blossomed in him, it wasn't right.

He couldn't drop the wood, his hands were bound up in something strange and too strong to resist. More of it came flying out of the darkness, more clicking, and he was firmly bound to the wall.

When he saw it come for him, he screamed. A guttural, fear laced scream that went on until the substance filled his mouth and choked him. Even without torchlight he could see it, squeezing through the opening of the doorway and unfurling until it touched the top of the tunnel.

It came for him, and all he could do was look on and struggle against the bindings that held him helpless.

"Did you hear that?" Skover looked over at the entrance. It was still going, a dwarf screaming in the mine. Yudoline shrank from the sound.

"What do we do?" Another scream pierced the quiet, this time closer. It was someone else, not the same as the first. A female dwarf. "Emelda," she whispered. They were in the farm cave, tending the crops.

There was no way out.

"Run." Skover got to his feet, dropping the bucket in his haste. It splashed out, soaking Yudoline's front. She scrambled after him, slower than he was. If she wasn't so afraid she might have wondered how he moves so fast. "If we hurry, we can make it to the entrance."

They ran, Yudoline following Skover, passed the cave berries, through the opening to the caves, and turned down the tunnel back to the entrance. Yudoline was lagging a few feet behind Skover.

The torches were out in the tunnel up ahead, but their eyes were accustomed to the low level of light. Her breath was fast and her heart pounding, matching the panting of Skover.

"We'll get to the exit and be safe," Skover said through his husky breathing.

"Wait for me!" Her eyes danced around, starting at shadows. Running wasn't something she was used to, but she couldn't help it. Her legs felt like stone already.

Skover was almost at the corner of the tunnel. It turned left, and would take them past the dining hall and to the crossroads. One more left would take them out to safety.

But what about Kimec, was he safe? The thought made her feet stumble, and she fell. Skover reached the turn. As she looked up, he disappeared around the corner.

Yudoline was about to scramble to her feet when he reappeared, flung back into the wall. He crumpled to the ground, folded unnaturally.

"Skover?" She got to her feet, never letting her eyes leave his body. Out of the darkness a long stream of white shot out with a hiss. It hit Skover, covering his body.

She took a step back. What was that? Why wasn't he getting up? She knew the answer to the second question, but didn't want to think it. Skover wouldn't be getting up ever again.

The white substance continued, covering his body until it had disappeared in a mound. To the left was the door to the kitchens, the right was the opening to the store rooms.

There was no escape behind her.

Something clicked on the stone around the corner, and Yudoline froze. The sound struck her to her very soul. Everything in her mind screamed at her body to move, but she couldn't make her muscles move.

Then, it came out of the black. It moved gracefully and quickly, approaching Skover with determined strides. They were stories, they weren't real.

But it was here, standing right in front of her. The cautionary tales of her grandmother, told when she wasn't behaving, the nightmares of her childhood. It was real.

The top of its body reached up to the stone above it, it was hunched over and not standing to its full height. Within seconds, it was at Skover's unmoving form. She still couldn't move.

It sank a stinger into Skover, then turned him over and covered him in white webbing.

Finally, Yudoline gained control of her trembling legs and she ran for the kitchen door. The thing noticed, and turned to her. Bulbous black eyes fastened on her.

A stream of white shot for her.

The scream brought his apprehension fully to the surface and stoked it into fear. Dorian and Yander both turned toward the stairs. He was certain it had come from there.

Strange sounds echoed through the mine, clicking and swishes bouncing off the wall. The combination of the sounds and the smells made Dorian realize why he had been so uncomfortable.

And now they were trapped between it and the exit.

"Dorian, what is that? Are goblins invading?" Yander was unsure, there was more than a hint of fear in his voice. For once, he seemed to be exhibiting good judgment.

"Not goblins." His apartment was feet away, with the axe locked in the trunk at the foot of his bed. Dorian didn't want to move in, he preferred to let the others take the rooms first, but they had forced him when the couples were in place.

It would be so easy to pick it up, to slip back into his former life. *No, that's what put me in this mess to begin with.* He hefted his pickaxe instead. It had good weight to it, if they couldn't escape, it would work.

"Then what is it?" Dorian was about to answer him when another shriek rang out. Yander's eyes opened wide. "Emelda!"

He ran down the tunnel, but Dorian grabbed his arm, wrenching him back. "What are you doing? Do you even know what's up there?"

"I don't care, Emelda's in trouble." Yander tried to shake off his grip, but Dorian held it tight in a grip honed by months of mining. If he let him go Yander would be going to his death. "Let me go."

Staring into his eyes, Dorian was forced to confront his own past. "Please, let me go," Yander whimpered. He imagined Yolanda that day so many years ago and almost lost the strength to stand. Would he have done anything different if he could try and save her?

"Please, she's in trouble. I have to do something." Tears were in Yander's eyes, the cries were stopped. It might be too late already.

"To go into those stairs will almost certainly mean death," Dorian said.

"I don't care."

Dorian breathed in a deep, ragged breath, then let the dwarf go. "I'll help you save her. We'll do the best that we can do."

The expedition might be in danger, but he wasn't going to let them die. If he didn't, his plans and his children would be lost to him forever.

25

INVADERS

"Kragnak, hold on for a second." The ringing of the hammer stopped.

"You heard it too?" Daruik asked. Lumdir nodded. Suddenly, the air was tense in the room. With the ringing of the metalworking stopped, they could hear it clearly. Daruik's face hardened.

"That doesn't sound good," Kimec said, dropping his plane.

"Get the spears," Daruik said. They passed out the weapons, even a nervous Noreck taking one in shaking hands. They all hung back in the workshop, none wanting to take the first step.

Then there was another scream. "Emelda!" Noreck wailed. Daruik rushed forward into the darkness of the corridor. Noreck was right behind him. Their courage dragged the others with them.

Daruik ran down the hallway, turning left and then right to reach the main crossroads. He stopped there, and the rest of the dwarves bunched up behind him. He first looked left, then right.

"What is it?" Noreck whispered, barely audible in the unnatural stillness. He held up a hand to silence her. The door to the outside world was shut, but how easy it would be to open it up. A slight draft blew from the entrance tunnel, bringing with it the sweet smell of the meadow grass.

There was a sound farther down the corridor to the farm caves. Daruik's head jerked to look down, but there was nothing in the tunnel. He started forward, less eager than he had been earlier, but still moving at a decent pace.

Footsteps shuffling down the tunnel followed them, then Daruik came to the corner. He stopped, pulling up short, and the others nearly ran into him. Cautiously, he looked around the corner.

When he saw nothing, he started again at a fast walk. The spearhead wobble out in front of him, ready for something to come out of the dark. Odd sounds were growing louder, coming from the farm cave ahead.

They reached the opening, and again Daruik stopped at the corner to peer around.

When he did, he started trembling. Then he saw her.

"Emelda!" Daruik stepped out into the opening. A giant spider stopped weaving its web around a pale, limp form. Long hair emerged from the white coating, glistening in the glow of the golden moss.

Noreck joined him and screamed. The spider dropped its prize and aimed a blast of webbing at the door. The other dwarves, about the join them, jumped back as it whistled passed. Daruik was caught full on, and Noreck took a glancing shot.

The others fled at the onslaught, trembling and tripping over each other in their haste to escape. It was pandemonium, their cries echoed and amplified by the dark rock surrounding them. It was no longer a safe, protective shield.

It was a tomb.

Struggling in the sticky webbing, Daruik tried to move out, taking a step forward. The silk refused to yield to his foot any farther. He watched with wild eyes as the spider approached, trying to move his spear.

It was no use, the spider was too fast and Daruik's arms were bound by the web. The fleeing dwarves heard a wet, sticky slap and then the sound of Noreck screaming.

A few seconds later, the screams stopped.

Kimec was in the lead and scrambled through the tunnels until they burst into the workshop. Shots of webbing followed them the whole way, narrowly avoiding them.

Panting, and lungs on fire, Kimec readied the door to shut, urging them into the room. "Come on, get in."

Kragnak was the last to come down the tunnel, almost to the door, when the spider rounded the corner. They were all shouting at him, and trembling hands pointed behind him. He glanced back, then stumbled.

A spray of web shot over his head, plastering itself to the wall behind the door. Kragnak crawled the last foot through the threshold. The spider was right behind him, hunched in the tunnel and scurrying with long, sharp feet that clicked on the rock.

Pushing as one, Kimec and Barileth slammed the door behind Kragnak and bolted it shut, locking it. A second later the door trembled and shook with an impact, the spider hissing in an otherworldly screech.

"It won't hold," Kragnak wailed. Blood flowed from wounds and scrapes on his knees, and he clutched them tightly and rocked.

"Shut up, you fool." Lumdir looked around the room. "Over here, we'll use this to brace it." Barileth, Lumdir, and Kimec picked up the half-finished support and rushed it over to the door just as it shook with another impact.

Dirt rained down on them, scattering on the rock.

"We need more," Barileth said, eying the door frame. It had shifted several inches.

"It's not going to last long." Lumdir was pushing an unused section of rock over, and Kimec had grabbed a few raw lengths of timber. Another impact, another shift of an inch. They braced it as well as they could, then backed up.

Barileth hefted a spear, swinging it around and taking a few practice stabs. "A full set of armor would be better, and a nice war hammer. If I'm going to die, I'm going to take something else down with me." He smiled, silhouetted by the fire still burning in the forge.

"We're going to die?" Kragnak asked, still shaking but on his feet now. Barileth shoved a spear at his chest.

"No, the King and his army are going to ride in and save us all."

"Leave the dwarf alone," Kimec said. Now that the moment of adrenaline had passed, he was able to think. He was thinking about his wife, wondering where she was.

"Remember, you all asked for this, whether you thought you would see this day. Are you going to turn tail and run? Where are you going to go?" Barileth leveled a steady stare at each of them as another impact shifted the door even farther.

Lumdir ignored him, turning back to the door. "Keep bracing it."

"What are we supposed to do then?" Yander's question sent a whirl of thoughts through Dorian's head.

What to do? Send a fully equipped squad of seasoned dwarves after it, that's what they should do. How it even got in the mine was beyond Dorian's understanding.

But they didn't have a squad of dwarves. And all the weapons they had were two pickaxes and...an axe. The spears were up a level, stashed in convenient spots for defense.

From outside invaders.

An enemy from within the mine hadn't even occurred to them, there were no caverns for enemies to infiltrate. Unless...

Dorian fixed his eyes back on Yander. "Have you been mining below us?" Yander's pause told him everything he needed to know. "Fool."

He wanted to strike him, to take out his anger on him. Dorian should have known better, should have kept a closer eye on him or warned him of the danger to which he was ignorant. But he hadn't done what he should have, too caught up in worry about other things.

And now others would suffer the consequences of his inaction.

Again.

"We need to do something," Yander said, pleading with his eyes. It had already been a few minutes since the scream.

What were they going to do? Two unarmored dwarves attacking a giant cave spider would be certain death, and not for the spider. They had no traps that would work, unless they lured it out the entrance.

Which meant getting past it unnoticed.

His heart sank as he finished weighing the options. Every one left them dead. There was no hope of surviving the day.

The realization hit him hard, and he took a step back. *My children, my love.* Everything he had been working for was in vain. They would be destroyed, down to the last dwarf.

And his chances of ever seeing any of them again would be over.

More screams from upstairs came to his ears. He remembered more than those in the expedition. He remembered his past, of expeditions long over and horrors he wished he could forget.

He had survived all of them, but now he would meet his end in the cold, dark mine deep in the wilderness of Zirad. No family to mourn him, no one to comfort him.

At some point he had sat down, his back up against the cool stone wall. The heat leaving his body brought him back to reality. Closing his eyes, he breathed deep of the earth, taking in the last smells of the mine. A faint taint of the spider clung to the air.

Dorian wondered if he would see her again soon. A smile played on his lips as he could almost imagine her calling his name. *"Dorian," she was saying. "Live, Dorian."*

"Dorian, can you hear me?" He opened his eyes. Yander was shaking him, nearly yelling in his ear. The dwarves dirt covered beard was covered in tears, his eyes puffy and red. "I need you."

He waved his hand. "You don't need me, I can't do anything now." Another scream. Yander looked to the door.

"Why won't you help me?" Yander hit him in the chest with a fist. Dorian looked down, but he didn't care. It would be over soon, what was the point of getting mad? When he didn't respond Yander took up his pickaxe, shot him one last look, then raised it and ran for the door.

What is the fool doing? Dorian watched him go with confusion. *Doesn't he know he's going to his death?*

"Emelda, hold on! I'm coming!" Yander sprinted out the door, legs shaking as he ran.

Something snapped in Dorian. Yander was charging into death, willing to save the dwarf he loved, while he cowered on the ground. What would she say to that?

There was a mine filled with dwarves just above them, fighting for their lives. Dyeing. And here he was wrapped up in pity and ready to accept death?

Would he have no more meals with them? No quiet moments around the table, no more moments filled with laughter and amusement? If he gave up now he wouldn't feast with them, lift mugs in joy, or share in their sorrows. Skover and his cooking, Yudoline and her desire to create. The industry and workmanship of Lumdir, Kimec, and the Icebrewers.

Even the brash and prickly Barileth, eager for a fight, he couldn't imagine living without. And the youngsters, the migrants. Didn't they deserve to have a home where they could live?

It was painful when he realized how close he had become to them. Yander, so young and innocent, ready to work hard and eager to learn. He had spurned him for so long, lost in his own misery and despair, unwilling to see what was right in front of him.

Courage. Bravery in the face of certain death. Honor in the chance to save a brother, a friend, a lover. Dorian gnashed his teeth together and stood up. "Am I willing to throw them all away without a fight?"

His children. He couldn't give up on them. How was he to be a father to his own children if he would abandon them? Dorian walked to his room, anger rising in him and mixing with a desire to live.

It welled up inside him, burning away everything else. This monster had invaded his mine. It threatened the lives of those he held dear.

He ripped open the lid to his chest, pulling and throwing the meager contents on the bed. In the faint glimmer of torchlight streaming through the open door, metal flashed, one edge of the cloth pulled back in his haste.

As he reached his hand in to take it, he hesitated. *My oath.* His hand closed around the familiar oak handle. *No. It was sworn in vain.*

The weapon, perfectly balanced, threw back the light. "Never again will I let my unwillingness to fight endanger the ones I care about."

26

REPULSION

Barileth paced back and forth, the others behind him in the room. "Steady. When it comes through, you find any soft spot you can. Get in close to avoid its web, but stay away from its legs and stinger."

"Stay away from its legs, but get in close? What would you have me do, ask it to stand still?" Kragnak asked, still clutching a bandage to his legs. Barileth flashed his teeth, gleaming in the dying fire of the forge. It caught his attention.

As the door shook again, a gap appearing at the top, he walked over to the forge, picking up the hammer and hefting it. "This will do."

"It's coming through!" Kragnak scrambled to his feet. The dwarves held out their spears toward it with shaking and trembling hands. A leg slid through the opening, scraping and clawing at the door frame and shifting it in.

Barileth gave a mighty roar and charged, jumping at the last second and bringing the hammer down with all his strength. It caught the leg with a glancing blow with a sickening crack.

An unworldly noise on the other side accompanied a flailing of the leg. It lashed out and struck Barileth, who tumbled to the floor and rolled back, dazed with a blow to his head from the fall.

The spasming limb went back into the dark hole. Kimec rushed over, spear outstretched, to protect him while he got to his feet and retreated with the rest of them. "Are you hurt?"

"It'll take more than that to bring down a Steeleyes," Barileth said, grinning but weary. A trickle of blood ran out the side of his mouth. They helped him up, he groaned as he stood. "On second thought, a rest would be nice."

Dorian ran out of his room and down the hall, intent on catching Yander before he could do anything stupid. The weight of the axe was reassuring, but put off his balance. *It's been too long.*

He took the stairs two at a time, ignoring the possibility of death up ahead. The effort of it made him breathe harder, sucking down air to fill his lungs and keep his muscles moving. His heart had been pumping from fear and beat harder with the exertion.

Yander was at the top of the stairs, clutching his pickaxe, back pressed up against the wall and looking around the corner. Dorian was relieved to see him alive and joined him in waiting.

"What have you seen?" Dorian whispered.

"Nothing." Yander squeezed his eyes shut and then opened them. "I hear it though." There were thuds and clicking and scratching issuing from the tunnel to the right. "I'm going."

"Wait." Dorian caught Yander before he could move, holding him back. "Rushing in isn't going to help us. We need a plan." The path up ahead was clear, the door to the outside world shut tight. All their traps were useless in the tunnel, unable to stop an enemy from inside.

"I'm scared, Dorian, but I can't wait and do nothing." Yander's hands were firm, clasped tightly around the handle. Only his legs shook.

"No, we'll act." A strange thought occurred to him, a plan bubbling up from somewhere strange. Another thud down the tunnel. "Did Daruik ever tell you the story of the spider and the bees?"

"What does that have to do with now?"

Always too eager. Dorian ignored the question, swinging his axe in the air. It swished happily, almost eager to fight.

"One day he was out checking on his hives when he noticed a spider climbing up to the beehive. It was larger than the bees, and intent on feeding. It found the opening and at first killed the bees with impunity. One by one, the bees fell to the invader, and Daruik started forward to save them. But before he could, something strange happened. The bees fought back. The first died, overwhelmed by the size and strength of the spider, but as the bees fought, they worked together. One bee was nothing, two wasn't much better, but when ten, then twenty bees attacked at the same time, they overwhelmed the spider."

"He didn't have to stop the spider, did he?" Yander asked, eyes downcast.

"No, although some of the bees fell, they killed the spider before it could get inside and kill their queen. We stick together and we'll kill the spider." Dorian hoped the old dwarf was fine. *A beekeeper, providing a lesson to an expedition leader.* He shook his head in wonder, then regained focus.

Yander shifted from one foot to the other. "There's only one prob-lem."

"What's that?"

"We don't have a hive of bees." The dwarf had found the one fatal flaw in his plan. If he had a dozen armed dwarves outfitted with the best weapons and armor, they might stand a chance. But two dwarves with an axe and a pickaxe?

"A few bees is all it takes." His mind raced, thinking of how they could lure it down the trap filled corridor before it would kill them. They would need to get in close to avoid the webs.

Which meant they needed a distraction.

What could they use? All they had were their tools. Then his eyes rested on Yander. The pieces of the plan started taking shape, then they fell into place. The tenor of the thuds changed. Something was shifting down the hall, and dwarf voices drifted out.

The tunnels were too tight to fight in, too easy for the spider to get off a clean shot. The hall would work, but he didn't think they could lure it in through the small door. That left the food cave, and its larger entrance. It would have to do.

"Can you do something that is dangerous?"

"What is it?"

"I need you to lure the spider to the farm cave." Yander's eyes opened wide. Dorian cut him off. "Before you say anything, know that I'll be there, waiting in ambush and ready to attack. It's the best option we have."

Yander swallowed. Now his hands were trembling. "I don't think I can do that."

"Will you trust me?"

"Dorian — "

"Take this then, you'll have to get in close. Avoid the stinger and the legs, they'll kill you in an instant." Dorian held out the axe, but Yander shrank back. "Yander, if you listen to my directions, I'll keep you safe, I promise."

27

RETREAT

Yander crept down the cave, more afraid now than he had been in his entire life. He held onto the pickaxe for dear life, hands clenched and heart pounding so hard he thought it might come out of his chest.

The smell got worse as he crept forward. The sounds were getting louder too. He could make out Barileth's voice, then Lumdir's. There wasn't a female voice coming out, and he wished again that Emelda was safe.

If only he could be sure.

He forced his legs forward, step by wobbling step. The corner was just ahead, a few feet more, and he would be there. Something shifted ahead of him, a new sound that made him jump.

A different leg came back, clawing through the opening, then another. Together, they shifted the door frame farther into the room.

"What do we do?" Kragnak asked.

"Back, to the dormitory. We retreat as much as we can." Kimec started to go, but Barileth reached out his hand and grabbed his shirt.

"No, we need to stay here and stop it from coming in. There's no way out." The frame was holding on, but it creaked and groaned against the stone it was set into.

"That door isn't going to last long," Lumdir said, anxiously watching it. "The stone is only so strong."

"We need to attack while we still can." Barileth picked his spear back up.

"Are you crazy?" Kragnak asked. Another leg joined the others in the gap. The frame cracked and shivered, sending a spray of stone chips over them. "It's too big to fight."

"Then die like a dog lying down. I'm not going to. Where is your steel dwarf? Where is your fire?" Barileth glowered at him.

"He's right, Barileth," Kimec said. "We can't fight it. Not with these sticks."

"We hurt it once, we can do it again."

"You hurt it, and look what it cost you."

Barileth was wheezing from the pain of trying to stand, kept on his feet by the hands of Kimec. He was about to say something else when they heard a strange sound from out in the tunnel.

"What is that?" Lumdir asked. The spider's legs shifted and twitched, moving against the frame. An inch more and it would come off, letting the foul creature in.

"Look!" The legs were coming back out, one by one.

"Come on, you stinking beast. You're slower than death itself."

"Is that...Yander?" Lumdir and Kimec looked at each other in wonder, but it was him. His voice was retreating, getting fainter every second.

"What is that dwarf up to? Robbing me of a well-earned kill?" Barileth sank back down, sitting on the floor and resting against the side of the forge. They couldn't make out what he was saying now, it was too faint.

"He's luring it away from us." Kimec approached the door, spear still in hand and ready.

"Fool." Barileth spat, blood and spit shimmering on the rock.

"May the gods save him now," Lumdir said.

He ran for all he was worth. The sight of the spider in the glow coming from the crack nearly made him wet himself, but Emelda could be in there. It had taken all the courage he could muster to sound his cracked and pitiable scream, but it had worked.

Yander almost wished it hadn't.

The spider clicked after him. Through the tunnels he fled, straight across the crossroads that led to the entrance tunnel and stairs to the mine. He didn't stop to look either way, remembering Dorian's advice.

"Just keep running," Yander said through his panting. "Don't look behind you." Every fiber in his body not dedicated to running wanted to. It urged him to look, just a twist of his head, only a second. "No!" he cried out. "Keep...running."

Past the dining hall he ran, then turned right. As he rounded the corner, he felt a brush of air behind him. It wasn't until a few steps later that he realized it was webbing, and it almost caught him.

Muscles straining, he kept going. The glow of the farm caves beckoned to him up ahead, welcoming him. He almost tripped on something, but kept going, turning into the relative safety of the cave.

There were...things hanging up ahead. They were covered with webs and dangling, not moving. Yander swallowed and ran toward them, running about halfway into the cave and spinning. The weight of the pickaxe had slowed him down and he saw a spear resting on a support just off to the left.

He took it, dumping the pickaxe in favor of the longer reach and went into the center of the room. Pointing his spear at the entrance, he planted his feet and readied himself.

Yander waited, breathing hard, heart fluttering rapidly. The crushed golden moss gave off its fragrant smell, which mixed with the scent of the spider all around. It was repulsive.

Something shifted. Yander tightened his grip on the spear, knuckles almost white. There it was again, a shadow on the cave wall. Clicking, steady and rhythmic, approached.

It was coming for him. A wave of fear washed over him, he couldn't do this. Then he saw Dorian, crouched at the entrance and ready to spring. The shadow shifted on the wall, then glowing eyes came out of the darkness.

Yander almost fled, but something held his feet in place. *Just like we talked about, steady now.* This was the moment of truth.

He felt fear. Not overwhelming, tamed by his steady breathing. Long ago he learned what being overcome by fear could do to you, and he had much to live for now. From the entrance, the spider made its odd hissing sound, readying its web to strike.

For some reason it held off, maybe it was blinded by the light of the golden moss or maybe seeing a dwarf standing its ground was something strange and unusual to it. Whatever the case, the spider advanced into the room.

It's got a hurt leg. One of the front legs was held off the ground, tilted at a strange angle, like it was broken. Still breathing slowly, in and out, Dorian waited.

"Dorian?" Yander was shaking, and he retreated one step. The spider raised its body and brought out its spinner.

Now.

Dorian raised his axe and sprinted forward just as the abdomen aimed at Yander. He couldn't see what the young dwarf, but he darted beneath the spider's legs just as a white stripe of web shot out.

With a battle cry, Dorian swung his axe, its dark head cutting the air silently. Less than a second later the webbing stopped, and the spinner dropped to the ground, liquid pumping out from the wound.

He didn't have time to celebrate, though.

The spider collapsed on him, even though his momentum was carrying him forward. Dorian tried to roll away, but something sharp bit his leg as he went down.

28

CORNERED

Yander charged. He screamed, mostly out of fear, the rest in anger. Dorian was beneath the monster the last time he saw him. The thrashing spider took all his attention now.

Great fangs loomed above him as it twisted its head, searching for the thing that had wounded it. The body wriggled and churned, and the legs flailed.

He was going too fast now to stop, even if he wanted to. Yander gritted his teeth and aimed his spear at the spider's abdomen. The spear hit resistance, went another inch, then stopped.

It hit the spider, but missed the body, and lodged in the leg. The spider, already enraged, fastened its beady red eyes on Yander. He felt his heart grow cold, and time seemed to slow as he pulled against the shaft of the spear.

His hands slipped, wet from sweat. The spider lashed out with a front leg. Yander tried to duck, but it clipped him in the side and knocked the wind out of him. He flew sideways and hit the ground, and the world went dark.

The painful weight on his body shifted, the hairy abdomen pressed against his face and scratching his cheeks was gone. Dorian rolled left, ignoring a throbbing in his leg, out from under the spider.

One of the supports was hit in the spider's throes and slammed to the ground with a crash, bringing down a waterfall of dirt that kicked up dust in the air and made the already dark room harder to see in.

Dorian searched desperately for his axe, gone when the spider had come down on him. Avoiding the sharp legs that were searching him out, he finally spotted a few feet away. A quick glance at the spider made his heart sink.

It had turned its eyes on him, and they glinted with ravenous hunger. Its legs sunk into the dirt as it repositioned between him and his axe. *I'm not going to make it.*

He had his regrets, thinking back on the last few years. Dorian's fear fled, and he got back to his feet as the spider advanced. *If I had been a better dwarf, this would not have happened.*

If he could go back and do it all again, he would. He wouldn't be so cold, so angry, and withdrawn from the others. He would have talked to them more, gotten to know them. Their hopes, their dreams, what they desired more than anything.

He wished he had been a better leader, one they deserved.

Brushing up against the ceiling of the cave and scattering dirt down below, the spider came at him, trailing bile from its abdomen.

Dorian backed up, then spied Yander off to the side. He was crumpled on the ground, not moving. "Yander!"

He didn't stir. The spider had killed him.

A torrent of anger came over him then. Dorian reached down, looking for a rock, a tool, anything, but there was only dirt. He grabbed a handful of it, anyway.

"Come on you fell beast, do your worst." The spider opened its mouth, sharp fangs dripping with venom. Dorian flung the dirt and the spider hissed.

"For Ironstrike!" Dorian dove out of the way of the spider's attack, hearing the battle cry off to his left. Barileth? What is he doing here? He expected another attack, but when none came, he seized his chance.

More voices joined in the cacophony as he dove for his ichor-stained battle axe, grabbing the shaft and spinning to see an unthinkable sight.

Four dwarves were locked in battle with the spider, long spears stabbing it wherever they could. The spider didn't know where to attack first, swinging legs wildly.

This was his chance. He couldn't stop now, they would die. Instead, he rushed to join them.

His axe sheared the first leg off completely, sending the spider off balance. The follow up swing didn't have as much power, but it bit deep into the one right next to it.

The spider was screaming now. Barileth had lost his axe and was using his fists to pummel the spider's abdomen. Dorian wrenched his axe free and took off another leg, then another, then finally the last two.

When he was done, the spider had curled up, trying to protect itself. While the others kept its fangs at bay Dorian walked around, raised his axe high, and brought it down.

The final blow to its head killed it. The light went out of its eyes and with one final twitch it contracted and stopped moving.

Dorian gulped down air, trying to calm his beating heart. His hand came away wet, and when he looked down it glistened black in the dusty light. Blood came from his leg, and he felt lightheaded.

"Barileth, what happened?" he asked, and sat down.

"You don't look well." Barileth leaned down, face covered in spider blood. He tore off a piece of his shirt and wrapped it around Dorian's leg. "Hold this here."

"Tend to Yander first." He still wasn't moving. Now that the adrenaline from the fight was fading, sadness and horror replaced it. I wasn't good enough, I didn't make it in time. The other dwarves had been turned into hanging webs. "Check the others."

Kragnak limped over to Yander, who groaned when he turned him over. "He's still alive." A wave of relief washed over Dorian, but he wasn't the only dwarf in the room. Dorian struggled to his feet to join Lumdir and Kimec.

They were cutting down the webbed dwarves. The first one came down in Lumdir's arms, and Dorian helped him lower it to the floor. He scraped away the webs. Daruik.

Fingers went to his neck. There was still a pulse, faint. Daruik opened his eyes and his lips moved, a whisper too quiet to hear. Dorian leaned in, pressed his ear next to the lips. "Poison...salve. Save my wife and daughter."

"We'll save both of you," Dorian said. There were tears glistening in Daruik's eyes. "Lumdir, go to the Icebrewer's apartment, take a bottle from his chest." They had cut down the last body.

"What is it?" Lumdir asked as he set the large webbed body of Skover down.

"A salve." Daruik's unseeing eyes looked up at the ceiling. "He used it to extract poison from his bee stings. Go now and be quick about it."

While Lumdir rushed off, they checked the others. Skover and Narfac were dead. Noreck's heartbeat was faint and slow, and Emelda alone seemed to be holding on.

But she wouldn't for long.

"Don't you die on me," Dorian said. Yander couldn't take it, the death of his love. He couldn't bear being responsible for that. Dorian wiped Emelda's hair back, eyes stinging. "I won't be able to forgive myself if you do."

29

DEATH

Emelda was graying by the time they applied the salve. It was too late for Noreck, her other wounds were too great. They waited, anxious to see what would happen, and she took rough, ragged breaths.

"Yudoline, where is she?" Kimec asked. Dorian realized she hadn't been with the others. He feared another body would be added to the row of dead dwarves. "Yudoline?"

Kimec's eyes darted everywhere, into the stalls of dead chickens and goats, around the wrecked farm caves, with the crops churned and destroyed. There were no other dwarves in the cave, alive or dead.

"We'll find her," Dorian said. "Barileth, you go with Kimec and look for her." Barileth nodded, lit another torch, and took the trembling dwarf by the elbow.

"Yudoline, where are you?" Kimec shouted.

"She's fine, just hiding somewhere safe and sound." Barileth forced the torch into his hand. "Take this." He grabbed another, and they headed for the entrance.

"Kimec?" There was no mistaking it, although it was very quiet.

"Yudoline! Where are you?" Kimec and Barileth bolted forward.

"In the kitchens." *Not dead after all.* Dorian was relieved, that was one less tomb to carve. He turned his attention back to Emelda, whose breathing had evened out.

Yander groaned again, then coughed. Kragnak helped him sit up. He clutched at his side, then saw Emelda.

His eyes grew as large as saucers, and he scrambled over to her. "No, no. It can't be."

"She's alive, lad," Lumdir said as Yander took her hand, pressing it to his lips.

"Emelda."

Dorian drew back, letting them have some room. The look in Yander's eye he knew well.

"Yander?" Like the flapping wings of a butterfly, Emelda's eyes fluttered and opened. Yander put a hand on her cheek, tenderly caressing it with his thumb.

"I'm here." His lip trembled. Emelda looked around, and her eyes widened.

"I remember it..." She shuddered, and her eyes went wild, searching.

"You're safe now, it's dead," Dorian said. "It won't be hurting anyone ever again." Yander reached over to take her other hand, flailing wildly, and groaned.

"You're hurt," she exclaimed. Emelda sat up, then fell back as her eyes rolled. The dwarves rushed forward, catching her before she did.

"Rest here, the poison is still strong." Dorian held her in a sitting position, and she recovered.

Yudoline, Kimec, and Barileth entered the cave. When she saw the spider's body Yudoline shrank back and clutched at her husband.

"Is it really...?"

"No need to fear." Kimec patted her hand. They joined the others, Yudoline fretting about each of their injuries. Yander didn't let go of Emelda's hand.

"Where are mother and father?" No one said anything, and a weight fell on Dorian's heart. Then her eyes found them. "No, it can't be."

They straightened the tunnel at the end, taking care to smooth out the rock. Yander wanted to dig out the niches, and after showing him the best way, Dorian let him.

The dwarf worked without stopping until they were done, his pickaxe singing a slow, steady dirge throughout the mine. Dorian left him to oversee the construction in the lowest level of the mine.

"How is he?" Barileth asked when Dorian joined him and Kragnak, each covered in bandages and Kragnak leaning on a crutch.

Dorian shook his head.

Before Lumdir started work on the coffins he had cut enough stone to seal the unintended opening. Dorian knew it was more important than putting the dead to rest, but the decision hadn't been easy.

They worked in silence. It took half the day, but when they were done two layers of rock stood between them and the inhabitants of the deep cavern. Dorian couldn't take pleasure in the act, not now.

Life had to continue, mouths had to be fed, and defenses had to be finished. There would be time to mourn later, for him at least.

He was worried about Emelda. She had lost both her parents in one day, wouldn't he mourn too? She had withdrawn, refusing to leave her room. Yander and Yudoline were the only ones she would see.

Lumdir finished the coffins the next day. Dorian gathered the dwarves. They picked up the dead, putting each one gently into a coffin, and carried them down the tunnels to the stairs.

Skover was the first to go down. The coffin was tied up and swung out over the edge. It spun slowly as they lowered it, the group silent as the rope creaked and the pulley squeaked.

Solemn and stately, Skover in his rock coffin was swallowed by the mine into the darkness. One after another the others joined him. Narfac next, then Noreck, finally Daruik.

Through the winding tunnel they carried them, torches casting a pall glow along their path, until they reached four black squares cut into the rock.

The group hesitated here. Dorian stared at those holes, remembering others. He hadn't even been there when they put her in the ground. Now he was exiled from her.

"Dorian?" Barileth was by his side, whispering in his ear. Dorian roused himself, realizing that the others were looking to him. He looked down at his hands, calloused and rough. What could he say that would extinguish their pain?

"Too soon." He looked back up, eyes burning. He would not cry. "They were taken too soon." His voice came out as a rough whisper in the dark. Emelda sobbed silently into Yander's shoulder.

"You were friends, parents, children." He touched the edge of Skover's coffin. "You leave behind mourning friends. We commit you to the earth."

Kimec cleared his throat. Heaviness hung in the air, sadness clung to them. Dorian swallowed, knowing he couldn't let it continue.

"Know that you did not die in vain. We will not succumb to the evils that visit us. We will not turn back in cowardice from this path. We will live on." He gritted his teeth, choking back the tears. "We will survive. Day by day we will miss you, but know that we will not forget you."

30

A GLIMMER IN THE DARK

Golden moss was scattered everywhere, cave berry bush leaves, too. They removed the spider's carcass, cutting it up where they could so it would be easier to carry. Dorian had them save the carapace on the abdomen and the spider silk scattered around the mine.

"Do we have enough to salvage?" he asked.

"The damage was not as bad as I thought," Yudoline said. She continued picking up clumps of moss, turning it over in the light of the torch for her squinting eye to examine. Those deemed acceptably free of blood and...other fluids were set aside. The others were tossed into a bucket. "We lost a quarter at most of the golden moss, and only a few cave berry bushes."

"Enough to last the winter?"

"I'm not sure, Skover — " She dropped another clump of moss into her bucket, cleared her throat, and continued. "We were going to have enough for everyone if they grew like they were supposed to."

Now we have four fewer mouths to feed. Dorian knew saying it would be useless and rub salt in the raw wound. He would have to do his own inventory, decide if they could make it without rationing what they had.

They worked together in silence until the fields were picked through that had seen the action and everything not fit to eat or use was discarded. It would be burned later, outside and far from the mine.

If aid were coming, he wouldn't have to worry about it, but he knew that was unlikely to happen. They were on their own, there would be no reinforcement or supplies sent to them.

All their efforts focused on staying alive and finishing the defenses for the mine. A week was all it took, and combined effort of all of them, to finish the wall. A few more days for Lumdir to puzzle out how to carve a drawbridge and then another few more to make all the components and the defenses were finished.

They were protected from attack from the outside, and from within. Or at least that was Dorian's hope. He had felt secure before, but after the spider attack his sleep was fitful and interrupted at the slightest sound.

The last few weeks of autumn went by fast. The first harvest was plentiful, bringing in more than they expected. The above ground crops were untouched by the attack and provided the bulk of the harvest. With a majority of the work complete, the blowing winds of winter signaled a slower time for the expedition.

Dorian gave everyone a break, slowing the pace of assignments. They finished the apartments and furnished them, and the connection between Emelda and Yander grew.

Harsh blizzards and difficult conditions trapped them inside the mine for all except the most essential reasons. The winter crawled by, month after month, and the expedition recovered.

The snows started to recede, and the sun came back. Dorian was reminded of the anniversary of the expedition, and he remembered his promise. The preparations took a full week, each dwarf pitching in and contributing something to mark the event.

Lumdir carved them magnificent plates, each one solid stone with graceful swans, flowering plants, and busy bees. Kimec and Yudoline worked on the food and drink night and day, getting everything cooked and ready with the help of Yander, Kragnak, and Emelda. Dorian finished mining the great hall and carved the entrance with the names of the fallen in remembrance.

Yander ambushed him with Emelda one night after dinner was over and the dishes cleaned up. They were holding hands, an unusual sight, and cut off his escape to his room.

"Dorian." Yander looked unusually solemn. Emelda squeezed his hand, and he cleared his throat.

"Yander?" He squinted his eyes, trying to discern his intentions.

"Emelda and I would like you to...marry us. Will you?"

Dorian's jaw dropped. At first he couldn't believe he heard right. The signs had been obvious over the last few months, the late nights, how inseparable they had been, but he had taken it as a sign of Emelda's mourning, not her interest in Yander.

"Please, it would mean so much," Emelda said.

"I'm not sure I would be the best choice to do something like that." He felt embarrassed, and saddened. It was a reminder of his own marriage and wife. But they wouldn't take no for an answer. Eventually, they wore him down. "Yes, I will do it."

Yudoline rummaged around the supplies. She thought she had seen one last sack of potatoes back here, deeper in storage. When she moved an empty crate a dusty cask caught her eye.

She brushed off the dust and cobwebs, squinting in the dim light. When she tried to move it, something sloshed around inside. "Sticks and stones, what could this be?"

The ale was stored on the other side, which they had plenty of thanks to her newfound skill of brewing. This was different, but seeing it tickled something in her mind. She tipped it over and rolled it out into the busy kitchen bustling with dwarves preparing for the feast.

"What is that?" Kimec asked, hands covered in flour.

"I don't remember. Here, Kragnak, help me open it." He pulled out the wooden stopper and together they tipped it over into a bowl. A deep crimson fluid poured out, splashing against the bowl and sending up a fragrant and unmistakable smell.

"It's wine," Kragnak said. Yudoline felt a flutter inside her and rushed over to get a cup. She dipped it in the wine and pulled it up to take a taste.

Sweet cave berry wine flowed into her mouth and over her tongue, tingling her taste buds and bubbling her insides. It was good, really good. Yudoline laughed and passed the cup to Kragnak, whose face lit up when he tasted it.

"I had forgotten all about this." She clapped her hands in joy, nearly jumping into the air with giddiness. "Now, we can have a proper celebration!"

Epilogue

A great fire roared in the dining hall. Laughter echoed around the table. Half-eaten dishes and empty plates kept company with mugs that emptied and filled.

Dorian sighed and leaned back in his chair, forgetting the cares of the expedition for a time. It would come back to him soon enough to burden him down again, but tonight was a night of celebration.

The wine and ale loosened lips and lowered inhibitions, and he even told a joke or two of his own to the delight of the other dwarves. Emelda rested her head on Yander's shoulder, cheeks flushed with laughter and wine. Yander had a huge, sloppy grin on his face.

It filled Dorian's heart with joy to see them so happy. For the first time in a long time, he found he was content.

It surprised him.

He turned the realization over in his mind, examining it and savoring it. Faint memories of his life before his imprisonment came back. The good times he had had with friends and his family.

Quiet evenings beside the fire. Playful meals filled with stories and cheer. Even the desperate times when they had to rely on each other.

He thought about his wife. Some of the heartache had gone away, and he wasn't sure what that meant. Could he rebuild a life here, away from her?

Lumdir broke his musings, filling up his mug with the wine Yu-doline had made. He took a sip, sweet and flavorful, letting it wash around his mouth as Kimec shared a story from his youth about being chased up a tree by a bear.

He might not be ready to let the memory of her go just yet, but tonight he forgot his pain in the company of his beloved companions.

A long pale hand trembled as it approached an equally pale forehead. A deep incantation reverberated in the room, echoing and hissing with power.

Visions flashed, and a misty cloud dissipated from his sight. His servant flew high in the air and the view made him dizzy with vertigo.

Down below on the side of the mountain a strange construction had been erected. It was hard to make out at first, but with further urging the semicircular wall was visible in the night.

"Interesting." His own voice disturbed him, as it had for many years. "What wind blows my way through the night?"

With a wave of his hand, he dismissed the vision and leaned back in his leather armchair. He stroked his chin with his hand, thinking and pondering.

At last he arose and walked over to the crystal table, laying a hand along its edge. "This change of circumstances may be to our benefit. We will watch and wait." A smile played across his blackened lips.

"And in time this may...further my research."

Ode to the Survivors

Surviving the Second Year

Eric Kercher

1

ILL NEWS

The sun was casting setting rays of orange and red when Dorian was shaken awake.

"Dorian." The voice was distant, but the urgency that filled it brought him from his dreams to the real world. He opened his eyes slowly, reluctant to leave. Barileth stood over him, dripping with blood.

That brought him out of his sleep and he jerked up, almost knocking Barileth back to reach for his axe.

"Don't," Barileth whispered. "You need to see this before the others." Heart pounding and mouth dry, Dorian nodded. Quickly, he dressed and followed Barileth of his apartment and up the central staircase. When they were far away from the other sleeping dwarves Barileth began his story.

"I was standing sentry and heard them coming a mile away. Well, I thought I would catch them in the act and even get some information out of them." They walked through the entrance hall and Barileth opened the entrance door.

It swung open with a groan and the two stepped out into the night. Stars twinkled up above between the sparse layer of clouds, and the half-moon washed the courtyard with its pale light.

"What was it?" Dorian asked, but Barileth only gave him a grin and pointed.

At the far end of the wall, tied to a rocky protrusion, an injured goblin shrank back from them. Green blood seeped from its left arm, the other hand holding it tightly.

Dorian's eyes narrowed. "One?" Barileth's grin faded, and he looked down.

"There was another one, but it got away. My spear broke attacking that one." He spit at the ground. "Pitiful cowards wouldn't even put up a fight. This one dropped his weapon and gave up when I sliced him."

"Ill news on a night like this." The wind was blowing down from the north, a vestige of winter trying to recapture hold over them. Spring was yielding to it. "Have you found out what it knows?"

"No, I came here as soon as I had it secured. Didn't want to raise a ruckus if I didn't have to."

"Let's go see what it came for." Together they marched over to it, and the goblin shrank back even more. Its glittering eyes darted in the darkness, searching for escape. There was none.

"Well, friend. It seems you wanted to come in and have a chat, so let's have a chat." Dorian stopped well short of it, but close enough to menace. It wouldn't have been taller than them if it had been standing upright, but shrunk down, it was half their size. Barileth kept a loose grip on the spear he held, unbroken. The goblin looked at it.

"That's right, I got a new one just for you."

The goblin hissed at Barileth, who made a movement forward. Dorian held out his arm, holding him back, as the goblin winced.

"No need to get any more violent than we already have."

"I tell nothing." The goblin spoke in broken common, barely intelligible.

"You'll tell us or lose a few more teeth," Barileth growled. The goblin shook, but didn't take his eyes off Dorian.

"You heard the dwarf. Better start talking now." The goblin's eyes flashed all around, but it didn't say anything. Dorian shrugged. "Shame about the teeth."

Barileth cracked his knuckles, his left side scraped and covered with dried blood already. He took a step toward the pitiful creature. "Be my pleasure."

"No, wait!" It raised its hands above its head and ducked down. Barileth stopped and shot Dorian a grin. It took a few more moments for the goblin to realize it wasn't being hit, and then it peeked out.

"Tell us what you know."

"Me told to get it. I listen to strong leader."

"Get what?" Dorian's eyes narrowed.

"Good stuff, food stuff, shiny stuff if it around. No supposed to touch stink--" it cut itself off and gulped, "nice dwarvesses."

"Where did you come from?" Barileth demanded.

"Away and far, moons away."

"Be more specific," Dorian said.

"No be able. Over here come from." The thing waved a hand to the west. "We no stay in spot. Move it up sometimes."

"How convenient."

"Now let me go? I no took nothing."

"No, we aren't going to let you go." Dorian crossed his arms to think. The face of the goblin twisted up and for a second. It lost its fear.

"You pay. Me, others come get me. Then you pay."

"Oh really?" Barileth leaned down and grabbed the goblin by its collar, tugging the strange leather chest plate up until it was standing. "And I suppose they'll come with friends, won't they?"

The goblin cowered, legs trembling. Blood seeped out of its wound, reopened by the rough treatment. Dorian put a hand on Barileth's shoulder.

"It isn't worth the risk," Barileth said.

"We'll lock it up. Keep it around until *we* decide what to do with it."

Barileth looked back to the goblin, tensed, then let it drop to a quivering mess. Dorian nodded and turned to go. Barileth followed.

"You can't be considering letting it go. It will bring friends in a heartbeat."

"It's too late for that if it is going to happen. Killing it won't accomplish anything."

"What? Keep it alive?" Barileth spat. "We have to kill it."

Dorian chewed on this thought, turning it over in his mind. A thief coming in the night to steal deserved justice. But with the other escaped, what good would that do? "We'll transfer the goblin to a cage. It will get rewarded in due time." His mind was fuzzy with tiredness and he yawned.

They reached the entrance, and Barileth stepped in front of him. "You must kill it. We can't waste our precious food and supplies keeping it alive. The cut I gave it might do it in anyway in a few days, it would be a mercy."

His tone was sharp and stuck in Dorian. How he wished he could turn the goblin over to someone else to make the decision, to strike the blow. Barileth glared at him, and a not so suppressed irritation bubbled up inside him.

"I didn't say we were going to keep it alive, did I? This was the first chance I've had to get some sleep and I intend to take advantage of it." The late nights had worn on him, draining away his energy and sapping his strength even after a partial night sleep. "I'll make the decision in the morning. Put it in a cage."

Barileth made one last stand, then uncrossed his arms. Dorian was glad he didn't make it into more of a fight than it already was. "Before you go you should see this." He opened the door, and they went in.

He reached in to grab his spear stashed behind the door. Dorian had expected the shaft to have snapped, but it was still strong and solid. The tip, however, was a different story.

"Not good." Dorian ran his finger along the bent blade. The copper had given in, and there was barely any edge to it any more. The tip was mushroomed and wouldn't make a mark even if it tried.

"Bent on the stone, I think. It could have been the bone, too."

"Even more important to find solid iron now."

"We need them, badly. If those goblins come back in force..."

"I already said it, we need better weapons. Would you have me pull good steel out of thin air?"

"I know you're working, but couldn't something else give? Or can we send someone to barter for it?" Dorian ran a hand over his eyes, even more tired now.

"We don't have a dwarf to spare. I was hoping that there would be some sent with supplies, but I think we all know that isn't going to happen." They were on their own, the lack of action from the King had made that perfectly clear.

"We'll make do then and make more traps."

More traps. More food, more goods, more supplies. Everything needed more, there was never enough to go around and never enough to spare. After over a year in the mine, the expedition was starting to look even more hopeless than it had.

"The door first, then weapons, then training. Do you need someone else to take the watch?"

"No, the goblins didn't even land a blow on me. Just ran." Barileth lowered his eyebrows. "Go get some rest."

"We'll get better weapons and armor. I know it's important, Barileth." Barileth nodded. They said good night and Dorian turned to go back down to his room while Barileth went to get a suitable cage from the stores.

Glad I thought to ask Kimec to make more. Dorian trudged back down the tunnel, his footsteps echoing in the empty halls. The rest of the mine was quiet, no ringing from the anvil, no scrape of tools on wood and rock.

A goat baaed distantly, then was quiet. Even as he reached the tunnel crossings, he knew he wasn't going to be able to go back to sleep. His mind was too awake, and he was too alert.

Instead, he turned right, going into the farm caves. Beneath the ground the seasons had little effect and the cave moss was growing thick and full. Chickens were asleep in their pen, the flock struggling to recover after the spider attack.

The goats hadn't fared much better. Now down to three, a breeding pair and a kid, there wouldn't be much to live off of if they had to slaughter them. Hopes of a stable of milkable goats were dashed now.

Dorian sat down in the center of the caves, letting the smells of the moss flow into him. Now, so soon, they were faced with another threat. What else was in store for them? And would he make it to his third year and win his freedom?

What was Ruby doing now? What about Xanther? For the last few weeks Dorian had thought of them every night when the work was done and the storm of the day was over. He hoped they had a good life, that they were happy and healthy.

Would they have told him if they were dead? The thought struck him, sending a chill down his back. Remembering the cold eyes of Lightaxe made him doubt it.

The light of the moss wasn't as welcoming anymore, and the sounds of the night turned more sinister. A creak to his right, a shuffle ahead of him. His head swiveled, chasing ghosts. *Nothing but shadows.*

There were others to think about. Living, breathing dwarves that were depending on him to survive, and who he needed to finish his task and see his family again. *What were they going to tell them?*

Dorian chewed on possible words and options. They wouldn't be happy to hear about a goblin almost gaining access, and there were some who might panic to know one had gotten away.

Having chosen not to kill the thief put him in a worse predicament. He had to go back, find out where Barileth had put it. Dorian made up his mind and left the farm cave and went back to the entrance.

The air had chilled more since he had left, at least a half hour had passed, or more.

"Barileth." Dorian kept his voice quiet, not wanting to startle him. A shadow shifted to his right and Barileth emerged from his hiding spot.

"Here."

"Where is it?"

"Over there." He had found a cage, the goblin was locked inside. Its eyes glowed with hatred through the stout wooden caging.

"We'll take it inside, hide it for now. Help me move it into the tunnels." When they approached the goblin, it swung out its hand, trying to claw them, but a quick hit from Barileth tamed it. Together they picked up the cage and its inhabitant and pulled it inside.

The goblin was heavier than it looked, but the two of them were able to bear the load. Dorian shut and locked the entrance door behind them, giving them time to rest. They worked through the tunnel, careful to avoid triggering the traps with their load.

"Down the stairs. I've got one in mind." The stairs forced them to go one at a time, and Dorian rotated to the lower position to take the brunt of the weight.

"It'd be easier my way." Barileth grunted as they took another step. "Less questions too."

Dorian ignored it. He didn't regret his decision. Barileth was about to say something else when there was a snap that echoed down the tunnel. Their heads jerked toward the sound. At the same time they realized what was happening.

"Invaders," Barileth said.

2

ALARM

His love glowed in the center of the room, encased in the crystal that preserved her body. Vasknar sat in a decaying armchair, caressing the side of it. How little time they had together.

But they would have time again, he knew it. He had come too far to abandon her to death. Thunder rumbled outside, the rain dripped through holes in the roof.

Remains of his most recent experiment were scattered among the filth on the table, a disappointment. He sighed. Pushing too fast again. It never worked out well, but he couldn't help himself.

"Something a little...smaller?" A finger tapped his chin. Thoughts drifted back to the tantalizing thought of the hole in the mountains. It was so rich with opportunity it sent a shiver down his back.

He could try one, then perfect his art on the others. Maybe he would take one at a time, surreptitiously. Would they notice? He might need to take all of them at once.

"I'll need more help, my love." He cast a loving glow down at her, imagining her smiling at him. "I must leave, but not for long. I'll be back soon."

He stood, gathering the supplies he needed for the journey. His raven had found it first and he was saving it for a time like this. Vasknar swept a cloak on his shoulders, took up his hat, and stepped out into the stormy night.

"Back up the stairs!" They pulled the cage back up, dumping it to the side.

"I'll hold them," Barileth said. Dorian nodded and headed back down.

"Up, wake up," he shouted. He regretted they weren't able to hide the goblin, but now was not the time to worry about it. "We're under attack. Everyone to arms."

When he swept into the apartments the dwarves were in a variety of states of readiness. Lumdir was ready and dressed, but Yudoline peered sleepily outside the door as Kimec rushed past her in his nightclothes.

"Get your weapons, defend the mine." The others spilled out of their rooms, and Dorian rushed in to get his axe, slinging it over his shoulder to lead them up the stairs. Their footsteps echoed around the tunnel, startled eyes hardening with resolve.

When they poured into the entrance tunnel, they drew up sharply. A sheepish Barileth met them, no evidence of invaders anywhere.

"What is it?" Lumdir asked. They looked around, but there was no danger in sight.

"False alarm." He pointed to a hammer trap. Its head was on the ground, no longer raised in readiness.

"There aren't any attackers?" Yander asked. Barileth cringed. Dorian was relieved until Yudoline spoke up.

"What was that goblin doing in the cage, then?" A hush fell over them. Dorian's heart sank. In the rush he hoped that they wouldn't have noticed.

"Cage? I didn't see a cage." Kimec scratched his head and shifted in his nightclothes.

"It was back at the top of the stairs," Yudoline said.

Trying to hide it now wouldn't do any good. "It was a thief. Barileth captured it earlier tonight." At first, they stood there. Finally, when the realization of what he said registered, they started talking all at once.

Dorian was overwhelmed by the sound, and the exhaustion from the earlier events of the night was catching up with him. A slight throbbing at the base of his neck started, spreading further up to his head. He tried to calm them by holding up his hands.

They still talked over one another, yelled across the tunnel at each other. "Enough," Dorian said. It wasn't loud enough, so he raised his voice until it thundered. "Enough!"

"Were you going to tell us?" Lumdir asked. There was a hint of anger in his voice, and his arms were crossed, beard jutting in anger.

"I can explain everything, give me a moment." He held up his hand to silence Yander who was beginning to speak. "Barileth stopped goblins from coming in the mine tonight."

"Look, this did it." All eyes swiveled to Barileth. He was holding up the severed end of a rope, the strands cut. It was supposed to be intact and holding up the giant hammer. For a moment Dorian was glad Barileth had distracted them, giving him breathing room.

"We must have bumped it with the cage." Barileth rubbed the back of his head as he stood over it, and inwardly Dorian groaned. *So much for the distraction.*

"You brought the cage in here?" Kimec's eyes were wide and open now, a few veins standing out on his forehead.

"What were we supposed to do, leave it outside?" Barileth scowled and crossed his arms.

"You were going to hide it from us, weren't you?" Kimec was about to launch into another speech when Yudoline stopped him.

"Hold on, he said goblins. I only remember seeing one goblin. How many were there?"

Dorian looked around, back to the intent eyes staring at him. The wall was behind him, and after a small step back he bumped into it. The door was starting to look very appealing. He decided not to hide it from them, it was too late now.

"From what we could tell only two of them." On the inside, Dorian was cursing himself for his slip up. "Barileth apprehended one and the other one got away."

"Got away? Where did it go?" Yander asked. Dorian pressed his lips tight together and hesitated. Yudoline answered for him.

"It's going back to tell the others about us." Her brow was pressed down against her eyes, tight lights around her eyes.

"You let it get away?" The vein on Kimec's forehead was throbbing now.

"Well, you didn't do a lot of helping, now did you?" Barileth retorted. Kimec's jaw worked, muscles bulging.

"Calm down, dear." Yudoline put a hand on his chest.

"If it tells the other goblins about us then we're in danger, aren't we?" Yander drew Emelda close. "What are we going to do about this, we can't just let them come and kill us."

"We don't know that they're going to come and kill us. It didn't get into the mine so as far as they know there could be an army of dwarves in here." Dorian could see what was happening and wanted to calm them down.

It wasn't working.

"We've got to get ready, we have to be ready for the attack." Yander's eyes were wide too, and his hysterics were starting to affect the others.

"Let them come," Barileth said. "More things for me to kill."

"You're the one who got us into this mess in the first place," Kimec said, almost shouting.

"Did not. They were bound to find us eventually, and I stopped them from even getting in the door. You should be thanking me."

"Thanking you? I'll show you what I'll do to you." Kimec started to roll up his sleeves and turned to Barileth, but Yudoline was holding him back.

Barileth laughed at him. "Come on, old dwarf, I'm not going to roll over like you would in a fight."

"That's enough, both of you." Dorian had to raise his voice. "And everyone needs to calm down. Barileth is right, they were bound to find us this close to the border. That's why we built the wall." *But not the only reason.*

"The wall doesn't have a gate," Lumdir said.

"We'll make one tomorrow." Lumdir's eyes narrowed, so Dorian hastily added, "As soon as we can." Yudoline had managed to back Kimec up farther away from Barileth, and Dorian stepped in between them. "It's almost time for watch change anyway, I'll take the next watch so you can all get to bed."

"Sleep at a time like this?" Yander asked.

"I don't think I can sleep," Kragnak said.

"Go back to bed, we can deal with this in the morning. At least get some rest. We have the traps and I'll lock the door when I'm not outside checking on things."

"But they'll come for us."

"Not tonight they won't, it's too early. Besides, goblins aren't known for their courage. I doubt the escaped thief tells anyone about us for a while."

"He's right, coming back empty-handed wouldn't work well for it," Barileth said.

"We all signed up for this. Each one of us knew the risks." Dorian forced eye contact with each one of them as he talked. "Go back to bed, get some sleep."

Kimec looked like he was about to say something, but Yudoline nudged him and he shut his mouth. Yander looked worried, but less so than he had earlier.

"I'll go first, keep a good eye on things." Barileth tossed Dorian his spear, which he caught with one hand, and he forced himself through the crowd. At the doorway, he turned back. "Leave it here?"

"For the night, yes," Dorian said. One by one the others followed Barileth. Kragnak was muttering under his breath, Dorian only caught a few words. What he heard almost made him smile, if the event wasn't so serious, it would have.

Yander and Emelda were the last to leave. "I'll catch up to you," he said, giving Emelda a hug. She gave him a look, but left anyway. Yander turned back to him, eyes haunted.

"Dorian, I can't handle more death. Not like this, not right now." Dorian was moved, and put a hand on his shoulder. "Promise me no one else will die."

What am I supposed to say? He thought back to all the other leaders in his life, wishing any one of them was here instead of him. But they were all either dead or gone, and he was in this place.

"Get some sleep Yander, I'll be up here watching out for you." The words came out hollow, empty. He wished he had the courage to tell him the truth, or some way he could wriggle into a lie, but said nothing else.

Yander nodded after a few moments, then turned and followed his bride. He paused at the doorway. "I'm depending on you."

Long after he was gone Dorian was thinking about those words. Spoken so lightly, but they felt so heavy.

The morning found them with heavy feet and tired eyes. Dorian barely got any sleep and was feeling it, sluggish and dull. He knew what they had to do and, after a quick breakfast, the entire expedition of dwarves was outside and helping to finish the gate.

Dorian directed the efforts, while Lumdir focused on carving as fast as he could. They had to patch rock together to make it big enough to fit the opening, but near mid-day it was finished and ready for fitting.

Barileth had devised the raising mechanism earlier, and now that they all were focused on it, worked with another group to set it up and use the last of their longleaf rope and a good portion of what they had been able to make earlier in the spring.

While they were setting everything in place, and Lumdir was leading Kragnak and Kimec to move the door over, Yander pulled Dorian aside.

"Can I speak with you?"

"Yes." Dorian wiped the sweat off his brow and sucked in a heady breath of air warmed by the early spring wind.

"In private?" Yander looked serious, even after Dorian peered into his eyes. He nodded and they went a respectful distance from the others, far out of earshot. Dorian watched the working groups while Yander shifted on his feet.

After a few moments, Yander worked up the courage to speak. "After what happened the other night, and last year too--" his gaze shifted to the ground, then hardened. "I wanted to ask you to train me to fight."

Dorian's mouth almost dropped open. "What?"

"Please, you have to teach me." Yander took a deep breath and continued before Dorian could interrupt. "I need to be able to protect Emelda and everyone else. You know what happened, how I wasn't prepared the last time, and with the invasion imminent-"

"There is no invasion," Dorian said.

"There could be, any moment, and you know that I'd be useless. What good am I in a fight with a pickaxe when we'll be facing goblins with swords and spears?" Dorian didn't know what to think.

"A pickaxe is a fine weapon in a pinch." Dorian crossed his arms, worries rushing through his mind. Yander was old enough to look out for himself and others, but teaching him to fight? How would he use his newfound skills?

"You know that it won't be enough. Look at all the others." Yander swept his hand over to the workers. "Almost all of them can fight somehow, but I'm the useless one. I can't bear seeing Emelda get hurt again."

His heart twinged, and he closed his eyes. The face of his dead wife drifted in his mind, how he wasn't able to protect her. Could he relegate Yander to the same fate? He would have died protecting her rather than not be able to protect her. Wouldn't the young dwarf feel the same way?

But he wasn't ready to teach Yander that, not now. Not after his skills were useless to protect his own family.

"We'll talk about this later, after everything is taken care of here."

"Dorian, please teach me. I know you care about Emelda, too. You can't be everywhere, and you can't protect us by yourself." There was desperation in Yander's eyes now. Had he expected Dorian to say yes?

"Let me sleep on it, I'll give you an answer in the morning." Dorian clapped Yander's shoulder. "I can see the fire in you, the desire to protect."

Yander wasn't happy. "The morning then." He turned to walk back to work, and Dorian watched him go. The young dwarf had a weight on his shoulders now that he had never carried before.

Dorian passed a hand over his eyes. *Three years, that's all I have to last. Then, I can be with her again.* He joined the others, unsure of what he was going to do.

3

DWARVES ON THE HORIZON

The gate rose with a creak, straining against the ropes pulling it up. Dwarves heaved at the winch, straining against the weight.

"Almost there." The door went faster now "A few more feet." Yudoline urged them on from her vantage point on the wall.

The gate whined and snapped shut with a bang. Dust drifted off the wall, and Yudoline clapped her hands. "Done!"

The dwarves let out a cheer as one, the sun sinking to the west and turning the gray of the wall a brilliant reflection of pink, yellow, and red. They had done it.

"I'll sleep soundly tonight," Lumdir said.

"You have many reasons to." Kimec rubbed his arms. "My bones will be aching in the morning."

"Break out the ale tonight, we celebrate." Barileth finished tying off the rope, securing it in place. "All we need to do is undo the rope and it'll open."

"Won't that be easy to open?" Yander asked. "Which would be bad if something got in?" Barileth shot him an angry look.

"It isn't going to stay like this, I'll figure out a way to have it work better. When I get more time, of course."

"You'll have to work on it in your spare time," Dorian said. With the work done and dinner waiting the group had turned to the mine and was going back in. "I need you to hunt tomorrow. We need the meat." Barileth groaned.

"That's right. Don't tell me it's just rockbread and potatoes again?"

"We won't tell you that then, you'll find out when we get inside." Yudoline winked at Yander, who managed to crack a smile.

Barileth groaned again. "Someone save me from this tediousness. At least give me an extra foaming mug of ale tonight. I'll need it."

"The faster you teach someone else to use that crossbow the more likely we are to get more meat," Lumdir said. Dorian winced at that, but everyone was inside so he busied himself with shutting and locking the entrance door. That made him feel better.

"If I could trust you not to shoot yourself in the foot, I would."

"Now there, that was uncalled for." Barileth laughed at Lumdir's reaction and clapped him on the back, making him misstep.

"Who is there to teach? Everyone is busy with their work. You have the stone, Kimec the wood, and Kragnak has the metal." Dorian frowned at the reminder. It was going to be more difficult now that the last frost was over.

A hush fell over them and they trudged to the dining hall in silence. Times were going to be hard, they knew that, but they didn't have to like it. As food was brought in on steaming platters they perked up, but there was no joking or conversation.

"Will you join me in a toast?" Dorian raised his mug into the air. He had to do something and it was the only thing he could think of. The others followed suit as Yander and Emelda joined them with the last of the food.

"To stone as thick as a dwarf, and to walls that keep out the enemy."

"To stone," the others echoed. Without waiting for the others Dorian took a pull on his ale. Better than the last batch, this had hints of oak and was smoother, with only a hint of bitter aftertaste.

Yudoline was getting better at this. Conversation began then, enough of the weight of the day broken. Good ale and good food helped, although Emelda wasn't as good a cook as Skover had been.

They would make it. With enough hard work and a little luck, they would make it.

Dorian avoided Yander the next day. His question had kept him awake until the exhaustion had consumed him, but he was no closer to making a decision. Instead, he divided out assignments, choosing to help with planting aboveground instead of mining.

The earth was hard and he put his skills to good use breaking it up for the others. Emelda and Yudoline joined Kragnak, who had been enlisted to help, in planting the seeds they had saved from last season and foraged.

There would be a larger variety of crops growing this year. Potatoes, some kind of squash, hops, cucumbers, carrots, and a tomato plant with fruits the size of a thumb.

Clearing all thoughts from his mind, Dorian focused on the work. The others chatted as they worked, and the two dwarves managed to draw out Kragnak from his usual distant self to take part.

Less than an hour before lunch Emelda spotted Barileth in the forest.

"Why is he back so early? I don't think he's caught anything." Dorian rested and shielded his eyes against the sun to look. Barileth was empty-handed and moving fast up the slope.

"Probably just laid out some traps this morning, nothing to worry about. I'll talk to him and find out." Dorian left his pickaxe in the dirt and picked his way down the slope back to the gate. He untied it and let it down, they had decided to leave it shut unless it needed to be open.

Barileth emerged from the tree line and hurried over. "What happened?"

"Migrants coming, from the north."

"Already?"

"It is well into spring. They probably left after the worst of the winter storms to get here." Dorian rubbed his beard, thinking through their stores. They might have enough food for them.

"How many were there?"

"Six or seven, maybe up to ten. It was hard to tell. I came back as fast as I could." He still had his crossbow slung against his back.

"We'll have to put them in the dormitory." They weren't completely unprepared, Dorian had anticipated another group of them would be coming this year and with less to do in the winter they had made more beds, furniture, and dug out apartments to accommodate the possibility.

He had expected four, five at most. If there were this many though... Either life was getting harder at Zirad or someone wanted to send more dwarves this way. Was Seventh Hall an expedition for ore or something else?

"I'll help with the gate." Barileth started for the winch, but Dorian waved him off.

"No need. It might send the wrong signal to our new guests. No need to scare them off before they even get here. But get the weapons ready and waiting, just in case."

It took them another hour to get up the mountain, and by the time they reached the edge of the trees word had spread through the mine. Everyone was milling about outside waiting for the new arrivals.

Dorian thought about sending them back to work but knew that it would do more good. He asked Emelda to prepare for ten more for lunch though, which sent her back in and out of the way.

As the migrants were coming up the trail that Barileth had made from his trips to hunt, Dorian was glad to see that they looked healthy and strong, for the most part. They could use the help around the mine.

"Welcome to Seventh Hall travelers." The packs on their backs gave away their intentions, and they had a few pack goats with them that included cages of ducks and chickens. He was glad to see they hadn't come unprepared.

A tall, burly dwarf with red hair at the front of the line eyed him and the others before moving forward. After he looked around, he turned back to greet them. "This is Seventh Hall? We were expecting something...better."

Dorian clenched his fist, but then forced it to relax. "I am Dorian," he held out a hand. "And you would be?"

"Mughan Mithrilbasher." His grip was strong. "Isn't this wall a little weak? We were expecting better defenses than this."

Flashing his teeth, Dorian let go of the dwarf's hand. "It will hold, like the rest of the dwarves here. Enemies have misjudged us in the past and regretted it so I understand your hesitation. Please, come inside and join us for lunch."

"Sometimes things are what they seem though." Mughan jerked his head and the line of dwarves behind him moved up and into the wall.

"And what would your expertise be to judge?" Dorian frowned at him.

"I know my stone and I know how it cuts. After all, I was the head of the stonecutters for the Royal Quarry." Lumdir bristled and was about to say something, but Dorian stepped in.

"Ah, the quarry that has plenty of time to fuss and preen about the stones they cut, and can always through them to the rabble of the common man if they mess up." The smile on Mughan's face was wiped away. "We don't have the luxury here."

Dorian raised his voice and turned to address the others. "Everyone inside for lunch, make them comfortable and happy and show them where they can set their goods. Barileth, please help me with the gate."

Mughan didn't follow the others, but crossed his arms and watched them raise the gate. "I see you're planting the spring crops. Other than the haphazard rows it looks fine." Dorian focused his frustration on the winch, pushing hard and clenching his teeth.

There were ten of them in all. Ten more mouths to feed, ten more dwarves to house, but ten more bodies that could be put to use. Dorian was painfully aware that they now were outnumbered by the new arrivals.

Although the gate could be raised by two dwarves, the weight made them strain. While Mughan watched they brought the gate up until it crashed into place.

"Why are you so unpleasant?" Barileth asked, after catching his breath. "Abused as a child?"

Mughan's eyes narrowed at the comment. "Barileth, that was uncalled for. I'm sure a good night's rest and some food and drink will set everything right." Dorian motioned for him to go inside.

"Your arrogance will be your downfall...Barileth, was it?"

"Speak for yourself dwarf." His reply was cold and quick.

"Inside, both of you." Dorian had enough. Barileth turned and went in, but Dorian didn't wait for Mughan and followed. When they slipped inside the cool of the tunnels he waited.

Sure enough, the new migrant followed them. "Watch your step, we have traps in this tunnel." Dorian led him through, pointing out the various triggers to avoid.

They joined the others in the dining hall, who had already dumped down their packs and started eating. Dorian was glad to see there would be enough to go around, the golden moss was growing well and there was always plenty ready to be ground into moss flower for the rockbread, which was fresh and still steaming from the ovens.

The migrants weren't complaining at the lack of meat though. They tore into the bread, slathering copious amounts of goat butter on it that melted in seconds. Barileth joined them, but Mughan hung back.

"Where are we to live?" he asked.

"I don't have everything ready yet, but we'll find a place for you."

"You weren't expecting us?" There was an undertone to it that poked at him.

"This many? To such a small, remote expedition such as ours?" Dorian smiled. "No, we were planning on you coming sometime next month when the weather was better for travel. It appears you were eager to join us though."

"Ready, not eager."

"Traveling in winter, bold I would say. Perhaps you were running to us? Or away from something?"

Mughan ignored the question. "The tunnels seem rough, and ill-suited for habitation. If these are your best efforts in furniture making and mining, it's a good thing we came."

"Watch what you say about my dwarves." The others continued to eat, blissfully unaware of their quiet conversation. Dorian wasn't smiling anymore.

"Oh, that comment isn't directed at the makers." Mughan looked around the room. "And this chamber, not much foresight for the one who placed it here. Doesn't account for the future, I'm afraid. We may have to change that."

The hair on the back of Dorian's neck was standing up now, and his emotions roiled inside him. He kept calm, though, suppressing his anger. "I'll be more than happy to put you to work, you can count on that."

Mughan bared his teeth, then leaned in and whispered words only Dorian was meant to hear. "I'm not sure you're fit to lead this expedition."

4

MIGRANTS

Dorian held Mughan's gaze. "You can think whatever you like. That isn't my concern. What is my concern is the health and future of this expedition. Now I intend to keep everyone alive." He pulled back his lips, revealing his teeth. "You aren't going to be a problem, are you?"

Before Mughan could answer Dorian turned away. "Yudoline, would you please show our new guests around after they have finished?" He resisted the urge to turn and read Mughan's face.

"Of course, are you not eating?" He had already turned to walk out.

"I'm not hungry. Everyone else meet me in the supply room when you've finished." Inside, he wasn't sure there would be enough food for all of them. *Just when things were starting to level out and we had started building up a surplus this happens.*

He shook his head. No reason to get disheartened. Being alone helped him think and clear his head. The first group of migrants hadn't been all that helpful, these were dangerous. He'd have to keep a close eye on Mughan.

In the supply room they had a few of the older beds still around, enough for the migrants at least. Kimec's newer beds were sturdier and stout compared to the old ones, and were in the apartments.

There were two apartments free, with beds and dressers to go with them. Dorian shifted some of the supplies off to one side of the supply room, which used to be the old dormitory.

He envisioned the space, thinking there might be enough room if they took some of the supplies out and put them back in the workshops. It would be cluttered again, and impede production, but it was better than nothing. He was still thinking about it when the sounds of the other dwarves came from the tunnel.

"Kragnak, please take the chests down to the empty apartments. Yander, you take the old bedding down." He tasked them as soon as they came in the door, and they got to work. "Everyone else, we take care of this."

"Back into a dormitory again," Barileth said. "Can we put a lock on the door to keep them in?"

"To work everyone." Dorian ignored the comment and they got busy. By the time Yudoline brought the migrants around for their tour they already had all the beds set up and arranged.

"Well done," Yudoline said, leading the pack into the room. They crammed themselves among the remaining boxes, crates, and barrels. "This is where you'll all be staying, except the Thunderheads of course, and they'll be one other apartment open."

"That will be for Mughan," a big dwarf with a red beard said. Mughan smirked as Dorian fumed.

"Your name was?" He tried to cover it up, being as polite as he could.

"Dozotaine Brightbasher," he said, crossing his arms.

"We'll set you up over here. That reminds me, we still have introductions to do."

"We did most of them in the dining hall," Yudoline said. "Everyone, please introduce yourself."

They went around in a circle. There were the Thunderheads, Hukgras and Thurbag, Yutatir Coinmaul, Thardegith Emberhand, Olgim Merryfal, Kuddick Beryljaw, Fimroul Anvilhorn, and Glorithoid Flintbrow.

"Welcome, I'm sure we'll be using all your talents over the coming months and years." A few looked like they had fighting experience, Dozotaine and Yutatir, and Dorian made a note to find out later if they had.

"These are ours?" Fimroul asked, going over to one of the beds.

"Yes, of course," Yudoline said. "Make yourself at home."

"Fantastic, they warned us that there might not be a place for us right away." He laid down on the bedroll. "Not the worst I've ever slept in."

"In a few days we'll have the rest of the apartments finished and you'll move in there. Now, if everyone could move back to the dining hall we can talk about work."

The dwarves talked amongst themselves and headed out as the founders put the finishing touches on the dormitory. Yander hung back and tried to catch Dorian's attention before he could follow the migrants.

"Have you thought about it? About what we talked about yesterday?"

Dorian sighed. "Now isn't the best time Yander. I've got to get them set up with tasks and figure out how to feed and clothe them. There isn't time to teach you how to fight." Yander looked down, crestfallen. It made Dorian feel bad. "Give me a few more days, I'll think about training you when everything is settled."

Yander nodded and followed the others. Dorian still hadn't decided what the right thing was to do.

"Why do you do that to the boy?" Barileth asked, carrying a crate out of the converted dormitory. "Don't you see how much he looks up to you?"

That made Dorian stop short. "Looks up to me?" He furrowed his brow. "He doesn't look up to me, I'm just the one he has to bug."

Putting down his crate Barileth raised an eyebrow at him. "I'm not afraid to tell you the truth like the others are. If he wanted training in how to fight he could have asked me, or even Lumdir. You know the reason he asked you. He looks up to you, respects you."

"What? No, it's just because I taught him to mine." Dorian shrugged. "I'm no more of a leader than the next dwarf."

"Fool yourself all you want," Barileth said, picking his load back up. "You're going to have to face the reckoning sometime. There are worse things than goblins out here."

"He'll learn himself."

Barileth started walking. "If he's alive," he said over his shoulder.

Heart full of conflict, Dorian remembered an earlier time in his life. The echo of the present reached back from the past and drug him into his own mind.

The grizzled, burly dwarf tapped him on the head with his stick.

"Remember to guard yourself. Focus on what your enemy will do."

"Right, focus on the enemy," Dorian said, lifting his own axe into the preparation position he had been taught.

"And keep your feet farther apart." Dorian shifted his feet. "Keep your back straight. Head up. Keep your axe ready, don't droop."

As he focused on raising his axe Kazal dropped down, faster than Dorian expected, and lashed out a foot. It swept under him, taking his legs with it, and Dorian flailed wildly.

When he hit the ground Kazal was over him in an instant. Before Dorian could take a breath, the practice stick was drawn across his throat. "You're dead."

"That's not fair, I wasn't ready."

"Not ready?" The gray-haired miner narrowed his eyes. "Weren't you warned to watch your opponent?"

"Well..." Dorian rolled over to get up but a whack on his fingers stopped him. He dropped his axe and brought in his hand to cradle it, now pulsing with pain.

"You don't get to decide when your opponent attacks. You either react or die." Dorian glowered. Wasn't Kazal supposed to be teaching him? He failed to see how this was helping.

"I'll be prepared next time."

"Prepare now. War won't give you any time to get ready."

Kazal. It had been years since he had thought about him. A faint smile played on his lips as he recalled better times.

Without his mentor ship Dorian might not be here. He took me in, showed me what I needed to survive, not what I thought I needed to know.

The others were waiting though, so Dorian left his memories and indecision behind to hurrying to the dining hall. The others were waiting for him, Mughan included.

He questioned each in turn, learning about their previous occupations and skills. As he suspected these migrants would be more useful.

After a few hours he had a good idea of how to employ them and released them to prepare their quarters.

"How are the new arrivals?" Yudoline asked, joining him in at his table, sweat streaming down her head.

"Promising."

"Oh?" She raised a tankard of water and took a drink. "Tell me about them." Her eyes glistened as he started to talk.

"We've added a furnace operator and smith's apprentice, a bowyer, a miller with other farm experience, a cheese and butter maker, another miner, and a few other odds and ends."

"Who is the miner?"

"Dozotaine, but I suspect he has some fighting experience from the few questions I was able to ask him. An experienced miner would have caught some that he missed."

"Sticks and stones, we have a mystery on our hands." Dorian laughed, some of the tension leaving his body.

"There are many reasons for a dwarf to want to leave the city and all its riches to strike out on their own."

"There are." Something about the tone in her voice made him curious, but he wasn't going to open himself up to any questions down the same path.

Dorian rose. "I must prepare though, how is the planting?"

"Hot, and sweaty. We'll finish by the end of the day though, if I have anything to say about it." She joined him and they parted ways, Dorian deeper into the mine and Yudoline to the exit.

After he bade her farewell and good luck he checked on the migrants. The Emberhands were happy with their apartment, and even Mughan seemed satisfied with his.

He retreated back to his room to work through his plans for the new arrivals. With an additional miner they could dig deeper to discover more ore, or concentrate on mining the veins of copper that were already discovered.

Yander was below him, carving out the rest of the apartments right now. Dorian should be with him, but couldn't bear to be around him. What would he say?

Dorian squeezed his eyes shut. He had told himself before he started that there was a good chance the dwarves with him would die. He told himself he wouldn't get attached, and now look at him.

They had already lost dwarves and it affected him more than he thought it would. He had to keep them alive, just for another two years at least.

If I had taught him what I knew the others might still be alive. The thought crackled through him like lightning because he knew it was true. Yander might have opened the hole, but Dorian invited in the spider by his inaction.

Is that why I'm so hesitant to teach him? With no one else around and nothing else to distract him Dorian was forced to face himself. His axe was hanging from pegs carved into the wall.

Had another dwarf, or more than one, been able to wield weapons like he was able to there might be more of them alive today. Shame and guilt washed over him.

"No." He tried to fight it off with anger. Anger at the King, anger at those who killed his wife, anger at his children being taken from him and all the lost years.

But it didn't cleanse him of his guilt.

If they were attacked today many would die. Too many. They weren't ready, and the danger that was out there knew them.

Dorian stood and walked to the axe. He ran a finger down the blade. Cold. Smooth. Sharp. It was molded from raw steel, shaped and hammered, quenched in fire and ground.

He had to do the same to Yander. He had to teach him, just like Kazal had taught him many years ago. He had to set aside his ego and his fears.

It was too late to not get attached.

A plan started forming in his mind, growing and pulsing. He had spent all those years alone struggling to keep alive. He wasn't going to waste it now.

And he wasn't going to let a bunch of monsters kill his friends and compatriots. Dorian's eyes lingered on the axe for a few moments more before he turned and grabbed his pickaxe.

Goblins were coming to kill them. He didn't know when and he didn't know how many. *I have to teach him, I have to make sure that he can survive.*

It was time to prepare.

5

A Promise

A soft knock at the door caught his attention and wrenched him from his thoughts. "Come in."

Emelda walking in and shutting the door behind her caught him off guard. "I need to speak with you." She turned, shoulders up and chin down.

"Have a seat." Dorian vacated his chair and gestured toward it. His movement made the candle flicker, sending an aromatic trail of smoke his way. She shook her head.

"Don't do it."

He cocked his head to the side. "Do what?"

"Yander asked you to teach him to fight. Please, don't do it." She came closer and grabbed hold of his shirt. Dorian recovered from his surprise and softened his gaze. He took hold of her hands.

"Emelda, be reasonable." Her nostrils flared and her eyes narrowed.

"You're going to get him in trouble, I know it." She shook her head. "I can't stand to think of it."

"What do you mean?"

"You'll take him to fight and he'll get hurt. He isn't like you Dorian, he can't wall himself up like you can." He jaw almost dropped, but he caught himself because tears were in her eyes. "His heart is too tender."

Dorian couldn't help himself. He let go of her hands and put them around her. "I can't promise to keep him safe forever. What would you have me do? Leave him defenseless?"

"We're safe here, he doesn't need it." She shook her head against him, now on his chest. *What am I doing, what have I done?*

"That isn't true. The world is filled with evil. We can't avoid it no matter how hard we try. Only by facing it head on can it be defeated."

"I can't lose him, not after Mother and Father…" She sobbed against his chest and he tried to keep his own eyes dry.

What could I say? Any promise he made would ring hollow and untrue and he knew it. He already made up his mind to train Yander, could he even turn back now?

They expect too much of me. "I'm a weak dwarf. Without all of you I'd perish."

"No, you're strong. You fought for us, fought for…them."

"I'm supposed to be the one encouraging you." Her tears subsided and she wiped her face on his chest and stood back.

"You know the only reason we're still here today is because of what you did for us. I don't know what happened to you before you came with us but you're a good dwarf Dorian."

He couldn't hold her blazing gaze and dropped his eyes to the floor. "I can't promise you that I won't train him."

She sighed and slumped into the chair. "I had a feeling you wouldn't." Dorian sat on his bed, which creaked with his weight and patted her kneed.

"I can promise that I'll do my best to keep him safe. And you. No matter what happens."

Emelda smiled through her sadness and got up and hugged him. He hugged her back, a strange mixture of sadness and warmth flowing through him.

After she left, he replayed the conversation in his head. *Would she have said the same thing?*

He shook his head and tried to forget her, but his heart burned. How he missed her, and how he wished he could forget.

"Two more years and then I'll be free again," he whispered. "This time I won't fail to bring her back."

"Dozotaine, you'll work on the ore veins again today." Dorian watched him stand up and stare at him.

"Barileth, stay with me and Kragnak for the morning and then hunt in the afternoon. Dozotaine, are you waiting on something?" The burly dwarf hadn't moved and was standing with his arms crossed.

Mughan inclined his head slightly. "No, I'll go right away." Dorian didn't miss the exchange, and Mughan smirked at him. He resisted the urge to throttle him.

"Mughan you'll help with the planting outside." There was a pregnant pause before Mughan got up and left without a word, the last of the migrants to depart. "Next time I'll make him cleanup duty," he muttered under his breath.

"Are you sure that's the best idea?" Barileth asked. It had been three days since the migrants arrived and every day the same. Dorian ignored the comment.

"Kragnak." Dorian waved him over.

"You need to assert some control in a way that won't backfire. Divide them up, make them easier to handle." Barileth was picking his teeth with a splinter.

"We will be thinking of ways to strengthen our defenses this morning."

"Aren't they strong enough already? We have a wall and a gate and a row of traps. What else do we need?" Barileth laughed at Kragnak's comment. "Oh, right."

"There's no such thing as too much when it comes to protection," Dorian said. "We'll need better weapons, can you make swords and axes?"

"Should be able to now that we've gotten more metal from the mines. What were you thinking?"

"Enough to equip everyone. What about armor?"

Kragnak looked down and kicked his foot. "I...wasn't the best armor smith. I could try a breastplate."

"Work on the weapons first, and then try it." With the new arrivals they were ten weapons short of being fully equipped, but Kragnak more recent attempts had gone better. They at least looked like what they were supposed to and sharped up.

"Give the first one to someone other than me," Barileth said, spitting out his splinter and leaning back in his chair. Kragnak frowned at him but said nothing.

"You're hear for something else though. We need a better trap, something that will keep out the thieves."

"Were you thinking cage traps?" Barileth asked. Dorian nodded. Barileth leaned forward. "We're out of cages."

"That's why Kragnak is here." They both turned to him.

"Me? I can't make cages," he sputtered.

"Yes you can. You've got enough copper now to build a stack of them."

"But I've never made them before. Why can't Kimec make more wooden ones?"

"How long is wood going to last against a metal sword?" Barileth asked.

"Not long?"

"You are correct. Which is why you need to get to work making the cages. Barileth, can you come up with a mechanism to activate them?"

He leaned back and stroked his beard. "Hmm…I've heard of these working before. If I can get it to work right we can make it come down from the ceiling in two pieces and then clamp shut."

Kragnak's eyes went wide. "Or, we could have it come out of the ground and then shut at the top." They got wider. "Or perhaps we have it in two sections that come from either side of the wall and then lock in place after they slam shut?"

"Are you crazy? How am I going to make a cage that can do that?"

"Oh, it shouldn't be too hard I imagine. Add a hinge somewhere and it should work." Kragnak, practically frothing at the mouth, turned back to Dorian.

"Are you hearing this?"

"Yes, he has a good point." Dorian nodded solemnly.

"Thank you, it's already hard enough as is." Kragnak deflated a little, but he was still worked up.

"Which is why you should start right away," Dorian said. "A hinge would be fine." He patted Kragnak on the shoulder in a reassuring manner.

Kragnak's mouth dropped open. "Wait, but, no-"

"What are you still standing around here for dwarf? You heard the man, go start on it." Barileth tried to pull Kragnak to his feet. Kragnak sputtered, getting red. He was trying to make words, but it wasn't working.

It was too much. Dorian smiled, which broke Barileth who laughed. Peals of his hearty, rich laughter echoed around the room. Dorian joined him, and Kragnak couldn't stay mad for long.

"I thought you were going to make me do it," he said when at last the laughter died down.

"You'll still need to make the cage," Dorian said.

"Put a hinge on the top side and I'll have it come up from the ground," Barileth said. "Let me check the spacing in the entrance tunnel for size."

As Barileth was leaving Kragnak turned to Dorian. "I don't think I can do it. I've never done something like this before." He was deflated, hunched over the table. Dorian was glad the ale was already put away. He moved chairs, sitting next to Kragnak.

"I know it is hard for you, after everything that has happened." Kragnak refused to meet his gaze, playing with his heat hardened hands. Dorian knew he needed something, but wasn't sure he could give it to him.

Again, he wished someone else was in his position. For a brief moment he even toyed with the thought of Mughan leading, but the anger that burned up in response put that thought away quickly.

So instead, he fumbled for the right words to say. He wasn't Goldhand the Vanquisher leading his troops into battle, or the famous bard Salazn who could regale crowds for hours. He was just a plain dwarf with nothing special to offer.

"There is no one else to take your place," Dorian said flatly. "No matter how much you wish it weren't true." Kragnak lifted his eyes.

"I'm not good enough."

"You should give yourself more credit, and more grace. Think about the weapons, you didn't know how to do that before you started."

"And they didn't turn out well..."

Dorian shook his head. "They were good enough to fight off a giant cave spider and save the expedition. They were good enough for

Barileth to use it to keep the thieves away." That one was techni-cally true. "They are good enough."

"Do you think so?" There was a glimmer of hope in his eyes.

"Kragnak, you know how to make a bar. You can make a cage." There was a long pause as the unsure dwarf turned Dorian's words over in his head.

"I guess I can try." Dorian clapped him on the back.

"That's the spirit. Try away until you get it right." He couldn't help keeping the smile from his lips. Kragnak perked up and returned it. Dorian felt better about his chances.

"From what I remember we have enough copper for me to get started." Kragnak rose, and Dorian joined him. Just before he left the dining hall he turned back to Dorian. "Thanks Dorian."

Dorian was taken aback. "For what?"

"Believing in me, even when I can't believe in myself." With that he turned and was gone.

It left Dorian alone to think and dwell on the conversation that he just had. Once again he was left moved by the responsibility he had to the rest of the expedition.

They were relying on him to survive. He had to be good enough to make sure they did. As he wandered down the main stairs he thought about Ruby and Xanther.

His feet carried him the rest of the way, following the sounds of the pickaxes ringing on the rock. Yander and Dozotaine were hard at work on the copper vein, and had carved out a good chunk of it.

Piles of tetrahedrite lay in the tunnel. Yander's voice carried down the tunnel. "How goes the mining?" Dorian called.

They stopped, turning to him. "Good," Yander said. "I can feel it getting weaker as we go, we should be done by tomorrow."

"There's plenty here for what we need." Dozotaine's mouth was pressed tight and his eyes exasperated. Dorian almost chuckled, but stopped himself. Yander set his pickaxe against the wall.

"Is there anywhere else to mine?" he asked.

"Not yet, once this is done we'll move on." Dozotaine frowned and turned back to the rock as Yander motioned him further up the tunnel.

"Are you two getting along?" Dorian asked.

"Hmm, yes of course. Why wouldn't we?" Yander tugged his beard. "Although he isn't very fast, I would have thought he could use a pickaxe better too."

"Surprising." Dorian wasn't surprised. "Have you felt any other ore?"

"I keep thinking I feel it, but I'm not sure."

"Once we've dug out everything we need we'll go back to searching." Two years wasn't much time, and every day they lost was one day less. The King would expect results.

They were far enough away that Dozotaine's mining was fainter. Yander looked back and then leaned in close.

"Did you think about what I asked you?" There was an urgency to his voice, even though it was lowered for Dorian's ears to hear.

Thinking back to what Emelda said, Dorian hesitated.

6

NEVERENDING

Yander's tight lips pressed into a frown at Dorian's pause.

"Yes, I'll do it." Yander let out a whoop of joy, and Dorian held up his hand. "Don't make me regret this decision."

"I won't. Thank you, thank you, thank you."

"Go on then," Dorian said, shoving him away. "Back to work."

"When can we start?"

"After the work's done. Go."

"Done, we'll be done soon." Yander looked invigorated, flowing over with energy. Light was back in his eyes, and it gave Dorian a strange sensation and left a faint smile on his lips.

While they finished mining the tetrahedrite, Dorian took care of the pile of ore, carting it to the bucket winch and up the mining shaft to the top. From there he carted it with a different wheelbarrow to the forge.

Kragnak was at work, shaping bars of iron into rods at the anvil. They glowed a cherry red when he took it out of the fire and his hammer sent sparks flying.

"Hard at work I see, figured it out?" Dorian asked.

Kragnak jumped up at the sound of his voice and sighed. "You startled me. I was about to start work on a sword, actually. Thardegith is working on the ore."

The new dwarf was sweating hard and loading chunks of ore into the crucible. Dorian watched him work. He moved with the confidence of one who had done it many times before. "Glad to hear it's working out."

Luck gave them at least a few dwarves with useful skills. Maybe they wouldn't be such a drain on the expedition as he first feared. Dorian wandered over to him.

"You've done this before," he said.

"Oh yes. It's good to be back in the heat of the forge after such a cold trip." The steady ring of Kragnak's hammer punctuated his speech. "A bit smaller than I'm used to…"

"Where did you come from then?"

"South Danverland Forges. My grandfather worked them long before I, melting the iron flow of Three Forks." He finished filling his crucible, eyed it and added another load before scraping it off.

"Impressive, I've heard stories about it before. A large operation, if memory serves."

"No, not anymore. Tis a dwindling forge, running low on ore in the southern shafts." The smile that was on his face faded with the memory into a frown. "She's fallen on hard times."

And hence one of the many reasons for our expedition. Dorian kept the thought to himself, choosing to comfort instead. "We're glad to have you nonetheless, no matter the condition that brought you here."

Thardegith's eyes widened. "I'm surprised to hear you say that, with the rumors."

Dorian's eyes narrowed, and he forced himself to relax. "Rumors?"

"Oh, I wasn't supposed to let that slip." He hung his head in shame. "Bad Thardegith. We heard you didn't want us here, that you're thinking about expelling us and taking our goods. Please let us stay, I can't survive out there."

"We'll do nothing of the sort. You've come to join us and join us you have. Keep working the copper, I've got plenty more to feed you for a while." Dorian dumped his load in the stockpile and left to get another.

He looked back before he did. Thardegith was still working, clearly relieved at Dorian's reassurance. *But who had spread that rumor?* One dwarf came to mind immediately, and the hostile attitude suddenly made sense.

While he worked to bring up the ore he puzzled out what he could do to combat the new arrival's actions. He didn't get far, he wasn't cut out to play these kinds of games.

Unfortunately, they were happening anyway.

Kragnak's work in progress distracted him on the third trip. The shape of a sword had taken shape, but there was a small problem with the form.

While he watched Kragnak fought the copper, pounding down strange formations that left the sword lopsided. Whenever he would fix it the other side sprouted another hump.

It wasn't going well, and Kragnak was getting frustrated. He was using too much force, and the longer it went the worse it got. Finally, he had enough and thrust it into a barrel of water to sizzle. The smell of steam and hot copper filled the air.

He threw his tongs down and stalked off into the tunnel, mumbling under his breath as he went.

"He's too young and brash," Thardegith said, pulling the white-hot crucible from the forge.

"I can't disagree with you there, but I'm not sure brashness is his problem," Dorian said. The crucible tipped over and the molten metal poured into the sand molds, sending up its own clouds of steam.

"We don't have a lot of options," Kimec said, working with a plane to shave down his plank.

"Unless you can forge?" Dorian asked, turning to Thardegith.

"Me? No, I've never held a hammer before, just a foundry dwarf."

"That may change, we don't have many smiths," Dorian said. It would be better if Kragnak could just get his confidence. He wasn't a bad smith when he knew what to do.

"Were there any other smiths in the group?" Kimec asked, stopping and leaning up against his smooth wood. Dorian shook his head.

"I'm the closest there is," Thardegith said.

Dorian realized that dinner was soon and he still had the rest of the ore to bring up. He left the others at their work. Yet another task to do on a long list of them. Would it ever end?

Roast potatoes and venison wafted through the tunnels, pulling Dorian into the dining hall with the Yander and Dozotaine. Laughter spilling out greeted him.

Everyone else was there and seated already, spooning portions of steaming hot stew into bowls and taking freshly baked rockbread from a pile on a platter.

Stomach growling, Dorian joined them, grateful for the happily crackling fire in the main fireplace that warmed his muscles. Hauling the ore had taken a toll on his body and he slipped into the chair with a sigh.

When he did some of the migrants looked at him sideways. Olgim, the closest, moved his chair farther away. Mughan smirked at him. It dampened Dorian's spirits and he tore into a warm loaf of rockbread.

"As fresh as my mother made it," Kuddick said through his mouthful, half a loaf still steaming in his hand.

"Ah, but if we had strawberry jam it would make it all the more better," Dozotaine said.

"Strawberries? You must have come from the Gathiz," Barileth said.

"Journeyed to Zirad as a young dwarf looking to make my mark." Dozotaine took another loaf anyway and smothered it with goat butter. "Never could quite make it though."

"So, you chose to join us here and strike your fortune from the ground?" Barileth asked.

"If we manage it. I'm sure a take of the gold beneath our feet would be more than worth the risk."

"Gold?" Barileth guffawed. "You're more likely to get covered in dirt than to get a cut of that."

"Speaking of dirt, we managed to plant the rest of the furrows today," Yudoline said, ladling him a steaming bowl of stew and shooting Barileth an over-sized glare.

"Great," Dorian said.

"You forgot to mention the rest of the hard work you put in," Mughan said from the other side of the table.

"Oh yes, I almost forgot. With Hukgras and Thurbag's help we plowed another quarter stave of field. We'll run out of seeds planting at this rate."

"Sounds like you were busy," Kimec said, grabbing another loaf to dip in his stew.

"They worked hard. It isn't surprising given the right kind of direction." Dorian understood the subtext but tried to ignore it. He wondered if Mughan was trying to test him somehow, or if he was really that spiteful.

A hush fell over the others, and most became interested in their food instead of looking at the others.

"They do work hard, don't they," Dorian said at last. The taste of the stew had gone stale, even though it was filled with spice and salt. He kept eating, meeting Mughan's eyes. The dwarf was steely and revealed nothing but a hint of contempt. "You'll learn to do the same as well."

Mughan stiffened in his chair. Dorian knew it was his chance to move on or fight and he watched intently. "I've learned my lessons in life well dwarf. Can the same be said for you?" When he had no reply Mughan continued. "Or do you need someone to teach you?"

"I'm never too old to learn something new."

"Then you could learn a lesson on leadership and how to treat others with respect." Dorian opened his mouth to reply, but Yander interrupted him.

"Dorian's more of a leader than you'll ever be."

"Yander," Dorian warned.

"It's true." Yander turned back to Mughan. "You don't know what we've been through here, what horrors we've had to face." He started to choke up. "What sorrow we've endured." His sadness turned to something else.

"Dorian was with us every step of the way. If anyone deserves respect it's him." There was a ferocity in his eyes and a courage that Dorian had glimpsed once before. Yander had promise in him, but his words were too kind and Dorian didn't deserve them.

Mughan cleared his throat. "I mean no disrespect to anyone, and we don't know what you've been through. You are right. But you don't know what we've been through either, and haven't bothered to find out."

"We've opened our doors to you, haven't we?" Yander asked, eyes aflame.

"That's enough Yander."

"You can't let him treat you like this." Yander saw the look on his eye and sat back, crossing his arms. Emelda put a hand on his back and caressed him. "Fine."

The dwarf showed promise, but that's all it was right now. He could go too far sometimes. Dorian glanced around the room and felt how the atmosphere had turned frosty. The new migrants were on one half of the room and everyone else was on the other.

"I think the best thing to do is to have our dinner and call it a day," Dorian said. The laugher was gone, and so was the conversation. They finished in silence.

"If you're finished, we'll take you down," Dorian said when everyone was done.

"Down where?" Mughan asked.

"Follow me and you'll see. Yander, will you take care of the table please?"

Yander looked sullen, but nodded and started collecting plates. That would give him some breathing room, although he wasn't sure how it would turn out later.

While the new arrivals had been busy with their tasks the others had finished theirs. Dorian took a torch and, making sure they were following him, headed deeper into the mine.

They went down the stairs, but instead of stopping at the apartments he kept going one level below. He had stayed up late last night, and had Yander finish it this morning before he joined Dozotaine.

"I thought you could choose your own, except Mughan and the Emberhands of course." Dorian welcomed them with an outstretched hand, and the migrants complied.

"These are finished? I thought we would have to live in the dormitory for a long time," Olgim said, entering the first room.

"It took some work but we weren't completely unprepared. You just arrived earlier than expected." Dorian set his torch into the wall sconce while the others explored. "They're about the same."

Each room had a bed, wooden cabinet, and a stone chest. Mattresses filled with dried grass were topped with the last remaining blankets. They would need to make more, Dorian was planning on using goat hair if they could get a dwarf to work out how to weave it.

Mughan was walking through the apartments too, wordlessly following the others as they claimed a space for themselves. Dorian watched him carefully as he searched for something. *What is he looking for? Some failure perhaps, something to use against me in the future?*

"I'm impressed. I didn't think you'd be able to house us after seeing the state of the mine from the outside. You have my gratitude."

Dorian smiled at the humbled dwarf, ignoring the slight. "I'll remember that."

7

NEW LIFE

The furrows were dark against the green grass of the mountainside and glistened with dew that shimmered in the morning sun. Small, green buds were poking up from the rich earth and reaching their tendrils to lap up the sunshine and grow strong and tall.

Watching over them, Dorian turned the trouble over in his head. The expanded rows would be better than nothing, but if they had to account for failure and wildlife robbing them of their harvest, it wouldn't be enough.

He turned to survey the valley and, seeing nothing, returned to the mine while the sun continued rising. The others were up already and eating, and he joined them.

"What's the plan for today?" Yander asked as he joined them, making a plate for himself.

"You'll keep expanding the farm cave with Dozotaine." Food had risen to his primary concern again. The additional goats the migrants brought would help, once the doe gave birth, and they had a stock of golden moss built up but it wouldn't be enough.

The craft dwarves were easy, and he handed out their tasks. Dozotaine still looked to Mughan like all the migrants for approval. Dorian still hadn't figured out how to change that yet.

"I'll need some help," Yudoline said. "Their expanding the cave too fast for me to keep up."

"You've got the seeds?" Dorian asked.

"I've saved caveberry seeds and we can split the cave moss. That's all we have."

"Olgim, you'll work in the farm caves with Yudoline." The flora in the cavern sealed up behind the wall would yield more underground crops, but they weren't ready for that yet. He needed more time, but every day they lost was one more that they couldn't get back. "Is there enough to do?"

"Yes, sticks and stones, I've got too much to do already. I could use the help." Yudoline looked relieved. On more than one occasion he had happened upon her long after dinner working in the kitchen to brew the latest batch of her ale.

She needed the break, and with the migrants here he could finally get her some help. Without Skover life had been harder for Yudoline than the others, but the past was gone now and he had to focus on the future.

And that included a supply of food for them to eat. Dorian turned his attention to the other side of the table, where Yander and Emelda sat.

"Emelda, Glorithoid, you'll forage today. Gather as many plants as you can." Dorian was hoping Glorithoid's knowledge of plants would help with the food situation.

"We saw some edible plants on the trip up," Glorithoid said, after Mughan had given his approval. They could save the seeds to plant for next year, although they would have to expand the area for the farm.

It wouldn't help this year though.

"Good, gather what you can and note anything that might produce later in the season."

"And what about us?" Mughan asked. There were still four dwarves without assignments, Mughan the most prominent.

"Help Yudoline with the crops." Mughan frowned. He was probably looking for a better assignment, something with more effect, but Dorian was too worried about the state of the food supply to think of anything else. "We'll need to relocate the chickens and the goats. If you could find a place for them and lay it out we'll cobble something together."

"Fine." Mughan got up from the table, trying to be calm, but there was too much jerkiness in the way he stood up. He turned to the other migrants. "Finish up here and meet me outside the farm cave. We'll get right to work." The last comment was directed at Dorian, with a flash of his teeth to go along with it.

Clenching his teeth, Dorian watched them go. He tried to control his irritation, tamping down the actions he wanted to take against the dwarf. *Stubborn fool.*

"Everyone else finish up, we've got a long day ahead of us." Dorian got to his feet and walked out the door, dreading the tasks that lay before him.

Dorian hefted the training axe, staring down the handle and feeling its weight. Not too heavy in the front, but gave him plenty of heft to swing with.

"Not bad." He gave the axe a few test swings.

"Glad you approve. Here's the other one you asked for." Dorian took the outstretched weapon from Kimec. "Do you think he's ready?"

"Ready or not, he needs the training. Thank you Kimec." Kimec nodded, then returned to his work sawing down a large plank. More boxes would flow from his corner of the workshop, and barrels besides, to house the growing number of stone trinkets and potential foodstuffs.

Kragnak was working on a copper bar, drawing it out with steady blows that clinked over the roar of the furnace. The closer Dorian got the more he felt the heat kissing his cheeks, not unpleasant in the least.

"You're progressing I see." A partially completed cage was standing a few feet from the anvil, a skeleton that would be crossed with a lattice of copper to make it secure. Once he finished.

"I've been working it in." Kragnak stopped and wiped sweat from his forehead. "After I finish a weapon I give it more time." He crinkled his brow. "I'm not sure Dorian, it isn't turning out right."

Dorian reached out and grasped the partially completed cage. It was solid and didn't move when he shook it. "Seems to be coming along just fine. What do you have to worry about?"

"The cross bars are hard to work cold, and I'm not sure if I've joined them together right." Kragnak fidgeted. "What if it isn't good enough and whatever is supposed to be in there gets out?"

"Then we'll kill it with the weapons you've made." Dorian put his hand on Kragnak's drooping shoulder. "It's a cage Kragnak. It doesn't have to look pretty. It just has to work."

"It won't work."

"I've got an idea. Once it's done, we'll throw Barileth in there when he's sleeping. If he can't get out you've done a fine job." Kragnak sniffed, but then smiled. "Now get back to work, you have a lot more to finish up."

"I know. I've finished the rods," Kragnak mumbled. "I just need to put them together."

"Good." After one final pat, which stiffened Kragnak, Dorian turned. He looked back just before the door and after one final glance around the workshop Dorian walked out.

He took his time heading outside. Yander was waiting, pacing back and forth, and jumped when he spotted Dorian.

"There you are, I was worried you wouldn't come and you had changed your mind." He looked to Dorian with eager and expectant eyes.

"Take this." Dorian spun a training axe around and tossed it handle first to Yander. It flew through the air and into his waiting hands, which he then promptly dropped. After a scramble it was back in Yander's hands.

"Do I hold it like this?" Yander grabbed it with two hands, too far up on the handle. *From when he saw me holding mine.*

"Here." Dorian demonstrated the proper grip. "Farther down." Yander adjusted his hands.

"First lesson. Axe head, handle. You keep the handle, you give the enemy the head."

"Head. Enemy. Got it." Yander nodded, brows knit in concentration as he watched Dorian. He remembered that look. It was just like yesterday Xanther wore it holding his own training axe.

Fear for his son took hold of him. What was he doing now? Was he still alive? Would he remember me? Somehow teaching Yander felt like a betrayal to his memory. He should be with Xanther, not here.

It was his fault. He had wanted his wife back. What was he supposed to do in his sorrow?

"Dorian?" Yander's voice ripped him back to reality.

"What?"

"You were teaching me to fight, but then I lost you." Yander's eyes were opened wide and his axe was hanging down by his side. Dorian looked up into the sky to avoid his gaze.

"Hold the axe with both hands, make it a part of your body." Dorian ignored the look of concern, moving in closer to adjust Yander's grip. "Now, use the weight to strike. Lift up and come down. Like this." Dorian hefted his own axe, bringing it down in a deliberate arc.

Yander imitated him, if a bit shaky. "Good, only smoother. Don't fight it." He tried again. "Better." The months of mining had made that swing easy. "Just like swinging your pickaxe."

As Dorian worked Yander through the basics in the deepening evening he was impressed at how well the young dwarf took to it. *Not so young anymore.*

The sun cast a brilliant splash of red along the clouds, and Dorian wondered how long it would be until the attack.

Gentle clucking and soft calls of the goats echoed through the wide expanse of the newly expanded farm caves. Torches glittered and cast their light among the soft glow of the cave moss that was planted in patches along the ground.

Yudoline had done a good job staggering the moss. The plots closest to the entrance were filling up, and they shrunk as he walked down the cave to the other side where they were finishing up the last of the planting.

"Almost done?"

"With this section, yes." Yudoline straightened as Dorian approached, wiping her dirty hands on her apron. Olgim and Fimroul joined her for a break, only a few clumps of cave moss were left in the wheelbarrow. "We'll harvest what's ready when we finish."

"It's growing nicely."

"It's amazing what a few weeks of hard work will do for a farm, isn't it?" she asked, eyes sparkling.

"Let's hope it lasts." There was enough planted to feed more than double their number, if the full harvest came in. Always better to be over prepared than to not have enough.

"When we're done with this we'll fertilize— what's that?" Yudoline turned. Someone was shouting down the tunnels, and hard footsteps accompanied it.

Something was wrong. "Get your weapons," Dorian said, taking off for the entrance. *They weren't ready yet, the goblins had come too soon.*

He didn't wait to see if the others were following, but ran back to the dining hall where he was keeping his axe when he wasn't mining. As he got there, he made out Barileth yelling, coming from the workshops he thought.

"-arms, to arms. We're under attack." He rounded the corner and spotted Dorian, who had just come back into the hallway fully armed. "Coming from the south, I spotted them in the distance. We have a minute, or less, before they get here."

Dorian reached Barileth at a sprint. Yudoline and the others were following. "Get the others ready. How many?"

"Can't say for sure. More than I'd like to see." Dorian's heart was pounding now, and he was taking deep breaths, but he was alert and ready. They had reached the entrance to the mine when Barileth stopped him, pulling him back by the arm. "Dorian, I don't know how to say this, but they aren't goblins."

More dwarves had piled up along the entrance tunnel. Some looked determined and ready for a fight, but more were hesitant and nervous holding unfamiliar weapons in their hands. Dorian cursed himself for not preparing them better, but it was too late now to worry about that.

"If they aren't goblins, what are they?" Dorian whispered.

"You'll have to see for yourself." Barileth shifted his lopsided sword to his left hand and pushed open the door.

"For the defense of the mine," Dorian said. He had hoped it would be better, but hearing it come out of his mouth made him cringe inside. To make up for his embarrassment he charged out into the light.

Inside the wall was empty once he had blinked away the blinding light of the sun. He squinted, scanning the edge of the trees through the open gate as he ran to it, following Barileth.

He had to stop as Barileth pulled up short. A few seconds later, and with everyone else crowding into the courtyard behind the wall, he found what he was looking for and pointed. "There."

Something was moving in the trees farther down the mountainside, bleach white against the dark brown bark of the trees. The rattling drifted from them, and Dorian gaped.

"Are those...skeletons?" Mughan asked, shoving himself forward through the crowd. Dorian couldn't help but notice he had taken one of the better swords.

They were coming toward them, shambling skeletons armed with rusted and old weapons that glinted in the sun. Deep red balls of light burned where their eyes should have been and their mouths hung open, gaping black holes of death.

Someone screamed behind him, there was a thud that followed. "Over there," Kragnak shouted.

Coming up the mountain, with the skeletons in pursuit, Glorithoid ran with a limp and holding his shoulder. The skeletons were gaining on him and he looked exhausted. "They're going to kill him if we don't do anything!"

8

UNDEAD

Dorian didn't hesitate, but swung the axe to his hip and started out a run. Everything disappeared except Glorithoid ahead of him and the undead behind.

He had a faint awareness of others following, but they faded into the background of breathing. Glorithoid was pale and stumbled less than a dozen feet from him.

The skeletons got to him and raised their rusty swords to kill him. Dorian surged ahead, swinging his axe with a mighty roar, and crashed into the leader.

Bones crunched and shattered, and the axe continued with little resistance. Dorian's eyes opened wide and he nearly lost his footing as momentum carried him forward.

An axe wielding skeleton seized advantage of his surprise, taking a swing at him. He struggled to recover his footing, but it was too late.

Dorian dropped down and rolled under the swing. The air from the axe ruffled his hair.

The ground came up to meet him and he tucked his shoulder, cradling his axe, and rolled. The move brought him awkwardly to his feet.

Just in time to meet another spear wielding skeleton face to face. Red eyes burned into his, and he was afraid.

Shifting his grip, he hacked at it before it could move. His axe tore the shaft of the spear in two and continued through the skeleton, severing its spine right above the legs.

While he was preoccupied, two others attacked before the torso of the first could hit the ground. Dorian chopped at one to his left and countered the sword wing of the other at his right with the handle.

"Behind you!" Dorian turned at Barileth's warning, just in time to see the axe wielding skeleton attack again. It would have cleaved him down the middle, but with the warning he had time to side step it and bring his own axe up.

It smashed through the jaw and lodged in the skull of the skeleton with a sickening crunch, teeth tinkling along the blade as they fell. The light left the eyes, fading first to pink then to nothing.

Something grabbed his foot as he spun to face the remaining skeletons, but the nearest was still a few feet away. Only when he looked down did he see what it was.

The torso of the skeleton was clutching at his foot, rooting him in place. The other skeletons were rushing him.

Unfortunately, the skeleton had grabbed his other leg too, and its grip was strong. Dorian tried to pull free, but couldn't. He batted a sword away and ducked under a spear thrust aimed at his head.

If he didn't move now, they would cut him down.

"The head, go for the head," Dorian said, desperate to fend off blows. A sword broke through his defenses and scraped past his arm, he managed to bash the offending skeleton with a good blow to the head as punishment but felt something wet and warm flow down his arm.

The shock of it brought back his hearing. Besides the rattling beside him he heard Barileth's war cry and the clash of metal on metal.

Something flew by him, almost knocking him over, and after parrying another spear Dorian had a chance to see Barileth with his sword buried hilt deep in the half skeleton clutching his legs.

The fingers released him, and Dorian kicked his legs free. Now that he could move again he went on the offensive.

He swung his axe in powerful blows, loping off arms, legs, and heads. Barileth was at his side as they waded through the skeletons, extinguishing their burning red eyes.

And then, suddenly, there were no more.

Dorian whirled around, looking for more danger, but all that was left of the enemy was a collection of bones. His tunnel vision gone now, Dorian saw the look of horror on the migrant's faces.

Then, the pain caught up to him. A lance of it struck his left arm and he had to look. A flap of skin from the sword swing was letting out blood, and when he moved it gushed out.

"Get me a cloth, something. You." He pointed to Kragnak, who was farther back. Kragnak jumped, startled by the authority in his voice, and fled up the mountain.

Exasperated, Dorian tore a strip off his shirt as he directed the others. "Get him up the hill and be careful of that leg. Can he speak?"

"I can," Glorithoid said.

"Then speak." Barileth helped him, tying the strip around his arm tightly, sending a spasm of pain when he tightened it. Once it was tied the bleeding stopped.

"They caught us by surprise, I didn't know what it was." Yutatir and Kuddick put Glorithoid's arms over their shoulders and lifted him off his leg. A wash of pain ran over his face when they moved his leg.

"What do you mean us?" Yander asked, then his eyes opened wide. "Emelda." The look of shock made Dorian's heart fall. He waved Barileth away. Despite the adrenaline in his veins running like water he had to be level-headed.

"Don't jump to conclusions," Dorian warned.

"They took her," Glorithoid said. "They were going to take me but I ran. Damned skeleton took me in the leg with a spear when I was almost here too." Perspiration welled up on his forehead and he was looking pale.

"Where did they take her?" Dorian asked, keeping an eye on Yander. He hadn't said anything else yet and still had a dazed look in his eye. He would recover soon, and Dorian knew what was about to happen. Cooler heads had to prevail.

He took a deep breath of his own, slowing his pounding heart, and wiped the sweat from his face.

"South east, I think." Glorithoid wasn't doing well. "They went for her first. There wasn't anything I could do."

"Take him inside and let him recover. Yudoline will know what to do." The sun was still high in the sky, they had a few hours to sunset still.

"What are we going to do?" Mughan asked. He had grabbed a spear and was clutching it in his hands, watching Dorian carefully.

"Go and get her, we have to go and get her." Yander's dazed look was gone, replaced with a tight mouth and furrowed brow. "We need to leave now."

When Dorian didn't say anything Yander turned to look at him. "We could go after her," Dorian said before Yander could open his mouth.

"Could? We could go after her?" Yander's mouth gaped. "You mean we will go after her."

"They aren't the sneakiest of creatures," Barileth said. He had wandered to the trail the skeletons had left and was fingering a broken stalk of grass. Crouching down he traced something.

"Do you think you could track them?" Dorian asked.

"If you leave the mine will be completely unguarded. What if they come back?" Mughan broke in. "We'll be completely defenseless."

"Not quite defenseless," Dorian said.

Mughan bristled. "You can't take us away and expect everything to be fine." He had a point. So, what was he supposed to do? Yander was getting more agitated, and likely would every minute they waited.

Most of the dwarves were with him, with the exception of the group that was taking care of Glorithoid. The sun was fat and yellow in a cloudless sky, barely a breeze blew to cool them. "Let me know your thoughts about it."

"We need to leave now. I have to get her back," Yander said. It was what Dorian expected, and a twinge of guilt came with it. She hadn't pleaded to keep herself safe, but it felt like he broke a promise anyhow.

"That's a foolish idea. Here we have a wall we can defend, and a place to retreat to that our enemies can't follow." Mughan crossed his arms and looked around to the migrants that surrounded him.

"Don't listen to him," Yander said, voice full of anger.

"Hold Yander, let him speak." Dorian put a hand on his shoulder to comfort him, but he twisted away.

"I can follow them," Barileth said. "Even in the night. I say the sooner we leave the better. Besides," he smiled wickedly and played his fingers along his sword blade, "I didn't get a chance to whet my appetite for bones.""

"She's one of us," Lumdir said. "We can't leave her to die."

"Didn't you see those things? She's probably long dead by now," Olgim said. "Mughan's right, we should prepare here."

"Prepare for what?" Kimec asked. "If we go out and kill them, we won't have to prepare."

"You don't think there are more of them?"

"Why would there be?" Dorian wasn't as sure as Kimec was, remembering the traps he had discovered the first year. Now this. Something was out there, and it was powerful to be able to project this kind of magic.

"Walking skeletons don't seem unusual to you?" Mughan asked. "Something evil had to raise these from the dead. Something powerful had to send them here."

"If we keep babbling like this we'll never find her." Yander paced back and forth. "I'll leave myself." The young dwarf would do it too, if Dorian didn't do anything.

"Who would be willing to go on a rescue party?" he asked. All of the founders present raised their weapons, gleaming a pretty orange. A few seconds later Dozotaine and Olgim raised theirs too. Mughan glared at them.

"She was kind. Always treated me nice." Olgim wilted under the gaze.

"I can't stomach leaving her to die," Dozotaine said, standing strong.

"We would travel light," Dorian warned. "And we don't know what we're up against. There could be too many for us to handle and I want you to know the risks."

How could he be thinking about risking half the mine for this? Even if most of them did survive they would be decimated and probably wouldn't last the year.

"We know," Barileth said. "Better get on with it though."

"This isn't a good idea," Mughan said. "You're responsible for all of us, not just one dwarf." He voiced the argument Dorian was having inside. His children were depending on him to finish this. So was his wife.

"And would you like us to leave you to die, if it was you instead of Emelda?" Yander's eyes were shining with a blazing light.

"I would have the good sense to know my fate and accept it," Mughan said, too defensively. His hand went to the spear, and Yander started to raise his axe.

"Steady now," Barileth said, grabbing Yander from behind to restrain him. Dorian stepped between them both. Mughan, although angry, had retained his composure.

A nervous shift ran through the group. Several dwarves stepped back, and others fidgeted and looked between them.

Mughan turned to Dorian. "Make up your mind then. Do you risk our lives for one? Or are you going to be a leader and keep us safe?"

Now all eyes turned on him. This test would not be easy to pass. Dorian looked back up the mountain and the rough walls of granite that protected the mine.

They had worked so hard to bring it to life and to make it work. All those months of effort, of sweat and blood and tears. The dwarves that lost their lives, the others that gave up theirs.

And now he had 17 souls relying on him to keep it alive, to keep it going. He looked back to where the skeletons had come.

Emelda was out there, captured by an invisible foe. What would he want done if it were him? And did it even matter what he thought?

What duty did he have to the others? What did he owe them? Mughan could make all the demands he wanted, and he had a point, but didn't the mine mean more than the rock and the earth it was carved from?

"You're right," Dorian said. Mughan started to smile. "I do have a duty to the dwarves that have given up so much to come here. What kind of dwarf would I be to let them die?

He turned away from his shocked face, back to Yander. "We're going after her." Relief flooded into Yander's eyes, and Dorian felt the weight of his decision. "We're going to save Emelda."

9

A Choice

"If you're going I can't blame you, but I'm not about to join you on this foolish adventure." Mughan's eyes were slits and his mouth tight beneath his beard.

Dorian took a gamble. "You'll be in charge of the defenses then. Lumdir, Yander, go get supplies for the journey. Just enough food for a day and waterskins for the seven of us."

Yander nodded, his eyes watering up, and sprinted away. Lumdir followed, but at a slower pace.

"You don't expect any other attacks, do you?" Kimec asked, brows furrowed with concern. The ones that hadn't volunteered appeared to share his reticence.

"Expect any?" He hadn't expected the first one, or the thieves. Now, he wasn't sure. But there were a lot of eyes on him, and they needed answers. "No, I don't."

"Yet the possibility still exists, doesn't it?"

"We're still going. Anyone who volunteers can get ready, we'll leave as soon as Yander gets back." Dorian tried to do his best to ignore Mughan.

"You never answered my question. What are we going to do here while you're gone?" Mughan raised his voice, forcing Dorian to address him.

"We'll have plenty of weapons that you can use to defend yourself." Dorian turned to stare down Mughan, who refused to back down. "And the traps in the entrance tunnel. They're more than enough to stop any enemy that decides to try and attack."

"You know that's not true. What if there are more than the traps can handle? We'll be defenseless."

"He has a point," Barileth said. Dorian didn't expect him to take Mughan's side. He looked back to the mine, thinking.

"Then we decide to lock down the mine. Take everyone inside while we're out and lock the gate and doors. Don't open it until we give you a signal. Three loud knocks followed by us scraping the door with a blade and then three more knocks."

"That assumes you come back, what happens if you don't?" Mughan asked.

"We'll come back. And we'll have Emelda too." Inside Dorian wasn't as sure, but he tried projected confidence as best as he could. It seemed to partially mollify the others, but Mughan wasn't buying it.

"You'd better leave us the new weapons then. The old ones aren't good enough to repel an attack."

"Keep what you have, they will do."

Mughan turned to the others. "I tried to keep us safe, remember that. If anyone is foolish enough to go with him then be my guest." Dozotaine shifted, but didn't leave the group of volunteers. The wind rustled the leaves in the trees.

Dorian turned to look back down the valley, following the path the skeletons had laid out for them. What would wait for them when they came to the end? "I can't promise the safety of any dwarf who comes with me, nor can I guarantee the safety of those who stay. You all knew the risks when you came out here willingly."

Mughan had turned back to look at him, a strange look in his eye. The others were watching him too. "There is only one dwarf here against his will. Whatever desires you came here with," Dorian watched Mughan carefully, "or troubles you were running away from doesn't matter to me." He thought he perceived the slightest widening of the dwarf's eyes. Is my mind playing tricks on me?

Without a word Mughan turned and stomped up the mountain back to the mine. The migrants who hadn't volunteered followed him at a slower pace, turning to glance back at their group from time to time.

"That one's trouble," Barileth whispered in his ear. "Give me the word and we can have a happy accident in the mineshaft."

It was more than tempting. Dorian still roiled with anger, both at himself for allowing Emelda to be captured and {Glorithoid to be hurt, and at Mughan for his constant undermining. "We stay together, whether we like it or not. Alive. We have more than enough enemies to fend off without hurting ourselves."

Barileth shrugged. "Suit yourself." As the migrants entered the gate, Yander and Olgim returned, carrying bundles under each arm and slung with waterskins.

"Take what you can carry," Dorian said. They distributed the bundles of food. Dorian took one, Kragnak and Dozotaine the other, while Yander kept one for himself. "Follow them."

"Hope you can keep up," Barileth said. He took off at a trot, not bothering to check where the tracks were. Even Dorian could see where they went. Together they set off down the mountain.

The tracks led down the mountain northeast for a while, then turned east to follow the slope of the valley. Farther to the east, another peak of the Tremble range towered over them. The sparse trees on the mountainside turned thicker here, and more wildlife roamed beneath their branches.

"We aren't going south?" Yander asked when Barileth turned them.

"No, the tracks lead east."

"But Glorithoid said they came from the southwest."

"He did," Dorian said. "They had come out this far to forage." He didn't realize they had been so far from the safety of the walls. A better dwarf would have warned them to not go this far. He didn't.

"Up ahead," Lumdir said, pointing to a break in the underbrush. A basket lay at the edge, berries spilling out of it. They stopped in the clearing. Branches were broken and the grass was churned up.

"This is where they attacked," Barileth said, picking up a berry and popping it in his mouth. "The trail turns south here." He took off without another word, and the group followed him.

It looked like they had put up a fight, some of Glorithoid's blood had been spilled onto the undergrowth as he fled. Yander was running, a look of determination on his face. Dorian had to look away.

He wasn't far enough along in his training for this. Dorian wasn't sure he would be able to defend himself if they came upon the enemy. *Don't even think* if. *We'll find them.*

And what would they do once they did? An oppressive silence hung between them as they followed the tracks, only punctuated by the heavy breathing of the dwarves as they strove on. They would need rest soon.

The skeletons had taken a meandering path, almost like they were looking for something. They doubled back a few times until the trail finally led south through a gap in the mountain pass.

As they climbed, Dorian worried about Emelda and how close the skeletons had been to the mine. If they would have turned west right after going over the pass they would have been at the wall within an hour.

"Keep going, up ahead," Barileth said. He dropped back as he let Yander take the lead, the trees were gone this high and they only had to crest the range and pick up the trail again on the other side. "Do you see it?" he whispered when he was at Dorian's side.

Dorian shook his head. "They were too close. I'm surprised they didn't find us sooner." He had a feeling lingering at the back of his neck, like someone or something was watching them. It drew his gaze upward where he scanned the sky.

"What do you see?"

A few clouds, blue sky. Nothing flying in it, making lazy arcs and tracking their progress. "Nothing, let's keep moving."

Barileth looked at him as if he was about to say something, then nodded and worked his way to the front as they crested the mountain range. The trail spit them out onto the other side, with a view of the valley stretching out below them. Zirad was behind them now.

In a few minutes they were at the timberline again and small, scraggly trees gave way to larger pines. Dorian was glad to be back under cover of the forest. The openness of the treeless mountainside was discomforting after living so long underground.

"The trail is turning southwest." Barileth had bent down to examine the ground. There were less signs here, and it looked like he was having more trouble tracking them.

"What are they doing?" Kimec asked. Barileth shrugged and took off at a trot.

"Could be slowing down, or maybe they've changed something. I can't tell for sure." There was little undergrowth in the forest, the canopy of the pine trees was too tight. The smell was thick in the air and not unpleasant.

"Keep going, we can't lose them," Yander urged. He still had the look in his eye of fear and anger, and his body was tense. He was the only one who didn't look tired from their fast pace.

If we stop now, will we catch them? Dorian's own legs were aching, screaming at him to slow down or stop. The running was taking its toll. It was hard to see the sun through the leaves and he wondered how long it had been.

Dozotaine stumbled and caught himself, but that was his sign. "We'll stop here, rest for a few minutes." Dorian kept a close eye on Dozotaine. He was sweating more than the others. "Barileth, can you scout ahead? Take your time and rest as you need it."

"We can't stop now!" Yander was near the front of the group. The others had stopped at Dorian's command and he was pacing ahead of them. Dorian caught up to him, shed his load, and took him by the arm to lead him away from the others, who were slumping down to the ground.

"Look at them," Dorian said when they had gone far enough away to not be heard. Yander looked. They were panting, slurping down water as they leaned up against trees or lay on the ground. "What good will we be if we catch them and can't fight because we're too tired?"

Yander dropped his gaze and his shoulders slumped. "None," he mumbled. Dorian put a hand on his shoulder and squeezed.

"I know this is hard for you. Whoever did this, I'd like to take my axe to them." Just thinking of it made his blood boil. "But don't give up hope." Yander looked back up and met his gaze. He nodded. "Now, get some rest with the others."

As he walked back Dorian was left to wonder if he was doing the right thing. The weight of responsibility for her loss hung on his shoulders, and he was glad when Barileth disturbed him as he came back.

"Going slower, I think." Barileth took a swig from his waterskin, which brought his own thirst into focus. "If we can keep up this pace we might be able to catch them."

Mouth dry, Dorian unstopped his own water and let the lukewarm liquid flow into his mouth. It washed the dirt away and he spat it out. The next drink spread warmth all through his stomach. "Any idea how far ahead they are?"

Barileth shook his head. The others had recovered somewhat from the rest. "Can you keep going?" Dorian asked.

"You can't stop me."

"On your feet, let's move." Yander was the first to respond to his call, jumping up and urging the others on. They returned to the chase, a little worn for wear.

The trail continued south west, now a steady line that only changed to go around rocks and obstacles. Light faded in the forest, then disappeared. They kept going at a steady run, and Dorian was thankful for the years of cave life as his eyes quickly adapted.

Moonlight filtered down through the trees as they started to spread out, the forest thinning. There was no conversation now, only determined breathing as the chase took its toll.

His own feet felt like lead now, but he kept put one in front of the other. Calls of the night creatures surrounded them and he wasn't sure if they were cheering them on or making fun of them.

With the moon bright, they were able to see the tracks of the skeletons well enough to follow. Barileth led them on, until he pulled short and signaled for them to stop.

"What is it?" Yander asked as the others took the time to collapse and rest. The water was gone. Barileth motioned for him to be quiet.

Dorian looked up ahead in the night, staring intensely as he listened.

Then he heard it. A strange mixture of emotions rose in side him and he readied himself.

It was the rattle of bones, faint but distinct.

10

AMBUSH

Dorian nodded when Barileth looked back, who slipped away into the night ahead. Yander gripped his axe handle and brought it to bear, but Dorian held him back.

"Wait for Barileth," he whispered. Yander looked like he was going to take a step forward, but nodded. "Eat what you can now," he told the others.

Now that they were still, the sound was more obvious, but it was growing faint. Dorian choked down a half a loaf of rockbread and some goat cheese by the time Barileth slipped back into camp.

"It's them."

"How many?"

"Dozens, I think. It's hard to tell."

"Is Emelda there?" Yander asked, eyes wide in the moonlight.

Barileth nodded. "She's unharmed, as far as I can tell. They're carrying her like a dead hog, though."

"Any idea why they slowed down?" Dozotaine asked.

"No."

"Still headed in the same direction?" Dorian asked.

"Yes, no change. I think we can sneak around them, get ahead of them, and then surprise them." Dorian turned and scanned the terrain ahead of them.

They were still on the slope of the mountain as it made a wide descent down to the plains below. Rocky outcroppings were scattered few and far between, but the natural changes in the terrain might be useful.

"Over there," Dorian said, pointing to a small hillock with trees farther down. Judging from the gap in the trees it would be open terrain. "We'll set up an ambush there, but we need to be quick."

He started off at a brisk jog, and the others followed. Instead of going downhill Dorian looped them around uphill to try and cut them off. "How are we going to do this?" Lumdir asked in between breaths.

That wasn't something Dorian had thought about. He assumed once they got there it would be clearer. "We'll attack on my command."

"Are we all going to be above or should we have another group below them to the south?" Barileth asked. He wasn't nearly as winded as the others and looked ready for the fight. "If so, can I be there?"

Dorian thought about it while they ran. Two attacks would be more confusing to the skeletons, and wouldn't give them time to group and form a defensive position. He was glad Barileth was there.

"Yes, we'll split up. Quiet now." The rattling had grown louder as they approached. He estimated they were the closest they were going to be in a few yards. The dwarves gripped their loads and weapons, stopping them from clanging and giving them away.

On they ran in silence, until they came to the base of the hill. Dorian motioned for them to stop, and more than one dwarf collapsed in exhaustion. He listened carefully to the distant sound of the approaching enemy.

"Still sounds like the right place," Barileth said. He ran a hand along his blade greedily. Yander was right there beside him, straining at the place where they would emerge from the break in the trees.

"Barileth, you take Dozotaine and Lumdir. Everyone else with me." He grabbed Barileth's arm before he could go too far. "You'll know when the attack starts. Good hunting." Barileth smiled and clasped Dorian's arm.

"Break them like rock." They were gone in an instant, blending into the night and the underbrush of the trees on the other side of the clearing. Dorian took the others up into the forest, about twenty feet away, and they took up hiding positions.

He dropped his food and calmly unhooked his axe. "Yander, with me." He beckoned him over.

Yander came, watching the trees as he did, until he crouched down beside Dorian. The moon was almost full and bright, washing the gently swaying grass in a pale white light. "Stay safe tonight, don't do anything rash."

"I'll make them pay." Dorian knew only a small part of what he was feeling. He grabbed his arm, catching Yander by surprise.

"Find Emelda, kill the ones who have her." Yander nodded. He released him and together they turned their attention back to the forest.

The skeletons weren't quiet, but Dorian thought they could be mistaken for the rattling of sticks if you weren't paying attention. The sound grew louder as they approached, but the glowing red of their eyes was what he saw first.

Dorian tightened his grip on his axe. *I haven't given her a name yet.* Taking a deep breath of the crisp mountain air, he thought it would be a good night to do it. *Bonesplitter.* It felt right, and he ran a finger along its razor-sharp edge. She would have plenty to do tonight.

The anticipation of the fight ran through him, a strange buzz that heightened his senses and narrowed them all at once. The stones leaked warmth to him beneath his feet. It was almost like they were lending him strength.

The lead skeleton entered the clearing. "Ready," Dorian whispered. His heart was pounding now, and he felt Yander's anticipation next to him. When the dwarf stiffened, he laid his hand on his back. "I see her too."

A skeleton in the center of the group had her slung over its shoulder, and her head and hands hung limp behind it. *No, it can't be.* He swallowed the fear and tried to ignore it. She could be sleeping, or unconscious. Anything but that.

Licking his lips to re-wet his dry mouth, Dorian whispered in Yander's ear. "Wait for my signal. We have to catch them by surprise." The taste of the dust of their chase lingered on his lips. The skeletons had come within a hundred feet of them now.

Dorian waited until they were almost to them, then he waited some more. Every muscle in his body screamed at him, ready to attack now, but he resisted the urge. Only when the skeleton carrying Emelda passed their tree did he stand up and run down the hill.

"For Seventh Hall and vengeance!" Yander was right beside him, screaming in rage, and they closed the distance before the skeletons knew what was going on. Right before Dorian got to them he heard Barileth's guttural yell, and then the world erupted into chaos.

His first blow took a skeleton apart from the midsection, and he reversed his swing to take out the one next to it before the others could react. Then, the skeletons recovered and counterattacked, three at once.

Dorian parried one blow, dodged the other, but the last was too fast for him to avoid completely. A sword caught his arm, but he shrugged it away.

With all his strength he brought his axe up on the offending skeleton and cleaved it in two. Before the two halves he was already bringing his axe down on another, only to get it stuck in its skull.

Great. Panting and heavy from the exertion, Dorian ducked down to avoid a spear, then wrenched his axe free. He took a second to search for the skeleton carrying Emelda, who he had lost track of, but was forced back from an attack.

The red eyes left glowing afterimages in his sight as the skeleton attacked with its own axe. Steel rang on rusty steel as Dorian blocked it and swung a counterattack, but the skeleton was too fast and stepped back in time to avoid the blow.

Moonlight reflected off the white bone, half its ribcage had been broken and chewed up by time, and its jaw hung loose off of one side. The gruesome sight stopped Dorian for a moment.

"Dorian!" The warning was too late. Something smashed into his right arm, and he fell sideways. Another skeleton had attacked him from his blind side.

While he was on the ground his opponent seized the opportunity to attack. He saw the flash of the sword above him and rolled, ignoring the sudden pain along his arm. The sword sank into the earth his head had occupied seconds ago.

Acutely aware of the danger he was in Dorian scrambled to his feet. His surprise attacker was swinging a war hammer at him, but this time he was prepared. After ducking the blow he fueled his anger into a swing that smashed the skeleton apart.

Turning back to his original opponent, who was advancing with a swing of his sword, Dorian caught a glance of Yander fighting his way forward.

The young dwarf was clumsy, but determined. He was wielding his axe like a pickaxe, smashing through the chest of a skeleton.

Dorian parried the sword and attacked. His wounds were slowing him down though, and his axe only caught a piece of the skeleton's arm.

It jabbed forward with the pointed edge of its newly severed arm bone, almost catching Dorian in the eye. Bringing his axe low Dorian swept the legs from the skeleton, sending it crashing to the ground, and followed up with a crushing blow to the skull that ended its existence.

Yander had reached the center skeleton as Dorian took out another. He was going too fast and crashed into the fiend. All three fell to the ground and were lost in the confusion.

A scream of pain to his right drew his attention. Lumdir was clutching a spear in his leg with a skeleton advancing on him. It wrapped its bony fingers around Lumdir's throat, and he started to turn blue, scratching at the bones and trying to get a grip.

Dorian charged forward, hoping he would get there in time. He swung and decapitated the skeleton, and Lumdir took in a huge gasp of air.

And then it was over.

Dorian staggered as the moment of respite brought all his senses back. Pain lanced in his arm and from cuts all along his body. Blood poured out of Lumdir's leg as he grabbed it and pulled, causing Lumdir to grunt in pain.

From his shirt Dorian ripped a strip of cloth and pressed it against the wound, stopping the flow of blood. "Hold that there."

He turned back to the battlefield, strewn with corpses. Several skeletons were still moving, trying to get to weapons or to the nearest dwarf to attack. Barileth was moving among them calmly, smashing them with a large rock he had found.

The moon was hidden behind the clouds, bringing even more darkness to the scene. All the other dwarves were on their feet, but he only counted four figures moving.

Dorian searched among the bodies. Yander was with Emelda, cradling her in his arms and talking to her. The others were wounded as well, but most of them look superficial. He was afraid to look at Emelda.

"Please come back to me. I don't want to be alone in the world, I couldn't bear to lose you so soon." He caressed her face, brushing the hair back from her face where it had fallen. "Wake up Emelda, wake up."

It had come to this. All their effort was for nothing. Ignoring his pain, and ending the second life of a skeleton next to him, Dorian went to them. He leaned down into the cool grass, sinking next to Yander.

He didn't say anything. Yander was still talking in whispers and wipers. There was nothing Dorian could do or say to make it any better.

Why hadn't he stopped this from happening? Why hadn't he taken the signs seriously? There was a necromancer out here, and he was watching them. Dorian squeezed his eyes shut.

He never wanted to be in charge of this expedition, had resigned himself to his punishment long ago. It was a cruel fate to be given a second chance only to have it snatched away from him in the very manner that he had lost his freedom in the first place.

Then Emelda groaned. Dorian's eyes shot open, and relief flooded through him.

She was alive!

"Yander, Dorian?"

"I'm here," Yander said. The fog of sadness lifted from the other dwarves who had gathered around them.

"Where am I?"

"In the land of the living, surrounded by the dead," Barileth said.

"I knew you'd come for me," she said, touching Yander's face and stroking his beard. He kissed her in his joy.

"To the end of the world," Yander said. She wiped his cheeks and together they rose.

"Good to have you back," Dorian said, choking out the words. Why was he feeling so emotional?

"We didn't know what they were at first, that's how they surprised us." Dorian held up a hand.

"It wasn't your fault. I shouldn't have sent you that far out." Taking her hand in his, it was ice cold, he looked deep into her eyes. "They won't take you ever again."

11

Moonlight in the Mountains

Surrounded by the decaying remains of the skeleton raiding party, the dwarves gathered in the moonlight.

"How does it feel?" Dorian asked. Lumdir grimaced as he put his weight on his leg. He hobbled a few steps with help, then tried to walk on his own.

"Not good." He would have to be helped back. Emelda was able to stand, a thankful blessing. Other than bruises and bad memories she would recover.

"Barileth, Dozotaine, help Lumdir." A cold chill ran through him as he visualized the bones around him coming back together and back to life. "We need to make it back to Zirad before sunup."

"What happens at sunup?" Yander asked. He was holding Emelda's hands tight.

"Things can see better."

"We're in Guzan now. It isn't the friendliest to dwarves from Zirad visiting," Barileth said, hiking Lumdir's arm over his shoulder. They started north. "Who knows how they would take an armed band of us bloodied and exhausted."

"We could explain what we were doing," Yander said. Barileth snorted.

"You'd think they'd buy that we were chasing undead skeletons that had kidnapped one of our own from a mining expedition dangerously close to their border?"

"Better to not have to explain," Dorian said.

"How could they not believe the truth?" Yander muttered. Emelda whispered something in his ear, but he still looked troubled.

Dorian was glad to leave the grisly scene behind. They were slow, and the speed of advance was agonizing. At this rate they might not make it to the pass before day.

But there wasn't anything he could do about it now. What's done was done. He kept thinking about how it never should have happened. He wasn't prepared, too focused on other things.

They rotated dwarves, carrying Lumdir, who seemed to get progressively worse. The bandage that Dorian applied was getting saturated with blood. *We need to stop to rest.*

Lumdir never said a word of complaint and kept going, gritting his teeth as he hobbled along on one foot with support. So they walked on as the sky lightened, finally leaving the forest as the sun rose to the east.

Every few steps Dorian cast a worried glance behind them, expecting to see a random human to raise the alarm. Instead, he saw a peaceful forest devoid of watchers.

"We should cover our tracks," Barileth said as they approached the top of the mountain. Lumdir was fading and needed to stop, but they were too close now.

Dorian nodded. "Go." Barileth ran back, grabbing a branch and sweeping away the tracks behind them. He finished as they entered the pass, the sun over an hour higher in the sky.

As Guzan slipped out of view, Dorian breathed a sigh of relief. The entire party relaxed, the atmosphere of tension among them slipping away. They were back. All of them.

"Good riddance." Barileth threw down his branch, tucking it behind a rock.

"We're safe," Yander said.

"For now," Dorian said, still chewing on the troubling re-emergence of the dead. "We'll rest up ahead in the forest." It was only a few hundred feet away now, and the cover would hide them better.

"We need to do something about these weapons," Dozotaine said as they eased Lumdir down to lean against a tree.

"What do you mean?" Dorian furrowed his brows. Dozotaine held up his sword. The copper was dented along the edge, the previously sharp cutting blade reduced to a hunk of dull metal.

"The bones were too hard. It turned into a club after my first strike." Dorian took it, examining the edge in a slice of light that filtered down from the leaves. It was unusable.

"Mine too," Barileth said, throwing down his axe. It was flattened and might as well have been a hammer. The others were similar, the soft metal damaged by the battle.

His own axe was fine, both blades still sharp despite its heavy use. "This isn't good."

"That's an understatement," Barileth said. "It's the copper. Give me solid iron at least, that would hold an edge."

He was right, and Dorian knew it. "We'll worry about it when we get back. Speaking of." He got back to his feet. "Time to move."

Iron would be good and steel better. Neither of which they had. Another trouble to add to his pile. Dorian wiped his face. While the others carried Lumdir, he carried an additional burden.

It was almost noon by the time they made it back, the granite walls a welcoming sight. When they trudged up to its gate the others collapsed near, trying to get some shade from the now blistering sun.

Dorian knocked the code, using Barileth's dulled axe so that the sound would be loud enough inside to hear. It was quiet as they waited, the others struggling to keep awake.

They had been up for over a day now, traveled miles under pressure, and had fought a battle. Everyone was exhausted, Dorian included. All he wanted was a quick, hot meal, some water, and to crawl into his bed and fall asleep.

"Did they hear?" Kimec asked.

"I'll try again." Dorian picked the axe up, but then he heard something. It sounded like the mine entrance door. "Stand back."

The others moved away from the gate at his warning. Mughan appeared on the wall.

"You made it."

"Surprised we're still alive?" Barileth asked, more than a hint of anger in his voice.

"Somewhat." Mughan turned back behind him. "Open it up."

With a creak and a rumble, the gate rose. The opening welcomed the returning party, and they trudged through.

Mughan followed, coming down quickly from his perch to meet them before they got to the entrance. "What happened? You all look worse for wear." He eyed Lumdir. "I'm surprised you all came back at all."

Before he could help himself Dorian spun on his heel, got into Mughan's face, who stepped back. "Don't let me see you for the next few hours."

His eyes widened at the sharpness of his voice. Dorian didn't wait to for Mughan to respond, but turned when Barileth put a hand on his shoulder and stalked into the mine, slamming the door open.

Inside the familiar musty and cool space he struggled to control himself. *Calm, Dorian. What will the others think?*

"Give him some space," Barileth said behind him, and the others didn't follow right away. Dorian leaned his head against the granite support next to him, feeling how solid it was and the integrity of the stone.

He wanted to break something, to rage and rampage against the world and his own folly. Instead, he took a deep breath, let his eyes adjust, and headed for the kitchens.

They were empty when he got there, the fire burning low in the fireplace. It was almost reduced to red-hot coals, just a few tongues of flame licking the already burned logs. He added two logs and took a few loaves of rockbread, cheese, and a hunk of salted deer.

He took it to the dining hall, meeting the rest of his group along the way. Silently they entered, divided the food, and ate.

Yudoline rushed in a few moments later, followed by the rest of the expedition trickling in ones and twos. She ran over to Kimec, examined him head to foot, then embraced him.

"I'm home," Kimec said.

"And worse for wear. What happened out there?" Before anyone could answer, she exclaimed, "Lumdir!"

"Aye." He was leaning back in his chair, far enough from the table for everyone to see his injury and not trying to hide it.

"Your leg is bleeding." She was so matter of fact the entire room burst into laughter, even Dorian.

When the laughter had subsided, Yudoline was already treating Lumdir, after shooting a dangerous glance at her husband and Dorian. It was too late though, the laughter had dispelled her anger.

"We're lucky to be back at all," Kimec said. Dorian wolfed down his food, surprised at how famished he was and grateful for something to eat. There would be time to think about things when he wasn't as tired.

Yudoline was talking and asking questions as she treated Lumdir's wound, but it was all a blur to Dorian. The others were eating just as fast, as Mughan watched them with a searching gaze.

Look all he wants, I'll deal with him later. Dorian finished his food, pushed his plate away, and made sure that everyone else was getting their fill. They trickled out as they finished, and like a line of ants, they marched to their rooms and into their beds.

Yander and Emelda were the last to leave before Dorian, hand in hand slipping into the apartment they shared, a glimpse of the bed Kimec had made as a wedding present, and then he was past them.

His bed welcomed him as he dropped into it. Thoughts raced through his mind, but they slipped away into darkness as he slept.

"You can't think of any way to strengthen the copper?" Dorian wiped the trickle of sweat from his cheek that had gathered from the heat of the forge.

"All we have is silver and copper. Adding the silver back in won't help, but I'll try." Kragnak left it unsaid.

"I know," Dorian growled. It had to be down here, somewhere. After a week of exploration they still had nothing. "All we can find is tetrahedrite."

Kragnak shrugged. "Can't we ask for iron from the King?"

"We could buy some, if there were any merchants willing and able to find us up here." Seeing the look in Kragnak's eyes he regretted the harshness of his tone. "You didn't do anything wrong."

"I'll get back to work." Kragnak turned back to the forge, taking out a copper bar that he started to weld to the cage he was making. This one wasn't pretty either, some of the bars were warped and crooked, but it would hold just as well as the other three he made.

At least he is getting faster, if not better. It helped that Lumdir didn't have much to do with his injury and was able to help tend the fire. Seeing him working the bellows sent a twinge of regret in Dorian.

"How are you feeling?"

"Hot." The corner of Lumdir's mouth twitched beneath his beard. "Better than a week ago."

"Still healing?"

"Still healing."

"Yudoline tells me you'll be recovered in less than a month." The twitch was gone now, and Lumdir cast a glance at his workbench.

"Wish it were less. I hope she's right."

"Of course she is." They didn't have anyone else with any skill at healing, so she was the resident expert. The room was getting hot for Dorian, and not from the fire. He cast his glance around the room, all the craftdwarves hard at work.

The wounds he had gained were already healing, cuts and scratches compared to Lumdir. Most of the others had fared the same way, and Dorian was glad the skeletons hadn't been better. He wasn't sure they would have come back if they were goblins.

"I've got to go, try the copper and let me know." Dorian nodded to Lumdir, who returned it.

Kragnak stuck another bar of copper into the fire. "I will." Dorian slipped out of the workshop, troubled. Even though they had worked on the defenses of the mine he wasn't sure how well they would hold up.

They needed weapons that wouldn't break the first time they used them. Even if merchants came with loads of steel they wouldn't have enough to barter with them, iron was their only hope.

And they needed to mine it themselves.

Dorian didn't want to let Kragnak know about his doubts. There were no merchants the first year, he doubted they would show up this year. Even with Tufolin's helpful words, assuming he wasn't lying, they would have to make the trek up the mountains and across the same rivers they had made.

It wouldn't be enticing for a merchant unless they would find something special, something no one else would have. Or valuable ores and metals, not just a few hunks of silver and bars of copper.

And without their help spreading tales of wealth and treasure, Dorian wasn't sure they would even survive.

Which meant the chances of him seeing his children were disappearing every day.

12

An Empty Song

His children were still on his mind when he went to visit Lumdir the next morning, the exploration in the mine a failure.

Yudoline was there to swap the bandage for a fresh one. "Good morning."

"Morning," Dorian said. Lumdir was laying down, jaw tense under his beard.

"Get it over with." He looked more uncomfortable than Dorian had ever seen him. Yudoline exchanged a glance with Dorian and pulled off the old bandage. Lumdir sucked in a breath and Dorian saw why.

Red and aggravated, the wound had a crisscross of spider webbing flowing out from the cut that pulsed. Blood trickled from the wound, even though it should be healed.

The smell was what concerned him the most. A mixture of blood and an otherworldly stench. He kept a straight face as Yudoline cleaned the wound.

He was relieved as she wrapped it again, hiding it. "Feel better?" Dorian asked. Lumdir's face had gone red, but it was losing it and regaining its former pale color.

"That's one way to think of it."

"Stay off it today." Dorian patted his shoulder. "We'll manage. Just rest and recover."

"I'll bring you breakfast as soon as I take care of this." Yudoline stood, taking the bucket she had filled with water for the cleaning and dunking the old bandage in it. They left.

When they were safely out of earshot Yudoline turned back to him. "Did you see?"

"I saw it. He had to travel on it, that's what inflamed it."

Yudoline narrowed her eyes. "This is above my skill. No matter how it happened."

"You don't know what to do about it?"

"I've done all I know."

Dorian closed his eyes. If they had a true healer, they would know what to do about it.

At that moment Mughan chose to stroll by. "Good morning Yudoline. Dorian, may I have a word." Dorian opened his eyes and fixed them on Mughan.

"Now isn't a good time."

"It will only take a moment." There was an undertone in his voice, one Dorian didn't like. Yudoline was looking to him, uncertain.

"Go ahead, I'll catch up at breakfast." She hesitated, then turned and left, glancing back at them as she climbed the stairs. Everyone else would be at breakfast.

Turning back to Mughan, Dorian crossed his arms. This wasn't going to be a happy talk.

"What do you want?"

"No need to attack me." Mughan held up his hands and stepped back, giving him plenty of space. "We need to discuss the...unfortunate accident that happened."

"Discuss what?"

"Almost everyone else has recovered. Except one." Mughan glanced back to the apartments. "A dwarf wounded by the unde ad..."

At first Dorian didn't understand, but then the implication was clear to him. "He isn't going to turn."

"How can you be so sure?" Mughan fixed his gaze on him, watching him like a snake about to strike. Dorian knew the less he told Mughan the better. He shrugged.

"Wouldn't he already have if he was going to? It's been a week."

"Magic like that must be unpredictable."

Dorian narrowed his eyes. "What are you suggesting?"

"Nothing radical. Just some minor precautions, for the good of the mine. I'm sure that since you've never dealt with this you wouldn't know as much as me about it."

"Say it." Dorian was tired of always being careful around Mughan, and the words were terse.

"Keep him outside until he recovers."

"Outside?"

"We can make a tent, keep him comfortable." It was summer. The nights were cold, and the days were hot.

"He won't recover that way. He needs the earth around him. He needs to feel the rock."

"We need to be safe. Are you saying you're not willing to do what it takes to keep this expedition alive and thriving?" Torchlight flickered over Mughan's face, making a grotesque display of his features.

"Listen to me." Dorian took a step forward. "You don't run this mine."

"It doesn't look like you do either."

"You haven't been through what we've been through--"

"And I don't want to." His teeth shine in the light, predatory. "Do what's best for us. That's all I'm asking for." Mughan stepped by him and left him at the base of the stairs.

Inside Dorian was quivering with anger. There was something else though, something even worse. Deep down, no matter how he tried to force it away, he knew there was a nugget of truth in what Mughan said.

Something was wrong with Lumdir. They needed to do something about him. But could he be a danger to the mine?

For a moment, despite all he knew, he wavered in his conviction. *That's not how necromancy works.* In his mind he heard the question Mughan would ask.

How do you know?

A question he would dread answering more than anything. What if this necromancer was different, had found a way to spread his magic that no one else had discovered?

Even though it was still warm in the mine, he shivered and glanced behind him. The mouth of the mine gaped. Stairs surrounded it like teeth.

Turning swiftly, he walked upstairs, forcing himself to walk at a normal speed. Putting Lumdir outside the mine wouldn't be good for him, but would it be good for everyone else?

The others were eating when he walked in, and conversing in hushed tones. Some of the conversations died out when they saw him, and Mughan smirked at him.

Dorian ignored them and sat, took up a plate but didn't get food. There was too much rolling around in his mind for him to feel like eating.

"Dorian?" Yander asked.

"Yes."

"Were you going to hand out assignments?" Dorian had almost forgotten. He had worked out what he needed them to do last night, but now they seemed to escape them.

"I'll take the farming dwarves," Mughan volunteered, getting up.

"Yudoline will lead the farming dwarves this morning." There was a moment's hesitation in Mughan, but then sat down and waved toward Yudoline. Dorian was relieved that there wasn't going to be a fight, but Mughan leaned back in his chair, face clouded.

The rest of the assignments were given out without incident, and the dwarves left to work for the day. Dorian sat back when they were given out. Mughan was the last to leave.

He stood, staring at Dorian. There was something behind his eyes, and he wasn't sure what it was. *Could it be something other than anger? Hatred, even?*

"If you're going to tell me I'm wrong go ahead."

"That wasn't what I was going to say." Mughan crossed his arms.

"I'm not going to make Lumdir wait outside."

"I didn't think you would. It would take too much leadership to make that decision." It wasn't fair, and Dorian suspected even Mughan knew that. *What was he doing, trying to make him angry?* The blood pounding in his ears gave away the effect.

"You don't have what it takes to lead this expedition either. You haven't been out here like I have, seen the things I've seen."

"You haven't led for very long." A wave rose in Dorian, anger that bubble and simmered. *What does he know about me?*

"I don't care what you think," he growled.

"Turn to anger and violence." Mughan smirked and crossed his arms, which infuriated Dorian even more. "Do you have any other tricks or is that all you can do?"

"That's more than enough." The anger boiled, hiding the unease he felt.

Mughan unexpectedly turned on his heel and headed for the door. "Hate me all you like, it won't stop me."

The words rang in Dorian's ears. *Hate.* Did he hate Mughan? He was certainly angry at him, had a strong dislike because of what the dwarf had been doing to him and the expedition.

But was it hate?

Or was Mughan close to the truth, that it was hate that fueled him. Was it all the hatred that came from the death of his wife?

He didn't know and didn't want to think about it. Dorian stomped off, going down to the mines. The darkness of the main mine shaft comforted him, and he let his eyes adjust to it, not bothering to take a torch with him.

There would be a pickaxe for him, and he needed it. He couldn't feel the stone he was so angry, and the sounds of mining led him to Yander and Dozotaine.

"Dorian, what are you doing down here?" Yander asked, stopping to take a break. Stone dust settled around him, coating his skin with a granite gray. Dorian didn't answer, but took the extra pick from beside the wheelbarrow. "Is anything wrong?"

"Keep working and mind your own business." Dozotaine's eyebrows rose, and Yander recoiled.

"I'm sorry, I--"

"That's all you ever are, sorry. Leave me alone." He took some pleasure in Yander's reaction, but it quickly turned to shame. Dorian turned and stalked out of their tunnel to find an empty one of his own.

"Don't worry about him," Dozotaine said. "There's nothing wrong with you." Now a complete stranger was comforting Yander?

Dorian's shame grew. Their voices faded as he walked farther down the stairs, deeper in the mine, and he was relieved.

He went left at the next floor, following an abandoned tunnel that Dorian didn't think contained anything. Halfway down he turned to the wall and attacked it with the pickaxe.

Each strike shuddered up his arms, and he poured more and more strength into each blow. Rock chips flew as he took out his anger on the stone. The soothing feeling of mining stated to calm the storm that was raging inside him.

Anger. Shame. Fear. Hatred. They coursed through him like rivers, each one trying to take him over. Shame was the strongest, shame at being bested by Mughan, by letting Emelda be taken. Shame at taking so long to teach Yander and then lashing out at him.

Shame for his failures as the leader of the expedition. Shame at not being there for his wife. Shame at trying to bring her back using magic he knew was dangerous.

His arms weakened at the continual beating he was giving to the rock. His blows grew weaker in turn and his breath grew deeper and faster. Blood pounded in his ears.

Finally, his strength was spent and he stopped, gasping. There were no answers down here for him to find. There were only more questions. But, for the moment, the storm of emotions had calmed.

He went farther than he expected, surprised when he looked back to see the faint outline of the opening. It was too dark to see what he had dug out and thought about picking his way back over the remains of the rock he had mined.

Instead, he closed his eyes and took deep breaths. He tasted the rock dust and stale air, knew he was covered in it. He put a hand on the wall.

After his breath grew even and his heartbeat slowed he could concentrate on feeling it. He missed this. It had been almost a week since he had mined himself, letting Yander and Dozotaine work without him, and then the trip to rescue Emelda.

It was speaking to him now. Deep, powerful notes of strength sang out. There was no ore down this tunnel, at least as far as he could feel.

Dorian frowned and concentrated more, pushing all his thoughts away in an attempt to expand the distance he could sense. He felt the tunnels above him and below him, absent of the song of the stone.

Nothing. Still nothing. No ore, no gems, just granite.

He slammed his fist against the wall, willing it to yield its secrets. Why had they come up so short? Had the King's sources been wrong? Was there only granite in this mountain? Putting his back on the wall he slumped down and cradled his head in his hands.

That couldn't be true. His three years would be gone and spent if it were the case. His children would be taken from him forever.

Everything depended on them finding a better source of metal. Their survival and his family. He pulled up a handful of rock to feel it in his hand.

"If there is any iron in this blasted mountain, I'm going to find it."

13

ORE

The day yielded no ore. Lunchtime came and went, and then dinner. Dorian kept working on his tunnel, pulling the rock in great piles. Exhausted, he returned to his bed and slept.

His dreams were plagued by nightmares. Giant crows coming to gouge out his eyes. Rock monsters that cracked themselves off from the wall to devour him.

When he woke up the next morning he didn't feel rested, only covered in sweat.

And there was still the situation with Lumdir to deal with.

His room was the first stop as soon as Dorian was dressed. Lumdir was sweating and asleep, twitching and shifting. Dorian pressed a hand to his head.

Burning hot.

Was Mughan right? Dorian searched for the signs. With a thumb he pulled open Lumdir's eye. It was still white and rolled up to escape the light. He let it shut.

"He's getting worse." Yudoline walked to his side. "I'm afraid I can't do anything for him." She squeezed Lumdir's hand, but there was no reaction. His long, ragged breaths filled the silence.

"This is my fault. I never should have brought him."

Yudoline turned to him. "And where would that leave Emelda?"

"That was my fault too." He could tell her about the promise he made to her, to look after Yander. About how she wasn't selfish enough to ask the same about herself. She deserved better, they all did.

"You put too much on your shoulders. Let the others carry the load."

"Like Mughan?" The words snapped out of him before he could even think about it. Yudoline recoiled and frowned.

"Sticks and stones, do you really think that is how we feel?"

"I don't know what you feel." *I hardly know what I feel.* The atmosphere in the room was oppressive. He turned and started for the door.

"Dorian--"

"Keep him comfortable." He was gone before she could respond, shutting the door behind him with a click. There was something bigger out there, something that required his attention and he didn't know what to do about it.

And, deep down inside, he knew why this bothered him so much. First the dog, then the skeletons. This was his past coming back to haunt him.

Breakfast was passable, but he didn't taste it, and he gave out the daily assignments as quickly as he could. This time Mughan didn't say anything, of which he was grateful, but the others still looked to him before going off on their tasks.

He thought he saw some of the founders doing it too, but couldn't tell before he looked away. You're just imagining things. Yudoline started at him over breakfast and tried to talk to him, but he avoided her and hurried off down the mines.

His pickaxe was waiting for him down there and he picked it up, grateful to be alone. Yander and Dozotaine were working separate tunnels, each trying their own way through the mountain. The temperature was pleasant, and he soon was working up a sweat, chipping rock away from the wall.

Would their defenses hold? Or should he be devoting more resources to strengthening them? Dorian thought about his previous expeditions, how they had arranged their walls. He remembered how most of them had chosen to retreat deep into the mountain rather than expose themselves.

Was it already too late for them?

The entrance tunnel was surrounded by a wall, with plenty of room left in case merchants needed to set up with their caravan. As he thought about it, though that might not bet the best case.

It meant they were vulnerable, that the mountain itself wouldn't be able to protect them. *But, we have the door and can lock it. That will keep us safe.*

Unless it wasn't locked, or some determined enemy could knock it down. Each second he spent agonizing over it, thinking of different ways to improve their defenses.

"Dorian, are you coming?"

Dorian pulled up his next swing. "Coming?"

"To lunch," Yander said. Dozotaine was behind him, both covered in dust.

"Yes." He dropped his pickaxe and followed.

"We didn't find anything, again."

"The mountain seems like it's dry. Why did they pick this place to mine?" Dozotaine asked. Dorian shrugged.

Yander cleared his throat. "I was hoping you would have time tonight. To...you know." Dorian felt a stab of shame as soon as he realized what Yander was talking about. He hadn't practiced with him once since they got back.

"Tonight, yes." They trudged up the stairs. "Meet me after dinner outside, we'll practice there." Yander was behind him, but Dorian could tell from his footsteps he was happier. *That was all it took.*

"What are you practicing?" Dozotaine asked.

"Axe work. Dorian is showing me everything he knows. It helped too, against those skeletons I mean. I don't think I would have lasted very long without knowing what he taught me. Isn't that right Dorian?"

"You did fine on your own," Dorian said.

"Really? You don't mean that do you?" Dorian glanced back. Yander's eyes were practically glowing in the torchlight.

"Don't let it get to your head. You still wouldn't survive a real fight."

"I thought it was a real fight. Didn't you see them? They were walking skeletons. Brought back from the dead." Yander went silent. "Where did they come from?"

They had almost reached the top of the stairs, and Dorian stopped and turned back. "Don't you worry about that. They're back to being dead now, and we can rest easier." He grabbed the rope and started hauling, channeling his anger into it.

Yander looked more at ease and walked past without saying anything. Dozotaine stopped and waited for him to leave.

"Why don't you tell him the truth?" His eyes were hard.

"What truth?"

"You know whatever sent those skeletons to us is still out there."

"I don't know that. I don't know anything about it."

Dozotaine narrowed his eyes. "He has seen sorrow, why protect him from it?"

"You're right, he has seen sorrow."

"He isn't a child anymore." Of course Yander wasn't a child. He was a grown dwarf. He was married. He was blooded. The bucket appeared and Dorian yanked it over, dumping the tailings out.

"I'm going to go get lunch." He turned and left without saying another word, and Dozotaine followed him without saying anything either. He stewed along the way, dwelling on the myriad of problems that plagued him.

Yander walked into the room covered in sweat and slumped into the chair. He groaned.

"Did it not go well?" Emelda asked.

"I've got bruises in a dozen places I didn't even know existed. He didn't take it easy on me this time." He shifted in his chair and groaned again. The faint smell of beeswax comforted him.

Putting aside her knife and the block of wax she was carving, Emelda turned her chair toward him. "Tell me, husband."

It tickled him inside to hear it, sending a warmth that started in his chest and radiated out. He reached out and took her hand. "Something's bothering him. I've never seen him so distracted before. I mean, he's always been hard to read before but now I can see the anger around his eyes and the tension in his beard."

"And it makes you feel bad."

He nodded. "If something is trouble Dorian, what does that mean for us?" He stretched out his legs. "He's been this way since the...att ack." A twang of sadness at the memory.

Emelda squeezed his hand, a tear in her eye. He went on. "And ever since he's been troubled. The goblin and skeleton attack have made it worse."

"And Mughan."

Yander turned to her, tilting his head. "What do you mean?"

"You can't sense the tension between them?" she asked.

"No, I know they don't like each other and that Mughan thinks Dorian is doing a bad job, but I didn't think Dorian cared."

"He cares. He cares more than you think, and not just about Mughan. Dorian puts up his walls, builds his defenses, but just like mother used to say there is always softness beneath the shell."

"Are you still having dreams about them?"

"Every night." Yander got up, ignoring his protesting body, and pulled her to her feet. She came willingly, and he embraced her fiercely. There was nothing he could say to make that hurt go away.

He hated being beside her as she tossed and turned in her sleep. Hated when she woke up clutching him and whimpering, calling out for them. Deep down he knew their relationship was part of mourning for them, and wondered what life would be like if it never happened.

Would she still love him?

Sniffing, she reached up and caressed his beard. "Dorian cares for you too."

"Ha." He turned his head to the side. "He has a funny way of showing it."

"Remember that he has to look after all of us, that something else drives him too. He wouldn't be here if he didn't have to, and Mughan and everything else threatening him is another load he has to carry."

Yander thought about it, watching the torch flickering on the wall. "I hadn't thought about that before. I guess I can understand why he's so troubled."

"The skeletons, do you think they're coming back?"

He took hold of her shoulders, and looked her in the eye. "I'm going to protect you if they do, no matter what." They hadn't been able to stop him last time, and they wouldn't stop him in the future.

She nodded. "Have you asked Dorian what he's feeling?"

Ask him? Yander imagined walking up to him and questioning him. He had no doubt Dorian would throw him into a wall and probably stomp on him for good matter.

"I couldn't do that, you know how he is. I don't have the courage."

"Don't you say that." She pushed away. "Never say that. I've seen your courage." He didn't reply but cast his gaze to the ground. She put a hand on his chest, feeling for something.

"You fought for me, rescued me. This heart is too big for you to not have courage." It made his shame flee, even though he didn't quite believe everything she was saying.

How could a dwarf with courage not ask Dorian about his troubles?

"Thank you," he whispered, and drew her into a kiss. She giggled when he drew away and tickled her with his whiskers, and the warm feeling came back.

The lonely nights, the waiting and anticipation. It seemed like it was alone gone now for good and Yander didn't regret it for a minute. Even their small disagreements, like who got the left side of the bed, or who blows out the light at the end of the night, paled in comparison to the feeling he got when he held her close.

"I wish I had been stronger then. Things might have turned out differently." She drew back, gave him a stern look.

"There's no use in thinking that, no matter how much I want my parents back." Her eyes softened and she reached up to caress his face. "Maybe Dorian feels the same way."

Dorian feel regret for not being strong enough? Yander couldn't fathom it. The dwarf was as strong as steel, as unyielding as rock. It would take the whole mountain coming down on his head for him to feel regret like that.

"Will I ever know?" he asked.

"Ask him." Emelda said. Then, after a time, "At least think about it."

Yander wrinkled his nose, then rubbed his rough hands. "I'll think about it. If I can ever find him..."

"Still disappearing into the mines?"

"Yes. I can hear him working sometimes. It sounds like he's trying to kill the rock with how hard he strikes and how fast. It's roughed up his hands even though it has only been a few days."

"Still nothing?"

Yander shook his head. "No. The mountain refuses to give up its treasures. I can't feel anything, and I don't think Dorian can either."

"You'll find the iron, eventually."

"I'm afraid we don't have much time left. We have to find it now." He sagged and dropped back into the chair. After he ran a hand over his face Emelda took his hand and pulled him back to his feet.

"It's getting late, and you have the night watch tomorrow," she reminded. He had forgotten about that.

"Let's get some sleep," Yander said. "Dorian is up to something, I know it. And whatever he has in mind I think he'll do it soon."

14

REVENGE

Vasknar picked through the remains of his skeletons, stepping between their scattered bones. Shielding his eyes from the midday sun, he knelt down and picked up a femur.

One side of the bone dangled precariously from the other, then finally snapped as he lifted it. It had been shattered by something heavy, or something well swung. A raven, glowing red eyes peering, flapped to his shoulder and landed.

The talons dug into his shoulder, but the thick cloth of his black robe protected his skin. "Not a drop of blood to speak of." His voice came out as a whisper.

As he looked he found a few splashes, much less than what should have been there. The raven cawed at the scene.

"My love, you must wait a while longer." He looked over to the south west, feeling the pulsing heart that he knew would beat :again. "These dwarves have proved more meddlesome than I thought."

He stroked the raven. "They will pay for it." The broken bone in his hand toppled from his fingers, scattering a puff of smoke from where it fell. "With their lives, they will pay for it."

There were others in these hills that could help him. "Time to pay the goblins a visit."

Vasknar pulled his hood over his eyes to shield them from the sun and started back down the mountain.

Still no iron. It had been almost a week. And Lumdir hadn't recovered either. He was still burning up, tossing and turning, the fat and muscle melting from his body.

Dorian couldn't take it anymore, and got up to leave. A moan from Lumdir made him look back at the door frame. He clutched at it, then turned his back on him.

He had left Lumdir to die.

The others were at dinner. Dorian retrieved the item from his room, one he had kept as a reminder. Had it been something else it would not have been as painful a reminder, and he clutched its smooth surface.

Slipping it into his pocket, he headed for the stairs. Questions still burned inside him, tasks to do and things left undone. The others had cooled to him, and Mughan was winning their affection.

Their laughter greeted him down the stairs, wafting through the smells of roasted game and potatoes mixed with fresh rockbread. It died away as he reached the top, then came roaring back as he entered.

Mughan was seated at the head of the table, all attention on him. He was smiling as the others laughed, basking in the glow of their attention.

His smile lessened when he saw Dorian. Eyes left Mughan and reached him at the doorway until everyone was looking at him. Silence descended like a blanket, only the pops and cracks from the fire punctuating the stillness.

"Dorian, come to join us?" Mughan picked up his mug of ale and lazily took a sip like he didn't have a care in the world.

Dorian met his gaze, a cold flame of anger burning within him. He walked over to Mughan, who's smile slipped more, until he was standing beside him.

He let the silence grow uncomfortable. Dwarves shifted in their seat, but Mughan remained calm and kept smiling. Dorian wanted to hit him, take out all his pain and frustration, but knew that would only make him stronger in the eyes of the others.

Instead, he reached into his pocket. With all his speed he pulled it out, raised it, and slammed it down.

Gasps and a scream rang out, then a crunch. Mughan flinched, but met his gaze.

"Is that supposed to scare me?" He smirked. "Because it doesn't."

Dorian took a step back and folded his arms. A murmur was growing among the newest migrants. Dozotaine nudged Mughan, who broke off his gaze.

"What?" Mughan's mouth clamped shut when he saw the giant spider fang impaled into his meat and through his plate.

"Just in case you were wondering what's out here. There are more of them beneath us, and other evils above us." All eyes swiveled to Dorian. "If we want to survive, I suggest we get to work."

He wasn't sure if it would win them back, but he couldn't think of anything else that wouldn't drive them to Mughan. Violence, pleading, asking. It wouldn't work.

So, he chose fear.

"Aren't you going to eat your meal?" Dorian asked.

"I'm not hungry." Mughan tried to push the plate away, but it was stuck to the table. Dorian hadn't held back. Black venom was oozing out from under his plate.

Without another word Dorian left, heart pounding from their stares. *Would it work?*

He didn't know.

Instead of going back to his room he went to the workshop and sat next to the forge. Kragnak had tamped down the coals, but they were still glowing with heat.

Dorian stared into them, watching the colors play across the coals and ash. They were so fluid, it was like watching a stream that flowed any way it wanted. Red, yellow, black. He brooded, turning the problems over in his mind.

They were running out of time and he knew it. They needed better weapons, they needed more time training. He could use an army.

But what he had was a bunch of green dwarves. Some had faced adversity, but the newer arrivals had not. Their lives in Zirad had been too good. They thought coming out here would bring an end to their problems, but they had just traded them for new ones.

Kragnak found him, surprising him from behind. "Dorian?"

"Kragnak."

"Did you come to see the cages? I've almost finished them." They were lined up in a row, some of them already buried and set by Barileth.

"No, not for that." Dorian moved from his perch next to the anvil, giving Kragnak space to work again. Kragnak let out a sigh of relief.

"I'm still not very good at it." He grabbed the bellows and started to pump, breathing life into the flames. "I keep hoping the fire will teach me something, that it will burn away the weakness in me."

"The fire? How would it burn away weakness?"

Kragnak shrugged and added a few more sticks of charcoal. "Something we used to do back home. I'm not sure I believe it anymore."

"Go on." Dorian leaned in, no longer paying attention to the fire.

"It was part of my mother's religion. Whenever we would get sick she would put us as close to the fire she could get us. Said it would burn away the sickness." Kragnak took a long, round bar of copper and set one end in the fire. A spray of sparks rose with the smoke and died out before they could reach the chimney.

"One time my brother cut himself bad, almost to the bone. Mother warmed up the fire poker in the flames and, when it was red hot, shoved it into the wound." Kragnak shuddered. "I can still hear his screams." Dorian's hope faded.

"I'm sorry to hear that. How old was he when he died?"

"Oh, he didn't die. He was fine in a few weeks. Mother said the fire burned away the evil, but he still bears the scar to this very day."

"Burned it away?"

He picked up a hammer and took the bar out of the fire. "That's what she said." Kragnak started to beat the copper, flattening it as it cooled.

"Do you think it would work with fevers?"

He paused to think about it. "It might, we never tried it. We didn't have many fevers when we were growing up."

There might be something to this. Dorian watched Kragnak work a little while longer, attaching the bar to the cage and bending it around to make it connect. It still wasn't pretty, but the smith was improving.

"You're making progress. This is a much tighter turn than the first one," Dorian said. "You'll learn, don't give up."

Kragnak brightened some, but he still wore a frown. "I'll keep trying." At least Kragnak was firmly on his side, and most of the founders. It was the others who worried him. Dorian left to visit the kitchens.

It was a visit he had been dreading to make. With so many extra mouths to feed it was inevitable that they would run into another issue with food. The increase crop planting would help, but they still needed to grow and ripen before they could gather the harvest.

"Good morning Dorian, would you like something to eat?" Emelda held out half a loaf of rockbread, which he took gratefully. She was the only dwarf in the kitchen. He expected to find others, then remembered he hadn't assigned anyone that morning.

"Cleaning up from breakfast?" He took a bite. It was stale, but not hard enough to not eat. The resistance slowed down his chewing.

"Getting ready for lunch and dinner."

"Already?"

"I'm not as fast as Skover was." His name dampened Dorian's spirits, and a look of pain flashed across Emelda's face.

"He was a good dwarf." Dorian set down the rest of the bread, tearing off the chunk that he had bitten off of. He stared at it with no appetite anymore. "What do the stores look like."

A tight frown pulled down her face. "Come see." She led him to the store room. It was as he feared.

"How much is left?" He fingered the edge of an empty potato sack. There were plenty of boxes, bins, and barrels. Most of them were empty or half empty. Somewhere in the back of the dug out room he thought he heard a creature skitter. *There were a lot of storage containers, maybe it isn't so bad.*

"I haven't been able to count it all, but we might be able to last a few more months."

Dorian frowned. "We can't make it if that's all we have. Harvest is at least four months away. I'll send out more dwarves to forage." As soon as it slipped out of his mouth, a cold chill ran up his back. Who would he send? And how would he keep them safe?

They had lost the element of obscurity. Things had discovered their mine, things that were better left not knowing who they were.

"Foraging would help. The crops are growing well and the golden cave moss should be able to sustain us, but…"

"Don't worry about that. I'll handle the supply." He wished more than ever there was a caravan coming their way, loaded down with food. Great round wheels of cheeses, salted pork stuffed into barrels, tubers and potatoes to last the winter. He glanced at Emelda.

She looked smaller, her arms crossed and her shoulders hunched. "I won't send you," he added hastily. Emelda tried to smile.

"I'm fine." There wasn't much to say, but the silence grew long between them. Dorian shifted, feeling the tension. *Should I apologize?*

"You had nothing to do with it." It wasn't true, but he appreciated the thought. He dropped his gaze.

"How has it been?"

"I'm glad I have someone to come back to, if that's what you mean." He thought about leaving, about escape back into the tunnels where his pickaxe was all that he had to care about. Was this better than the dungeons?

"My dreams…nightmares." She shivered. He couldn't stand to see her so vulnerable. Dorian wrapped his arm around her as she shook. "I keep seeing them taking Yander. Over and over in my nightmares."

"Then it turns into my mother and father. They come back from the dead and come after him. Then, they turn on me." He couldn't imagine it and squeezed his eyes shut. He knew he should say something, but no words could ever overcome her pain.

And his.

Would that be what his wife would be like? A shambling skeleton with glowing red eyes? Could he do that to her, or to himself?

"The dreams will fade," he said at last. *Don't think about that.*

"But will the danger?" She had stopped shivering and pulled away. "Mughan is right. There are things out here that we need to be protected from."

"Are you saying that I can't protect you?" He drew back.

"I'm not sure anyone can protect me out here." She turned her back on him. "I'm thinking about leaving, going back to Zirad."

Dorian's mouth dropped open. "What about Yander? What about us?"

"He's the only thing keeping me here. This was my parent's dream, and they're gone now." She wiped something from her face. "I've got to get back to work, I have a lot of food to prepare while we still can."

Knowing it was the right thing to do, Dorian laid a hand on her shoulder. "Emelda, please stay with us. I promise to keep you safe to my last dying breath."

15

A Dwarf in Agony

Dorian chipped at the rock, breaking chunks of it away that fell onto the rough stone hewn floor. He replayed the conversation between him and Emelda over and over again.

"Give it up Dorian. It's been days." His voice echoed down the empty tunnel. He had dug this one deeper than the others, loathe to approach the cavern but feeling the necessary pull.

So far he had found another vein of tetrahedrite, a few gems here and there, and no iron. No tin, no lead, nothing but rock and copper. The others had done the same, with little to no results.

And it didn't feel like the mine was any more secure. Barileth had finished with the cage traps. Kragnak still fretted over his smith work, and Lumdir grew worse every day.

It was lunchtime. Dorian worked a while longer, then when he knew he couldn't put it off any longer, dropped his pickaxe and trudged up the stairs. Each step felt like a cliff, his legs felt like two large weights.

Everyone else was far into the meal by the time he entered the hall. Some greeted him, the others cast cool glances in his direction. He didn't blame them. They still paid him respect, for now.

How long would that last?

Dorian crossed the room under their gaze, listening to the conversations as he took his seat and collected his food.

"It is a lot smaller than I expected," Mughan said, casting a glance around the room. "The whole place, not just this room." Most of the migrants nodded.

"What do you mean? There's plenty of room for all of us, we even finished enough apartments for everyone to have their own." Yander looked hurt at the comment, but Dorian knew who it was really for.

"I'm not saying you didn't do a good job Yander. With what you have to work with I'm not surprised. It just feels...cramped," Mughan said.

"No like the halls of Zirad," Dozotaine added. "They had a grander feel to them too. An engraving here or there wouldn't hurt the place."

Dorian bristled, but let the comments slide by. He took a deep swig of ale. The flood of its hoppiness helped tamp down his anger. For long, he didn't know.

"That isn't fair and you know it," Yudoline scolded, waving a spoon in his direction. "Sticks and stones, we've only been her a year and a half. They had centuries to build Zirad."

"I didn't mean offense."

"They dwarves have worked hard to clear out what we have already. If you ask me I think they did a good job of it too." Yudoline gave Yander and Dorian a friendly nod. Dozotaine didn't see what Dorian could.

This hall would be three times as large, with columns that stretched up to the expansive ceiling. Around their circular frame would run a tapestry of carvings. Tales of yesterday would be told, the Great Hunt of Everlong, the Battle of the Horn.

And when they found the gold and silver that had to be hidden from them it would gild the tables and chairs, expertly crafted and of the highest quality. They reflected the light, dazzling the occupants as they feasted and drank and sang of the good days and hard times that would try and stop them.

The image in his mind faded, replaced with the hall as it stood today. It was dark, cramped, and gray. Dwarves huddled around the tables that were too small to hold them all, something Dorian was meaning to ask Lumdir to do.

They ate rockbread and a meager portion of vegetables. Where they should have been feasting, they were barely surviving. No wonder everyone wasn't happy with him.

"Surely that could be remedied though?" Mughan asked, his words pointed and his stare hard.

"We have enough room." Dorian stuffed a chunk of rockbread in his mouth and jammed his teeth together on it. It was fresh, thankfully.

"You might, but we have different tastes." Mughan flourished his fork with a spin, gesturing around the room.

"Then you should have stayed in Zirad. I hear they have plenty of room there." Dorian skewered a too-small potato with his fork with such force he wondered if it would be left in the plate. It wasn't.

"We could do with some more room. I'm always frustrated trying to move logs around the workshop," Kimec said. His wife shot him a look and he shrugged and scratched his head. "I wouldn't mind it, that's all I'm saying."

"Sounds like we could all use some room. How about making this place bigger?" Mughan asked, leaning back in his chair. He was relaxed, his left arm drooping back below him.

"Not enough time." Dorian savaged his bread, clamping down on it and tearing a piece off. Mughan's smile grew.

"Come now, surely we have enough time to dig out the workshop at least? Or maybe split them, make a new one deeper."

Dorian shook his head. That was something he was planning on in the future, but not now. He swallowed just as casually as Mughan was sitting before he answered, aware of the eyes on him. "When we find iron."

"But Dorian, how long will that take?" Yander asked. "After all the digging we've done we still haven't found anything."

"It's here."

"The dwarf has a point," Mughan said. He leaned forward now, a hunger in his eyes. "We have a wall and a stout door that we can lock. What do we really need the iron for?"

"Did you see our weapons?" Barileth asked.

Mughan waved a hand at him. "I saw them. We've got defenses already, let them come."

"We need it for armor," Dorian said.

Kragnak's face turned white. "You don't mean that, do you?"

"Armor? I don't see any armor smiths around to make it." Mughan waved his arm around the room.

"Hold your tongue," Dorian snapped and rose to his feet. Kragnak was frowning and cringing. "We have a smith." Kragnak might struggle, but there was promise in him. *I might be the only one who sees it, but it's there.*

Mughan held up his hands. "No offense meant." The founders were frowning at him. "We should be focusing on what we can control. Right now we can't find iron, so we should make life a little better for all of us."

Dorian cooled his anger, letting his grip on his table knife loosen. *I'm playing into his hands.*

"Offense was given," Barileth growled. Dorian put a hand on his shoulder.

"Mughan is right. We have gone too long without expanding." Mughan's smile slipped a little. "Yander, Dozotaine, don't worry about exploring for iron. After the meal you'll expand the workshop. Dig out a room the same size on the other side of the corridor."

"Without hitting the mineshaft?" Yander asked.

"Without hitting the mineshaft." Dorian dropped his knife on the table. "I'll explore by myself if anyone needs me."

Before he could hear any arguments or objections Dorian left. He heard Mughan talking behind him. "That went better than I expected. After the workshop we'll work on the dining hall, and then-" His voice faded as

Too worked up to go straight to work, Dorian went to visit Lumdir instead of going to the mine.

As soon as he walked in the room he wasn't sure it was a good idea. His breath was ragged, painful draws of air. After some hesitation Dorian reached out to touch his head.

Burning.

Feeling even more hopeless, Dorian turned and went to the mine. He thought about the troubles they had run into and tried to think of solutions. After reaching the end of the stairs he turned into a side tunnel he thought might lead him to iron.

It was quiet and dark. Dorian set the torch he brought with him into a pile of rubble and picked up the pickaxe.

Lumdir. Mughan. The necromancer. Goblins. No food. Which of these would be the end of them? Which would kill his chance to see his children and his lover forever?

Dorian stared down at the axe. *Could Lumdir turn?*

His knowledge of that dark art did not help him, so he closed his eyes and took in the cave.

The smell of damp and stone dust. The feeling of the coolness of the earth on his skin. He reached out with one hand, letting go of the smooth and well-worn handle of the pickaxe, and touched the wall.

The wall was raw granite, and rough under his hand. How long had had this mountain been here? How long had it remained undisturbed? What secrets did it hold?

He banished the questions from his mind and concentrated on feeling the rock. *There isn't enough time to be distracted.*

But the feeling was slipping.

"Concentrate." Dorian pushed away the thoughts swirling in his mind again, just trying to feel the rock. It was warm, and solid. Then, he pushed deeper.

The cracks in the rock were there, underneath the feeling of solidness. He sought out the warmth of ore or the shimmer of gems.

The gems would be useful for trading when the merchants came. If they came. He would take anything. Garnet, ruby, iron. *Ruby.*

He remembered the day she was born. It was so long ago. He had been so young. Yolanda was exhausted, but beautiful. The glow she had holding their newborn child. It was radiant and the memory of it made him smile.

Then, the scene flashed into another memory. Yolanda's face. Empty. Cold. Dead.

It had been his fault. He never should have asked for her to come. He should have gone home. But it was Lightaxe that asked him to go, it was Lightaxe who failed to keep his promise.

And it had been Yolanda who paid the price.

None of this was helping to find the iron though. Dorian took a deep breath and pushed them away, reaching farther into the rock. He was more successful this time.

Deeper, farther into the mountain he thought he may have sensed something. But the vision of his wife's face came back to him. It lingered in his mind.

He couldn't take it anymore. Opening his eyes he stepped back and swung his pickaxe at the wall and yelled.

The head struck home, right at the intersection of two cracks, and half the wall slid to the ground. Dorian stepped out of the way as it tumbled to the floor, raising a cloud of dust and crash as it hit.

He knew he should try again to sense the ore, but was afraid to. What if he saw his wife's face again leering at him from the grave? Was she mocking him, or accusing him?

Again, he struck the wall. Again, rock fell. He kept going. Soon he had to move the rock out of the way to continue. Some were too big to move alone so he broke them up and shoved them off to the side.

Dorian kept up a steady rhythm, turning down and burrowing deeper toward the faint hint of a trace. He lost himself in the work and was surprised by Yander.

"Any luck?" He asked. "Dinner is ready."

"None." Dorian wiped the sweat from his brow. It dragged along his head, filled with dirt and dust. "I'll come back tomorrow."

Tomorrow came and went, and the day after that. The workshop expansion was finished, and the great hall started. Mughan was smug every time Dorian saw him, and it grated on his nerves.

He took out his anger on the rock, pulverizing it as he worked. It helped to picture the smiling dwarf plastered across the wall. He found it drove him to mine faster.

Now he was sure it was ore, and it was close. After a hearty breakfast a few days later, he knew it would be revealed for whatever it was. He was hoping for iron, but couldn't tell.

Halfway through the morning the rock sang to him. It was pulsating with every blow of his pick, urging him on. He worked through the dust and tang of stone on his lips and got so close he felt like he could reach out and touch it.

Chunks flew, and his muscled strained. Sweat poured down his beard, tickling him as it dripped. It was close.

Then, a chunk of ore and rock fell to the ground. Holding his breath, Dorian reached down and sifted among the rock and dust. They closed around something and he smiled.

That warmth he knew so well, that feeling he was searching for. Dorian opened his fingers. Shining in his arm was a small chunk of hematite.

16

Training

With a chunk of ore in his grasp, Dorian turned to the vein of iron. His momentary joy faded when he felt it out. Within a few minutes he had excavated the ore.

All of it.

He stacked chunks of the ore into a pile. It wouldn't fill a barrel, let alone a wheelbarrow. Even after a further exploration in to the wall he had to admit the vein was exhausted.

Dorian wasn't sure if it was good that they found the ore or if would have been better if he hadn't found anything. He spent a few troubled minutes getting the wheelbarrow and transferring it to the bucket.

The trip up the stairs was hard. The creaking rope sounded like the gallows rope and the ore tumbled out with a crash.

Footsteps sounded in the tunnels as he gathered it back into a bin, making a mental note to ask Kimec to make another wheelbarrow.

Yutatir was the first to find him, eyes searching for danger in the relative dark. "What was that?"

"Me. Help me with a torch." The bin was heavy, but not as heavy as he would like.

After pulling a torch from the wall Yutatir peered into the bin. "What is it?"

"Iron."

"You've found it!" Dorian gave a rueful smile at Yutatir's happiness.

"That's all I've found."

"Oh. It isn't much?"

Dorian didn't answer, and they walked the rest of the way to the workshop in silence. As soon as they entered they were swamped with curious dwarves buzzing with questions.

"Settle down. It's iron ore."

"Iron!" Kragnak exclaimed, and a round of clapping on his back and laughter followed. It died away with glances at Dorian's expression.

"Melt it down," he said. Kragnak's smile faded, a question in his eyes. Dorian nodded.

The joy in the room slipped away. Kragnak stoked the furnace and prepared the ore, cutting away as much stone as he could. Into the crucible went even less than Dorian brought up, a pile of stone shavings where it had rested.

Kimec had already moved his workshop to the new expansion and there was more room in the workshop for storage. Dorian took up a spot on a large chunk of rock next to Lumdir's station to watch.

Word spread through the mine as if by magic. Dwarves trickled in until everyone was there but Lumdir. Dorian stared into the fire, left alone by the group, and thought.

Fire. Rock. The combination of the two yielded a substance crucial to their survival, and the survival of the dwarven race. Kragnak stirred the crucible.

Lumdir's empty workbench pained him. He knew there was little time left, and he wouldn't get better on his own. The fire danced and spun. Gouts of red and yellow leapt up and disappeared.

Burning heavy, the fire melted the ore slowly. Lumdir was burning. He couldn't stand it anymore. Dorian got up and walked across the room, as far away from Lumdir's workbench as he could get.

Every so often Kragnak would scrape off the top of the molten metal and tap the impurities off his tongs. He had a small pile of slag growing. *Too fast.* Each tap took more off the top.

Finally, the metal was ready. Dorian stood at the back of the group of dwarves, watching with all the rest as Kragnak grabbed the crucible in tongs and pulled it from the furnace.

"Stand back," he warned as he turned. Waves of heat distorted the air above the crucible, making the view behind it pulsate and shimmer. Dorian tugged at his beard.

Yellow liquid poured from the lip as Kragnak tilted the crucible into sand he had formed while the ore melted. He had made four indentions, but the liquid only filled up one and a half.

Less than two bars of iron, and the vein was exhausted. Dorian felt like throwing something across the room.

"I thought there would be more." Kragnak had set the crucible down. "There was too much slag. I tried to be careful..."

"It isn't your fault," Kimec said. "That's what you had to work with."

"Can we even make anything out of that?" Mughan asked.

"I could make something, a sword maybe," Kragnak said. The metal had cooled from red to gray. Waves of heat still came from them. "It would have to be a short sword."

One weapon. Dorian slumped up against the wall.

"We'll find more," Yander said. "We know the mountain has it now, we don't have to worry about that. There must be more beneath our feet just waiting to be dug out of the earth."

"There is no more," Dorian said. "That was the whole vein." Eyes swung to him, but he didn't care anymore. His chances of seeing his children again had been scraped off as slag.

"Surely there has to be more," Mughan said. "There's a whole mountain underneath us."

"I said that was it." Dorian fixed his empty stare on Mughan. He didn't feel hate for the dwarf at this moment. Mughan's downcast look inspired no feelings other than pity.

"Yander, you said we would find more." Mughan turned his attention from Dorian back to the group of dwarves. "We've expanded the caverns too. It might take longer than we thought originally, but we'll find more metal."

Would they find more iron? Dorian wasn't so sure. The mountain had been fickle, giving them only pain and heartache, not treasure and safety.

"We'll build our defenses. Prepare for an attack," Dorian said, pushing himself off the wall. "Everyone back to work."

"We're almost done with the hall," Yander said. "I can come down and help you?" The other dwarves were leaving as they came in, in small groups and alone, but he had held back.

"No."

"But with extra hands--"

"Dig out the rest. I don't have any more hope of finding more iron where I was mining."

After a long look Yander nodded. "If you change your mind."

"I won't."

He smelled them before he heard them. The stench rose from the hole in the ground, a mixture of rotten meat and refuse and the lingering smoke of fire. It couldn't be helped though, and he went forward as planned.

They posted no sentry. Apparently they believed that they were safe, hidden by their remote outpost and camouflaged entrance. They would learn differently.

"Forward," Vasknar whispered, his raspy voice carrying to his servant, not three days dead. It shambled forward, and he admired its rippling muscles and powerful form. Following it, he entered the cave and dropped down into the muck, his boots squelching in the mud and filth of the cavern.

Repulsed, he followed his companion. Now he could hear them, chattering and arguing up around the bend in the tunnel. It was hard to make out their language, it had been so long since he had heard any tongue it was difficult to make out.

The screams of terror, on the other hand, were easy to interpret. The first goblin to notice was the closest, and went flying as it reached for a spear next to it. Vasknar noted that it was the sentry, and the other goblins scrambled to mount a defense.

One large goblin, covered in scars, rose in defiance. He picked up a sword almost impossibly large and studded with bone along the chipped blade, and shouted out orders. Vasknar's bear roared, and the sound echoed through the cavern inspiring another dose of fear from the goblins.

"Hold." They weren't being cooperative. The bear had stood on its hind legs, towering above the creatures. Vasknar put a hand on its flank and it calmed. "I wouldn't do that if I were you. My pets can be quite dangerous when threatened."

From behind Vasknar he heard the sounds of footsteps, and the second bear shuffled into view. This one was not as fresh. Half its ribcage reflected the bleached white light of the goblin's fire. Something bubbled in a pot above the fire. Vasknar wasn't about to ask what.

The scarred goblin lowered his weapon. "Kill us then. We'll put up a fight." He answered in the common tongue, ignoring Vasknar's attempt at conversing in his language.

"I have no intention of killing you, or else you'd already be dead." Vasknar approached the fire. The goblins retreated, except for the scarred leader. The unfortunate goblin that had born the blow of the bear lay unmoving.

Vasknar picked the cleanest spot of log he could find and gestured to it. "May I?"

The scarred goblin, eyes still narrowed, nodded. Taking a seat, Vasknar tried to ignore the smell.

"What do they call you?"

"Snarg." An appropriate title.

"Let me get to the point of the matter. Do you know of a colony of dwarves near here?" Eyes shifted in the group, and whispers rose.

"Yes." Snarg crossed his arms. Vasknar waved back, the bears withdrew."

"I said I have no intention of killing you. Not unless you try to kill me first. Please, sit." Snarg hesitated and then sat across the fire from him. Vasknar smiled. "Good. I have a feeling we'll be great friends."

"Set your feet farther apart," Dorian said. Yander shifted his stance, sliding his left foot out a few more inches. "Now swing."

Yander grunted and attacked the dummy. The dwarf was trying to use his top half for the force, twisting at his stomach. As a result, the dummy shuddered from the hit but stayed standing, weighed down by the rocks attached to the base. Dorian rapped him on the thigh with a fist.

"You did it again. Power comes from your feet, quickness through your muscles. Watch me." Taking his own practice axe, Dorian took up his power stance and swung. The dummy tilted and then fell over.

"I did the same thing," Yander protested.

"Root yourself in the earth. Become like a tree, ready to resist the wind that tries to tear it down." Flashbacks of his own training, how Methar spoke similar words to him, came back. Dorian could taste the blood, still feel the bruises. *I'm going too easy on him, he needs to be pushed harder.*

After taking a few practice swings, this time turning from the hip, Yander prepared for another attack. He was concentrating too hard on his turning, and not enough on his footing. Right as he reached the end of his back swing Dorian swept his foot out from under him. Yander bellowed out as he struck the floor.

"Ow. What was that for?" Yander glared up at him from the ground.

"Does a tree think about how it stands firm?"

"That doesn't make sense."

Dorian reached out a hand to help him up, which Yander grasped angrily. "You are thinking. Stop thinking and feel. Here," he motioned to Yander's legs, "and here." He motioned to his heart and head.

"Why shouldn't I think? Haven't you told me the opposite in the past?"

"Fighting is different. Your body has to know the answers already, which is why you're training now." Dorian lifted his axe and swung it in a gentle arc. "You let your body take over when the call of the fight sound and it drains your ability to think clearly.

"The heat of battle will take you to a time before you were able to think, an ancient and primitive time. Prepare now, and you allow that primitive creature inside you a chance to survive."

"I'll prepare," Yander said, turning back to the dummy and setting his stance. "I want to survive when the time comes."

"As do we all. Again." Yander attacked, this time with better form. "Better." He kept going, and Dorian stepped back to watch. *Do we all want to survive?*

This life was filled with misery and pain. Maybe it was better if he left it. He could be with his wife again in the afterlife, enjoy a world without all the sadness and bitterness and tears.

Get a hold of yourself. What would Yander do without his help to guide him? What would happen to the mine? How long could they last on their own?

I still have hope to bring her back. "Now attack from above." Yander changed stances in response to Dorian's command, shifting his left leg forward. The axe swung down on the dummy, blow after solid blow landing.

The heat of the battle. The heat of the battle is what had gotten Lumdir injured. The heat of battle might get them all killed.

Or it could heal them.

"Keep working." Dorian turned, his body buzzing with energy. It might work. At this point, even if it didn't work there was nothing to lose.

"Where are you going?" Yander asked.

"To the forge," he said over his shoulder. "It might not work, but we're going to burn Lumdir's sickness away."

17

Cleansed by Fire

Lumdir's body was light, too light. His ragged breath was shallow as Dorian carried him up the stairs. *I hope I'm not too late.*

It wasn't difficult, and when he entered the workshop all eyes turned to him.

"Dorian, what are you doing?" Emelda asked, setting down the wooden bracelet she was carving. Kragnak, startled by the question, stopped hammering.

"Get that forge hot," Dorian said, and brought Lumdir closer to the fire. "Clear me a space."

Kragnak hastily put the copper bar he was working on and hammer down and moved his cages out of the way. Emelda and Kimec joined them at the forge, curious.

"Do you remember what you told me about your mother? Was that true?"

"Yes, every word."

"Good, then heat up that bar." A flash of recognition flickered across Kragnak's face, then he turned and thrust it into the fire. Dorian sat down next to Lumdir, gently pushing back the robe they had tied on his leg to keep him comfortable.

The wound was angry and crisscrossed with red. He breathed a sigh of relief to see no signs of necromancy. Lumdir wouldn't be turning. Then, a thought struck him. *As long as he is alive.*

"We're going to try and burn him."

"What?" Kimec said. Emelda's jaw dropped.

"You can't do that," she protested.

"We can and we will," Dorian said firmly.

"Kragnak," Emelda turned to him, "speak some sense into Dorian."

"It might work," Kragnak said. "I've seen it help before."

"We don't have any other choices left," Dorian said, brushing back Lumdir's hair from his forehead. *Hotter than fire.* "If we don't do something now he will die."

Kragnak pulled at the copper bar, sending a shower of sparks up from the coals. "It's ready. I don't want to get it too hot."

"Kimec, help me hold him down. Emelda, you too, take his leg."

"Put something in his mouth," Kragnak said. "To keep from swallowing his tongue," she explained when everyone looked at him.

"NO, you can't do this to him," Emelda said. She was flustered, but still got down to hold Lumdir's leg.

"We don't have time for arguments," Dorian said. Kimec placed a stick in Lumdir's mouth and then grabbed the other leg. "Kragnak, do it."

The copper slid from the forge, held by tongs. It was glowing white, searing his vision. Kragnak turned to bring it close, then knelt on one knee. He hesitated and looked at Dorian.

"Please don't," Emelda whimpered. A flush of uncertainty ran through him and he squashed it.

"Look away Emelda," Dorian said softly. He nodded at Kimec, then Kragnak. He still hesitated. The copper was cooling. "Do it."

Kragnak plunged the bar down again Lumdir's skin. As soon as the metal met it Lumdir recoiled. Hissing and crackling came from the skin, and the smell of burnt flesh followed.

Dorian was amazed at the strength Lumdir still possessed and had to press down on his shoulders with all his might. "Keep going."

Emelda was crying, and he felt her sadness, but he couldn't do anything about it. He wished that the copper would burn away his weakness too, that the evil in him would be quashed and destroyed.

Lumdir thrashed and struggled, clamping down tight on the wood between his teeth. His eyes flashed open, and Dorian felt a second of hope, but then they rolled to the back of his head and he passed out, leaving only the whites of his eyes and a limp body.

The deed had been done, and Kragnak dropped the still smoking bar of copper into the sand next to the forge.

"Is he...?" Kragnak asked. It was quiet, so quiet they could hear the sound of someone running in the corridor. Dorian moved the back of his hand to Lumdir's mouth.

His eyes had closed again, but a faint breath stirred the hairs on the back of Dorian's hand. Relief flooded through him, but he tempered that too. "He's alive."

"Sticks and stones! What did you do to him?" Yudoline rushed in, followed by Olgim. She rushed over to Lumdir and pushed Dorian to the side, giving him a nasty glare.

"Took a chance with the fire," Dorian said. He rose to his feet. "He'll need some rest."

"And something to drink, go get me some ale," Yudoline said. Olgim jumped and rushed out. She wrinkled her nose at the smell as she examined the wound.

Dorian wasn't sure, but he thought some of the red spider-webbing had eased. *Just my mind playing tricks on me. Don't get your hopes up.*

"There wasn't anything else we could do for him." Dorian wasn't sure why he felt like justifying his actions, but the words slipped out of him.

"So, you burned him? How is that supposed to help?"

Dorian shrugged. "It burned him, but it might burn out whatever is causing his illness."

Yudoline snorted. "You think he'll just up and get around, same as before?"

"I've seen it work before," Kragnak said, crossing his arms.

"What's done is done. No use arguing about it now," Dorian said. "Everyone back to work. We've got a lot of work to do." He knelt down beside Yudoline and scooped up Lumdir, still too light for a dwarf.

"Send Olgim down to his room when he gets back with that ale. I'm not letting this dwarf out of my sight." Yudoline leveled a stare at Kragnak, then turned it on her husband.

"Yes dear."

Yudoline sniffed and followed Dorian out of the workshop. He waited for it, preparing himself. It didn't come, even as they entered the apartments.

"Go on, speak your mind." Dorian laid down Lumdir on his bed gently, pulling up the blanket over his hot form.

Yudoline was still at the door, arms crossed and eyebrows drawn down. "You acted impulsively." She sighed. "But I'm not sure it was the wrong decision. You're right, there is nothing else we could have done, and it pains me to say it."

"You did everything you could. It's a miracle he's lived this long." Dorian offered her the chair, and she sat. "I know about the extra time you've taken with him, feeding him drop by drop because he couldn't swallow."

"I want him to live," she said, voice trembling.

"So do I." They waited in silence until Olgim came with the ale. Lumdir's chest rose and fell, sweat trickling down his brow. *Such a strong dwarf, laid low by one wound. A wound that was my fault.*

"I've got to go," Dorian said when Olgim arrived, also sweating and hauling a full cask. "When you're done with him I'll be in the farm caves. If you could show me how things are going I'd appreciate it."

"I can show you," Olgim said after catching his breath. Dorian looked at Yudoline, who nodded as she poured a cup of ale.

"He can."

"Lead the way then," Dorian said, somewhat surprised.

"My family grows mushrooms in our cellar," Olgim explained as they walked. "It wasn't something I thought would be important when we arrived, but it has proved helpful."

"Mushrooms?"

"Mostly buttercaps." Olgim sighed, taken away. "What I'd give for a big bowl of buttercap soup right now, thick and creamy. So rich with flavor, the soup my mother used to make."

"Sounds good." Dorian's mouth was watering at the thought.

"If we had some spores I could grow them again, but I haven't found any mushrooms good enough to raise." The turned left at the top of the stairs.

"If you find some we'll make the room." Olgim's eyes lit up.

"Do you really mean that?"

"Yes. We'll shift dirt to a rock cavern if you need it."

"No need to do that. We raised them on logs, it didn't matter what kind of cave they are in, as long as it stays dark."

Dorian laughed, the pressure in his chest lifting just a little. "That won't be a problem."

"I'll hold it to you then." Olgim shook his head. "A little taste of home way out here. I'm looking forward to it." They walked into the expanded farm cavern, now a cavern in name as well as in size.

Rows of support columns ran in every direction, holding up the mountain above it. Yander and Dozotaine had dug to within a few feet of the surface to the north, and had braced it.

"We'll look at the newer crops here." Olgim pulled him to the right. The dirt walls still looked damp and shiny. Small bunches of golden moss glowed in plots, a row of them lining up in between the supports.

They had already started sending out tendrils of moss, feeling their way along the damp dirt floor. "Looks like they are doing well."

"For just starting, yes. It's amazing how much the moss acts like mushrooms. We need to feed them, water them, and keep them happy and everything else they do on their own."

"Any problems?" The other plots of moss were almost full or half full. Dorian thought they might have enough of it to feed an army.

"No, the fertilizer is keeping them growing nice and tall." Dorian looked again. The moss didn't seem taller than what they originally planted. *Must be something I don't know about.*

Dorian decided not to ask about it. They walked on and inspected the rest of the crops. "All healthy then?"

"Yes, we should have enough to last the winter and then some if we just harvest what we've planted." Some of the golden moss was growing so well it had started creeping up the supports and walls deeper in the mountain side of the room.

"A ray of light in the dark," Dorian murmured.

"What was that?"

"Nothing, just glad that they are growing. As long as we can keep the moles away we might have a chance."

Olgim cocked his head to the side. "I don't know anything about moles, but we'll be eating rockbread until the goats come home." Dorian half smiled and patted him on the shoulder.

"Let's go see the goats." His mind wandered as they walked over, partially put at ease seeing the farms doing as well as they were. It was one burden lifted, but the other was still there. They had to harden the mine against the goblins, who would be here.

Dorian suspected it was sooner rather than later.

The goats and chickens were doing fine, the kids were growing and there were plenty of eggs to last for a while. For the first time in a while, he thought they would have enough food.

But would it matter? His thoughts wandered back to Lumdir, back to the attack and ambush by the undead. He thought that they would be hidden for longer, undiscovered by their enemies, but he had been wrong.

And it had cost them. Dwarves he had barely learned to love were hurt and may even die. Mughan had a point, he wasn't sure that he was able to lead them anymore. And it would only get worse as more migrants came, if they did come.

The baaing of a goat broke his attention and the spiral of his thoughts. He held out a hand and it came over to him, leaning over the wooden fence that kept it segregated from the crops. While it smelled and searched his hand for food Dorian hardened himself.

They would fine more iron, make better weapons and armor. With a fighting force they would be able to repel the things that lurked in the world that would love to devour and destroy them. All he needed was an army.

What he had was a group of migrants. He stared at Olgim. Short, stocky, but not muscular like Barileth or Dozotaine. How long would it take to train him and get him into fighting shape?

Even if they did get him trained in time, would he stand up under the pressure of battle? Dorian chewed the thought in his mind, and the goat nipped his hand. He drew back from the bite, his hand pooling a small drop of blood.

The realization dawned on him. They would never have a professional army capable of fighting off their enemies, and his heart sank.

18

IMPROVEMENT

Dorian shut the door behind him and motioned Barileth to sit. Barileth complied, eyebrows drawn down. After thinking about sitting down, Dorian decided to stand.

"How many more traps do you think you can make?"

Barileth sat back and looked at the ceiling. "Oh, I suppose I can put a few more together. Why do we need more? Why now?"

"Even if we do find iron, manage to make it into steel for, we wouldn't be prepared for what's out there."

"What do you know?" Barileth's eyes narrowed.

Dorian crossed his arms. "Enough." He let the silence continue, uncomfortable.

"Don't tell me then. I can assume the answer."

"Give me an answer, I need to know."

After scratching his beard and tilting his head up, Barileth finally answered. "I can make more, depending on how much supplies you're willing to allow me. Rock gears would be easiest to use."

Who would cut them? Lumdir was still in bed, looking better but still on the edge of the knife of death.

"We have copper, I'll get Kragnak to start working on more cages."

"That would be a start. I'll put together some more hammer traps and dead falls. I'm assuming this means you don't want me hunting then?"

"The traps first, and then the rest can come later. Make the entrance a killing zone if you have to, and plan for the door to be breached."

Barileth sat up straight. "You are serious, aren't you?" Dorian met his gaze without blinking. "How many goblins are you expecting?"

"It isn't the goblins I'm worried about."

"You think they'll come back?"

"I know something out there has found us. I don't intend to let them take us by surprise or take us without a fight. We will stop them when they come."

"If they come?" Dorian kicked himself inwardly.

"If."

"I'll work with Kimec to draw up some plans."

"Take the time you need. If we find iron Kragnak's priority will change. You'll be leftover at that point."

"They won't take us," Barileth said as he stood. "I won't let them, and neither will you."

Dorian nodded, but wasn't so sure.

"Just like old times again, isn't it?" Yander raised the torch above him, a pale light cast in its weak flame.

"And I'm already regretting it." Dorian couldn't keep a straight face though, and after a few second broke into a smile.

"You wanted to go down, right?"

"That's the best way." Dorian lifted his pickaxe and brought it down on the floor, taking a chunk out. A few more swings squared up the cut and left serviceable walls. "Take that side."

Yander took up his place across from Dorian, swinging true. His side of the stair was cut out almost as fast as Dorian's. "You've been working, I see."

"I try," Yander said, a happy smile on his face. They worked down a flight of stairs, continuing the mineshaft, and then turned to the right and deeper into the mountain. After a few feet Dorian stopped, stepping back from their handiwork.

A new tunnel, about two feet deep and almost perfectly round, stood before them. "Feel the rock, tell me what you feel."

"I'll try." Yander stepped forward, dropping his pickaxe to his side, and put his hand on the wall. He closed his eyes and concentrated. "I feel the wall. It's rough under my skin."

"Think less, talk less." Dorian watched him concentrate. "Breathe."

"It's warm. But dry." Yander furrowed his brow, eyes still closed. "There's a glimmer of something, off to the right. It feels...different somehow. Not like the copper."

Dorian stepped up to the wall too, feeling it. Yander was right, there was a glow there. "That's where we dig to."

They started to work, and the minutes slipped by. The joyful ring of pickaxe on rock kept up a steady cadence, a drumbeat, and rock slipping to the floor made up a chorus. Every so often they removed enough rock to keep it from clogging the tunnel.

Even with the stress and strain on his body, Dorian enjoyed it. Sweat started to pour down his face, the coolness of the earth licking away his heat.

"Dorian," Yander said softly. He almost didn't hear him over the sound of his pickaxe.

"Yes?"

"I...I don't know how to ask." His face was drawn and tight.

"It's about Emelda, isn't it." Yander nodded. "Go on then, it doesn't have to be perfect." A painful stab of longing for his dead wife hit his heart.

"She's worried about me, and I'm worried about her. Ever since..." he took a deep, shuddering breath, his hands trembling. "I can't get it out of my mind, or my dreams. They take her Dorian, every night."

Yander raised his head, his eyes full of so much anguish it tore at Dorian. "What am I supposed to do? How am I supposed to protect her?"

Dorian was washed in emotions. How was he supposed to give Yander the advice he needed to protect the dwarf he loved when he couldn't protect his own wife? The memory of her tore at him, and he drew a deep breath to try and recover some semblance of control.

"You do what you can," he said at last, his voice coming out of him in an otherworldly feeling. He hadn't thought of the words before they were out, and he wondered who he was talking to. "You do what you can."

"What if that isn't enough?" Yander slumped down, dropped his pickaxe against the wall with a clatter.

"It might not be enough." It wasn't enough for him. Dorian never even had a chance to fight to protect her. "You might die." Dorian's legs were weak, and he joined Yander. His head hit the wall, keeping it from spinning.

"I'm not afraid to die. I'm afraid to lose her."

"I know."

"You might not know this, but I've been practicing every chance I get." Dorian noticed Yander's hands, covered in blisters. "It doesn't feel like I'm getting any better."

"You are. I've seen it."

"It isn't fast enough, I need to be stronger."

"I understand."

"How do I protect her like I am?" Yander curled his hands into fists. "Weak."

"Yander, you have been getting better." Dorian's emotions were coming back in check. He was forced to focus on Yander's problems. He had no time for his own. "Your swings are harder and faster, your footwork more stable."

"Then why in all my dreams do they stop me from protecting her?"

"Dreams are a tricky thing. Sometimes they show us the past, sometimes the future. But most of the times they show us an image we want to see."

"I don't want to see Emelda taken from me."

"I didn't say you did." Dorian kept his voice quiet, not responding to Yander raising his. "You have the skills and strength you have. You might not be able to see it, but it's enough." He looked over at Yander.

The dwarf was still and staring at the ground. Dorian rose. "Come on, get up and follow me."

"But we need to mine. Where are you going?"

"There will be time for that later. There is something I want to show you." Dorian had been keeping it in reserve, waiting for when Yander was ready. He wasn't quite sure Yander was, but he needed something that would bolster his resolve.

And so, Dorian led him to the makeshift training room they had set up in an empty apartment, ignoring the protests and trying to address them as they walked.

"There will be time for that later," Dorian said. "This is more important now. Pick up an axe."

Yander picked up the oak training axe, his anger gone and his brow furrowed. "What are you going to teach me?"

"The most important lesson I can." They squared off. Yander raised his axe to match Dorian's stance. "Feel the axe in your hand. Feel how the handle touches your skin. It's warmth or coolness, roughness or smoothness."

"I feel it."

"See the blade, where it is."

"I see it."

"Smell and taste the axe." Yander shifted his stance, then concentrated.

"I smell it."

"Hear it. How it parts the air as you move it, the anticipation it has when it's stationary."

"I hear it."

"Good. Now, forget everything you hear, feel, taste, smell, and touch." Yander's eyes widened.

"Forget everything?"

"Everything," Dorian said. "Focus on how the axe moves and nothing else."

Yander shifted again, narrowed his eyes and fixed on the axe. Dorian attacked, streaking forward and knocking away Yander's axe before he had a chance to react.

"You're thinking. Stop thinking and feel." Yander took a deep breath. His eyes went blank. Dorian attacked again.

This time Yander was able to bring up his axe, deflect the blow. "You're still thinking. Again."

They reset. Again, Dorian attacked, but again Yander was still too slow. They continued the exercise over and over again, heating up the room until they were both breathing hard.

"Your body knows what to do. Let it do it." Dorian attacked again, but Yander was flagging. Dorian knew he was feeling the strain. "Now, when your muscles refuse to respond and your thinking is too slow you must fight by instinct."

"I don't understand," Yander said. "I've spent so much time learning how to attack and stand and block, and you say this is the most important thing to learn." He threw down his axe. "How is this supposed to make me stronger."

"It won't. Pick up the axe." Yander crossed his arms.

"If it won't help then why am I doing it?" *That was the question, about everything.* Dorian leaned down and picked up the training axe. The handle was smooth from where it had been worn by hands.

All the hours they had spent in this room, with these tools. All the time Dorian had spent in his youth training. Had it saved the ones he loved?

"When you feel the stone, what do you see?" Yander paused.

"I think I see where the ore is."

"But when you look at the tunnel wall what do you see?"

"Just rock, I suppose."

"Would it be better to use your eyes to mine, or feel it?"

Yander took his time to respond, and Dorian waited for him. *What lesson am I trying to teach him? That he shouldn't use his senses?*

What was he doing?

He looked down at the axe, a weapon that wouldn't hurt anything. Just like him, ineffective and useless.

But he had made a promise to Emelda, and he owed her that, as little as it was.

"I think I see your point," Yander said. "I'll try to do what you ask, but it's so hard. All of these thoughts keep swirling around my head and distracting me from it."

Dorian nodded. "Let them go, and refocus. They will come back, no matter what you do, but you must not let them linger."

Instead of more questions, Yander brought his axe back into guard. Dorian cleared his own mind, letting himself feel the axe in his hand.

He attacked.

This time, Yander brought up his own to counter. The two training axes met with a solid thunk that traveled down Dorian's arm.

He did it.

Yander's eyes widened and the two stood still in time. Then, Yander started to smile.

But Dorian was prepared for this and, even as pleased as he was, knew Yander had committed an act that that needed to be corrected. Dorian let the thought go and dropped his axe.

"I--" Yander's words were cut off as Dorian brought down his shoulder and shifted his weight, striking Yander in the chest with a shoulder.

The words and air went out of the dwarf, who fell to the ground and lay there. Dorian felt no satisfaction as he stood over Yander, but he was prepared for his foot.

With a quick snap Dorian brought down his axe on Yander's ankle as he tried to sweep Dorian's legs out from under him. It stopped the fight as Yander groaned from the blow.

"You're learning," Dorian said.

"Not fast enough." Yander took the hand that Dorian offered and struggled to his feet, wincing as he felt his left foot. "I did it though, did you see?"

"I saw." Dorian couldn't help but smile back, infected by Yander's joy. "And I'll keep teaching you until you learn."

19

FORGED

The stone gave way and piled up along the tunnel. Down into the mountain they carved a great path, pickaxes ringing like bells deep in the earth.

"I feel it," Yander said during a break. Dorian guzzled a flask of Yudoline's ale, the drink quenching his thirst and washing away the stone dust coating the inside of his mouth.

"Feel what?" Dozotaine asked, sitting and chewing a loaf of rockbread. The others were having their lunch in the main hall, but Yander had volunteered to bring food if they were able to work more effectively.

"Ore, I think. It's up ahead."

"How can you feel it?" Dozotaine tore off another chunk. Yander gave him a puzzled look.

"You can't feel the earth?"

"Sure, I can feel it," he said through a full mouth. "It's hard and rocky."

"Not everyone can," Dorian said. "Back to work, though."

"Have you felt it?" Yander asked, grabbing his pickaxe.

"I have." Dorian had a glimmer of hope, he thought it was a big vein but it was hard to tell. He struck the wall with his own pickaxe, a chunk of rock falling to his feet. "Clear this out so we can work."

Yander nodded and ran off to get the wheelbarrow. They had cleared out a big chunk by the time he returned, and it took all of them a few trips to fill and remove the rest of the rock.

All while the song of the ore called out, getting stronger.

Dorian stepped back when it was too strong. "Yander, you do the honors." He wiped the sweat from his brow and relinquished his place. Yander took it, examining the wall for a moment before he hefted his pickaxe.

The pick struck in a shower of sparks. It lodged into the rock and with a grunt Yander dislodged a chunk.

There it is.

"By the beard of Valknar," Dozotaine said, getting to his feet.

This vein started at Yander's midsection and went to at least his head. It glinted black in the torchlight with what could only be the glow of hematite.

Heart beating faster, Dorian stroked his beard and took a deep breath. His mind was racing already, tallying up the weapons and armor this would make. *Slow down, we can't see it all yet.*

Yander, however, had no such thoughts. He let out a loud roar and flung his hands in the air. "We did it!"

"Calm down," Dorian said, but he couldn't stop the smile from spreading across his lips. Yander's excitement was infectious, and they were laughing and clapping each other on the back in seconds.

"We have to tell the others, come on." Yander took off down the tunnel, whooping as he went.

"Yander, come back!" Dorian grabbed his pickaxe. "We need to get this out of the wall first."

"Can't it wait?"

"I'm with Dorian. Let's get as much out as we can." Without missing a beat Dozotaine joined Dorian and they struck at the wall.

The ore fueled their work, a vein that grew as they dug it out. Yander talked the whole time as they took turns at the wall, and Dorian didn't mind at all.

Soon they had barrowfuls of ore piled up in the main mineshaft. Dorian dropped the last load. "We've gone too long, I think they'll be wondering what happened to us soon. Take a few loads up to surprise them."

They piled the bucket high while Dozotaine ran up the stairs to lift it.

"Ready?" he called down.

"Bring it up," Dorian said. The bucket lifted with a spin, and they had to step back as a few chunks of ore fell out. They smiled at each other as the bucket disappeared.

"Do you think they'll be surprised?" Yander asked.

"I know they will. We'll have a feast tonight in celebration, with real meat." Dorian paused, and frowned. "I hope they haven't had it already."

"Don't worry," Yander said. "We'll have it again." Dorian laughed.

After a few trips most of the ore was hauled to the top of the shaft. "Where should we put it?" Dozotaine asked.

"Grab a wheelbarrow, we'll put it in the workshop." Dorian was expected to be mobbed with questions when he rolled the first wheelbarrow load, but it was empty.

Yander and Dozotaine were close behind. "We missed dinner, didn't we?" Yander asked.

"Not all of it." Dorian grabbed a particularly large chunk of ore. "Let's give them something to celebrate." He was relishing the look that would be on Mughan's face when he came in with it, and rolled it around in his arm.

"I could eat a goat, I'm so hungry," Dozotaine said, and they all laughed, Dorian picturing him trying. Together they went to the dining hall and entered together, while Dorian hid the ore behind his back.

The other dwarves were seated, eating the evening meal. It wasn't much, rockbread and cheese with carrots on the side, but it smelled heavenly to him. Dorian realized how famished he was when his mouth started watering.

"What happened?" Yudoline asked, a chunk of rockbread halfway to her mouth. "You look like a pile of dirt."

"And late, I see," Mughan added.

With a smile of contempt at Mughan, Dorian strolled to the other side of the table. "While you were having a good time, eating without us."

"We waited as long as we could," Emelda protested.

"We found it!" Yander yelled, spoiling the moment.

"Found what?" Mughan asked. Dorian brought out the ore and rolled it onto the table, right for Mughan's plate. It bounced once, slowed, then stopped as soon as it hit the edge.

"Is that--"

"Iron!" Kragnak stood up and reached across the table. He held up the chunk to the light. "And a big chunk too, where did you find it?"

"In the mine," Yander said. "At the bottom, we had to go down a lot deeper than we were expecting." The excitement grew in the room.

"And to celebrate, we're going to have a feast," Dorian said, taking a seat at the table. "Enough meat to satisfy everyone." Mughan didn't react like Dorian was expecting. He was calm and reserved, contemplative even. There's no way this won him over.

"Without rationing it?" Kragnak asked, a look of hope in his eyes.

"For everyone but you." Kragnak drew back, askance. "You've got work to do in the forge." Dropping his head down, Kragnak sagged.

Dorian's chuckle and waving hand caught Kragnak by surprise. "Come now, you'll get your meat." His chuckle turned into a laugh, which caught up the rest of the room. Then Kragnak finally joined in, filling the mine with sounds of true joy.

The hammer rang on the anvil, beckoning Dorian into the workshop. Everyone was hard at work, including Kragnak at the forge. Sweat streamed down his body.

His arms had grown with the heavy work at the forge. Dorian noted with satisfaction that he would make a good smith yet, no longer the skinny dwarf that had arrived so many months before.

Sparks flew from the iron glowing red as he hammered, a look of concentration on his face to rival that of a rock.

"Dorian, what are you doing here?" Emelda asked, rising from her workbench. She set down the bracelet she had been carving, the bin next to her work area filling.

"I've come to check on you, of course." He walked to her and took a peek behind her table. There were four more bins, almost completely full of crafts. "Staying busy I see."

"Let him work without bothering him," she said.

"I don't know what you mean."

"He gets so nervous when you're around." The comment surprised him, and he had no response. Kragnak was absorbed and hadn't noticed him yet.

Finally, after a pause, he spoke. "How has he been doing?"

"Better. I'm sure you're going to want to see what he's made today."

"I hope it looks better than the last batch. They'll do in a pinch, but I've never heard of anyone fighting well with a lopsided sword."

"Be kind, you know that was his first one."

"He's trying, I know it."

"Then let him be." Dorian knew that Kragnak was trying, but the sword was pretty bad. He imagined that he could hammer one out at or equal in quality, and that was with almost no training at all. Kragnak had been trained by the Forger's Guild, some of the best smiths in all of Zirad, and should be better.

"I wonder sometimes what happened to him. Why he has such a fear?" Kragnak was still working, sweat pouring down his face, lips contorted in wild concentration. The heat from the flames and the orange glow gave him an almost demonic look, if not for the fear in his eyes.

"They told him he wasn't good enough, that he would never amount to anything." Emelda's voice was soft and lonesome amid the hammering." How cruel a fate, to be destined to work at something you hate.

"We don't have much choice now, I'm afraid." Dorian hefted the sword. "Melt it down and start again, that's all we can do now." He turned back to Emelda. "Thank you."

Her eyes widened. "For what?"

"For caring, as much as you do. Not just for Kragnak, but for all of us." She dropped her eyes and hid her hands behind her. "I've noticed, and so has everyone else. Cooking meals that the dwarves prefer, that remind them of home. Cutting fresh flowers for Yudoline and leaving them at her bedside."

"I didn't think anyone saw me..."

"Be the soft touch, the one everyone needs." He squeezed her shoulder. "I can't be it, but we need it."

"You don't have to be so hard on yourself." Dorian gave her a half smile, then picked up the bracelet she was working on.

"Bees. They remind me of him. It's beautiful." They flitted among tiny flowers that grew on a vine encircling the band. He turned it over in his hand, ignoring the tears in Emelda's eyes. "Don't give it Mughan though, I know he'd like it. It's too good for him."

Mouth open, Emelda was about to respond. "Dorian! When did you come in?" Kragnak's voice was uncertain and wavering. Dorian turned back to the forge.

"Just a few moments ago. I see you're hard at work." He slipped the bracelet back on the table and gave Emelda's arm a squeeze. There was something in her eyes, but the moment wasn't right and she shut her mouth and let him go.

"Oh, yes." Kragnak slicked back his hair, shaking the sweat from his beard. "The iron is good, but hard. It doesn't want to form like the copper did. I always had trouble with swords." He shrugged and plunged the creation into the quench bucket. It sizzle and sent gouts of steam up into the already humid air.

"Keep at it. What about other weapons?" Dorian walked over to check on the rest of his work, looking over some more iron glinting next to the forge.

They weren't good. Not at all.

"May I?" Kragnak nodded, shifting from one foot to the other. Dorian selected an axe with lopsided blades, and picked it up. "Got some heft to it," he said. The balance was off, and would need to be fixed before it could be used, but the iron was hammered into an...axe shape.

He looked back at Kragnak, who was watching him expectantly. It meant that he wanted some affirmation, something that wouldn't make all his hard work seem like nothing. *How am I supposed to tell him to melt it down and start over again?*

"You don't like it." Kragnak sagged.

"No, I didn't say that." Dorian struggled to find something to compliment, glancing back at Emelda, who shot him a look of warning. "It has a nice curve here." He pointed out the larger blade. The sweep was well formed, not lopsided like the sword.

"I spent hours on that. I had some trouble getting the sizes right, but I'm working on that."

"You're working hard." Dorian couldn't tell him he was doing a good job, not with weapons like these, but the dwarf would be crushed by the truth. "You're our smith, the Seventh Hall smith. You put raw ore into the fire and a weapon comes out the other side."

"Do you mean it?" Kragnak looked up, relieved at his words.

"Every word." Dorian laid the axe back on the table gently, not knowing if it would shatter. A thought struck him that might solve his dilemma. He surveyed the group of odd-looking weapons. "And I know exactly what to do with these."

20

PROVING GROUNDS

Yander huffed, leaning over his weapon. "I didn't think it would be this hard."

"Stop your yammering and get back to it." Dorian gave him a gentle kick to the backside to bring him to his feet.

"Now that wasn't called for."

"Attack."

"Arrrgh!" Yander charged back in, weapon raised high above his head. Mere seconds from meeting his foe he struck with a cleaving overhand strike.

The hit was true, striking right on the face. "Again," Dorian said. Blows fell, metal rang out, sparks flew. When he had finally given everything he could, Yander followed it up with a two-handed chop from the side.

With a crunch the axe gave, half of it flying off as it yielded to the rock. It left a nice cut, almost a quarter inch deep, as evidence of the final blow.

"Good." Yander drew back, panting. Dorian walked over to see his handiwork, counting the strikes. "An extra four notches that meet the criteria. You're improving."

Yander grinned. "Couldn't do it without you. Are we really going to go through all of these?" He held up the broken iron axe, the stunted back head all that remained after the training.

A few more broken weapons were already piled on the table, and Dorian grabbed the broken axe head to add it to the pile. The stone had mushroomed the blade, a few notches missing from the crescent.

"Every last one." The metal rang as it hit the pile. Dorian rounded on Yander, sensing an opportunity. "Unless you'll volunteer to tell him his work isn't good enough?"

"No, no." Yander held up his hands, going a shade paler. "We'll use them."

"Good. We've got one more to go to today before we send them back to the fire to be remelted." Dorian tossed him a lopsided sword, one side deadly sharp. "You've caught your breath, so get back to it."

In a few moments it joined the others. "That's it," Yander said, still trying to catch his breath.

"We have to cut the training short today. That's enough for now."

"Already? But we barely started." Dorian chuckled at the comment, eying the pile of broken swords and axes.

"Take these back to Kragnak to have him melt them down and reforge them into something new. I've got to go." Dorian turned to leave, but Yander grabbed his arm.

"You want me to take them? What if he asks who destroyed them? What am I supposed to say then?"

"Tell him the truth."

"But then he'll think I did it on purpose!"

"You did do it on purpose."

"That's not what I mean. All his hard work trying to make these weapons and I've gone and destroyed them in a few hours. Won't he be dejected and sad?"

"He might be, but I need to leave." Yander dropped his eyes to the floor. Dorian was hoping to avoid it, but it looked like he would have to take the blame anyway. "Tell him that I told you to do it, that we were testing them to see how strong they were. Tell him they were made well, solid, and took a beating against raw stone."

"I still don't think it is a good idea..."

"Trust me," Dorian said. He patted Yander on the shoulder, who started to slink toward the pile, grabbing an empty bin on his way. Shaking his head, Dorian left the room and headed for the kitchens.

What would Kragnak think? Would he be angry, sad that everything he made was destroyed? Dorian didn't think he would, he thought that he might be relieved. Starting over wouldn't be the most palatable thing in the world, but he would get a second chance to start over.

A second chance, something he would never be afforded had he stayed in Zirad. Dorian shook his head as he walked. There was too much corruption in the capitol, headed by too big a fool. No wonder there were dwarves willing to risk their lives just to leave it.

Would he ever return? Or would he keep to himself on the edges of the wilderness, maybe find another expedition where he didn't have to lead it? The thought of it excited him inside and he had to rein himself in.

"Don't get too ahead of yourself, Dorian. I still have to survive this." That meant feeding all the dwarves, the subject of his early departure.

"Dorian, good morning," Olgim said as he entered the kitchen, looking up from a pile of potatoes. Skins coated the ground next to him. "I'm peeling potatoes."

"I see that. Good morning."

"Good morning," Emelda said. She stirred the pot one last time and hooked the large wooden spoon up, wiping her hands off on her apron. "You've come to see it?"

"Yes, what do we have?"

"The harvest was good," Olgim said, picking up another potato and slicing away the skin. "The best was the southern plots."

"We managed to fill four barrels up," Emelda said, following him to the storeroom. They were at the front, heaped to the top with the golden moss that was starting to lose its luster. It would darken to gray soon, what gave rockbread its name.

Dorian moved around the re-arranged storeroom. They had taken out the empty containers like he asked, laid them against the wall in the corridor, and it was easier to see what they had. "Let's count it up."

"I'll get the paper," Emelda said, disappearing out the door.

"I think we'll have enough," Olgim said when she was gone. "And the outdoor crops are growing well. Soon enough we'll be able to harvest the carrots, and then a few weeks after that the potatoes and squash."

"I thought you raised mushrooms?"

"My extended family are farmers. I don't see them much, but when we do the talk is all about growing things."

"Consider yourself the head farmer then," Dorian said, shifting the top of the golden moss away to see what was underneath. It looked good and healthy.

"Really?" Olgim drew himself up and puffed out his chest. "I've never been head of anything. They wouldn't let me back home."

"Who wouldn't let me?"

"Everyone. I wasn't much of a miner so they tried to keep me out of the way." Olgim tossed his potato into a bucket. "Father was a master, though, could almost taste the way rock split. He almost became a stone worker, too."

"Did he teach you anything?" Dorian felt a mixture of hope and disgust at thinking of replacing Lumdir. *He's doing better, he'll survive.*

"Not much. Didn't trust 'em with the rock." Emelda returned.

"I've got it here." She waved the parchment and charcoal, then joined Dorian.

"Let's get started." While Dorian counted their food, Emelda recorded the amounts. All the vegetables, every block and wheel of cheese, the buckets of milk, meats and skins from Barileth's hunting, they were all accounted for.

Emelda handed him the final tally and he looked it over, thinking about how many dwarves they had and about how much each one would eat.

"Enough to last the winter and most of spring," Dorian said when he had come to his final conclusion, scratching it out on the sheet.

"Without anything else? It seemed so little," Emelda said.

"We dug a big storeroom for when the mine gets bigger. It might not look it, but this could hold enough food for a hundred dwarves or more."

Emelda's eyes widened. "That much?"

"That much." One weight lifted off his shoulders. The chickens had hatched another brood, and would continue to lay. The goats seemed to be doing fine and were still giving milk. "Barileth has the fall to hunt, too. He might get us some meat for long nights and dark times."

"That must make you feel better."

Dorian gave her a half smile. "It doesn't make me feel worse. We have a few more years to go, though. Who knows what will happen in the future?" There was a commotion from the hallway.

Together, they entered the kitchen, just as Yander burst into the room.

"Come quick, there's a caravan arriving!"

"A caravan? Where is it coming from?"

"The north," Yander turned back as Dorian and the others caught up to him, following him out into the hallway. "Barileth sent me down to find you. They have a few oxen and are carrying a lot of stuff."

He did it. I didn't think he would. He looked back to see Emelda and Olgim following with downcast eyes. "Come on then," Dorian said to the others who were lagging behind. "No use in trying to hide that you don't want to come. I have a feeling we won't get much work done anyway."

They walked quickly to the entrance and out into the blinding sun. Others were already gathered at the gate, along the makeshift walkway they had constructed to be able to see out. Dorian and his group joined them as the rest of the dwarves streamed out.

Mughan had already taken the prime vantage point. "Not as many as I was expecting, but there are more than one," he said as Dorian climbed up the stone ramp. Able to see above the wall top, he searched out in the direction that everyone was looking.

They were there, trudging their way up the slope. Barileth sidled up next to him. "Saw them when they were farther off." He looked over at Mughan. "I tried to get you out without raising up a fuss, but it looks like I sent the wrong dwarf for the job."

Three forms led at least four oxen through the trees, backs laden with barrels. Everywhere around them dwarves were talking, and laughter broke out once in a while.

"I hope they have steak, or anything other than eggs and goat's milk," Dozotaine said.

"Thanks for trying." To the others, Dorian raised his voice. "Clear out a path, we need to have somewhere they can rest and spread out." Olgim was the farthest down the wall, closest to the exit. "Olgim, go get some rope. Mughan, get some stakes in the ground that they can tie up to."

"Yutatir will get them." Mughan nodded to him, and he brushed past the others to follow Olgim down into the caves. It got under Dorian's skin at how easily he cast off his order.

"Everyone else, get everything we've set up for trading out here as soon as you can." That spurred them to action, dwarves scattering off the ramps and down into the mines. Except Mughan and Dorian, much to his dismay.

So together they watched as the dwarven caravan ascended the slope. Dorian thought of what he wanted to do to Mughan, how he would put him in his place when the time was right. That was more than he could handle right now, though, and he said nothing.

"It looks like they have plenty of goods to trade, will we have enough to barter with?" Mughan asked.

"We have enough." Dorian crossed his arms, refusing to move from his vantage point even though he wanted to leave, go anywhere else.

"I suppose you'll want to do the trading too?" Mughan gave him a sideways look and then turned away when he didn't answer. "A shame, a more adept dwarf would have gotten more for the meager trading stock we have."

Dorian ground his teeth together and watched the caravan approach, plodding along. Behind him the mine was a flurry of activity as dwarves swarmed out with the trading goods they had been building.

"Two years of work is no meager trading stock." He spat the words out, making Mughan turn back to face him.

"I mean no offense, it's just that what we have..." He shrugged. "I'm used to more, I imagine. You seem like you're used to less. A lot less. Care to explain why?"

"You wouldn't understand if I told you.

"I'm not your enemy Dorian." *You could have fooled me.* "There are more deadly things we should be concentrating our time on, but with your distractions and coddling of the dwarves unable to contribute have jeopardized all of us for too long." Mughan was smiling, but it was cold and never reached his eyes.

"Lumdir is getting better. He might not be able to contribute right now, but he built this mine." Dorian clenched his fist, then released it, and took a breath. "You'll never understand what it was like in the first days, you've only just showed up when things were easier."

"This is easy?" Mughan let out a sharp bark of a laugh. "I'd hate to see what hard was like."

Now it was Dorian's turn to smile. "Continue on the path you're on. I'll make sure you find out."

21

VISITATION

"Ho, Dorian." A familiar voice from beyond the wall broke up the moment, allowing the tension between them to release for a moment. Dorian turned to it, trying to smile a more natural smile.

"Tufolin. What did you do to the King to have him send you out here again?"

Tufolin laughed a deep, hearty laugh that carried up the mountain. "You don't want to know."

"I'll come down to greet you properly." As Dorian turned, Mughan caught him by the arm.

"Don't think I won't forget this," he said so that only Dorian could hear.

"Release me." Dorian stared hard, and Mughan relaxed his grip. He left, a sinister look brooding on the other dwarf's face. Of all the things that Dorian had said, that was the one that made him angry?

He had been hoping to get some sort of reaction from Mughan for a while, but even his entrance with the spider fang hadn't elicited one. It didn't make him feel good, but Dorian left to greet the merchants anyway.

There would be time to have that fight later, but not now.

"What news from the expedition?" Tufolin asked as Dorian drew closer, the rest of the dwarves in tow. They swarmed the three merchants, and Dorian pulled Tufolin out of the fray. "Anxious to see me? I haven't been gone that long."

"We're progressing."

"Fast, I hope?" Tufolin drew aside his coat and took a swing from his water skin.

"There have been some... complications." They walked through the gate and were led into the makeshift marketplace the dwarves had set up inside the wall. The gate swung shut when they were all through, slamming in place.

"I imagine that might have something to do with it?" Tufolin raised an eyebrow. "Goblins, perhaps?"

Dorian nodded. "That's not all. We've been visited by a necromancer's ilk. Have you heard of anything in the area?" The merchants stopped their oxen and were unloading their goods. Crates and barrels were untied and set down on the grass, and out of them came samples to show.

"Necromancy? I haven't heard of anything." Dorian wasn't sure that he would have, but it still felt like a letdown. Any information would be better than what they had now.

"I've forgotten my manners, please go inside and make yourself comfortable. Rest from the journey and we'll meet when you're ready."

"You'll have your hands full with those ones. I'll leave you to it, I could use some rest." Tufolin mopped some sweat off his brow and sideburns. "That isn't the easiest journey, as you know."

"I know." Tufolin went inside and Dorian joined the throng crowding around the merchant's wares. A glint in the sunlight caught his attention.

It was silver, well made, and was perfectly balanced from the look of it. The steel pickaxe was tied up to an ox, along with a bundle of other tools. He eyed it longingly, wanting to feel its weight and heft.

But there were other things to look at, and supplies they needed more. The merchants had brought cloths and leather, string, and rope. All goods that were in short supply.

"Look at this," Yudoline said, picking up a shirt. "Well crafted, and softer than butter." She felt along the arms. Dorian looked down and was keenly aware of how ragged his own clothing had become.

In fact, he could tell the migrants from the original founders by their dress alone, and in what year they had arrived. Mughan, of course, had the best-preserved clothing. In his mind Dorian knew what would happen.

The bargaining was hard, but even the silver bars they had smelted hadn't been enough to get everything that Dorian was hoping for. The entire time Mughan had been there watching, giving him a scowl every time the merchants refused to come down on their price.

They were left with empty bins that had once been filled with crafted goods, and in exchange received clothing, cloth, rope, and several dried meats and cheeses. Emelda and Olgim were excited at the barrel of seeds, with additional types of cave crops and one particularly interesting find.

"Butter mushroom spores." His eyes lit up when he opened the sack. "Enough to grow a feast of them!" Olgim took them with delight, disappearing into the bowels of the mine.

Orders were given to take the rest away and the merchants invited into the mine to rest and sleep. They planned on leaving in the morning, as soon as the sun was up, no matter how hard the dwarves tried to persuade them to stay.

The steel pickaxe was packed away, far outside their bargaining power. Dorian wished they had kept the iron weapons. They might not have gone for very much, but they could be melted down as scrap metal.

Would that have been best? He didn't know anymore. The sun set, casting up a fire of red, yellows, and oranges. With the day spent, Dorian felt no closer to feeling good about the future of the expedition.

Dorian knocked softly. "Come in," came the weak reply. He opened the door and went in.

"How are you feeling?" Lumdir was looking better, although he was far too thin.

"Better than yesterday."

"Good." Dorian wrung his hands and sat down.

"I was able to stand up. And my teeth stopped aching as much. I think I'll be able to eat a whole mammoth tomorrow."

Dorian smiled, relieved. "Sorry it's taken me so long to come visit you. Things have been busy and..."

"No need for that. I know how it is. You're probably wanting me back to work tomorrow." It was Lumdir's turn to smile. "I'm sure my list will be long."

"Longer than you think." Dorian put a hand on Lumdir's shoulder.

"It wasn't your fault, you know. We all wanted to go after her, and I wasn't quick enough to avoid the strike."

"I don't know what you mean." *Yudoline had been talking too much again.*

"You've changed. I used to hate you when we first got here."

"I deserved it."

Lumdir let out a sharp bark of laughter, that quickly dissolved into a coughing fit. He waved away Dorian's efforts to help. "That you did." He looked into Dorian's eyes. "But now? I think there is only one dwarf left in the mine who still hates you."

"And he's a pain in my side." After leaning back in his chair, Dorian turned back to Lumdir. It was worth a shot, and he did need some advice. "How do you think I should deal with Mughan?"

Lumdir shook his head. "I wasn't talking about Mughan."

"But who else hates me more than him?"

"He doesn't hate you. He thinks you aren't making the best decisions for the expedition, that's it. In some ways he's jealous."

"Then who were you talking about?"

"I was talking about you."

"Must we do this at all?"

"You know how it goes. If you'd like me to keep it brief I can, but the full report will be going back to the King regardless of whether you hear it or not." Tufolin arched an eyebrow as he looked over the parchment he was holding.

"Then get it over with," Dorian said, taking a swig of his ale. His cup echoed in the empty dining room as he set it down, the remains of the smell of lunch still in the air, rockbread and roasted vegetables.

"Well, there was much improvement since last year." Dorian snorted at that. "Food provisions seem to be on the rise, I estimate you'll have enough to feed everyone through winter and keep a stable supply of underground crops growing in that time."

"Provided it isn't eaten by vermin."

"This evaluation is for now only. Disasters aren't included."

Dorian waved his hand. "I know, I know. Go on."

"Enough rooms and beds for every dwarf." Tufolin checked off his parchment. "Space for industry, with a plan to expand." Another check. "Defenses seem adequate, considering the threats in the area."

That struck Dorian, and he wasn't sure why. A wall, a gate, and some locked doors and traps. "Against everything?"

"Even considering your reports? Yes, I think so." Tufolin returned to his parchment. "Ores discovered. Iron, copper. Rock veins. Granite layer, adequate earth for farming."

"And here comes the best part." Dorian drained the rest of his cup. Tufolin cast him a glance.

"Necessary improvements. Area and means to treat wounded." Dorian sat up at that, a pain striking his chest. He tried to forget their conversation, but it kept clawing at him.

"We're working on it," Dorian growled.

Tufolin held up his hands. "Don't be offended. It's what I see. What happens in the future is up to you. Weapon production is... lacking. Areas for entertainment and feasting can be improved. Faster production of alcohol is required, a dedicated worker is recommended. Gemstones need processed. Textile production is non-existent and endangers the growth of the expedition.

Stonework has been delayed due to exigent circumstances, but a secondary stone worker is required to meet demand. Growth will be delayed without adequate stone work."

Another hit below the belt, but Dorian was glad he didn't list out what happened. "Silk work is possible, but hasn't been explored."

"It's been explored," Dorian said. That wall would stay blocked up until they were good and ready to venture into the deep, with plenty of protection set up.

"And finally." Tufolin paused and looked up from his parchment. "Ore exploration is behind pace and the mine is too shallow."

Dorian sat in silence now, staring at Tufolin.

"You need to dig deeper Dorian. What you seek is far down, and the King is relying on you to find it."

"Then the King can come out here and do it himself."

"I'll leave that out of my report. There are dwarves waiting for your success here. Are you going to let them down?"

"You're treading on dangerous ground, Tufolin. I suggest you leave off the threats."

"I have nothing to do with it. I'm simply here to advise you and make recommendations." He shrugged. "What you do with them, from my outside perspective, I have no control over. And yes, your children are being withheld from you. It wasn't the King's first choice in action."

"For which I'll never forgive him."

"You never would have, and he knows it." Tufolin's expression softened. "He spared your life, Dorian."

"The world might be a better place had he not."

"I doubt it." Tufolin rolled up his parchment, put it into a scroll case and sealed it. "I'm leaving now, with the merchants. They were relatively pleased by their visit, and I suspect may spread the word about it."

"So, they could come rob us too?" Dorian muttered. Without responding Tufolin stood up and patted him on the shoulder.

"Delve deeper Dorian. Delve deeper."

"This is a quiet kind of night," Olgim said. "Nothing's been happening."

"Good to hear," Kuddick muttered.

"Get anything good from the merchants?"

"A pair of socks, that's it."

"Do you want the spear?" Olgim held out the funny-looking iron spear in offering, but Kuddick shook his head.

"No, this will do for me." He patted the iron war hammer.

"That's the best one I've seen so far. It actually looks like a hammer."

"It's been a while since I've used one of these." Kuddick spun it around, taking a few test swings.

"I can tell."

He stopped swinging, then turned back. "Wait a second. You don't mean that in a good way, do you?"

Olgim scratched his head and looked down. "That isn't the way I meant it to come out." Stars twinkled in the sky, a gibbous full moon laying fat along the horizon.

"It's different, isn't it?" Kuddick gazed out over the valley. "Peaceful. Empty. Quiet."

"It is."

"None of the busyness of the capitol."

"Do you miss it?"

Kuddick stuck the hammer back in the loop on his belt. "Some parts of it. Most of it I could do without."

"I miss it," Olgim said. "I wish I could go back most nights, but..."

"I know." The world was silent. Not even the crickets were singing. Something wasn't right.

Olgim looked around, watching the tree line carefully. Kuddick stepped closer beside him.

"What is it?"

"I don't—there in the trees."

"What?"

"Something moved."

"I can't see it."

Olgim was about to respond, but a whistle sounded out and something flew past his ear.

"Get down!"

More whistles, and then clinks as arrows rained down on the wall and around the dwarves. Olgim pulled Kuddick down, and they dropped behind the wall.

22

ATTACK

"What are we going to do?" Olgim asked as the still of the night was shattered by the wild howls of creatures just outside the wall. More arrows flew, and they covered their heads.

"We've got to go get help." Kuddick eyed the entrance door. "How many are there?"

"I don't know."

"Well check then."

Olgim glanced up at the top of the wall. "I don't want to."

"Bearded lizard, I'll do it then." Slowly, Kuddick rose and peeked his head over the wall. More cries rang out from the goblins and he ducked his head back in before a clatter of arrows hit the wall and just where his head had been.

"Not good. Too many. Forty, fifty maybe."

"Fifty." Olgim clutched at his chest. He checked the gate, still locked tight and up out of the way.

"They have ladders too." Olgim met Kuddick's eyes.

"If they get in we're all dead."

"If they get in," he agreed. Olgim handed him his spear.

"I'll go get help, keep them off the wall." Kuddick took it, hand shaking, then nodded.

"Go fast." Olgim was gone though, rolling off the wall and stepping down the ramp that led into the courtyard. Just over the wall the sound of the goblins was getting closer. They were yelling, jeering at the wall. Taunting him they called out to have him show himself in the common tongue.

Kuddick gathered his wits and quieted his mind, drawing out the war hammer. "Come on then, just like practice. You knew this could happen when you came out here, they warned you before you left."

Olgim was halfway across the courtyard now, and going fast. In a few moments he would reach the door. That might be all the time Kuddick could give him.

There was a creaking and bending sound from the other side, then the crash of wood on stone from a few feet down. Kuddick got to his feet and ran over to it.

He braced himself on the wall, dug the spear into the crude, wooden ladder that now poked above the wall, and pushed with all his might.

It resisted at first, then moved. As he pushed it away it was shaking, and the surprised face of a goblin appeared at the top. Kuddick smiled and gave one final shove, sending the ladder toppling back and taking a screaming goblin with it.

A mighty crash ended the scream, and Kuddick smiled. "One down."

An arrow flew by his ear, and he ducked. More ladders creaked up and down the wall, and he swore to himself.

One by one they struck home. Kuddick looked at the mine entrance. No Olgim, and it was shut tight. He thought about running for it, but then turned to the wall.

Better to stop them here if he could.

The first ladder went down faster than the first, but the second was harder and shook more violently than the other. Kuddick finally gave up, tossed down the spear, and drew his hammer.

A goblin face rose out of the darkness, bigger than the others, and Kuddick swung with all his might. His hammer connected with a crunch, and he let the momentum take him forward and pushed against the ladder.

The weight of the goblin clutching at its face and pulling back from the blow helped bring the ladder back away from the wall to crash down. Kuddick took a moment to peek up over the edge.

Goblins swarmed the area outside the gate, barking and screaming at each other in their foreign tongue. They were already picking up the other ladders that had fallen, rolling their dead companions out of the way.

And there were at least four more ladders.

Kuddick paled, then ducked down as a goblin archer took aim at him. He slammed his back against the wall.

It was no use, there were too many. His lungs were burning from his breathing and his heart was beating fast.

Clutching his hammer in both hands he decided. He got up and ran for it, bashing a ladder on his way to the ramp.

He tripped at the edge and tumbled down, scrambling to get up when he hit the bottom. Looking back, he ran for the door.

Goblins were coming over the edge now. Twisted, curved swords were on their backs, in their teeth, and in their hands. One stopped at the edge and yelled something back, but Kuddick turned away from the frightening scene and to his salvation.

The door beckoned to him, and he hoped it was still unlocked. An arrow streaked by him, startling him out of his course. Kuddick twisted and turned, slowing his advance but trying to avoid more arrows coming his way.

Pain lanced up his leg, sending him to the ground. He looked back at the arrow sticking out from his leg and the goblins rapidly advancing on him.

What is that sound? Dorian looked up from Tufolin's report. There was some sort of commotion in the hallway. The hairs on the back of his neck stood up and he searched around for his axe. Something was wrong.

It wasn't here. It was back in his room. *Or is it in the old dormitory with the rest?*

The sound got closer, and Dorian hoped he was being paranoid, that everything was fine. It was getting late and he was probably imagining things. He should have been in bed already, today was a long day.

Then, he heard Olgim through the corridor. "- someone has to help." He remembered putting the axe down in his room, but that was a long way away. Dorian got to his feet, knocking the chair to the ground and ran out of the dining hall.

"Olgim!" He had to shout his name a few more times before Olgim turned and stopped his yelling. "What happened?"

"Goblins," Olgim said, panting. "Goblin attack."

"Go wake up the others. Come now dwarf. No time to rest." They weren't ready for this. The wall might be done and the gate finished, but they could scale those. Only the entrance door stood between them and the enemy he feared would be here.

Dorian pulled Olgim along, checking that the door was closed. "Did you lock it?"

"Kuddick is still out there."

To his left was the entrance, to the right the stairs down to the others. An unlocked door, but with a dwarf outside. If he were to close it now all hope would be lost for Kuddick. But, on the other hand, they would be safe inside.

Until when? Would they be stuck in here forever, waiting to be rescued? There was no way to fight if they locked that door.

But they would survive. The thoughts ran through his mind in a split second. He knew what Mughan would do, but he couldn't bring himself to do it.

Dorian turned right, following Olgim, down into the mine and where the dwarves were sleeping. Together they yelled and raised the alarm, and when they got there dwarves were standing outside their rooms, blinking the sleep out of their eyes.

"Get your weapons and get to the entrance tunnel. We're under attack by goblins!" That got their attention, and soon they were scrambling to get dressed. "No time for that, to your arms."

Rushing by the others, Dorian went into his room. There, on his desk, his old friend lay where he last put it. He didn't waste a second, but picked it up and ran back outside.

Some of the dwarves had kept their weapons in their room. Yander, he saw, was one of them. "How many?" he asked as he fell in behind Dorian.

"I don't know."

"Fifty, or more," Olgim said.

"How will we survive?" Yutatir asked, panic in his voice. Dorian stopped long enough to grab him by the beard and shake him.

"You won't, if you lose your wits. Get your weapon and fight."

"I left mine in the dormitory." Others said the same.

"Get up there and put on any armor that you can find." Kragnak hadn't made much, just started on the helmets, but there might be enough for all of them. "Kuddick is still out there."

"You don't mean to go out and fight them?" Mughan asked. He was fully dressed, ready to go. Dorian wondered how he had done it.

"No time to talk, get up there." Dorian ran out the door, and the others followed him. They were loud as they rushed up the stairs, clamoring and clawing away as a ragtag group.

Once again Dorian wished he had more time to train them, or have Barileth train them, or anyone. Even Dozotaine showed more promise than anyone else.

And they were still one dwarf short. Lumdir had to be in bed, still recovering his strength.

Which meant the odds were even less in their favor than before.

"Fifty goblins, what are we going to do?" Yudoline asked.

"We fight them off," Barileth said. His gruff voice was a welcome sound in the darkness. "Wish someone brought at torch though." He grunted, and someone else yelled.

"Sorry," Kragnak said.

"That was my stomach," Barileth said.

"And my foot," Mughan added. Dorian tried to repress his feeling of welcome at his complaint. "You're going too slow. We need to get to those weapons now."

They were at the top of the stairs now. The door was still shut.

Dorian breathed a sigh of relief. They still had time, although he didn't know how much. "Don't get distracted now, we've got some surprises waiting for them."

The dormitory was only a few more steps away, but Dorian was kicking himself for not having someone mine out another entrance to it. It never seemed important, but now that they had to go through the workshop to get there, it would add precious seconds to their preparation.

"The first helmet is mine," Mughan said as soon as they entered, and he walked over to the stack to hand out, right after he grabbed a sword. Clanks and crashes filled the air as the dwarves descended on the supplies.

Everyone else was taking their weapon of choice. Kragnak had been busy, and there was enough for everyone to have a weapon with some of the old copper spears and axes left in reserve. Kragnak started to pick them up, but Dorian stopped him.

"Leave those. We won't need them."

"Are you sure?" Even among the commotion Kragnak stood still.

"We've put them up against the worst we can throw at them. They'll be strong enough." Kragnak smiled at Dorian's words, and he thought his eye might be watering, but dismissed it as a trick of the low light.

"Is everyone ready?" Dorian raised his voice above the sounds. "We need to go now."

"Not yet," said a few. Every second that passed would mean less change for Kuddick to survive. Still the dwarves helped each other with the meager iron and copper armor.

Mughan sidled up to him and leaned in close to his ear. Dorian resisted the urge to get farther away. "Why even go out there? Wouldn't it be better if we stayed inside?"

"The entrance hall is the best chance we have. The traps will only hold them off for so long, and once they have control of the mine then we won't have a chance."

"But we have a fortified position here, we can hold them off indefinitely."

Dorian leveled him with a steel gaze that Mughan returned. "And what about Kuddick? Do we leave him outside to die?"

Mughan shrugged. "That would be unfortunate, but Kuddick knew his chances when he came out here just like the rest of us."

"No, I won't do it." Dorian twisted his hand around the handle of his axe. "I've left loved ones behind, and I'm responsible for this expedition." He turned to the door, looking back over his shoulder.

"I'm going to help Kuddick, even if it's the last thing I do."

23

RESPONSE

"Who will come with me and fight?" Dorian turned at the doorway to look back into the room. Kimec, Yander, Kragnak, Barileth, even Emelda and Yudoline stood clutching their weapons. The new arrivals were grouped behind Mughan.

"We won't go with you," he said.

Dorian recoiled. *Surely, they must want to protect one of their own.* "You'd leave Kuddick to die?"

"I would leave Kuddick to his fate." Mughan crossed his arms. "We have a better chance of survival if we stay here. The goblins will have to come to us, and when they do, we'll be ready."

"What load of --" Dorian held up a hand, cutting Barileth off.

"And what of Lumdir? What will he do when the goblins come pouring in?"

Mughan shrugged. "The mine will survive without a few dwarves, especially one who hasn't pulled his weight almost since we got here. No, we should all stay here and fight where we have the best advantage."

The migrants nodded and clutched their weapons close. None of them looked particularly eager to fight, even Dozotaine.

"Now is not the time to hide. What if it were you out there Mughan? Would you be so callous then?" Dorian growled.

"I would know that my sacrifice was for the good of everyone else. And I'd fight as long as I could."

"You would run and hide like a coward," Barileth said, starting to advance. Kimec stopped him, grabbing him across the chest.

"I would do what was right for everyone else. Dorian, on the other hand, is willing to kill us all. All for a single dwarf."

"Would you do the same, if you were in his place?" Dorian spoke past Mughan, hoping to move the others. He couldn't protect them with only a handful of dwarves, he needed them all. "Is it right to abandon those we care about, all to save our own skins?"

He paced back a few feet closer to them. "Do you have the courage to protect those you love? Or will you stay here and die anyway, a long slow death of starvation and hunger. All while the goblins cackle and celebrate right outside, taking everything we've made as their own." He pointed toward the door.

"That is the future that awaits you if you refuse to come with us and fight them in the entrance tunnel. A long, slow and agonizing death."

"Save it," Mughan said. "That won't scare us."

"Do you speak for everyone?" Dorian looked to Dozotaine. "Dozotaine, is that what you want?" Dozotaine didn't meet his gaze. "Olgim, what about you?" Silence.

Dorian looked at each, all of them refusing to look back at him.

"See, it looks like I do speak for them." Mughan gloated, a half-smile on his lips. "Had you been a better leader you could have done the same."

"Remember this day in shame, however long you live," Dorian said. *There wasn't enough time. I can't waste what little we have trying to move dwarves that refuse to move.*

"Dorian, we need to go," Kimec said.

He turned to address Mughan. "Remember what you told me about protecting the others. About the hard decisions that leaders have to make." Mughan didn't reply, nor did the others. There was only a small shuffle.

"For Seventh Hall," Dorian whispered. Then, he turned and ran to the door, only a small handful of dwarves close behind him.

With only a heartbeat separating him and the others they rushed through the workshop and rounded the corner of the entrance tunnel.

"Kuddick!" The dwarf was inside and at the door, but Dorian noticed the blood right away. Arrows were sticking out of his back and one in his left leg, and he was leaning against the door.

Too late Dorian realized he wasn't leaning against the door.

He was holding it shut.

"I'm sorry," Kuddick said as he was pushed by the door. Goblins rushed in the new opening.

The mine was breached.

Dorian screamed out in anger as the first goblin in stuck his sword through Kuddick's chest. The dwarf crumpled, and another came in hacking with an evil-looking axe.

He was too far away to do anything about it and had to watch it. Time seemed to slow, and his chest felt crushed.

I was too late.

It was just like Lumdir, only this time there would be no chance Kuddick survived.

The body fell to the floor, and more goblins crowded the tunnel. One, two, three more came in.

There was no time to mourn, for only a short distance separated them and the attackers. Dorian felt the excitement and fear rise in him, his already elevated heart pumping faster. He tightened the grip on his axe, feeling the smooth, warm wood beneath his fingers.

"Come on you stupid goblins," Barileth was yelling, urging them on. "Come and get it."

"Hold here," Dorian said, waiting at the end of the long hallway. They had an advantage at this end of the hallway, as long as they kept their bows in check. The entrance hall was only wide enough for two, maybe three of them at a time.

And it was dark. Their eyes glinted in the darkness as the twisted creatures walked closer to them. They were talking in their own language, a mixture of hisses and growls, and Dorian wished he knew what they were saying.

Then, he saw a new goblin step through the door, bigger than the others, cast a look at Kuddick, the turn its attention to Dorian and the other dwarves. His body was covered in scars, and he held an axe in each hand almost as large as his head.

"Can I have that one?" Barileth asked.

"He's huge," Yander said. The goblins parted for the new arrival, pressing forward into the tunnel.

Only a few more feet. Behind him the other dwarves had formed a tight circle, sounds of their fast breathing breaking his concentration. Dorian slowed his own, forcing himself to calm down. *Just a few more steps.*

"What was that?" Olgim bolted upright, clutching at his spear.

"Calm down," Mughan said. There were strange noises coming from behind the door that they had shut and locked. The coals in the forge still glowed, casting an orange glow from it.

"We shouldn't leave them out there," Olgim said, spear chattering against the floor.

"Are you going to go out there and risk your life for them then?"

"But what if he's right?"

"He isn't." Mughan shot him a stern look, and Olgim wilted under it.

"They did put their lives on the line for one of ours," Dozotaine said quietly. He was sitting in a corner, running a stone against the edge of his axe with a steady rhythm.

Mughan looked back to the door. The stone scraped against the axehead, leaving it sharp and honed. "Did we ask them to?"

"No. We didn't." He kept sharpening, even though the blade was as sharp as he was going to get it.

"Then we wait here, defend our position, and let them break on the edge of our weapons." Mughan hoisted his sword, swinging it with a few test cuts. The blade was awkwardly weighted, and difficult to control.

"Wouldn't we have a better chance if we were all fighting together?" Olgim asked. He had sat down against the side of the forge, huddling underneath its mass.

"He has a point," Dozotaine said.

"We need them for the mine," Thurbag added. "We can't survive on our own without them."

"We can and we will."

"I don't like it," Fimroul said. "Sitting here in the dark while they fight. It doesn't feel right to me."

"What is going on here? Don't you want to survive to live another day?" Mughan turned on them, his eyes flashing. "We fight here, stand here where we're safe."

"I saw them in the valley," Dozotaine put down his stone and rested the axe against his shoulder. The edge of it glimmered in the light of the forge. "They didn't hesitate against foul hell spawn. Charged right in, even though we were outnumbered."

Mughan was getting a sinking feeling, and something even worse was rising inside him.

"Don't say it."

"We need to fight with them."

"No." Mughan crossed his arms, but he knew it wasn't right. Maybe Dorian was right. What would be the point of surviving the fight only to waste away and die like rats in a cave?

"Mughan, you've been telling us that Dorian isn't fit to lead this entire time. So why is it that he's the one risking his life for everyone else while you stand here behind a locked door?" Dozotaine looked at him with a hard gaze.

"I--" Mughan tried to respond, but there was nothing he could say. His mouth opened and shut.

"What are we going to do?" Dozotaine asked, then quieter, "What are you going to do?"

Mughan turned his back on Dozotaine and the others, a wild churn of emotion running through him. Goblins were yelling and screeching outside the door, and dwarves were yelling back.

Soon they would meet in pitched battle, while he was here locked behind the door.

He wanted to survive. He needed to survive. Death could be wait-ing outside the door.

But it could also be in here.

Dorian wondered if today was his last day alive. He wondered if he would ever make it out of the mine and see the light of day again, or if he would ever be able to see his children.

He had missed so much of their lives, and now he might not ever see them again.

"Here they come," Barileth said, just to his right. "Wish I had some better armor. Those weapons look like they might hurt."

"Sorry, I couldn't do it," Kragnak said.

"Don't think like that. We've got everything we need right here." Dorian straightened, afraid to show any semblance of fear to either the goblins or the dwarves behind him.

The goblins were smiling and shouting insults at them, forming up into mismatched ranks. The scarred one pushed and shoved his underlings into position.

They were advancing.

Dorian wished he had prepared more, that they had put in more traps or made the walls higher. Everything he had been meaning to do or have done was a heavy burden he had to bear.

Because now it all mattered. More than food or drink or beds to sleep in.

He cursed himself over not doing more sooner.

"One more step," Barileth said, then yelled, "I can smell your breath from hear you filthy cretins. The goblins advanced.

And then the first trap went off.

24

TRAPPED

A boulder swung down on the lead goblin, and its glee for blood turned to surprise and a crunch. The force knocked it into its followers, who toppled in a heap.

The dwarves let out a cheer that rocked along the passageway, and the goblins shrank back. But their leader refused to let them retreat, landing blows to urge them on.

"We've got more where that came from!" Yander said.

"Magnificent." Dorian took a moment to cast a quick glance back at Barileth. His face was aglow in satisfaction.

The goblins kept coming, and then they reached the cage traps. They snapped up from the floor, capturing a few goblins and closing on another few.

"A few more down, how many are left?" Kragnak asked.

"Too many."

"We've got more surprises in store. Let them come," Barileth said. He raised his voice. "You hear that? Come on you filth, come and get it."

The goblins, still coming in through the door, obliged. Some-what pushed, they ran the gauntlet.

Cages sprung, and more hammer traps smashed. The smell of goblin blood permeated the air now, thick and vile. Still, they came in, and Dorian lost his confidence with every trap activated.

Goblins climbed over and around their brethren trapped in cages, and shuffled over bodies that littered the tunnel. The scarred one at the back pushed them on.

Then, they were over the trap area. "Wait here," Dorian said. "The widening of the tunnel will work to our advantage. They'll have to come one at a time."

Dwarves packed the tunnel, shoulder to shoulder, but only in sets of three. There wasn't enough room for more.

The first goblins made it through the traps, cautiously approaching the dwarves. Dorian was almost glad they were fighting here. If they would have tried to take the courtyard outside the door, the goblins would have been able to use their numbers to their advantage.

He raised his axe as the first goblin neared. Its yellow eyes glowed with blood lust and greed, but Dorian was prepared for it.

Thrusting forward, the goblin howled in victory. But it was too soon. Dorian knocked the blade away with a downward strike then brought it up, using the other side to cleanly cleave off its head.

Then chaos erupted. More goblins took its place, howling and cackling in anger and frenzy. Grunts and screams took their place as Dorian lashed out, attacking while he had room.

With a bash to the face Dorian struck another one down. A goblin with a curved blade took its place and parried several blows and Dorian found himself fending off blows and strikes.

He struck back where he could, but with the tight quarters he struggled to move effectively. Some of them found a way past his defenses, a cut to his abdomen, a stab in his leg.

The goblin sneered at him, eyes flashing with glee. Its sword was faster than the others.

Dorian fell back, forcing Barileth with him. With a quick glance he realized that Yander was gone, and a stab of fear struck his heart.

He didn't have time to dwell on it. The goblin pushed him farther back. Blow after blow he narrowly avoided death.

And they were falling back. Inch by inch they lost ground to the goblins, who came on in a fury. It felt like a never-ending wave washing up on the shore.

Breathing hard, Dorian struggled to keep up the fight. He landed a strike to the goblins' left arm, but it just kept fighting, letting the arm hang limp.

Barileth yelled out in pain, then made his opponent squeal in return. Dorian fended off another blow, this one cutting into his shoulder.

He had to do something. All around him dwarves were taking wounds. In desperation he let out a war cry and charged, dropping his shoulder.

It caught the goblin off guard, and he landed his shoulder into its abdomen. The goblin fell and gave him all the opening he needed.

Dorian took it, swinging his axe above his head. The goblin tried to stop the blow, but there was too much power in it.

With a swish the axe ended its life.

The smell of blood was thick, and the sounds of struggle overwhelming. Dorian yanked his axe free and was able to catch a brief moment to recover.

His heart sank, even as it was screaming in his chest.

The goblins had pushed them to the crossroads. Barileth was bleeding in several areas, he couldn't find Yander, and the scarred goblin was walking toward him with a sinister look on its face.

But worst of all he caught a glimpse of Kragnak holding his arm. His right hand was gone, a stump that ended below his elbow.

Never again would Kragnak hold a hammer. His dream of becoming a smith was gone, shattered.

Then the scarred goblin was attacking him, and he was forced to defend himself.

Dorian parried the first strike, and he felt it shudder through the axe and up his arm. His eyes opened wide as the second axe came at him.

Ducking, Dorian felt the goblin's axe cut off his air. He had to give ground, backing up.

The goblins pressed forward. "Back to the stairwell," Dorian shouted above the melee.

He couldn't afford to let the goblin land a blow, and after parrying another hit tried to strike back.

But the fight had exhausted him, and his arms weren't responding like they should have. The goblin knocked away his attack and smiled.

It should have enraged Dorian, should have made him dig in and fight harder.

Kragnak won't survive. None of us will. Goblins were still coming down the entrance tunnel, howling and cackling.

Dorian parried another strike, then counterattacked. The goblin ducked and laughed at him.

"This no challenge. Human deathraiser promised good sport," the goblin said. "Dwarvesess not fight well." He attacked again. "We will see how they die."

Human. Something struck Dorian about it, a fear that ran deep in him. Dorian gave more ground, blocking the goblin's strikes with slower reactions.

They were behind the crossroads now, just a few more feet to the edge of the stairs.

Yudoline was helping Kragnak behind the line of dwarves. His hand was wrapped with a blood-stained cloth. He couldn't see everyone.

There were too many of them. *We're all going to die.*

He wondered if this was what his wife felt before her final moments. He was tired, his muscles weren't responding like they should, and his energy was failing.

I won't be seeing my children again. After all the struggles, the death and hardship, it was coming to an end.

This goblin was too strong, too fast, and too good. *I'm no match for him.*

With a nasty smile, the goblin toyed with him. It hissed in delight and batted off Dorian's feeble attacks.

The goblins would take the mine. They would destroy what they had built, turn it into a warren of evil.

They would trample the crops, break the furniture. The forge would be converted to build weapons of war, and who knew how many innocents would die by their blades.

All their work in the mines would be stone and pillaged. The dead would have died in vain for a dream that would turn into a nightmare.

Dorian fell back, his arms aching from blocking.

I'll never see my family again.

He wanted to sink down to his knees, rest one final time. Dorian's lungs were on fire and wounds from earlier in the fight were beginning to ache.

It would have been better to die in the prison than here. Dorian knocked away another blow, knowing that it was probably the last he would be able to avoid.

Yander kicked away the goblin's sword and struck out with a vicious chop. It went low and true, taking off the goblin's leg.

It let out a scream of pain, and Yander ended it with a final blow to the head.

Panting, he looked back to make sure Emelda was still safe. She was helping tend to Kragnak and Kimec.

The tunnel was awash with sound and confusion, and Yander turned back to the fray, but something caught his eye.

The ugliest goblin was attacking Dorian and winning.

At first Yander couldn't believe his eyes, but Dorian was pushed back a step, then another. Barileth battled another goblin and blocked Yander's view of Dorian's fight.

Barileth dispatched his opponent with a growl, then pushed back and out of the way.

Dorian was down on one knee, pressed up against the wall. The goblin hammered away at him, blow by blow, and Dorian's parries grew weaker.

He was going to die if Yander didn't do anything.

Goblins pressed in the tunnel ahead of him, threatening the others, but he had to act.

He swept out his axe, forcing the goblins back, and it gave him enough room to cross the tunnel.

"Dorian!" The ugly goblin raised its axe high, readying it for a killing stroke. Dorian gazed up, on one knee.

Yander swung in desperation, off balance but without enough time to set himself right.

The two axes connected above Dorian's head. Yander managed to deflect the blow, sending it careening into the wall.

Then the goblin turned its attention to him, eyes blazing in anger.

Fear struck him, but his fear for Dorian overwhelmed it. Yander let out a war cry and found his footing. His own rage burning, Yander went on the offensive and lashed out.

Dorian gasped for breath, time seeming to slow. Yander was driving the scarred goblin back with a flurry of strikes, but he knew Yander was no match for the goblin in a drawn-out battle.

It was only a matter of time before Yander would be killed. A motion from the stairs made him look back.

Lumdir walked forward with his spear like a crutch, too weak to hold it upright. Something inside him kindled.

"Go back Lumdir, you're too weak," Dorian said.

"Can't...let you...have all the fun." With a weak smile Lumdir hobbled past Emelda and Yudoline to the fighting line.

A spark ignited in Dorian, a glimmer of hope. They were dwarves of Seventh Hall. They had carved through the rock and shaped it into their own.

They had overcome struggles and defeated enemies more dangerous than this before.

And Yander and Lumdir wouldn't give up, not in the face of almost certain death.

What kind of dwarf would I be if I let him die? Here he is, fighting for me when I'm in trouble.

And I'm about to give up and die?

Deep inside him a flame that was almost out sprung to life. An infusing energy flowed through his body. He couldn't let them win.

Dorian stood, forcing away any thought of pain and failure. Yander's attacks had waned as the goblin deflected them, batting them away like they were a fly.

"You invade our home?" Dorian raised his axe, now lighter than ever before. "You threaten our lives and what we've built?" He rushed to join in the attack, swinging his axe in a vicious side cut.

The scarred goblin blocked it with his own, but a shudder went through him. Dorian smiled his own smile now, as Yander followed up with another strike.

It was working. Before the goblin could react, Dorian was swinging again, this time an overhand slice to get it to step back.

"Go right," Dorian said. Yander stepped over and attacked, forcing the goblin left and into the wall. It gave them a moment of respite. The goblin no longer looked haughty and confident, its eyes shifted quickly from one to the other.

And it gave Dorian enough time to take stock of the situation. Barileth was waning, Lumdir was fighting but only enough to ward off attacks for Barileth. Kimec and Yudoline were paired together fending off another goblin.

But still the goblins came. Down the hallway, spreading out into the side tunnels of the mine. There was no way out for then. Their numbers were too overwhelming.

Without help.

"Look out," Yander said. While he was distracted the goblin was attempting a rush attack, but Dorian sidestepped the blow and batted its axe away.

"We need the others," Dorian said. "We can't do this without them."

25

DESPERATION

The tunnel was crushed with bodies, the stink of battle and death filling the mine. Dorian wiped away sweat from his head, and the back of his hand came back bloody.

"Push them back, we'll make for the dining hall." The mineshaft was behind them, but being stuck on the stairs wouldn't help their cause. Barileth nodded and yelled, pushing back a goblin and stabbing another that had come up behind it.

"Emelda, stay back!" Yander parried a blow from the scarred goblin, then another.

"I can't let you fight alone." She struck out with a spear from behind him, but the goblin batted it away easily. She was too slow.

Dorian eyed the distance to the crossroads. They would need to fight back a few more feet to regain the ground they had lost. He followed up an attack from Yander with his own, and the goblin took another step back.

It was barking orders out in its own tongue, but Dorian couldn't understand it. Goblin reinforcements were more hesitant now that their companions were falling, and the floor was getting slippery from the blood.

The dwarves, however, held their ground and were even gaining some. Dorian shifted the grip on his axe and lashed out, catching the scarred goblin by surprise and cutting its arm.

More goblins appeared, and Dorian broke off his attack, letting Yander step in, to strike at a smaller one that had come up behind its leader.

The goblin tried to stop his blow, holding up a leather shield, but Dorian put as much power behind it as he could.

Steel ripped through leather, and his axe lodged into the side of the goblin's head.

"We aren't gaining ground," Barileth yelled. He was right, with the call for reinforcements the goblins were pushing them back down the hall, closer to the stairs and farther away from any defensible position.

"Keep fighting. We can't get pushed to the stairs." The crush of bodies made him step back. The scarred goblin fell back, letting his soldiers shield him, its left arm hanging limp at its side.

"They won't stop coming," Kimec said. He grunted as a goblin kicked him, connecting with his arm. Dorian had to look away before he could see what happened to him.

He parried a thrust by a new goblin, batting away its curved sword. There were more down the tunnel, an impossible amount for them to survive.

They needed reinforcements.

Anger rising inside, Dorian counterattacked, swatting away the goblin's sword and charging in.

Less than a hundred feet away. Can't they hear us?

His shoulder caught it on the chin, knocking it down to the ground. Dorian's axe made quick work of ending the fight, and he took a brief second to recover, gasping for air.

The scarred goblin was gone.

Hope once again welled up in his chest. *If I can get them to attack, we might have a chance.*

Then Dorian saw the scarred goblin. It had retreated farther back down the hall and was driving the other goblins on.

And it was very much still in the fight.

Goblins drove him back, and the others along with him. Dorian growled and tried to strike back, but they were fresh and he was not.

"Mughan, we need your help." Dorian ducked, avoided a spear, and raised his voice even louder. "I swear that if you fail to fight, you will not survive this night."

"For the glory of stone, and a life worth dying for!" Barileth bashed a goblin and took place on his left side.

"For those lost and those who survive!" Yander struck out with his axe, giving him enough room to join him on his right.

"Dwarves of the Seventh Hall hear me and heed my words. It is not today that we lay down our arms, though we may lay down our lives." Eyes blazing bright, Dorian fought and bellowed with all his might. "We fight for what was lost, and what might be!"

"Wait," Mughan commanded, holding up his hand. The battle had moved farther down the entrance tunnel. They all had heard Dorian's plea to him, and the dwarves in the room were already on edge.

Now they were surrounding him, on their feet. He didn't know what to do.

"Mughan, we can't let them die," Dozotaine whispered.

"I--" he stopped. Wouldn't more dwarves die if they tried to fight too? He looked around the room and felt the shift.

Was Dorian right? He heard Dorian yell, voice as clear as if he was beside him. "Dwarves of the Seventh Hall hear me and heed my words."

Hands clutched at handles, and Mughan's eyes shifted around the room. He had worked so hard to get here, and now it felt like it was slipping away. His chance at a new life, wasted.

All because of that stupid dwarf and his inability to see what was before him.

"It is not today that we lay down our arms, though we may lay down our lives." The sounds of fighting almost overpowered him. Metal rang on metal. Screams punctuated his words.

"We fight for what was lost, and what might be!" Mughan dropped his gaze, remembering the life that he had lost. Hadn't he done it himself? Hadn't his inability to see what needed to be done drove him here?

And yet Dorian was the one willing to stand up and fight, while he slunk away and hid. Just like he promised himself he would never do again.

A hand on his shoulder. Dozotaine.

Mughan straightened. "It is time. They need our help." The mood in the room shifted. He raised his sword and saluted the dwarves in the room, they turned to Dozotaine and nodded.

Together they unbarred the door. The thick wooden beam that had held it shut crashed to the ground. Mughan stepped through.

Goblins littered the tunnels. Mughan took a deep breath and raised his sword. "The light take you Dorian."

26

REMEMBER

Dorian smiled. Whatever he thought of Mughan, he would not back down from the fight now.

The goblins sensed something was wrong, and he was more than happy to take advantage of it, cutting off the sword arm of his opponent.

"About time," Barileth said.

"You're just mad it'll spoil your fight," Kimec said. Barileth laughed.

Together the three of them advanced down the hall, pushing back the uncertain looking goblins.

However, their advance came at cost. Blood ran down Dorian's head now, and the other's weren't in much better shape.

"Keep fighting," Lumdir said, leaning up against the wall and gasping. A large gash ran down the side of his arm, and he clutched his spear tight.

Dorian shifted the grip on his axe, so that he could hold it better though it was slick with blood. "We'll never give up." He swung, knocking away the goblin's sword. "Never." He swung again, knocking away the shield.

Over his shoulder the spear came through, stabbing the goblin in the chest. It was down in an instant.

"Thank you," Dorian said. Lumdir nodded, then collapsed behind him. "Emelda! Get Lumdir!"

"Dorian, ahead of you." He turned, just in time to see another goblin swinging down with both hands clutching a sword. Dorian sidestepped, just in time, and shoved the beast back.

The momentum carried him forward a few steps, and he found himself between two more goblins focused on his companions.

They turned on him, and blood pumped through his body as his heart sped up. Dorian hacked at the one on his left, but the goblin to his right was fast.

It's sword lashed out, catching Dorian in the forearm he raised to stop it. It bit deep, and the goblin hissed and twisted. Pain lanced down his arm and Dorian yelled out.

An axe crushed its head, and the pressure on his arm let up for a moment. Yander appeared over him, with Barileth fending off the other goblins ahead. "Dorian, you can't stay down now."

"Help me up." Yander reached down and grabbed him by the wrist, making the pain worse. He quickly let go when Dorian yelled again, then shifted his grip to the back of his arm.

A quick pull and Dorian was up again, shifting his grip to his good arm. Blood trickled from his wound and down to the floor, the dripping lost in the chaos of the fighting.

"Go back to Emelda," Kimec said, stepping forward into his place and roughly pushing Dorian back. "I'll hold for now." He swung at an approaching goblin, forcing it back.

Dorian wanted to protest, but she was already next to him, tearing at her skirt and tying it around his arm.

"Don't you think about giving them an inch." She worked furiously, conviction in her voice. "We can't give them control."

The momentary lag in the fighting brought all the tiredness and exhaustion that had been lingering at the edge of his consciousness to bear. There was blood all over her hands and clothes. Great splashes of it that tuned the brown back.

She cast a nervous glance at Yander, part horror and part pride. It gripped his heart, and in the darkness he almost mistook her for Ruby.

His breath stopped for a moment as time seemed to slow. *Would she be about this age now?* Shame washed over him. He couldn't remember.

Ruby wasn't here now, Emelda was. She tightened the bandaged, sending a momentary flare of pain up her arm. He ground his teeth together and tried to ignore it.

"I'm not going to let them live." Standing back up he prepared to rejoin the fight.

She caught his arm. "Remember."

Their eyes met and something unspoken passed between them. Dorian nodded, then charged back into the fight, favoring his left arm.

Not a moment too soon, he lashed out his axe and blocked a sword coming for Kimec's throat.

"Could use a break," Kimec said.

"I'll be happy to take your place." Dorian felt renewed, as tired as he was, and slipped around Kimec to strike. Axe met wooden shield, and the goblin hissed at him.

"About time you joined us. I thought you were taking a nap back there," Barileth said with a wicked grin.

"They aren't stopping." Yander hacked at another goblin, who refused to yield. It was saying something back, but none of them could understand it.

"We'll make them stop, then." Sparks flew as Dorian parried a blow, sending sparkles of black across his vision. "If we can drive them back to the traps it might give us an edge."

"Most have already activated."

"Not all." His opponent kicked out, but Dorian saw it coming. He grabbed the goblins foot and pulled, feeling a shriek of pain in his left arm. Ignoring it, he brought his axe down to end its life.

The scarred goblin was back there, still directing his goblins. They had bows out, but the tightness of the tunnel made them useless unless he wanted to hit his own kind.

So far they hadn't loosed a shaft.

But they were fighting to a standstill. Neither side gave ground, no matter how many blows landed on the dwarves or how many goblins died.

We're going to be overwhelmed. The thought struck him after he ducked another attack, the tunnel still filled with the shrieking and screaming of goblins that smelled blood.

"They aren't going to give up. Not like this," Dorian said. He searched around the tunnel, desperate to come up with a solution.

"Neither are we," Yander said, pushing a goblin back against the rush.

They had no exit, and they weren't getting far enough down the tunnel to get to the dining hall.

And then a great cry went up in the tunnel.

At first Dorian thought it was the goblins readying for a final attack, but he was confused. It didn't sound like goblins at all.

"What is that?" Barileth asked. He leaned up against the stone support.

For a moment Dorian considered bringing the tunnel down, but quickly dismissed it. They would stop the attack, yes, but there would be no way to know how much would collapse.

He might bring the mountain down on top of them.

Dorian growled, then slashed into another goblin going for Barileth. "Let them come, we'll take them all."

27

Vengeance

"Those aren't more goblins, look." Yander pointed.

Goblins were looking back, confused. The sound crescendoed, then above it all he heard a familiar voice.

He wasn't sure if he should laugh or cry.

"For the iron of the mountain, and the vengeance of Seventh Hall!" Dwarves crashed into the left flank of the goblin forces, Mughan leading the charge.

Barileth did laugh, then waded into the front ranks of their enemy.

"Seventh Hall," they were crying as they attacked. The goblins weren't prepared for the dwarves, and a line of them fell.

"He did it," Dorian said. "I didn't think he would." The goblins they had been fighting had heard it too, and they were turning.

Dorian seized the advantage. "Forward, push them out."

They were running now, or trying too. The crush of bodies in the tunnel had nowhere to go, because Mughan and his group had cut off their retreat.

Panicked, the goblins were easy pickings. In a few minutes Dorian was face to face with a goblin blood covered Mughan.

He was smiling that smile, the one that Dorian despised, but he was glad to see it again.

Mughan held out a hand. Dorian let go of his axe and clasped it, smiling himself. Despite all the chaos, understanding passed between them.

"Lead on," Mughan said. They released each other.

The goblins were in full retreat now, despite the scarred goblin lashing them and kicking them forward. They were throwing down weapons and sprinting to the door.

And the dwarves weren't far behind.

Dozotaine whirled with a practiced hand, calmly cutting down goblins with speed Dorian hadn't seen with a sword. Barileth wasn't far behind, and Yander took the remaining space in the tunnel.

"We aren't done yet." Dorian charged, Mughan right beside him.

His focus was on their leader, who was regaining control of the goblins. With a few more kicks he ended the rout, turning it into a tactical retreat.

They were streaming out the door now.

"They mean to fight in the courtyard," Mughan said.

"I see it."

"Open ground."

"I know." Dorian surged forward, taking Yander's place and attacking in a fury. He held back some of his strength, saving it.

Mughan took Barileth's spot, letting the dwarf rest, and the three of them pushed the goblins back. The scarred goblin was at the end of the tunnel, escaping with the rest of his kin.

"Watch the traps," Barileth cautioned as an unsprung hammer smashed a goblin to bits with a satisfying crunch, catching another's leg and sending a spray of dirt and rock shards into the throng.

"Going left," Yander said. Dorian ducked down, and let the axe fly free of him as Yander struck at another goblin, shearing off its nose. It hissed and attacked, but Dorian blocked it.

He pushed forward, keeping the momentum they had gathered, and the goblin fell back with the others. Only a few more feet stood between them and the outside world, and with a mighty roar Dorian led the charge.

Two goblins were trapped inside and dispatched quickly by the dwarves, but even though the corridor was strewn with dead goblins, there were still far too many outside.

"Shields to the front. Take them by surprise." The only two dwarves with shields, Olgim and Dozotaine, were let through. Only a few seconds had passed since the lead goblin had slipped out the door.

Mughan nodded. "Go," Dorian said.

With the two in the front, the dwarves rushed out of the mine. Moonlight scattered along the courtyard, not overpowering his vision.

Goblins were forming up at the end of the courtyard. The scarred goblin was yelling and cursing at them to fire their bows, but there weren't enough ready.

"Seventh Hall!" the dwarves cried. Arrows were nocked, and two or three let loose.

But it wasn't enough to stop them.

The dwarven line crushed into the goblins, spreading out now. No longer confined to the tunnel, they were free to fight one on one.

And the goblins didn't have the upper hand this time.

Dorian went for the scarred goblin, lashing out with a mighty two-handed sweep. With his hurt arm he had less power, and speed, and the scarred goblin stepped back and knocked it away.

His enemy tried to carry his attack forward and sweep him off his feet, but Dorian had seen the move coming. Shifting his weight, Dorian swung his axe back around to in front of him just in time to parry an axe blow.

He didn't have time to avoid the elbow to his face.

It hit him like a rock, the taste of blood flowing into his mouth, spinning him to the left. Dorian blinked, caught by surprise. The sounds of battle had faded in a ring, but he thought he heard his name.

Another blink. Something was coming at him. Dorian dropped down and shook his head to clear it. Another attack by the scarred goblin. Another close call.

Then Yander was there by his side, stopping an axe.

I can't let him be here. It's too dangerous. Dorian shifted the grip on his axe and dug deep inside himself for his last remaining reserve of energy.

And then he went on the offensive.

He poured all his anger, all his desire to survive, all his will to protect the others into his axe. Blow after blow he swung, the scarred goblin giving ground.

One of its axes was flung away, and it tried to use the other with two hands.

But Dorian wouldn't be stopped. Seeing an opening, he feinted left and then attacked right.

His axe sheared off the goblins hand, and it bellowed in rage. "You will die," it screamed in the common tongue, reaching for the weapon it had dropped.

"Not today," Dorian said. He chopped its head off.

Ready for more fighting, Dorian turned to see that the fight was over. Goblins ran down the mountain, the few that remained fleeing now that their leader was dead.

Olgim was groaning near the entrance, a shaft sticking out of his leg, with Mughan right beside him.

Yander.

He searched. His eyes found Yander just behind him, leaned over. Fear struck him, and he rushed to his side. "Yander?"

The young dwarf looked up, then back down to his side. He peeled away his hand, which reflected the moonlight. "Goblins got me."

28

WOUNDS

"Is it deep?" Dorian kneeled down, peeling back the shirt. It oozed blood, but didn't look bad.

"I don't know."

"Come on, let's get you inside and tended to."

"No, tend to the others first. I have to find out where they came from," Yander said, taking a step forward. He stumbled, but Dorian caught him.

"Barileth, take him back in."

"Give him to someone else, I can chase down those goblins." They were still fleeing, but already to the forest by now. Out of the fifty or so that came, less than ten were still alive.

"Over here! This one's still alive," Kuddick said.

"We've got plenty of prisoners, and we're in no shape to chase them down." Barileth, like all the other dwarves, was covered in wounds. With the adrenaline from the fight draining out of him, his own were starting to throb and burn.

He tried shifting his arm and paid the price for it. Barileth grumbled, fingering the edge of his sword and staring longingly down toward the fleeing goblins.

There was nothing Dorian wanted more at that moment than to hunt down the remaining goblins and kill them one by one. His anger raged, and visions of the pain he would inflict flashed by.

The groans of Olgim brought him back to reality. Swallowing his anger, he turned back to the mine. "There are dwarves to attend to. Come on Yander."

Slinging Yander's arm around his shoulder, with Barileth doing likewise, they shuffled him back into the mine.

Kuddick's body was gone, a dark stain of blood remaining. The victory had cost them, and now Dorian was going to find out how much. The darkness of the mine enveloped him, one part comfort, one part sadness.

The trapped goblins hissed at them and stammered something in their language, but the bars were too tight for them to do any harm. Mughan and Dozotaine were carrying Olgim, and Lumdir stood at the crossroads leaning on his spear.

"Take the wounded to the old dormitory, they've set up a hospital there," he said, pale and dark bags under his eyes. Dorian felt a stab of shame, remembering Tufolin's assessment.

One more thing he failed to do, one more reason he wasn't fit to lead this expedition. He stared at Mughan, watching him carry Olgim and comfort him.

"Everyone needs a good arrow wound to make them distinguished. Think of the tales you'll be able to tell for the ages, and how the ladies will react." He smiled and chuckled, and it brought a grin to Olgim.

"You think so? Oww." Olgim groaned from a wrong step.

The smile Mughan wore was real and was the first Dorian had seen. After everything Mughan had done, after the division he had sown, Dorian never thought he would respect him.

But he had seen him in battle, had seen his courage. Mughan was a true leader, not like Dorian. The feeling churned in him, pulling him in two different directions.

The dormitory buzzed, almost all the dwarves inside. Yudoline and Emelda had taken charge, and Emelda rushed up to Yander as soon as she saw him.

"Yander!" They set him down, only to be mobbed by his wife. He groaned as she squeezed him. "Oh, I'm sorry. You're hurt!"

"Not much, I hope. They caught me in the side." Emelda shot Dorian a glare of anger, then led her husband by the hand to one of the old beds.

"Sit down, I'll have a look." She turned him to the light of a torch, then peeled back the fabric with her slim fingers. "Barileth, get me a fresh bowl of water from the pot in the kitchen, as hot as you can get it. Dorian, take out this old one." She nodded to the bowl on the floor, full of a red liquid.

Barileth looked like he was about to argue, but then thought better of it. Dorian arched an eyebrow at him, then did as she commanded.

Yudoline had taken Olgim, who had let out a groan of pain through the stick he had between his teeth. One hand was wrapped at the base of the arrow, and with a quick flex she snapped off the back.

Dorian had seen something like it before, but taking the bowl gave him a good excuse to get out. Back outside he went into the moonlight and a still night.

It was surreal, how peaceful it was. He tossed the bloody water outside the wall, a noise above him catching his attention.

Lumdir was up on the wall, looking down on him and the view of the valley.

"Lumdir, I didn't see you there."

"Thought I'd keep a lookout."

"You're not hurt?"

"Not like the others. I've had a nick here or there, nothing as bad as before." Dorian nodded. "Thank you Dorian."

"For what?"

"You kept us together. You kept me alive. Hold on." Lumdir held up a hand before he could protest. "I wouldn't be here today if you hadn't done what you did. None of us would be." He nodded back to the mine. "Go on, you still have some work to do."

Dorian searched for words, part shame and part pride fighting inside. "Keep a good watch," he said at last, and went back inside.

The arrow was gone from Olgim's leg when he came back, and Yudoline had moved on to Dozotaine.

Yander was laid out on the bed, and Emelda was cleaning his side. He was staring at her with such a look of love that Dorian almost felt like he was intruding.

Watching them was painful and pleasing all mixed into one. How many times had he stared at his own wife with the same look in his eyes? He wanted it back, more than anything in the world.

She gently wiped around the wound, dipping her cloth into the steaming bowl of water to keep it clean. Yander reached up and touched her arm with a trembling hand and she looked up and smiled at him.

There was a bud of hope in watching them, and another of a long-remembered desire. *I'll get back my love.*

29

RECOVERY

"How are you feeling?" Kragnak opened his eyes at the sound of Dorian's voice.

"Could be better." He was pale, his left hand clutching what would have been his right. "I can still feel it. Like it should be moving, but it doesn't."

"I'm sorry."

"Well maybe now my hand won't shake so much," Kragnak said, with a forced laugh after. "Never could hold it still enough to get a good hammer blow in."

Dorian pulled up a stool and sat down beside him. The smell of battle still permeated the air, but it was quieter now that everyone had been tended to. His own bandages itched, but he tried to ignore it.

"I'll never be able to use a hammer again, will I?" Kragnak was staring straight ahead, eyes toward the ceiling but focused on something else.

Without a right hand? Will he be able to do anything? Dorian had his doubts, and considered airing them. *What good would that do?*

"I don't know."

Kragnak let out a long sign. "I know I won't. All those years spent chasing being a smith. It was all for nothing."

Dorian reached over and put a hand on his shoulder. "Not for nothing. Look around you. These dwarves wouldn't be here if not for your hard work."

"Not good enough."

"It was good enough, and more than we could ask for." Dorian looked around the room. There were too many injured, and too few to take care of them. "I fear we've all been asked too much of us."

"I knew what I was getting into." Some of the sadness in his voice had fled, replaced by anger. "Besides, this place has become a home I never thought I'd have."

Dorian smiled at him. "Rest easy, and recover as soon as you can. We still need you."

"Like this?" Kragnak held up his stump.

"In whatever way you are." Dorian patted him on the shoulder and got up to get some fresh air.

Yudoline was checking on the dwarves, and he stopped her.

"How are they?"

"Beaten, bruised." She smiled. "I think they'll all recover."

"But will they heal?" he asked.

"Go get some rest. You haven't slept and look it." She patted his arm. "Lumdir will be in to help me."

"He also needs rest."

"He's a spring chicken compared to you right now. Go on, get out of here." She pushed him gently to the door, and he obliged her. Slipping out into the darkened tunnel, the sounds of the wounded faded.

Now, the goblin's words came back to him, haunting his mind. *Deathraiser... It had to be a necromancer.*

What would be the odds of another one? Low, even though the power of necromancy knew no bounds of race and class.

It had to be the same one.

Was this punishment for what he had done? An electric feeling ran up the back of his neck, anticipation perhaps, or something else.

There still might be a way. If I get her body.

But that meant they would have to survive. And it meant that whoever was after them wouldn't stop. And would likely be angry that all the attempts on their life had so far failed.

The sun was up, morning halfway gone, when he emerged out of the mine. The courtyard was still splashed with blood and strewn with goblin bodies, another thing they had to take care of.

A cloudless sky greeted him, the chill wind of an early autumn drifting up the valley. Another season gone, another to survive. After the heat of the mine, it felt good on his skin.

Up above something black caught his eye. *Vultures already, they can't even wait for us to mourn our dead.* He looked closer.

It flew in an erratic circle, but it wasn't a vulture. And there were no other birds in sight, which struck him as odd. Squinting, he could just make it out.

In a lazy circle, it flew around the mine. He could just make out that its head was turned toward him. Eventually he realized what it was.

Another feeling began to creep up the back of his neck. The bird was watching him. It was watching the mine. He was sure of it.

For a few more turns the black bird circled, until it was satisfied, or called back.

Dorian stood outside the mine, heart heavy. They had survived, for now, but at what cost? Wounded and dead dwarves, defenses breached and exhausted.

Another gust of the crisp wind, the smell of fall beginning to slip in. He took a deep breath, trying to stay awake.

There was nothing he could do right now. The warmth of the sun on his closed eyes, Dorian put aside his cares.

Now was a time to recover. Now was a time to rest.

He went back inside to his own bed, stripped off his soiled clothing, and slipped beneath the covers. Above him the sun cast golden rays as he was taken to sleep.

Epilogue

Yander sat back and laughed, then groaned from the strain.

"Too weak to even laugh. You need to toughen up dwarf." Barileth took a deep swig from his glass, cheeks rosy and eyes bright.

"It only hurts because of how ugly you are."

"Hush now," Emelda warned. "Before you say something you regret."

"Aye, make sure your lady keeps a hold of you." They were grinning at each other, and Yander took a bite of his rockbread dripping in butter.

They looked a rag-tag bunch, all around the tables covered in bandages and wrappings. Dorian's arm itched, still burning a little. He was thankful to have some of the least of the injuries though.

The discomfort made him look at Kragnak to see how he was doing. Lumdir was beside him looking much better than he had and helping him to eat. He wasn't used to using his left hand and was working out how to use a knife with it.

"Friends, for I feel like I can call you that now," Mughan said, rising to his feet. His left eye was covered with a bandage, but it didn't hamper him. "I want to raise a mug for each and every one of you. You fought valiantly, and bravely, and kept the faith in the darkest of nights."

"With little help from you!" Barileth shouted in jest.

"You know we saved your bacon." Dozotaine elbowed him.

"And we raise a glass to you," Dorian added. "For fighting when we needed you."

"We're all dwarves of Seventh Hall," Yudoline said. "Let us always remember."

"For the dwarves of Seventh Hall, then." Mughan raised his own mug high above his head.

In unison, they cried out "Seventh Hall!"

Hand tightening, Vasknar felt the pleasure in inflicting pain. The goblin struggled under his grip, clawing and clutching at his arm with vicious little claws.

He squeezed tighter, clenching down tight, until he felt a crunch of the goblin's wind pipe, then a few more moments and the life fled out of its eyes.

"That was not the news I was hoping for." Vasknar threw the body to the side, advancing on the other two goblins. He wanted so very much to hurt something, and his arm hurt from the scratches.

Blood dripped down his arm, making him angrier. Why is it all going wrong?

"They are hundreds of dwarffssess," a goblin whimpered.

"Excuses. I know how many there are, I've seen it." Vasknar looked at his skeleton, and it shambled into action, stabbing the goblin through the heart in a few seconds.

The other tried to scramble away, but the other skeletons grabbed it, holding it tight. It begged for its life, squirming under the firm grip of the undead.

Vasknar turned away, already thinking and plotting. These dwarves were more trouble than he first thought, and for a moment he considered letting them be.

But his experiments on the humans had failed every time. He needed something smaller, he needed those dwarves.

Waving a hand over his shoulder he left, the cries of the goblin silenced. He picked his way through the goblins' cave. They were foolish to try and hide from him, thinking that he wouldn't find out.

With a squawk his raven alighted on his shoulder. He had grown fond of the bird, and grateful he could use its eyes for his seeing.

That one dwarf. He was going to have him. And he was going to accomplish what he had set out to do. No one was going to stop him.

BASTION OF THE DEEP

SURVIVING THE THIRD YEAR

ERIC KERCHER

1

Dirge in the Deep

Down into the gaping mouth of the tomb the dwarves descended carrying coffins on shoulders. They went single file down the rough carved stairs. Torches spitting and footsteps falling were the only sounds.

The steps were rhythmic, slow. The torches cast their light on the final resting place, two holes staring out like eyes.

One by one, they shuffled off the steps into the flat cave. Spread out, they made a ragtag ensemble. Barileth and Dozotaine put down their coffin, Dorian and Mughan theirs. They struck the ground with merely a whisper, cradled and gentled into place.

Dorian took a deep breath. The air down here was stale, cool. Untouched and un-breathed, it still was thick with granite dust that their feet had kicked up into the little swirls around their leg.

He wished he were here to mine.

The silence stretched into discomfort. Mughan cleared his throat, catching his attention. He nodded when Dorian looked at him.

Dorian took a few steps forward and turned back to the crowd of dwarves. He had been through too many of these.

And it wouldn't be the last if his suspicion about the necromancer was correct.

"A great evil took our friends, our families," Dorian said at last. "In the earth they have toiled, to the earth they return."

"To the earth they return," the crowd repeated, voices echoing off the barren walls. Dorian felt like there was something else he should say, but couldn't find the words.

Instead, he stepped forward and picked up the casket with Mughan. It was heavy.

They lifted it over their shoulders and slid it down the opening, scraping stone on stone. He tried to avoid looking at the names carved into the tombs below it.

The casket slid in and hit the back side of the niche with a dull thud. Barileth and Dozotaine finished putting in the other casket. All four stepped back.

Lumdir walked forward, favoring his injured leg, and with Yander's help, set the first cover in place. He tapped it into position with his hammer, then struck out. The cover rang out like a bell.

Again, Lumdir struck. The door rang and shifted farther back. The hammer blows sounded a mournful rhythm.

A voice from behind him started singing the dirge. Softly, at first, it grew. Others joined in the lament.

Dorian added his voice, singing the ancient song filled with sadness. For the lives that were cut short, for the loved ones lost.

He hadn't been at his own wife's funeral. Now, in this place he called home, he felt the full force of his loss.

Tears came then, streaking through the rock dust on his face.

Lumdir finished the first and moved to the second. The second verse of the dirge began.

It almost overwhelmed Dorian, and he struggled to keep on his feet.

All the time lost, all the memories they could have made. The protection he should have provided, not just her, but everyone.

The deep voices of the dwarves rolled through the tunnels, returned and magnified by the stone. It intertwined with the hammer blows, a dull, steady rhythm.

He wouldn't be able to protect all of them, and it pained him to know it. There would be more.

There would be more.

The cover clicked shut. The funeral was over and the song faded.

One by one, they departed without a word. Dorian wiped the streaks from his face and beard. There was still hope, a chance to see her again.

It called out to him, and it threatened those he held dear.

Dorian stayed until long after everyone had gone, thinking. When he had finished, he walked over, felt the carved names on the covers, and then walked away.

He didn't go to eat like the others had, and then to sleep. He went deeper into the mine, down as far as he could into the virgin tunnels that hadn't seen living things.

He found a pickaxe and wandered the tunnels aimlessly. After a while he realized it wasn't doing any good and lit a candle and picked a tunnel.

There was something at the end, an ore of some kind hidden behind another few feet of rock, and he set the candle down and got to work.

The pickaxe rang with a steady rhythm, and he couldn't get the sound of the dirge out of his head. That haunting melody, the words that spoke of life and death and the sorrow of the lost.

Death wasn't final.

The words that brought him here, the words that sealed his fate in Zirad and brought forth the King's judgment.

Just a few words, spoken to be comfort, and turning into something more.

The King had to have the book locked away still. He wouldn't destroy it and bring down a curse on his kingdom.

And if it was still there, Dorian could use it.

But there was another way. Dorian pushed aside the chunk of rock that fell to the floor and returned to digging.

The same necromancer that threatened him offered him an opportunity. This human had discovered something powerful, and if he could get his hands on it, he wouldn't need the book.

All he would need was his wife. And that would be easier to get than the book. All he had to do was survive this year and finish the King's task.

"Dorian."

He paused, pickaxe in midair.

"Yes?"

"Can I join you?" Lumdir asked. Dorian wanted to tell him no, to go away and leave him to his sorrow, but he said nothing. Lumdir took a seat on a chunk of rock, settling in beside him.

Dorian pursed his lips, but turned back to the wall. Candlelight flickered, caught by the ore and reflected to him.

Iron ore. A big vein of it too. Without thinking, Dorian had excavated the rock around it.

"Enough for a few weapons, nice find," Lumdir said.

Dorian cleared his throat. "Why are you down here?" His voice was blessedly even.

"To see how you are doing."

"Fine."

Lumdir shifted and crossed his arms. "I've seen the look in your eyes. You've changed since the attack." Silence stretched, punctuated by the pickaxe ringing against the wall.

What right does Lumdir have to meddle? Dorian channeled some of his frustration into his pickaxe, and each blow shattered rock and sent it flying. Some of the shards hit his face, stinging him, but he ignored it.

"I have no right to pry into your mind. However, you saved my life. I'm not about to let you give up yours."

Dorian spun on him. "Is that what you think?" Lumdir locked eyes with him.

"I'm not sure what to think. Tell me what I should be thinking."

"It isn't like that."

"Then tell me, what's bothering you?"

The pickaxe drooped. Dorian wasn't sure how long he had been down here now, and his body felt drained.

"Nothing."

"I don't believe that."

"Are you going to work me over like one of your rocks?"

Lumdir snorted. "The rocks are softer than you are. I've no tool to break you."

"Tools don't break dwarves."

"What does?"

"Life. Life breaks us."

"Not death?"

Dorian narrowed his eyes, but Lumdir gave up no information. No searching glance, no twitch.

"What are you getting at?"

"We still have enemies out here that can kill us. After almost dying the first time, I'm not keen on repeating it."

Dorian still bore wounds from the battle. "Neither am I."

"Good." Lumdir stood up and walked off.

"That's it?"

"You aren't ready yet. I'm satisfied that you'll keep fighting. Besides, it's late and I should be sleeping." Lumdir paused and looked back. "As should you."

He left, leaving Dorian perplexed. Exhaustion came over him then, his muscles worn out and tired. He would get the other dwarves to collect the ore tomorrow.

Lumdir was right, there was enough here to make plenty of weapons. Enough to equip all the dwarves, and maybe enough left to forge armor.

But all of that could wait for another day. Now, as he trudged back up the tunnel, was the time to sleep.

The pen scratched as he wrote, tallying up the record for the day. Another harvest of golden moss, another splitting of the harvest, and the other dwarves had finished their tasks.

Words on the page lightened, and then he ran out of ink. Dorian dipped his pen in the ink jar, tapping off the excess, then stopped to think.

He wasn't sure where to go next. They had worked so hard to get the mine up and running, put in so much time and effort that if they weren't threatened by a necromancer, they would be in a good position.

So now what do we do?

He mulled the question, pondering their options, when there was a rap on his door.

"Come."

Mughan walked in, striding confidently and sitting down on the open stool.

"I wasn't expecting you."

"No one ever does," Mughan said, then glanced to the page. "Am I interrupting?"

"Yes, you are." Dorian returned to his work, writing down the furnishings Lumdir and Kimec had made. Mughan stared at him and leaned back, interlacing his fingers and putting them behind his head.

Dorian ran out of ink again and set the pen down on the desk, turning to Mughan. "You aren't going to leave, are you?"

Mughan grinned at him. "How long have you known me?"

"Long enough."

"What are we going to do about this predicament we're in?" Mughan studied his face.

"We'll survive."

From deep inside his clothing, Mughan produced a pipe. Six inches long and carved from deep brown wood, the pipe had strange carvings all over it. Intricate, but small. "Do you mind?"

"Didn't know you smoked." Dorian didn't stop him as Mughan reached into another fold of his shirt and took out a pouch of shredded tobacco.

"You don't know much about me, Dorian, but we can change that." Mughan stuffed the leaf into the pipe, crushing it down with a thumb. The smell of it washed over him, rich and earthy. "My line comes from that of royalty, of the same lineage of King Lightaxe himself.

"His ancestors kept power and the favor of the gods. Mine, not so much." Mughan gestured around at the walls. "Hence, you see me here on a wild expedition instead of sitting on the Emerald Throne of Zirad."

Dorian crossed his arms across his chest. "I'm not interested in a history lesson. Least of all, about kings."

Mughan chuckled, adding his final wadding to his pipe. "That is what I like about you, and I can't say I'm not surprised." He shrugged and stood. "Had my fortunes been different, I might feel the same way, but although we didn't keep the power, the name of Mithrilbasher still lives on."

He took the torch from the wall sconce and brought it to the mouth of his pipe, sucking in puffs to get it to light. Dorian watched him, wondering where it was all going and growing impatient. "Enough to give us an estate and partial interest in the mines, we live a comfortable life.

"But a third son, what lot in life can he have in the inheritance?" Mughan returned to his seat, smoke drifting lazy circles around his head and stinking up the room. Dorian wanted to tell him to put it out, but held his tongue.

"And so I was forced into a different life. One that has granted me many positions and many acquaintances.

"Like the others, I'm curious about you. Unlike the others, I have connections that give me more answers." Mughan leaned back.

Dorian's blood ran cold. "Answers? Or rumors and lies? Talk is cheap when the subject isn't present." He gripped the edge of arm-rests.

"Perhaps, but I know something about you." Mughan drew a deep pull on the pipe. The tobacco burned cherry red and cast a glow on his face, which faded as his breath slowed. His eyes glowed. He let out the smoke in a long exhale. "The one who hunts us. He isn't the only one who's dabbled in necromancy, is he?"

2

PROTECTION

"I don't know what you're talking about."

"Do you?"

"Why do you think that?" The look in Mughan's eye wasn't malevolent, but it was something else. *Was this ambition, or a play for power?*

"The merchants came bearing more than commerce, for me, they brought information." Mughan slipped a piece of parchment from his pocket clamped down on his pipe. It hung from his mouth as he unfolded the page. "Shall I read you what it says?"

"I don't care what it says," Dorian growled.

"Dorian Ironstrike, a preeminent colonizer and miner. Excellent dousing skills and able to find even the faintest traces of precious ores. Prized by King Lightaxe for his ability to lead successful expeditions."

Dorian turned away, back to his notes. The words rung in his ears. "Let it be."

"Wife killed by goblins on her way to his last colony. You turned to necromancy to bring her back, stealing the book of the dead from the Royal Library. The incantation was thankfully interrupted before it could do too much damage and you were sentenced to life imprisonment. Is that true?"

Hand shaking, Dorian tried to pick up the pen again as a distraction.

"Dorian, is it true?" When he didn't answer, Mughan continued. "I wondered why the King wanted you on this expedition, dragged from the bowels of the dungeons. What could compel him to bring you out in such a time as this?"

"I don't know what the king thinks. Frankly, I don't care." Dorian turned on him.

"An interesting position to take, considering he judges the success or failure of our expedition. You're deflecting though." Mughan took the pipe from his mouth and leaned in. "Is it true?"

Of course it is true. Every day he had to deal with the consequences, the pain and sadness. A life lost. A love destroyed.

For not the first time, Dorian envisioned violence upon Mughan. However, unlike before, he knew that Mughan had the interests of the expedition at heart.

What would lying get him? Mughan already believed his report, however he managed to get it, and Dorian thought through ways of trying to persuade him it was a lie.

But he knew it wasn't going to work. Mughan would see through it. Dorian's heart pounded and his hands sweated.

That only left him one option. The most bitter of them all.

"It's true," Dorian whispered. His voice caught in his throat and he dropped his eyes to the floor.

"I'm sorry for your wife." Mughan's words were soft, and not what Dorian was expecting. The tenderness made him look back up. Sadness reflected in Mughan's eyes, echoing what he felt in his heart.

"You didn't do it," he said roughly, "No need to apologize."

Pipe glowing again, Mughan took the time to exhale out another cloud of smoke. "That may be, and I assume you still live with the pain, but we need you here and present. You've been distracted since the attack, not yourself. What are you considering?"

"I don't know what you mean."

"The others suspect, just as I did. Maybe know more than they're letting on." Dorian immediately thought of Lumdir. "We all have a right to keep our past hidden, as long as it doesn't affect us." Mughan tapped his pipe on his teeth. "Your past is affecting you."

Dorian put the pen back down, hand still shaking. "I don't know what to say."

"Tell me it isn't too much for you. If it is, I can take over."

So it is a play for power, after all. "It isn't too much for me."

"I'm not after your job, not anymore, at least. Not yet."

"Is that the first truthful thing you've told me?"

Mughan let out a bark of laughter, eyes twinkling. "I've revealed some of my own secrets, the shaft is level between us. The game has changed, though. Any necromancer willing to recruit goblins is a bigger threat than any of us suspect."

"Agreed."

"Here's what I ask. Call a council, bring everyone together, and tell them the truth about what we're up against. They have a right to know and might surprise you." Pipe spent, Mughan tapped out the ash and tucked it away into his clothes.

Dorian stared at the pile of ash on his floor, a black spot on the gray stone. "I'm up to the task. As you know, this isn't my first expedition."

"But it is in quite a few years." Mughan stood and offered a hand. Dorian took it, his grip strong. "I have plans and I need to stay alive to see them to fruition."

"Don't tell anyone." Dorian gritted his teeth. "Please."

Mughan nodded. "I'll keep your secret for now."

He left. Dorian thought long after, distracted. He tried to pick up his pen, but never dipped it into the ink again.

Thoughts swirled around, threatening to overwhelm him. What did Mughan want?

What did he want?

He knew his deepest desire, the temptation that was before him. Turn back on the path that led him here, or choose to give it up.

Turn to the earth. Turn to the deep. Tufolin's advice, delve deeper.

If he was going to do that, he needed to train Yander better, unlock the glimmering potential he had inside. The young dwarf had learned the song of the earth fast.

Another thing to do, another task on his list. But the one that held the most promise.

Yander could help him find the ore.

Dorian drifted into a fitful sleep, plagued by nightmares of his wife and children suffering horrible deaths.

She was soft and warm. Her hair tickled his chest, but he didn't care. Yander leaned back and relaxed, enjoying the moment and breathing deep.

Emelda shifted on his chest and looked up and smiled. He smiled back and hugged her tight. She snuggled up to him again.

The cool of the apartment caressed his skin. His mind wandered, thinking about the future and what it held.

Soon, it took him to dark places. Potential dangers, real and imagined, ran through his consciousness.

Yander swallowed, heart beating faster.

"What is it?" Emelda hugged him tighter.

"This place. When we set out, I was so young and ignorant. I thought it would be a grand adventure, full of gold and jewels and an easy life of wealth. Reality was different."

She took his hand, interlacing her fingers with his. He went on. "Instead of a life of ease, we have this. Dangers below us, dangers above. The mountain doesn't want to give up its most precious treasures, and it has been difficult to find any ore at all."

"We'll find it, I know you will," she said. "They didn't choose this place without knowing what was here."

"I thought that, too." He shook his head. "Not anymore. I'm not sure the King's Explorers had any idea about what was here, that they might have picked it for another reason."

"What do you mean?"

"Do you want to stay?"

"Yes, of course. Why do you ask?"

His mouth was dry, and he licked his lips. "If we have merchants this year, will you do me a favor?"

She looked up at him with a questioning look, but a sultry smile on her lips. "Go on."

"Will you go back to Zirad with them?"

Emelda eyes narrowed, then she sat up. "You're serious, aren't you?"

"Yes, I am."

"No, I won't do that."

Yander sat up too, gripping her arms. "It isn't safe here Emelda. Zirad is a walled fortress, almost impenetrable. You'll be safe there."

"I know Zirad, and I know my place. This is my home. Everyone needs me. You need me."

"I can't have you hurt for me," Yander said, shaking his head. "What would I do without you?"

"Would you send me away to not be with you, anyway?"

"It wouldn't be for forever, just until I'm done here." He had said the wrong thing. Emotions shifted on her face.

"Why would you ask this of me?"

"Because I love you." It churned inside him, the desire to keep her and the need to push her away.

"If you love me, you wouldn't ask this of me."

"Do you think I haven't thought this through? That I haven't laid awake at night thinking of what's happened?" His body tensed up, remembering those sleepless nights. "If there was any other way to keep you safe, I'd take it."

Her eyes widened. "You can't do this to me, Yander, please." The pleading in her voice made the hardness go out of his body, and he slumped down. "We still have time, we still have hope. My parents didn't bring me here because they thought it would be easy. They brought me here for opportunity."

He looked away as she wiped her eyes. "There is nothing to return to in Zirad. Not for me. I have no family there, no hope, no prospects."

"I'll find someone to take care of you."

"Who?"

The silence stretched on in the night. The one candle they left burning was flickering down to a stub.

"Are you going to send me to your family?" she asked.

His mouth opened and shut.

"I didn't think so."

"It's still safer this way."

"We've survived this long." She reached out and touched him, and he swung his gaze back to her. "Despite all the work, the pain, the loss." It played across her face. "We've built something. We're a part of something new and grand and bigger than I thought possible before."

Yander shook his head. "This mountain refuses to give up its treasure. All we've found is iron and few jewels here and there."

"That's what's bothering you, isn't it?" She put an arm over his shoulder and leaned her head on his.

"No." He paused. "Well, not all of it, at least. It seems like no matter what I do we never make any progress."

"That isn't true. Think about what we used to have and where we've come from. When we got here you hadn't even found ore at all, but since then you helped discover copper and iron."

"What good are they against the undead and goblins? We need steel and more armor. I'm not the only one who sees it," Emelda rubbed his back.

"You're tired, let's get some sleep and talk about this in the morning."

Yander set his jaw. "I've made up my mind."

"Have you considered that I might be safer here?" Her voice was soft.

"No."

"The merchants talked about the goblin raids, that they had come closer and closer to the city. They said Zirad wasn't as safe as it used to be, that dwarves were getting fed up and thieves were on the loose."

"Speculation, stories to scare us."

"And why would they need to do that?" She asked. He didn't reply. "We'll talk about this in the morning," she said firmly.

At that, she got up. Yander didn't see any reason in arguing about it now. She crossed the room, bare feet padding on the stone, and blew out the candle, leaving them in total darkness.

He laid back down. When she slipped into bed, he reached out for her and embraced her. She put her head on his chest again and he thought as he listened to her breathing even and slip into sleep.

Awake, his night vision revealing shapes and shadows in the room, Yander turned over his options.

She might be right, she could be safer here. It had already been two years, who knows what could happen in a city like Zirad? Politics and kings were no concern of his, but he couldn't help but think something was off in the kingdom.

But there was danger here, real and present. What kind of dwarf would he be if he couldn't protect her from it? After the death of her parents, he was all she had left, which was why she clung to him. Was it right to try and get her to leave?

If he could be better, if they could find more ore, she wouldn't have to go. He pictured them in gleaming steel armor, standing tall against goblins and undead alike.

That might be the only way we get out of this mess. He wondered what Dorian thought, what he wanted from the expedition. The way he had taught him to feel the earth.

If he could be better, if he could sense the ore like Dorian could, he could protect Emelda and the others. Yander scratched at a bandaged cut on his face, relieving the itch beneath it.

And if they had better weapons and armor, they could fight back.

"Dorian will help me." He clenched a fist, using it to relieve the pressure he felt inside. "Together, we'll find the treasure that this mountain holds."

3

ACTION

Chapter Three

Dwarves crowded around the table as Dorian unrolled the map. He asked Barileth and Yander to hold it down.

"Yutatir has been helping Barileth with this for the last few days." Eyes went to them both. Yutatir bowed a little, red creeping up the cheeks above his beard. "We'll need to fortify our position if we have any hope of surviving this year."

"Why don't we ask the King for troops or reinforcements?" Thardegith asked. Dorian exchanged a knowing glance with Barileth.

"We've put in a request with the king's liaison when he was here. Don't expect a reply," Dorian said.

A murmur ran through the crowd. "Surely he cares about our plight."

"He outfitted the expedition and gave us supplies. As you recall from your contracts, that is all he was obligated to do." Mughan turned to address Thardegith. "We share in the riches, we share in the risk."

Before any more whispers and dissent could occur, Dorian took back control, pointing to their outpost on the map. "Here's the mine."

He moved his finger just a little. "This is the border with Guzan. As far as I know, we haven't crossed it with any of our tunnels and I don't plan to."

"That's where we expect the attack to come from, that's where we need to protect." Dorian spread out his arms. "Like Mughan said, we share the risk, so it isn't fair for me to make all the decisions."

He looked at each in the eyes, drawing out the silence and letting his point sink in. "I won't blame any dwarf who leaves now, not after everything we've been through. A few more weeks and the passes back to Zirad will be open again and ready to travel."

"Anyone who wants to leave should go then." The fire snapped and cracked behind them. "Think about it." They all still bore signs of the fighting. Kragnak's stump of an arm covered in bandages, cuts, scrapes.

The wounds were still fresh, both visible and invisible.

"If I were them I'd take the pass and attack from the north," Barileth said, tracing up from Guzan. "The mountain is too tall to try and get over, and it's too steep above the mine entrance."

"What if they came from the other side?" Dozotaine asked.

Dorian shook his head. "It's possible, but harder to get across. A fighting force might have trouble with the grade and uneven terrain. I'd agree with Barileth."

"So cut back the forest, both above and below us," Mughan said. "Give us more room to see them coming." He drew an arc around the mine.

"I could use the wood too," Kimec said.

"Build walls all around," Lumdir offered. "Up the slope, around the above ground farms too."

"And a watchtower, with a bell," Yander said.

"Good ideas." Dorian nodded to Yutatir, who produced his charcoal stick. "The east side will give us the best view of the mountain." Yutatir drew a circle around the mine.

"If we cut down the trees, we won't be able to get the fruit," Yudoline warned.

"What if we made our own fruit?" Yander asked. "Plant them inside the wall?"

"An orchard would be wonderful." Yudoline's eyes sparkled. "If we had apples, we could make cider."

"We can transplant some younger trees," Dorian said, thinking through his previous experience. Memories he hadn't thought about in years came coming back. Harvest time. The apples practically falling off the tree. All the work that it too. "It's a lot of work to gather and process all that fruit. Machinery would make it easier. We'd need a room for it to go in."

Yutatir added one to the wall above the mine, "If we add it to the wall it cuts down on two sides."

"Speaking of walls, we should thicken the existing walls, and cut in crossbow slits to them," Mughan said.

"We don't have enough crossbows to go around." They had two, one Barileth used for hunting and a spare. "Kimec, do you think you could make more?"

Kimec stroked his beard and wrinkled his eyes. "I can figure out the wood."

"Anyone ever made crossbows before?" Dorian looked around the room, letting his eyes fall on Kragnak. "Could you try?"

Kragnak looked at his stump. "I'll need some help."

"We'll talk later," Dorian said. "This is going to take more work than we've put in, and more than I have any right to ask."

"This is our home. We aren't leaving it now," Emelda said, a strength in her voice and a fire in her eyes. Dorian was surprised, but pleased too. "I'll learn how to make crossbows, it can't be much harder than waxwork."

"Every hand helps." Yander was standing too straight next to Emelda. Dorian noted it and moved on. He would ask later.

"We should expect the wall to be breached," Dozotaine said. "We'll need better defenses inside the courtyard and mine."

Barileth grinned. "More traps. And holes for arrows."

"What about holes for dropping rocks inside? If they get that far," Olgim said.

"Easy enough to make," Dozotaine said, "As long as it's high enough or small enough that the enemy can't get through."

"Do we have any idea of what and how many to expect?" The one question Dorian didn't want anyone to ask, and Yudoline had asked it. There was no use in trying to hide anything now, they would learn one way or another.

"For some reason a necromancer wants us dead. He was behind the goblin attack, and the undead who tried to take Emelda."

"How do you know?" Kimec asked.

"Because the goblin told me. I have a feeling he isn't going to just give up, either. I expect he'll be back in force to destroy us. We can't let it happen." He wouldn't let it happen, not if he wanted to see his children again.

Or my wife.

Dorian pushed the thought aside, lest it betray him. The power that the necromancer had, he had never seen anything like it before.

"Why would this necromancer be after us?" Hukgras asked. "What did we ever do to it?"

"Those who reach out for the dead are driven by things that long should have been forgotten," Mughan said, watching Dorian as he spoke. "Trying to make sense of why they use the evil is a fool's errand, isn't that right Dorian?"

Dorian played along, nodding. "We'll never know what drives them, and there isn't any sense in wondering. We can either run away, or fight back."

"Why can't we reason with him, come to some sort of understanding?" Hukgras asked. Her question was sincere and betrayed her lack of experience.

"One does not attempt to reason whit those touched by death. It's unnatural," Mughan said. "We need to survive. We need better defenses. We need better armor and weapons."

"Agreed," Dorian said. "Which is why we'll have to split our mining between ore and stone. Two dwarves can supply the stone for the fortifications, the others will need to find the ore."

"We've plenty of ore. We need steel." Eyes turned to Kragnak at Mughan's remark.

Kragnak gripped his stump. "I need a flux to make steel. We can make the pig iron, but only that."

"So if we need flux, then let's get it," Mughan said.

"It isn't that easy. If we haven't found flux stone by now, there might not be any in the area, no matter how deep we dig."

"How do you know that, without exploring?" Mughan asked.

"Because we've hit nothing but granite so far," Dorian growled. "You can't make steel with granite for flux."

"Then why don't we find flux stone? How hard can it be?"

"Have you dug through a layer of stone lately?"

"Why dig through it when it's been opened already?"

Dorian's heart skipped a beat, thinking about the wall in the mine. "What's that?"

Mughan crossed his arms and cocked his head. "We've all seen it. It isn't hard to figure out why there is a stone wall in the mine. We should open it up and explore the cavern."

"No." Dorian's voice was flat, under control. The other founders and migrants were silent, but shifting and movement betrayed their discomfort.

"We can cover more ground that way, find out where the rock layers end and begin."

"It's not up for discussion."

Mughan drew back. "Why?"

"Because that was where the spider came from that killed our family." Emotion played across Emelda's face as Dorian spoke, but she held strong. He was keenly aware of the impact it had and was sorry for it.

But there was nothing he could do about it now. What was in the past was done.

"Surely we're better equipped now?" Mughan looked around at the others. The newer migrants nodded, but the other's faces were hard.

"Out of the question," Dorian said, almost grinding his teeth.

"This is about the survival of the expedition--" Dorian cut him off.

"We can survive without going in the cavern. It will take more work and effort, but it's safer." He couldn't bear another funeral, not so soon after the last one.

If he had his way, he wouldn't need one.

"Dorian," Mughan looked like he was trying to be patient, but the corners of his mouth drooped and condescension crept into his voice. "We have a squad of fighters now, all well equipped with iron weapons and armor. We'll have to go in there sometime."

Others murmured their assent. A flash of annoyance, and a reminder of why Dorian didn't like Mughan rose in him.

But the dwarf had proved his mettle and had stood strong when a weaker dwarf would have taken the easy way out. Dorian drew a deep breath to control himself and pushed away the thoughts.

"Back to the defenses. Since we already have the crops planted here, we should put a room on the south-west corner of the wall."

"We could build a windmill, let the wind do our work for us," Barileth said. Kimec chimed in about the lumber he would need, then others.

Dorian pulled back from the conversation, grateful for the respite. Mughan had pulled back, crossed arms, and was silent too.

They sketched out the general layout of the new wall and towers, put in the processing room, and decided on how big to expand the entrance tunnel to.

At the end, they had a plan to move forward. One that might survive a serious invasion even. Dorian, despite the dust up with Mughan, was optimistic.

If we can expand the ore exploration and processing, we might make it. They had another migrant wave to look forward to also, later after the winter snows had receded and the rivers weren't too swollen to cross.

That would bring more workers, and more help.

Enough to push them over the edge? Dorian still wasn't sure how worthwhile the king's promise was, or even if it was actually his word.

But that was far off in the distance, and they had a necromancer to deal with.

The conversation shifted to where they would place the arrow slits, and how many crossbows and bolts they would need.

Mughan was drawn back into the conversation. "What about an escape tunnel?" Dozotaine asked. "If we run into a bad situation, it would be nice to have."

"Better yet, why not use it to our advantage?" Mughan leaned in and drew all eyes. "We build it into the courtyard and give anyone who decides to attack and make it into the entrance tunnel a nasty surprise."

"Attack from behind, where they never expect." Dorian smiled. "A great idea, and one I hope we never have to use."

"We'll build a door they'll be hard pressed to breach." Lumdir raised his arm and made a fist. He was looking better than he had a few days ago, improving. Soon he would be back to work in earnest.

"We have a plan then." Dorian smiled and looked to the south. They would be making their own preparations, whatever that necromancer would throw at them."

They talked through the rest of the defenses, dividing up the tasks to those who would be most appropriate. The day drifted by, and soon it was time for dinner.

Dorian ended the discussions in a better place than they had begun. "Each dwarf has his or her mission." He made eye contact with each one again, and was satisfied to see resolute faces. They knew what was in the balance.

"Again, consider staying here carefully. If you do leave, no one will fault you. We all know what will happen if we fail."

They disbanded to prepare, and Dorian waited and watched them leave. For the others, it was poverty and disfavor of the king.

For him, it was the chance of ever seeing his children again.

4

A Proposal

Mughan grabbed his arm as he walked by, pulling him in close. "We need to talk." He looked at Emelda. "Alone," he whispered in his ear.

A question in her eyes, Yander nodded to her. "Go on ahead, I'll just be a moment." The others trickled back to their dinner preparations.

"Walk with me." Yander eyed Mughan warily. The other's footsteps disappeared as they passed the apartments on their way down the main shaft.

"Where are we going?"

"You'll see." Yander pulled up short on the stairs and crossed his arms.

"You'll tell me now."

Mughan scowled. "Down to the cavern entrance. I need to know about it and it's clear Dorian isn't going to tell me. Fool of a dwarf, all that land and won't even use it!"

"It's sealed for good reason."

"We'll talk here then. We all know that we don't have the numbers to defend ourselves against an army, and I expect that after a few failures an army is what we'll get."

"Steel." The torchlight flickered over Mughan's expression, one foot on the step above him with his hands folded across it. "We need it if we're going to stand a chance, both of success and survival."

"There are other ways."

"Have you found the gold yet? I haven't seen it if you have."

Yander's mouth pulled at the corners. "I haven't seen you in the mines helping any."

Mughan held up his hands. "No need to get defensive, it was no critique of you, or Dorian's, work."

"It sure doesn't feel like it is in good faith. Dorian may be fooled by your "acts" of good faith, but some of us see through it."

He did something unexpected then. Mughan laughed. Yander blinked. "You did it to save yourself and whatever reputation you still have."

"You're right, I did do it out of self-preservation." His eyes twinkled with residual mirth. "But we all do it, even you. Why did you come here?"

The question hung in the air, hung above his head. "Not willing to answer? Fine, then at least talk to me about the cavern."

"I'm not going in there." Yander was thankful his voice was so strong, glad it didn't betray his inner turmoil. "No one should."

"We have to survive, you know that, everyone else knows that. By the time you can find the flux stone by mining it might be too late."

"I'm still going to do it my way, not that way."

"Think about it. I want what's best for me, but I also want what's best for you."

"And what happens when those two things are different?" The cool air of the mine drifted on his shoulders. "You'd abandon us in a second if you had to."

Mughan shook his head. "You don't know me well. In time, you will."

"I trust Dorian and I have for a long time. I'm going to do it his way." Yander turned and walked back up the stairs.

"Take some time," Mughan called up after him. "We have some time left, but not much."

Yander didn't go to dinner right away, but turned into the apartments. He dragged his hand along the wall, touching the surfaces that he had helped dig out. This used to be solid stone.

What was it now? A mine? A place to live?

A home?

How long had it been since he had one of those? He pictured a few young dwarves, growing like moss on a damp wall.

What would they inherit? Would he take his money, assuming they finished the contract, and go somewhere else?

Yander thought he had been searching for riches all this time. For glory and legend, but now that they had come this far he wasn't sure anymore.

He had wandered to their room. The bed was made, blanket tucked in neatly. Emelda had straightened the small wooden desk that Kimec had made for them as a wedding present.

His eyes wandered over to the stone chest Lumdir had carved, rough but useful. Surviving and unlocking the treasures of the mountain were good, but he had to do it for more than himself.

For more than Emelda.

He would need to do it for everyone in the expedition, even Mughan.

And he would need Dorian's help. This mountain wasn't going to give up its secrets lightly. A plan formed in his mind, and he stayed a few more minutes.

He would find flux stone. They would make steel. The mountain would yield, no matter how strong and solid it would be.

He would be the one to conquer it.

Thardegith yawned, covering up his mouth with a hand. "You'll get plenty of sleep tonight." Dozotaine clapped him on the back.

In reply, Thardegith grumbled and swung his pickaxe over his shoulder. They trudged the rest of the way down the tunnels.

Dorian stopped the group at a branch. He pointed down the left-hand tunnel. "Dozotaine, take Thardegith down there. Mine as much good stone as you can for the others. We'll be deeper like we talked about."

They went down the right-hand path, curving down deeper in the mountain. Yander carried the torch, and Dorian's body blocked the light, sending a long shadow.

Stone crunched underfoot, remnants of past digs. The air was cool, and stale, down here.

"Can you feel it?"

"Not yet," Yander said. They walked on. "Can you?"

The stone was silent for him. Dorian had hoped this path would yield results. Soon they were at the end. A solid rock wall stopped them.

Dorian reached out his hand and touched the wall. Rough. Cool. Dry. He searched as far as he could feel, but felt nothing. When he opened his eyes Yander was crouched down, touching the floor.

"Anything?"

Yander hesitated. "Perhaps. A faint..."

He joined him, searching. "Why can't we find what we're looking for?" Dorian glanced up. Lips tight, eyes squeezed shut, Yander trembled.

"We have time yet, we will find it." Dorian hoped the words were true, that whoever had chosen this place had chosen well.

Thus far, he had been disappointed.

"Then teach me better." Yander's eyes snapped open. "How am I supposed to be useful without being able to sense what we're looking for?"

"You can't sense what isn't there."

"I can't believe that. I won't believe that. What am I doing wrong?"

This was one element that Dorian didn't know how to change. How was he supposed to teach something that could only be felt? Was he to scatter ore into the earth himself?

He had dwelt on it, puzzled on it, for days, weeks, months. He stood back up. "We'll dig here. We can use the stone, if nothing else. Come on."

Yander took the offered hand and rose. "At least it will feel good to dig again," he muttered.

They got to work, digging down to where Yander thought he felt something. Yander had improved, speeding up his rate of advance, and together they made a nice line of stone blocks before lunch.

After they had finished Dorian wiped the sweat from his brow and examined them. They would do for the wall, he would send others down to get them.

Yander was still striking at the wall, cutting off chunks of rock that tumbled to the ground with a hollow thud.

"Time to eat." Yander kept digging, focus in his eyes. "Yander, you need the nourishment."

He glanced back, but stopped. "I'll bring food next time."

"Would that be wise?"

"I feel it now, there is something up ahead." Dorian checked. He was right. It was faint to him, but it was there. Not gold, not iron, but something else. As they advanced, he would know.

"What do you think it is?"

His brow wrinkled. "I'm not sure yet. It doesn't seem like anything we've found yet."

"We'll know more after lunch." Together they went back to the dining hall and ate a filling meal of rockbread, eggs, and deer meat. Yander wolfed through his, only stopping to talk to Emelda about her morning.

He was also the first one out, kissing her goodbye as the others were barely halfway through.

"Someone's in a hurry," Mughan remarked.

"As should we all be," Dorian said through a mouthful of bread. That silenced him, but Dorian didn't like it.

Emelda shot him a worried look, but didn't say anything. He would have to talk to Yander about it. Dorian, not far behind Yander, told the others which tunnel they were at, but they still were hauling the stone Dozotaine and Thardegith mined.

It was good news, but he couldn't dwell on it long. He made sure the others were set and followed Yander back down the mine.

By the time he got there Yander had already advanced the tunnel another few feet. He heard Dorian approached, and turned, forehead already glistening with sweat and gray with rock dust.

"I think it's silver. It isn't quite like the hematite we found, but it has a similar feel and there isn't very much of it." His eyebrows drew down. "Do you think it's enough?"

"I haven't known a king to pass up silver yet," Dorian said. Together they mined until dinner, still far from the ore. Yander was right, it was silver, and he was stronger in sensing it too.

They ate a late meal, after all the others had finished. Dorian was tired, his muscles aching after the effort, but was surprised when Yander stood back up.

"I'm going back down."

"Rest tonight, the mountain will still be there tomorrow," Dorian said. But Yander was already gone, making no indications he heard him.

Something's changed. Dorian finished his dinner and went out to the courtyard to check the progress. A large stack of stone was in the courtyard, with dwarves brining up more every minute.

He shielded his eyes from the rays of the setting sun and gaged the amount. It wouldn't even be enough to expand the wall. He was captured by questions and his own tasks, and it wasn't until far into the night that Dorian had a chance to return to his room.

He knocked softly on the Helmsplitter's door. A few moments later Emelda cracked the door in her nightclothes.

"He isn't back?"

She shook her head. "I'm worried about him Dorian. He asked me to leave, to go back to Zirad."

It surprised him, made him grasping for words while she waited. "He just wants you to be safe I think."

She crossed her arms and looked down. "That's what he told me. Am I going to lose him too?"

"I would be sad if you left," Dorian admitted begrudgingly, patting her arm. "You do too much work around here to not be missed." He wanted to make her comfortable, to make her secure.

He didn't know if he could. *That's probably how Yander feels too.*

"If it makes you feel any better, I'll talk to him tonight. Get some rest, I'm sure he'll be up soon."

Emelda smiled at him, and nodded. She shut the door with a gentle click. Dorian stopped by the kitchens before he went down to the mine, filling a water skin with cold water from the bucket.

Yander was mining when he arrived, within feet of the silver. He looked exhausted and took the water without a word, gulping it down.

Dorian joined him. Together they made short work of the stone, and a small pile of silver gleamed in the torchlight.

Slumping against the wall, Yander let his pickaxe clatter to the floor. The torch had burned down, was now fluttering.

Dorian flexed his arms, feeling the heat and tension that he had built in them. His breath, once sharp and fast, was slowing, and he also put down his pickaxe to examine their handiwork.

He turned away from Yander, down the tunnel to the mineshaft. They had come so far, but he didn't want any of it for them.

"I wish things would have been different," he said, back still to Yander. He didn't want him to see the anguish in his face, the lives lost that fell on his shoulders.

"For whatever reason you all were caught up in this. Not what I wanted, not what I ever dreamed of." His legs throbbed with fatigue, and he welcomed it. It was what he deserved, it was what he needed.

He heard Yander stir behind him and anticipated his words. Lashing, painful, honest.

But the words he expected never came.

"I promise to be better than I was, for you and Emelda. For everyone." Those seeking their lives would not stop just because they repelled one attack.

"I will make sure that we succeed. I will give the king what he wants. I will keep everyone else alive.

5

FORGING

The chimney leered at him, reminding him of the tombs they had just buried their dead in. Kragnak shuffled in any way.

"Welcome back." A smile cracked Kimec's face, and he set down his saw. Within moments he was clapping him on the back, wood dust flying in the air and getting into Kragnak's nose.

He had missed that, he realized.

"How are you feeling? Ready to work?"

Kragnak nodded.

"We've kept everything clean for you, stacked up some charcoal and ore ready to go." They were neatly piled beside the foundry. "Thurbag has been waiting."

The other dwarf was using a rag to polish his tools, and Kragnak had a momentary pang of jealousy. But, as soon as his eyes shifted back to the forge and anvil it evaporated into fear.

"Thanks," he mumbled, clutching his stump.

"Are you sure you're ready for this?" Emelda had come up beside him, placing a hand on his arm and looking into his eyes. He didn't like how they were searching for him and looked away.

"I'm ready." He straightened his back and marched forward.

"If there is anything you need just let us know," she said, walking with him. Kimec also joined him, and he was inwardly grateful that they did.

He wasn't sure he could have made it on his own.

What good was he now? Unskilled before, now he was pitiful. And the worst part was knowing that it was everything he had been useful at before. His teachers at the guild had been right, he would amount to nothing.

But here he was, in the middle of the wilderness by himself, with nowhere else to turn and nothing else to do.

"Good morning, Kragnak." Thurbag held out his hand, then hastily pulled it back. It stung.

"Morning." Kragnak's voice was icy. He tried to soften it. "I see you've been busy."

"Kimec helped me on where to put everything." Thurbag wouldn't meet his eyes, and turned back to the forge. "I think I've built the fire right. They gave me some pointers but told me that you would know best how to arrange it."

Emelda squeezed his arm again. "Are you sure?"

He took a deep breath. "I'll handle it from here." At least he wouldn't have to worry about wielding his hammer.

That would never happen again.

"With Thurbag's help we'll have this forge up and running in no time." He tried to force a smile. Emelda gave him a pointed look, but returned to her workshop.

Kimec clapped him on the back. "If you need anything--"

"I'll ask," Kragnak interrupted. He also returned to his work. Emelda watched them over a bracelet she was carving, but he tried to ignore it.

"We've got to make the iron bell for the watchtower," Thurbag said. "I've gathered ore, but I saw that there were bars. I didn't know which to use."

"We'll start with the bar." His eyes went to the hammer. He walked past it, grabbing his apron and passing the leather strap over his head. When he went to tie it, the absence of one hand made him remember.

The slice of the blade. The sound of it falling.

The absence of pain, and the wonder, until it came later.

And now this, the memory of a hand that wasn't there anymore.

"I'll help." He added hastily, "If you want it, of course."

"You'll help me, and I'll help you. That's what we're here for, right?" Kragnak forced himself to be calm, to stay in the room even though he wanted to be somewhere, anywhere else.

Thurbag nodded. "You're right."

Fire flared and smoke belched from the foundry. The heat of the blast blew back Kragnak's beard and threatened to singe his hair.

"Too much," he said, waving his hand irritated. "You're going too fast."

"Sorry." Thurbag slowed down his work on the bellows, lifting up on the foot crank that made the leathery lungs billow air.

The fire died down, letting Kragnak poke and prod it with his left hand. It was awkward, and the scraper kept going everywhere except where he wanted it.

In the end he managed to stir up the coals to where he wanted, pulling off enough slag to be satisfied. He dropped the scraper in disgust and sat down on a stool.

"Keep going, a little faster." Kragnak watched the fire. "That's about right." It had been a rough start. He wasn't even that sure of what he was doing, but now he found himself in charge of teaching someone else to do it.

He struggled with the words, fumbled over the phrases that Thurbag found foreign.

It hadn't gone well so far.

Two lumps of iron, too burnt and misshapen to be of any use, lay on the dirt floor. Kragnak had given up on both.

This was going to be a long day.

Hammer struck iron, ringing out in the workshop. "No, you're hitting too softly."

Another strike. "Better." Then another. "About right." Thurbag shifted his grip on the hammer. "No, no," Kragnak said. "That's too high."

"What?"

"Here, hold it like this." Kragnak took the hammer with his left hand, finding it awkward to hold. "The top needs to be farther down."

"I put it farther down."

"No, your hand was up here."

"Isn't that what you told me to do?"

"No." Kragnak was finally able to wrestle the hammer into his hand to the proper grip. "Like this."

Thurbag squinted and rolled down his eyebrows. "If you say so." He took the hammer back and started to swing, but the iron had cooled too much.

"Hold on." Kragnak was too late, the hammer bounced off the ingot. He winced at the sound, and once again wondered how they were going to do this. He pulled it from the anvil and thrust it into the fire. Thurbag manned the bellows.

It would take a lot of forging to make the bell, and skill that Thurbag didn't have. Right now the iron was thick and held the heat, but as they worked it that would change. The thin iron would cool too quickly, and Thurbag was too slow.

If only he had his hand back. He would be finished within a few hours. Not to mention not having to be exasperated at every turn.

He caressed his stump, mourning the loss.

"Is it ready?" Kragnak looked down and cursed. He pulled the iron from the fire, sizzling and sparking. Thurbag rushed over as he laid it back on the anvil and took up the hammer.

The sparks left afterimages in his eyes, and Kragnak blinked them away as Thurbag attempted to shape the iron. He had attracted the attention of the others, who paused their work.

Kragnak ignored their eyes, feeling them burn into the back of his head, and tried to turn the iron at the appropriate times. Thurbag wasn't keeping a steady rhythm, instead beating as soon as he could.

"Every fourth for the anvil," Kragnak reminded.

Thurbag started and interrupted his hammering. "I forgot."

"Here, like this." Kragnak handed him the tongs and took up the hammer in his left hand. Although balanced in his right hand, his left wasn't used to the weight.

Or fine control.

Kragnak attempted to shape it, but like Thurbag he had a hard time keeping his hammering steady. "Give the metal time to rest."

It was like starting all over again, and the reminder of his training had him sweating, and not from the heat of the forge.

He thrust the hammer back to Thurbag. "Take it."

Heart beating, and taking short quick breaths to make him seem calm, Kragnak took up his place on the tongs. Thurbag imitated him, but Kragnak knew he didn't do a good job showing him.

Once again, Kragnak tried to walk him through the technique by words alone, but Thurbag wasn't getting it. "If I had my hand back I could show you better." Kragnak had caught his breath now, banishing the thoughts away. "Or if I could strap a hammer to this arm," he held up his stump, "I could show you."

"Now's a good time for a break. I brought you some ale." Kragnak whirled. Kimec offered him one of the mugs, frothy with foam. "Go on."

They both took a mug. Kragnak drunk deep, the bitterness of the hops refreshing him. It was also cool and slaked his thirst. Kimec pulled up a stool and sat.

"I heard what you said." There was a knowing gleam in his eye. "It isn't easy teaching someone else what you know." He took a sip from his own mug, foam coating his mustache.

"I'm afraid I'm not doing a very good job," Kragnak muttered into his own mug. A flash a panic shot through him as he realized he might be doing the same thing to Thurbag that was done to him.

"I'll pick it up soon enough," Thurbag said, cheeks cherry from the exposure to the heat of the forge. He wasn't smiling, but he seemed relaxed. "I've had worse in my life. One of the reasons I joined."

"You don't deserve it." Kragnak gripped the handle of his mug, grateful for its warmth and solidity. "No one does. I'm frustrated is all." He sighed.

"Patience, it will happen if you don't force it," Kimec said.

"We don't have time for that," Kragnak said. He wanted to throw something, anything. Chuck his mug into the fire and watch it spark into a thousand pieces.

But he didn't.

"What if I made you what you asked?"

Kragnak turned his head back to Kimec. "What?"

"I've been known to make a few things in my life." Kimec stroked his beard thoughtfully. "I might ask Barileth if he has ideas..."

"What I asked?"

"I could attach a hammer to your arm, given the time and materials." Kimec rose. "Give me a few days and I'll see what I can do."

Dazed, Kragnak put down his mug. "I--" he took a breath. "Could you do that?"

Kimec, face cracked with age, gave him a wink and patted Thurbag on the shoulder. "Just wait."

Lumdir paced off the wall, the morning sun beating down on him. They had another pile of stone stacked in haphazard piles next to the aboveground crops. Small shoots of green poked through the brown earth, and Yudoline tended them as the others worked.

"Right here," Lumdir said. Dorian crouched down and hammered in a sharpened stick at the point. He turned right, paced off a few more, and directed another stake be placed.

"Will it be big enough?"

Dorian squinted, estimating how big the final enclosure would be. There was enough space to expand the crops to double the amount, plus another double portion for the orchard.

"More on that side." The trees would need more space when they were fully grown. That wouldn't be for decades, but now was the time to think about it. "This is enough."

"The bigger we make it, the longer it will take," Barileth warned.

"Right." Dorian had thought about that, but he couldn't restrict the future mine too much either. "A double portion will be enough. We'll build the wall first, and the room after."

He called back to the others waiting at the crest of the hill. "Start digging." They started with the pickaxes, another day without the maximum complement of miners working below, and the earth churned.

Soon the turn was laying in rows to the side, the soft dirt yielding to the digging dwarves while Dorian and Lumdir laid out the rest of the walls.

By the end of the day they had trenched out the remaining defenses. Dorian stood up the slope with Barileth to survey the work. Rock wall had started under Lumdir's direction, a line of gray in the brown earth.

"Will we finish in time?" Barileth asked.

Dorian grunted. "We have to." The wind brought up the smell of the shedding trees from the valley. Most of the gold and red leaves had fallen, coating the ground, but a few brown trees stood out among the others.

He thought about everything they had, and everything they would need. It would take time to mine enough ore to satisfy the king. It would take time, and dwarves, to build the wall, let alone mine the stone and haul it to the surface.

It would take time to provide for the mine, not just their basic needs like food and drink, but small comforts and luxuries like clothes and shoes, leather and woodwork.

The more he dwelled on it, the more he knew down in his heart that they couldn't do it all.

So he sat for a few moments with Barileth, knowing that they would either suffer or die.

Or both.

6

NEVER ENOUGH

The darkness enveloped him, the mine quiet except for his movements and the steady beat of the pickaxe against the stone.

Rock crumbled and fell. Air took its place, and Yander advanced deeper into the mountain. Sweat ran down his brow and into his beard, dripping off and flinging off as he dug.

And dug.

And dug.

The others had left long ago, to go to sleep, but he couldn't sleep. Every swing of the pickaxe was too late already, every second he spent asleep would be too much to handle.

So he worked.

He paused, arms aching and screaming at him to stop, and obliged them. He was too weak, too easily overcome by fatigue and exhaustion. Dorian didn't seem to think so, but he knew it.

Pressing his hand to the rock, he reached out and listened to the earth. The stone sang its deep baritone, but there was precious little else.

"Why can't I feel it?" he shouted into the darkness, only beaten back by a small candle he used to see. "Why can't I do what I need to do?"

He kicked a chunk of rock, sent it careening down the tunnel. It knocked against the wall, skipping, until it finally stopped.

It was silent again.

But not inside his head. A million thoughts raged, swirled, stormed. No matter how hard he tried, he would never be good enough. No matter how hard he tried, he would not find the ore they needed.

He was so tired.

Thoughts of his warm bed came back to mind, and he longed to go there and join his wife. A pang of guilt hit him. She was why he needed to keep going. He needed to protect her, and he needed to provide for her.

So he returned to his work, chipping away at the stone and feeling for the ore he knew the mountain held secret.

"Yander?"

He stopped, turned to Emelda. She stood in her nightclothes wrapped tightly around her. A few strands of hair drifted out across her face. She wiped them away. "Please come to bed."

"You should be sleeping," he said, drawing a deep breath. He wanted to reach out, touch her. Wrap his arms around her and kiss her. Her arms were wrapped around her in a tight hug.

"I would sleep better with you at my side."

"I'm still working."

"I know. That's why I came to find you." She reached out her hand, took a few more steps to him. "Come on."

He wanted to go with her, his body ached and his eyes burned.

But he needed to work harder, needed to work longer.

"Just a few more feet, and I'll be done." He wasn't sure it was true, but thought it might placate her.

The corners of her mouth drew tight. "I'll stay then."

He turned back to the wall. "You should go back to bed, I'll be right behind you."

He heard her move, glance back to see her perched on a chunk of stone he had mined. "I want to talk to you."

"Oh."

"I haven't seen you very much. You're always down here working during the day and I'm working during the meals." Exasperation seeped into her voice.

He wondered what he could say, but kept mining. "I wish I could see you more too."

"You could see me at night. In our room before we go to sleep." The pickaxe rang on the stone as he worked, punctuating her pointed words.

"There's nothing more I would like," he said through gritted teeth, "but right now I need to focus on finding ore."

"You have been."

"Not enough."

"How much is enough?"

"I don't know."

"Then when will you stop? When the mountain is empty? When there is no more ore to mine?"

"I don't know." He thrust his pickaxe deeper, driving it into a seam. A huge chunk of stone broke free, and he had to jump out of the way to avoid it falling on him. "Why are you asking all these questions? You know I don't have the answers to them."

"Because I love you." Her eyes were soft, and...glistening? Yander blinked, taken aback. "And I know you love me, which is why you are doing this."

She got off the rock and approached him. He didn't resist as she touched his face, caressed his cheek and beard.

"I can't feel it, like Dorian can." He managed to choke out the words. She hugged him, squeezing him tightly. "The dwarf is unbelievable. It's like he can sense where it will be. He's been the reason behind all our finds, not me."

"Yander." He met her eyes. "Dorian has been mining since before you were born. Of course he knows more."

"But if I had those skills, we wouldn't be in such a bad position." He was glad of her closeness, could smell her hair and scent. He breathed deep of it.

"Is that what this is about? Jealousy?"

Yander snorted. "I'm not jealous."

"You are, I can see it in you. Yander, you don't need to be jealous."

He stopped hugging her back. "I told you, I'm not."

"You can't even see it, can you?" Her eyes searched his, but he looked away.

"This is about providing and protecting you."

"Don't cover up the reasons. If that's the reason you've been distant, been absent, then you need to acknowledge it."

"That isn't the reason." His voice was louder now, and he let go of her. He wanted to push her away, retreat somewhere else.

But she was in between him and the mineshaft. There was nowhere for him to go. Now her eyes were blazing, and she stood taller.

"You stop this foolishness right now. Dorian is a great dwarf. You're a great dwarf in your own right. Do I need to go into the reasons?"

He didn't say anything.

"We need both of you. But I need you more."

Yander had been working long hours, and he was tired.

"What do you want?"

"I want you to come to bed, to get some rest. To not work too hard."

"I can't promise you that I'll give up, but I'll come to bed." His eyes burned, but he picked up the candle and grabbed her hand.

She smiled, and they went to bed.

Even though the covers were cool, even though his body was exhausted, his mind kept turning and keeping him awake.

He was going to fail them.

He knew it. They needed a stronger dwarf, one who was better.

That wasn't him. He listened to the sound of Emelda's breathing and felt inadequate.

"Another one here, just like you said." Thardegith brushed back rock chips, revealing a glimmer of hematite. Dorian grinned and clapped him on the back.

"Good." The dry spell was broken. They were finding ore now. All they had to do was melt it down and turn it into steel, if they could ever find the flux stone.

"Haul it up as soon as you can." Dorian joined Thardegith in excavating it, and soon they had a good pile that Dozotaine and Yander took back to the mineshaft.

Wheels creaked, and Dorian stopped to take up his shovel. Yander wheeled his barrow next to the pile and started filling it.

"Dozotaine is stuck at the mineshaft." Yander picked up the shovel and started loading. "They're having a hard time bringing it up."

"Why?" Dorian leaned on his pickaxe. "There isn't that much here."

"They don't know where to put it." Dorian inspected Yander. There were circles under his eyes, his movements were slow and deliberate. Not like him.

"Keep working, I'll handle this." Yander nodded, but didn't meet his gaze. Dorian thought about asking him, but chose not to.

He didn't know what troubled the dwarf and didn't have time to figure it out.

Instead, he went up and found the issue was in the workshop. Ore was piled everywhere, and Dorian was shocked.

"They can't keep up," Kimec said, nodding over to Kragnak and Thurbag. They were bickering next to the forge. It looked like Thurbag wanted to do something and Kragnak wasn't pleased.

"How long has it been like this?" Dorian knew he wasn't getting much out of the forge, and was still waiting on his bell, but hadn't been down in days.

"Almost since they started."

"Water and oil?"

Kimec shook his head. "Worse."

"I could pull Thardegith..." Dorian stroked his beard as he thought. The dwarf had just gotten used to the pickaxe and was starting to increase in speed. They would be back to square one.

"I don't think that's the problem," Emelda said, joining them.

"Pile it in the hallway for now, off to one side." Dorian motioned Olgim to reverse his loaded wheelbarrow. He went with him and gave more instructions. Olgim dumped his load, taking up almost half the tunnel, and went back for more.

Dorian returned to observe. Kragnak was stewing off to the side and Thurbag wore a frown as he worked the bellows.

"What did you mean?" he asked Emelda.

"Kragnak's angry, unfocused." She shook her head and brushed off a few wood shavings from the sleeves of her arm. "It isn't Thurbag. Replacing him with someone else would be just more of the same."

"Then someone needs to set him straight," Dorian said.

Emelda's eyes widened. "No, don't do that."

"He's mourning his hand. It's only been a few weeks," Kimec said.

"We don't have time for him to mope around like this." Anger rose in Dorian, but he knew most of it was at himself. How long had he been angry after the death of his wife?

Since he had been there not a single ingot had been cast. The forms were ready to be poured, empty in the sand next to the fire.

"Would you be ready a few weeks after you lost your arm?" Emelda's pointed question struck a chord with him, and gave him a twinge of mild annoyance.

Dorian crossed his arms. "Fine. What do you propose?"

"Give him time to recover. Let him do something else until he's ready."

"No."

Emelda's eyes narrowed. "Then he will continue to act this way."

He was about to respond, but Kimec broke in first. "There is another option. I've talked to him about it but hadn't said anything to you yet."

"What is it?"

"Give me time to work on something to replace his hand. I've been thinking of an option with Barileth, and I think it will work."

Dorian imagined what life would be like without one of his arms. Gone would be his days of mining. He wouldn't be able to pick up most things.

Would he be just as angry?

He choked down the remnants of his own anger and knew the answer. If there was a way they could help Kragnak, he would be willing to try it.

"What do you need?" Kimec smiled.

"Leather and wood." He pulled out a chunk of wood from beneath his workbench. "I've had a good piece of seasoned oak I've been saving for a while. It was too small to use in the furniture."

"And too small for a crossbow?"

Kimec shifted. "I'm still working on that."

Dorian nodded. There were so many things to do, and he wasn't sure how much time they had left to do them.

All he knew is that there would never be enough time. The more they finished now, the stronger they would be when the inevitable attack came.

And he wasn't going to be unprepared this time.

"Make sure it doesn't take too much time away from your other duties."

"I'll work on it after I'm done for the day." Kimec cast a fatherly glance at Kragnak. "I can't bear to see him like this. It's not good for a dwarf to not be useful."

There was more than a little truth to that. Dorian knew what it felt like, remembered that first expedition. He had hardly known how to hold a pickaxe, let alone handle one.

And he had seen Kragnak struggle with his smithing, known that it had taken a lot of effort and work to improve even the little he had.

Now all that work was gone, cut off with the hand in the battle.

Rejected by his guild, cast out by his family, Dorian had an unusual bond with him. He wasn't sure why, other than he too had been in a bad situation and cast out.

He didn't want the same to happen to Kragnak.

"I'm afraid that if he doesn't improve, he won't want to be here anymore," Emelda said softly. "He feels like he doesn't belong."

"This is his home," Dorian said, face steeling. "Do what you need to do. Take the leather from the stores and let me know if you need anything else."

The fire of the forge played on Kragnak's face, forlorn and broken. *No, not while I breathe.* "We're not going to lose him."

7

Unlawful Entry

Another block of rock pushed into place, Mughan stepped back to rest. The sun was early in the morning sky, and the heat of summer had given way to cool.

He watched the sky and the surrounding scenery. Winter was coming soon.

"Give me a hand with this one." Fimroul struggled with a particularly large chunk of granite, and Mughan stepped in to help him.

Together they wrestled the massive block into place on the wall. Breathing hard, they both rested as the others continued work on the watchtower.

"How long will it take?" Fimroul asked.

"To finish?" Mughan surveyed their work. Perhaps halfway, more on the less side of it. They still had another story to go, at least. "Another month, if I had to wager."

"That long?" Fimroul patted the sweat off his beard with his shirt.

"We're spending too much time on these walls and not enough time finding that flux." Mughan glanced at Fimroul, watching him carefully.

"Aren't the walls more important?"

"If we were working on them, perhaps." He enjoyed a quick burst of chilled wind that cooled him. "But will walls help us with the King?"

"I guess not." Fimroul seemed chastened.

"Time for a break?" Yutatir asked. He added his stone to the pile and flexed his arms. "All day long, moving rocks from the mine to here. It would do a dwarf good to have more breaks."

"Aye, and to stretch your legs beneath ground again," Mughan said. "Perhaps a little exploration, even?"

Fimroul snorted. "I've done enough exploring of the mine, thank you very much. I don't intend to spend my free time there after weeks scouring the stone out of it."

Mughan shrugged. "There is another place."

"The farm caves?" Fimroul asked.

"Don't be stupid," Yutatir said, "he means the cavern they've walled off."

Fimroul waved off a bee that had discovered it like the dwarf. "Why would we want to go down there?"

"For one thing, it's easier work exploring than hauling," Mughan said. "More importantly, there are resources locked away behind that wall, and an easier way to find that flux stone."

Both dwarves were looking at him now, interested but unconvinced. "Imagine digging through layers of rock, weeks and weeks of exploration vertically and horizontally. You don't know what kind of layers you're bound to get."

"Now, imagine all that work was done for you, carved out over eons by dripping water and rushing rivers. A nice, fat tunnel that cut through all those layers, offering up their riches like a suckling pig with an apple in its mouth."

Mughan reached out his hand and pulled an apple out of his pocket. He took a bite. "All you have to do is take a little walk, and reach out and pluck it." He crunched away. "I've heard tales of gems shining in the walls, gleaming like eyes of fortune, ore veins flowing like rivers and ripe for the taking."

Fimroul licked his lips. "You think...it'd be like that here?"

"Why do you think the King's scriveners picked *this* place?" He had them now.

"It's too dangerous." Yutatir crossed his arms. Almost had them.

"There are dangers, to be sure, but without risk are there any rewards? We have weapons, and armor, to protect us."

"What about the spider?" Fimroul whispered.

Mughan tossed him an apple, then another to Yutatir. He shook his head. "Sad tale, I know. But cave spiders that large are one in a thousand, and drive off any others. They kill the competition."

"So you're saying there aren't any more? That it's safe?"

Smiling his most charming smile, Mughan invited them to sit. He took up a perch above them, looking down. "How long will it take the miners to excavate enough to find flux stone? Weeks, months, years?"

He shook his head. "I like Dorian, but we don't have that kind of time. We've got a year left on our contract, and we have to deliver. A half-finished wall won't protect us as well as steel weapons and armor."

"But Dorian said--"

"I know what Dorian said," Mughan cut off Fimroul. "And I like him. Difficult times call for difficult decisions, and once we explore the cavern and find the flux stone, he will realize what kind of good will come of it."

Yutatir looked troubled still, but Fimroul was mollified. "Come with me, give me one night of exploration, that's all I ask." Mughan's eyes glittered, and he leaned in. "Haven't you wondered what was behind that wall? What secrets it hides? ...What treasures?"

"Are there really gems just in the wall?"

Mughan smiled. "Come with me and see." They talked more, and he raised their excitement to a fever. He knew the founders wouldn't approve and strictly forbade them from talking to others.

However, they did convince Glorithoid and Dozotaine to come with them.

Mughan made the preparations in secret, gathering the necessary supplies and counting the cost that it would take. He stashed everything away for a night exploration and set it for a few nights later.

The others kept their promise and told no one else. Dozotaine was the most skeptical, but Mughan had played on his weariness of mining.

They gathered at the appropriate hour, after Mughan had completed his night watch. Each gathered their armor and weapons from the new training room, and Mughan removed his tools.

The night was quiet, all the other dwarves were asleep. Even Yander and Dorian had retreated to their apartments for the night, helped by the generous portions of food that Olgim had helped make.

Quietly they crept down the stairs. Mughan's heart beat and his skin flushed as they finally approached the wall. All it would take were a few strikes of a hammer, and it would be unlocked.

What secrets lay on the other side of that stone? What riches would they uncover?

They dumped the supplies and dressed up in the armor as quietly as they could. Breastplates, helms, and greaves, poorly made but better than nothing, would protect them from whatever was on the other side of that wall.

Mughan stepped forward, leading the group to the wall. He held out his hand. Fimroul handed him the pickaxe.

"Is everyone ready?" Not a single negative response. The torch crackled in the silence. "Tonight, we make history lads."

He shifted his grip and raised the pickaxe high.

It came down.

The iron rang out on the stone blocks, the tip lodging in a seam. Mughan wrestled it free, but the wall held.

"Come on," Mughan said, and struck the wall again. He thought one of the blocks shifted, and his heart raced.

Others joined in, with hammers, shovels, and bars of iron borrowed from the smithy. When the first stone fell, Mughan wanted to shout for joy, but knew better of it.

He peered through a hole the size of his head. The torchlight fell on moss and stone, but nothing living moved.

"More, and be quick about it." Mughan handed his pickaxe off to Dozotaine and drew his sword, who quickly widened the hole for them all to step through. "Just enough for a door, not too big now."

They stopped, listening with blood rushing in their ears for sounds in front of and behind them. It was still.

He took the torch in his other hand, and, firm grip on the pommel of his sword, advanced into the hole. His eyes darted all over, watching for any sort of movement.

His feet crushed the thick moss, almost like wool, that coated the ground. Nothing but stalactites and stone above him, and a few cobwebs.

Ahead of him the cavern twisted to the right, obscuring his view. It appeared to shrink, but that could have been a trick of the light.

Mughan was now a few feet into the cavern, and the others were holding back. He scanned around him.

In the distance something scurried from his light, no bigger than a rat. Squeaks confirmed it. Nothing else moved.

"Come in. It's safe." The others took a few tentative steps, weapons drawn and at the ready. "Come on, are you dwarves or are you men?"

Dozotaine, flushed, led the rest of them out and into the cavern.

"It's quiet," Fimroul said.

"Plenty of moss," Glorithoid said. "I bet crops would grow well down here."

"What else lives down here besides..." Fimroul swallowed, "you know."

"Many things could live down here." Mughan stepped forward carefully, picking his way and raising the torch up to examine around him. "Most of them are harmless, helpful even."

"I don't see any gems," Yutatir said. "You promised us gems and ore, right out in the open."

"Don't be daft," Mughan said. "We haven't even explored the cavern."

"This isn't it?"

"This is a small side tunnel. If I had to guess, the main cavern is up ahead, maybe through a few side passages. I've read about these places and not one is the same."

"Be on your guard," Dozotaine said. He was clutching a double-headed axe with two hands. Mughan felt better with him here.

"It's defensible, this would be a natural choke point if we had to stop anything." Mughan looked to both sides. "We could carve a few arrow slits, give us an even better position."

"Look," Yutatir said, pointing up to the ceiling. "Spider silk." A cave spider scuttled out of view, no bigger than their hand.

"Keep that in mind, we need to move forward," Mughan said.

Yutatir sighed. "I'd love a set of spider silk socks again. More comfortable than these goat hair ones." He shook out a foot, but followed Mughan.

They rounded the corner, the tunnel opening up again. "Quiet from here on out," Mughan said. "If there is anything down here, I'd prefer if it didn't know we were coming."

The five dwarves advanced down the tunnel in a line abreast, torches blazing hot.

The hand reached down, pulling him into the icy water. His lungs burned, ached, then filled with water, and right as he was about to die he woke up.

Dorian gasped, clutching at his throat. He sucked in the sweet air of the mine, drawing deep to settle his raging heart rate.

All a dream.

He wiped his face, stroked his beard with a trembling hand. In a few more moments he recovered his wits and shook his head.

"Nonsense." He was glad it wasn't a dream of Yolanda. Those were far harder to deal with than dreams of his own death.

Dorian got out of bed, relishing the cool on his feet, and splashed water over his face. It was early, but it was a good time to get a head start.

And a good time to raise the dead. Just before daybreak, when the night was at its peak and the darkest. That was when he would bring his wife back to him.

Something, however, was off.

He could feel it, an odd sensation. Maybe it was something prickling the hairs on his neck, or something else.

Whatever it was, something was not right.

Not bothering to get dressed, he collected Webcleaver and headed for the door. The hallway was empty, and so were the stairs.

He looked up, then down the mineshaft.

Without hesitating, he descended. The mine was quiet, just the rope of the elevator shifting in the yawing expanse.

His footsteps echoed around him, and he wished he had brought a torch. Even with his eyes adapted to the dark of the mine it was difficult to see.

Still, he advanced down the stairs.

The first level he stopped at for a moment, sensing the air.

He kept going.

Down, farther into the mine. There were new footsteps in the tiny layer of dust of the steps. Someone had come down.

Eventually he followed his instincts to a lower level, the same one that led to the cavern. The same one the spider had come from so long ago.

At the end of the stairs his hand found the small ledge he remembered. He lit the candle that was left for this very reason and held it aloft.

Momentarily blinded by its light, and axe prepared, he let his eyes adjust.

Chunks of stone littered the once clean floor. His candle bathed the area in light, and he saw it at once.

His heart rate spiked, sending a jolt of energy through him and his chilled core. There it was, gaping and ready to swallow him.

Wall demolished, the cavern was open.

8

RETURN FROM THE DEEP

Chapter Eight

In a split second he made a decision and turned. Running up the stairs, Dorian waited until he was within earshot of the apartments before bellowing out his warning.

"Rally to the mines! The cavern wall has been breached." Lungs burning, he pumped up the stairs even though his legs burned and ached.

Faces appeared in the mineshaft, blurred by sleep, and then torch-light. "Arm yourselves," Dorian shouted. They disappeared, replaced by a clamor and shouts above him.

The dwarves were awake now, and readying themselves. Yander ran down the stairs to meet him, axe at the ready.

"Get the armor. I'll hold off whatever comes." Thoughts rushed through his mind, the worst that could happen.

Was it another cave spider? He forced himself to slow, to take deep breaths and recall what he had seen. After he closed his eyes, careful to take one last look behind him to see it was clear, he remembered.

The way the stones were on the floor, how the wall looked. Some of his alarm fell, then flashed to anger. His eyes shot open.

"What is it?" Kimec asked, still in his nightclothes. He had a sword in one hand and a shield of iron in the other.

"The cavern is open." He counted as Yander arrived with armor in his hands.

"Most of it is gone," he said, shuffling down the stairs. Lumdir and Kimec reached for the box. They started distributing the iron armor. "This is all that was left."

"Where's Mughan?" They looked around. Dorian pointed to Olgim. "Check his bed." He ran back into the apartments as the armor was donned and questions flew. Dorian ignored them all, repeating what he knew and nothing more.

Olgim reappeared, cheeks flushed and red. "It's empty."

"Good for nothing--" Dorian finished his thoughts with a series of curses. They were missing five dwarves in all, and he knew where they were. "We're no longer a defense party."

Dorian spun on his heel and led them down the stairs. "What are we?" Olgim asked.

"A rescue party," Barileth said, smacking his sword into his shield. The clang echoed down the shaft.

It didn't take long to descend, but the questions came thick and furious. "Are you sure it's just them going out and not...something...coming in?"

"Can a spider use a pickaxe?" Dorian growled, tromping down the rocks. *The confounded dwarf! Could he not behave for once in his life?*

"No." Olgim looked relieved, but then tightened the grip on his spear.

"Keep your voices down," Barileth said. "We don't want to attract anything."

"Did you bring your hammer?" Dorian asked. Lumdir patted his hip. It swung in the moonlight. "Good. We'll need it."

"You don't mean..." Yudoline gasped, "you can't mean to shut them in."

"If it comes to that, I will." They were approaching the level, a few more steps away.

"They don't deserve that," she whispered, hand clutching at her necklace. "No one deserves that."

"They knew the risks, they had it coming," Dorian said, then softened his voice. "As much as I want to, it will be a last resort. Spread out."

The dwarves filed into a better fighting position, dropping off the stairs and into the tunnel. Dorian motioned for silence, and the voices dropped to whispers, then to nothing.

It was quiet, not a living thing ahead of him in the cavern. He motioned for a torch, and Yander gave it to him.

The opening leered at him, urging him in. *Why hadn't they just been patient? Didn't they know what crept in the dark?* He hadn't done a good enough job stressing the dangers that were down here.

IF they were dead now, it would be his fault. Equal parts bitterness and fear drove him forward into the breach. The others followed.

There was no telltale sign of danger. Nothing jumped out to grab him as he crossed into the cavern, stepping on the springy moss of the floor.

Still, his heart pounded in his chest, and his senses were sharpened to a keen point. His torch cast light into the darkness, but there was nothing there. Dorian hoped.

"We must go in farther," Dorian said, turning back to the others. "If I say retreat then be quick about it." He looked in each of their eyes until each acknowledged it. Yander was right behind him, protecting Emelda.

Dorian led them into the cavern. The tunnel turned, and he followed, keeping an eye and an ear out for anything suspicious.

"Hold." The noises behind him stopped as he held up a fist. They must be looking at him, for he felt their eyes on his back. Breaths too fast, too shallow. They were nervous.

But he thought he heard something.

There it was again.

A scratching, or something similar, up ahead. The tunnel turned left, obscuring his view.

It could be a million things. Rats. Cave birds. Dwarves.

Or even the scratch of eight legs on stone.

Dorian planted the torch in the moss, returning both hands to the axe. He raised it up and breathed deep, calming his nerves and strengthening his body.

The others shifted behind him. They heard it too.

Then, light up ahead. Dorian relaxed his grip and exhaled.

A few moments later Mughan and the rest of his band rounded the corner and stopped. "Oh," he said.

"What were you thinking?" Dorian held back his anger, his need to throttle the dumb dwarf.

"Of survival," Mughan said. He waved back down the tunnel. "It was as I expected, a massive cavern that stretches down into the depths."

"We even heard water," Fimroul said. Mughan shushed him.

"We thought you were..." Yudoline trailed off, voice cracking.

"Shame on you," Kimec said, turning to hug her.

Mughan stiffened, then drew himself up to his full height. "We took the risk for you. He certainly wasn't." He pointed at Dorian, who had to bite his tongue.

"There was a reason it was walled off," Lumdir said dryly.

"Everyone can go back to bed, or to work, as he or she sees fit." Dorian turned back to Mughan and the others. "I'd like a word with you."

"Say whatever you're going to say in front of everyone." Mughan crossed his arms and planted his feet. Dorian, despite his anger, was relieved that they were safe and didn't want to give Mughan the satisfaction of a fight.

He turned and nodded to the others. Yudoline had recovered, wiping her nose. That hurt him the most. He had been ready to wall them off and leave them for dead if the mine needed it.

She would never have even dreamed of it.

Barileth raised his eyebrows, but Dorian shook his head. The others turned and left.

"Wait."

"They aren't going to be here for you to influence Mughan." Dorian turned back to the stray dwarves. "And if you continue to disobey the rules that we have made then there will be problems."

"Those *rules*," Mughan spat out the word, "were made by weaker dwarves at a weaker time." He unfolded his hands and pointed back to the tunnel. "Out there we have a chance to explore at twice, four times the speed you can mine. We'll find flux stone in a matter of days, as opposed to months or years it will take you."

How long would it take them? Dorian shifted uncomfortably. "That gives you no liberty to endanger the others. Alone, I might have understood, but convincing them?" He shook his head.

"We weren't forced," Dozotaine said. "We came of our own free will. You know he's right, we need steel if we're going to survive."

"We'll make it through the winter and find it."

"What if it's too late by then?" Mughan watched him with narrowed eyes. "What if the dead already roam these halls by spring?"

Water dripped off the wall somewhere in the distance, plinking down into a puddle farther into the cavern. *What am I supposed to do with them? He has a point...*

"There were better ways to do this."

"Who would have done it?" When Dorian didn't reply Mughan continued, "When were you going to do it? Did you ever have a plan to explore the cavern?"

Dorian didn't like how this was going. How was it that Mughan always seemed to have an answer that cut him deep?

"We haven't found anything digging." Dozotaine piled on. "Despite how deep we've dug, there hasn't been a flux stone in sight."

"We could tell you what you've found, unless that would make you even angrier." Mughan tilted his head to the side.

"I'm disappointed, not mad. I thought we were all clear, that you'd had your chance to discuss this when we held council."

Mughan's eyebrows twitched at that. "And where you didn't listen?"

Dorian sighed. "What did you find?" He held up a finger at Mughan's smile. "But we're still going to seal the cavern."

"At least put in a door. It would make it so much easier to get in and out."

Dorian turned and started walking. "Back in the mine."

"Will you consider it?"

"What's at the end of the tunnel?" The others were crushing the moss behind him. Its odor was fragrant compared to the musty staleness of the mine.

"It goes for a few more twists and turns and feeds into a large cavern. We saw mushroom forests and plenty of moss from the top, but it drops off fast enough you would need good luck or plenty of climbing skills to get back up."

"Up or down." They were back inside the cave now, with Lumdir at the ready. "Seal it."

Mughan frowned, but continued relating his story. "Down. I'd say at least fourteen levels deep, by our reckoning, and about the same above. There were patches of golden moss deeper on the cavern bed, but too far to see properly."

"There is plenty of space to put in a few farms, and we saw huge caveberry bushes beneath the mushrooms," Glorithoid said, his voice quick with excitement.

"Any creatures?"

"None that we saw," Mughan said. "Or heard. Certainly no evidence of giant cave spiders."

"Just normal cave spiders, a good silk source," Yutatir cut in.

"I didn't expect any." At least, not this soon. "Unless we have a dwarf that can work it, I don't see a point yet. We might." He wasn't fully deflated, but Yutatir looked disappointed.

"We looked around, found a few possible paths down, but decided not to risk it for today and turned back." Mughan shrugged. "That's it. We only left an hour or two ago and I wasn't going to push our luck on the first attempt."

"You were going to cover your tracks and rebuild the wall."

"If we had a door, we wouldn't have to rebuild it every time." Dorian shot him a glare. Devious and cunning, but he did have a point. Did they have the luck to cut through the right stone layer?

And if they did, when would it happen? He assumed the necromancer had used up all his strength with the raid and goblin attack, but that might not be the case.

Dorian shivered as a cold feeling crept up the base of his skull. The necromancer might be out raising an army right now, creeping in among graves and battlefields long abandoned.

"Could you do it?" Dorian asked. Lumdir stopped his work and turned.

"A door?" He scratched his head, then measured the opening with his hands.

"I want it impenetrable."

"I can't do that." Lumdir scratched his beard, "but I could make it strong."

"Coming around?" The corner of Mughan's mouth twitched, and his eyes gleamed with a mischievous light.

"No more nighttime journeys. No more daytime journeys." He frowned, and added, just to be sure, "No more journeys out there at all, are we agreed?"

"How long do you expect us to hold this agreement? Until we're all dead at the end of a skeleton's lance?" Mughan asked.

"No, I don't expect that. You might be right, we may have to explore the cavern to find what we need. I'm willing to admit that, but for now we do it my way and dig."

That should buy me enough time to prepare them for what might be down there. But would it be enough?

"We have to know you're willing to do what needs to be done, when it needs to be done Dorian." Mughan crossed his arms again.

Dorian did some quick calculations, then guessed at how long he might need. A few weeks should be enough.

"Give me two months," he said. "If we haven't found it by then, we'll venture into the cavern and I'll take you myself."

9

THE ARM

The fire belched, and the bellows roared.

"Now." Kragnak reached into the fire as Thurbag gave up his spot and rushed over to the anvil and hammer. He bobbled it, then dropped it.

Frowning, Kragnak held the glowing iron on the anvil, ready for the strike to come. It did, as Thurbag recovered and started his work, but Kragnak only frowned and looked on.

"Stop," he said. The metal had lost its glow. It had only taken a few hits, but it was enough. Kragnak thrust it back into the fire to warm up.

"Sorry." Thurbag shrugged and deliberately turned away from him before taking up his post on the bellows. Kragnak stewed and burned like the fire, taking the chance to stir it and break up the coals.

They had abandoned the bell, for now, and had turned to the easier, less complicated forms that they still needed.

Thurbag had struggled with everything. It seemed he had more thumbs than fingers, and could never keep hold of anything.

On more than one occasion Kragnak had almost approached Dorian about switching to another dwarf, but every time he thought he had worked up the courage there was that chiseled face and dark eyes that stared into his soul.

So Kragnak never did.

"Working hard?" Kimec asked. Kragnak stopped staring blankly into the fire, realizing that he had wandered, and turned.

"Yes." He forced himself to relax his pursed lips, and to avoid staring at Thurbag. He was faster than him as an apprentice.

"Good news." Kimec was holding his hands behind his back. "Am I...interrupting?"

"Yes," said Kragnak.

"No," said Thurbag at the same time. Kragnak turned and scowled, leveling a cold stare his way. Kimec eyed both of them and pulled what he was hiding from behind his back.

"Sounds like you need this then." He offered up the strange assortment of wood and leather straps to Kragnak, who only stared at it.

"What is it?" Thurbag asked.

"I know it doesn't look like much..." Kimec scratched his head. "Go on, give it a try."

"Is this...?" Kragnak's eyebrows rose.

"Turn to your left." Kragnak complied, and Kimec slipped one of the straps over his shoulder. He fastened the other around the stump of his arm, making adjustments once they were all on and asking Kragnak how it felt.

When they had it situated Kimec pointed to the front. "That will hold a hammer, if you can make one with a tang."

"I can't." Kragnak stared helplessly at it. It felt awkward, and heavy, despite it being made of wood.

"I'll help."

"Good," Kimec said, slapping Kragnak on the back. "That takes care of it. Try it out and let me know how you feel." He rubbed his hands together, then patted them absentmindedly. "I'm off to work." He backed up. "Lots of orders to fill. You know how Dorian is with the...work."

Kimec was wearing a smile, but it was clearly forced. Kragnak looked back down at the contraption on his arm. How was this thing supposed to work?

He just threw in a hammer and that was it? He was a smith again? Fear clutched at his throat, another chance to fail. Again.

Thurbag was at his elbow. "I know I'm not a good smith," he said. "And you've been patient with me." Kragnak felt more than a stab of guilt and had to avert his eyes. "Show me how to do this. It's the least I can do."

"Come on then," Kragnak mumbled. "We've already got the iron heating." He stepped Thurbag through the process, how they would shape the hammer head and a small spike out the bottom that would attach to the small hole in the head of the wooden arm.

Thurbag claimed to understand, but like Kragnak expected, struggled with the shaping. Hammer rang out on iron as he over worked one side, then had to try and bring it back into form only to do the same thing again.

Kimec was watching, and pretending not to. Kragnak tried to keep his cool, grinding his teeth together. By lunch he was ready to walk away, but they almost had the top of a hammer.

He was silent through lunch as the others talked and told stories. The wooden arm was useless to him, and almost a hindrance, but he was able to rest it on the table.

After lunch, they went back to work on the spike that was to serve as the tang.

It went even worse than the hammer.

Kragnak was almost at his wits end by the end, but quenched the hammer. Steam billowed up to the roof of the cave and spread like his anger. When it was cool, he pulled it dripping from the water and dumped it on the anvil.

"Do you want to try it?" Kimec asked from across the room. Kragnak took a deep breath, bracing him and choking down all the words that came to mind.

"Yes." He inserted it and braced the arm as Thurbag tapped it in place. He was careful not to hit Kragnak, which he appreciated.

Now it was even heavier. Kragnak flexed his arm, swinging it around to get a good feel.

It was off balance, but not bad.

All it would take was one quick swing to test out.

"It's too close to dinner." Kragnak motioned to Kimec. "Would you help me take it off?

Kimec's eyes narrowed. "We have time."

"I don't think so." He was starting to sweat. He wanted it off.

"Kragnak, if--"

Emelda cut Kimec off. "After dinner would be fine. Isn't that right, Kimec?"

Kimec clamped his mouth shut and turned back to his work.

"I'll help," Thurbag said.

"Thanks." Kragnak heaved a sigh of relief when it was off, rubbing his stump where it had chafed.

For a long time he stared at the arm, afraid of what might be.

"Backed up again?" Dorian peered up the mineshaft. "What's going on up there?"

"Hold on. We're stuck up here." A few seconds later Dozotaine's face appeared at the top of the mine. "They can't keep up with us."

"Can't keep up? We aren't moving that fast." And they still had to haul it all the way up from the tunnels to the winch. *What could possibly be keeping them?*

"We've backed up the tunnels with stone. They need to be moved outside, but there aren't enough dwarves to keep up."

That didn't seem right. Yes, they had fewer dwarves working on the wall than they needed, but with a dedicated hauler and a floating builder to haul they over matched the one miner who did most of the hauling.

"I'm coming up." He started up the stairs, wondering what the holdup could be. When he got upstairs and saw the waiting row of stones for himself, it made it more real.

"Take my place," Dorian said. Dozotaine nodded and went back down into the mine while he went outside.

He met Hukgras in the entrance tunnel. "Why are these backing up?"

She heaved a chunk of rock up over her shoulder and balanced it. "The tunnel is too narrow for both of us to get through with a load. Glorithoid is waiting outside for me to finish." With that she turned and struggled to the door, picking her way through and over the traps.

Dorian saw what she meant. Even with the rock in front of her there wouldn't be enough room for two dwarves to pass side by side. Glorithoid held the door for her and waited for her to pass.

"You see the problem, don't you?" he asked. Dorian should have realized that moving all the stone would have made this problem, and he was kicking himself for not realizing it earlier. "I said we should have told you sooner."

"We can fix it, and I had planned to. With everything going on I forgot we needed to expand the tunnel." He stroked his beard. "It will make the traps less effective..."

"Whatever you're going to do, do it quick. We're buried beneath all this stone." Glorithoid picked up his own stone and struggled it to the door. The miners had built plenty of muscle over the past few months. The others dwarves would as well, but he never imagined it would get this bad.

Rocks lined the tunnel, stacked up as close to the door as they could get them. *A few more feet to either side will do it.*

"Dorian." Mughan sauntered into the mine. "They said you were here."

"How is the wall coming along?"

"It would be better if we could get stone faster."

Dorian squinted down the hall, thinking about the best way to do this. "Yes, I know. We have to expand the tunnel, and raise the ceiling while we're at it. Eventually we'll need a bigger door too."

"What for?"

"Wagons."

"Ah." Mughan scratched his head. "While we're at it, why don't we make some improvements?"

"How so?" Dorian squinted, and crossed his arms.

"I've been thinking about those bolt holes. That's well and good, gives us a nice chance for crossfire, but what about something from the top?" A gleam glinted in his eyes. "Something that might make an invader think twice about coming inside again." He winked. "Something to drink?"

"Something hot?" Dorian stroked his beard.

"Exactly."

"I like it." They would have to fortify the ceiling, but it could be done. "We may have to suspend the wall construction to get it in place, but I think Lumdir can supply stronger supports and flooring. A few holes would let us drop whatever we'd want."

Dorian turned. "Before we do, I need Barileth." He had to search the caves, finally finding him in the farm caves tending the goats. Dorian brought him back to Mughan, who had returned to his work constructing the wall with the others.

"The others are too slow," he said, dusting off his hands. "I wish they would move faster."

"Then make them," Barileth said.

"Focus," Dorian warned. "How do we make this place a killing floor and not an easy access point?"

"We'll be up against skeletons, so fire won't be much use," Barileth said.

"I'd assume more goblins too, and other forms of undead." Dorian didn't like it, but they needed to be ready for anything.

And it might not be pretty.

"Finish the wall," Mughan said bluntly, and then shrugged.

"Assuming they get through the wall." Dorian gave him a dis-approving stare.

"We can redo the traps." Barileth pointed near the door. "Set up the cages as close as we can to the door as possible. Once activated, they'll be a good barrier that we can use to funnel them where we want them to go."

"And we could set up choke points, concentrate our attacks there," Mughan said. "How much room do we have above us?"

"Once we raise the ceiling, not much, and even less if we're going to grow trees up there."

"What about keeping a line clear then? Just use enough space for access and nothing more." Barileth was still looking around the tunnel, plotting his traps.

"I'd put the holes there, there, and there." Mughan pointed above them, about a third of the way down the tunnel, and then divided equally to the crossroads. "We should also add a door to seal it off."

Barileth shook his head. "Holes would make us vulnerable, allow the enemy in. We should keep the arrow slits and traps. They should be good enough."

"And what if we run out of bolts?" Mughan arched an eyebrow. "Or they have their own. Windows go both ways."

"All the more reason to not have holes in the ceiling." Barileth's eyes narrowed.

"We'll do both. We can put a hatch on the murder holes, and make them lock." Barileth glared at Dorian. "He makes a compelling argument."

"Fine, as long as I get more traps."

Dorian let out a sharp bark of a laugh. "You'll get your chance."

They stepped through the room, estimating what the size would be and coming up with a natural flow. Once they had the choke points established, the arrow slits were easy to locate.

"It's a good start." Dorian envisioned the changes, then calculated the work it would take to bring them to fruition. "I'll bring up Dozotaine to start on the expansion."

"Now?" Barileth asked.

"The sooner we get started, the better." Dorian looked down the tunnel, the same direction that the skeletons had gone. "If we don't, I'm afraid we'll have to welcome an army."

10

A Spark in the Night

He waited until everyone else was asleep. The rough blanket scratched against his skin, but it was nothing compared to the tingling to where his hand should have been.

Rising from his bed, Kragnak slipped into his clothes. He carried a stone in the pit of his stomach. It was hard, unmistakable. He had to think of the others. He had to do this for them.

Dread grew as he went up the stairs. Each step he wanted to flee, to run back down to his bed and stay there. But he knew sleep wouldn't find him anymore than it had the last few nights.

So instead, he walked.

His hand on the door to the workshop, he hesitated. Even now, beneath the fear there was something else. A spark of excitement. It dawned on him suddenly, taking him off guard.

He almost said something, but gasped instead. For a moment, frozen in time, he couldn't move. Couldn't breathe. Spellbound, he waited in the silent corridor.

Eventually the feeling went away, and he had to remind himself of why he was here. It didn't matter that he had failed then, this was now. People believed in him here, so unlike anything he had felt in a long while.

He couldn't let them down.

The door creaked on its hinges, opening to reveal the barely perceptible glow from the fire.

Kragnak went in fast, before he could turn back, and closed the door harder than he wanted. It banged, and he winced.

He listened for noise, footsteps down the hall, a dwarf coming to check on the sound. All the while he stared at the forge and the arm.

It never came.

After taking a deep breath, and pushing down the fear, he approached the forge with hesitation. The banked coals gave off almost no light beneath the ash.

Without hesitating further he brought them to life. The fire sparked as he added charcoal, tiny specks of light that burned bright then disappeared.

Soon the fire was cheery and crackling away, leaving him only to add a chunk of iron to heat and work the bellows.

All the while he was keenly aware of the arm that sat next to the anvil. Wood and leather, with a hammer attached. Was that all it took to restore him to where he had been?

Hope, and dread, competed. He didn't know which one would win, but he had to find out.

The iron glowed in the fire now, ready to be worked. Kragnak stepped back, sweat trickling down his forehead.

There was nothing else to do.

Except that.

After building his courage, reminding himself that Dorian needed him to be able to work the metal they dug, he finally mustered enough to pick it up.

It was warm, not cold like the iron had been, and inviting. He was repulsed, but tried to put it on anyway.

Without help he struggled and fought with it. The leather straps kept shifting, just as he would get one set his movements would release another.

His frustration mounted. Some, at himself for not trying it while others were around, and some at something deeper.

But he knew he couldn't do it in front of the others, and they would have suspected something if he had left it on, so here he was.

And he wasn't going to give up.

After what seemed like hours, and a few paces around the room, Kragnak faced his foe and growled at it. Someone had said he was useful, and he wasn't going to let a piece of wood take it away from him.

So he pulled it up and set his teeth into the top strap, the most troublesome strap. The rough leather scraped against his tongue, flooding his senses with its smell and taste.

With his other hand he steadily manipulated the others. One by one he put them in their place, until only the top remained. That, while holding down the arm, he pulled tight with his teeth.

Almost overcome by the emotional and physical toll it had taken on his body, Kragnak slumped against the anvil and caught his breath. His heartbeat slowed, then left his ears.

Rising to his feet, Kragnak re-stoked the fire and brought the iron back up to temperature. With his left hand he pulled it from the fire and set it in place.

The hammer felt heavy at the end of the arm. He took a few test swings against the hammer, his heart beating fast once again, and not with exertion. Each blow made his breath catch in his throat.

He had the hang of it now, but the iron had cooled again. Mouth dry, he put it back into the fire to heat it up again.

He knew what he was doing. Kragnak scolded himself, trying to build his courage back up to do what was needed. He went through the names of the dwarves in the expedition.

He asked himself what Dorian would think if he couldn't even try this.

Iron glowing hot, he pulled it back from the fire.

It started to cool on the anvil.

Kragnak raised his hammer arm.

And stopped.

What if he failed? What if he wasn't good enough?

Were the others really right?

He almost stopped, almost walked away. But then Dorian's voice rang in his ears. The one dwarf that had believed in him.

Kragnak mustered all his strength, then brought the hammer down.

Iron rang out on iron. The blow shivered through the wood arm to his own, traveling up his shoulder until it dissipated into his chest.

Kragnak stared.

It felt...good.

The iron bore the imprint of the hammer. Right in the center, where he had aimed. Not too much to the left, or tilted too far to the right.

Right in the middle.

He held up his arm, awed.

It wasn't shaking.

That couldn't be. That had to be wrong, it was a trick of the light. But the more he stared, the more sure he was.

His left arm trembled. The wooden arm was steady, strapped in tight.

After all these years, and he hadn't even thought of it.

By now the iron had cooled too much to work. Fear forgotten, Kragnak hopped from one foot to the other while it warmed up.

He was brimming with excitement when he pulled it back out, and zealously attacked the iron. It seemed to melt under his hammer arm, spreading and forming faster than any other he had worked.

When he was done he drawn the bar into the beginnings of a short sword, tang and all. Kragnak basked in the glow.

Time slipped by. Heat and cool, hammer and form, Kragnak worked through the night. He finished one blade, then started another.

Axe followed sword. Sword followed axe. Sparks flew and the fire burned. He gathered more iron and started on a helm.

He stepped back, finished, and surveyed his work. The swords were straight and ready to be sharpened, the axe well-formed and balanced better than any he had made. Even the helm, short and squat, looked like it would fit well.

Kragnak sensed something and turned to see Kimec watching him from the door. "How long have you been there?"

"Long enough."

Embarrassed, Kragnak looked down and shifted his weight. "Thank you." The hammer glistened in the light of the fire." He expected to be exhausted, but instead he was energized. His body thrummed with it, flowing to his extremities.

Kimec walked to him, examining the arm. "How does it feel?" He checked the straps, adjusted one.

"A little sore on my... How long have I been down here?"

"Breakfast is finishing up."

Kragnak's eyes widened. "It's morning already?"

Kimec smiled and picked up the sword, running his eyes down it and feeling its weight. "Today is a new day."

Another chunk clinked onto the growing pile. Dorian stretched his back, rubbing it to ease the burning in it.

"Another good haul of galena," he said. Yander glanced back from the vein, brow furrowed. "But still, no flux stone."

He knew why, but the thought of what was down there...

"How do you overcome it all? When there's so much, I mean," Yander clarified, after Dorian's look.

"Learn to listen better." Dorian scratched his chin, and leaned on the handle of his pickaxe as Yander and Thardegith kept working.

"It amazes me that you can even hear it," Thardegith said, throwing another chunk onto the pile. He picked up a rock, examined it, and tossed it back down the tunnel. He was getting better at identification, but showed no signs of hearing the song. "Imagining being able to just listen like that." He shook his head.

"It isn't so easy." Dorian unstopped his flask and drunk deep. The ale washed away the dust that collected at the back of his throat, and flooded his senses with hopiness.

Yudoline was getting better at this.

"I wish it were," Yander said. A few flicks of his pickaxe brought down another chunk, almost as big as his head. That would make for good bartering by itself.

"We'll finish this vein up and head downward tomorrow." Dorian straightened and grabbed the handle, swinging the pickaxe to his shoulder. The squeak of Dozotaine with the wheelbarrow echoed down the tunnel. "We might get lucky and break through a layer."

"If we had the luck," Thardegith muttered. "Haven't seen anything but granite since I've been down here."

Despite how deep they had come, he was right. The mountain seemed to be a big chunk of it, one big rock that pierced the earth.

"It won't be like that forever. We'll break through."

"When?" Yander asked, irritation in his voice.

Dorian eyed him, but he kept on working. "Soon." *I hope.*

Dozotaine appeared around the corner, with an empty wheelbarrow. They stopped to load and send him on his way. Time slipped by, and the vein hollowed onto the tunnel floor, then was hauled away.

They finished the day and went to dinner. Yander went back down as soon as he was done, and Emelda gave Dorian a pleading stare. He nodded.

Yander was pushing himself too hard. It was in his face, in his slower walk, even the way he ate, like his muscles weren't responding fast enough. All of that was on top of the morning sparring sessions too.

He wasn't improving as fast as he had been. Yander might have even been getting worse.

Dorian caught Emelda in the tunnel. "How much sleep is he getting."

Her gaze dropped to the floor. "A few hours. Sometimes none at all, I think." Wrinkles spread from her eyes, almost as bad as Yander's.

"You asked him to slow down, haven't you?"

"He doesn't listen." Her hand trembled. He hated seeing her like this.

"Yander needs to be a dwarf and take care of himself." Anger made the words harsher than he expected, and Emelda's eyes widened.

She held up her hands. "No, he's doing this because he wants to take care of me, of everyone. He struggles, not being able to hear the ore."

Dorian was baffled. "Not able to hear it? He can already hear it better than I can."

"He doesn't think so."

"I'll tell him. I'll tell him to start taking care of himself better too." He turned to go, but she grabbed hold of his arm.

"I want the dwarf I love back, but please don't hurt him."

He softened, grasped her hand. "He might deserve it, but he will see reason. I can't drag him to his bed."

He pictured it, and the thought banished some of his anger. It almost made him chuckle, and Emelda's frown softened. He bade her goodbye and went back to the mine.

On the way he thought about how he could get to Yander, what he must be thinking. He couldn't blame the young dwarf. He didn't have the experiences that Dorian had, nor the wisdom of years.

But he had to survive to get there too. It was up to Dorian to lead him, to take him off this path. And a pang of knowing what it was like to be hot headed and prone to overwork also ran through him.

The sounds of the pickaxe led him to Yander, working alone in the mineshaft. He was cutting stairs deeper into the rock, and had already gone down almost a level when Dorian found him.

Even in the low glow of a candle, Dorian was struck by just how tired Yander looked. He tried to hide it, but it wasn't possible.

"Take the night off Yander. The mountain will be here tomorrow."

"Will it?"

Dorian shifted, standing a few steps above. "Don't be petulant."

Yander's brows furrowed, but he only swung harder. Chips flew. "It might not be here tomorrow."

"We have time."

"No, we don't." Yander rounded on him. "And I haven't done enough."

Dorian expected something, but the outburst took him by surprise. "That's what this is about?"

"I should be better. I should be able to hear it."

"You don't understand," Dorian said, taking a seat on the steps. "I'll just have to show you."

11

WINTER WINDS

A rock crumbled and fell. Yander left the pickaxe in the stone sticking out halfway.

"You're going to tell me? Like you've taught me everything else?" Fire filled his tired eyes.

"If you'll sit down and talk like a dwarf."

"What do I have to do to make you realize I am?"

Dorian was taken aback. He tried to find words to respond, but nothing came to him. Was this part of the problem, or the whole thing?

"It isn't enough," Yander said. "No matter what I seem to do. It isn't enough for you. It isn't enough for the expedition. It isn't enough for Emelda."

"Do you really think that?"

"I don't think. I know it." He pointed back up the mine. "I wasn't able to save Emelda's parents, or Skover, or Kuddick. I haven't been able to find anything other than a tiny bit of iron and silver, which won't satisfy the contract. What am I good for?" He spat out the words, pent up inside him.

"Then you are a bigger fool than I thought." Dorian hardened. "It's time to put away your youth and become a dwarf."

Yander clamped his mouth shut and went quiet.

"Get rest. You're no use to us if you're dead." He felt like there was something else to say, that if he were a better dwarf he would know it. But he wasn't. He could only be himself.

Yander's jaw worked, the muscles showing through his beard as it twitched. Dorian crossed his arms, expected some sort of retort.

Instead, he turned back to his work, yanking the pickaxe free and attacking the stone.

Stone gave way under his assault. Rock flew. Yander started to shout as he dug. He got louder and faster.

"Yander," Dorian shouted. "This isn't the time."

But he kept crushing the rock. Over and over again, as fast as he could. Finally, his crescendo could grow now louder. Yander gave one last shout that echoed through the mineshaft.

And then he threw the pickaxe down the tunnel. He keeled over, panting.

"I hope you see how childish you are."

Yander turned and rushed past him, knocking him in the shoulder and sending him stumbling.

Dorian caught himself and watched the fleeing dwarf. *This wasn't how it was supposed to go.*

He wrestled a stone into place, finally getting it to lock between the others. Dorian shivered as a cold winter wind blew up into his coat and under his shirt and wished he was back in the warmth of the mine.

Resting, he watched the others from his vantage point at the half finished watch tower. They scrambled like ants out of the mine with stone, faster now that the corridor was expanded, piling it onto the growing wall.

The first layer had been laid all around the upper portion of the hill above the entrance tunnel. Expansion on the original wall had been easier, and he was glad they had focused on strengthening the walls.

Now, he felt secure behind three-foot-thick stone that was even higher than before.

He glanced back at the horizon. Dark clouds massed far to the south. Soon they would bring snow and storm and drive the dwarves back underground. So they worked as fast as they could.

Even so, the upper wall was only three feet tall in most places, barely tall enough to keep out animals, let alone an army.

There was another storm growing to the south. So far they hadn't seen evidence of the necromancer, but that only made him more nervous.

Perhaps we should leave this half-finished, work only on the wall? He played with the thought, trying to keep his mind off the threat.

It didn't work.

He shivered again. What kind of death was he bringing? What would he do? Raise more skeletons? Or focus on more dangerous soldiers, with better dexterity and strength?

He hated not knowing, hated living in the dark.

Dorian turned his attention to the crops, trying to push those dark thoughts out of his head. They needed food next year, enough to feed the expedition and more.

There was still plenty of room for crops, the remains of the harvest still visible through the light dusting of snow. Stalks and dead leaves uncovered by the footprints of the dwarfs, laid in patches.

Next to those, on the other side of the entrance tunnel, small saplings transplanted from lower in the valley stood in well-formed rows. They had room to grow and expand, not enough to spread out but enough for the harvest of cherries and apple.

If they survived the winter.

Dorian wasn't too familiar with fruit trees, other than to tell one from another, and hoped getting them in the ground before the frost was good enough to keep them alive.

If not, they would need to wait even longer. But, he decided, that wouldn't be the worst thing in the world. They could always gather from the forest if they needed too.

Dorian turned back and finished the rest of his task, completing another layer on the watchtower. When he was done he went back inside, grateful for the warmth of the tunnels.

He wanted to check on Kragnak anyways, and the thought of the fire of the forge made him perk up. Sure enough, the workshop was toasty and it started to melt the cold from him.

After greeting Kimec, hard at work, he approached the fire and warmed his hands, watching Kragnak and Thurbag working. The hammer rang on the metal and the anvil, happy peals with a steady rhythm.

It was going better than it had. Kragnak was on the anvil as Thurbag turned the glowing red iron bar. It was starting to take the shape of a sword. The fire heated his face, down to his beard.

The iron cooled, losing its glow, and Thurbag took it back to the fire, working the bellows when it had been buried. Dorian stepped back from the sudden increase in heat.

"Hard at work?"

Kragnak wiped the sweat from his head. He had shed his shirt, and his muscles glowed. Gone was the lanky, skinny dwarf. Now, he was bulking up and starting to show signs of a true blacksmith. "Yes."

"Good."

Holding up his hammer hand, Kragnak breathed deep to recover. "It works nicely, although I have some modifications to make."

"You've already improved the hammer." The first one had been rough, bulky. The one he wore now was sleek, refined, and smaller.

Kragnak nodded. "It works better, and I don't tire as easily." He rubbed underneath the wooden arm. "Still chafes though."

"Is this the most recent?" Dorian gestured to a sword.

Kragnak nodded. "Just finished yesterday."

Dorian examined it, picked it up. The balance was right, and the blade straight. In the fire it looked sharp, and felt it too. It was like night and day to what he had made earlier.

Wearing a half-smile, Kragnak ducked down. "I never thought losing my hand would make me a better smith."

"You never gave yourself enough grace. Very little of you has changed Kragnak." Dorian tapped his head. "Either here." He pointed to Kragnak's chest. "Or there. You have the heart of a smith, and I saw it in your eyes the first time I saw you working."

"I--" He stopped. "I don't know what to say."

"Say you'll get better. Say you'll become a master smith."

Kragnak looked up, eyes shining. "I *will* become a master smith."

Dorian laughed. "Good." He picked up a bar of iron. "Then become one with the metal, and fashion it with a strong hand." He tossed it to Kragnak, who caught it with his hand.

The bell caught Dorian's eye. "Finished?" he asked, motioning to it.

"Yes. I was hoping to polish it more, but I've lost track of time." The iron surface shone in the light of the fire, gleaming from burnishing. It was still sitting in the sand. "Here, let me show you."

Kragnak set down the iron and picked up the bell. With his hammer he tapped it. A light peal rang through the workshop, clear and crisp.

"That will do," Dorian said, stroking his beard. "Now, we just have to have a place to put it."

"How is the watchtower coming?"

"Well." *But it won't matter much, not if what I suspect is true.*

Kragnak set down the bell. "What is it?"

Dorian hesitated. "We need armor. Prioritize that."

"You don't think the walls will hold." It was more of a statement than a question. "You expect us to fight."

"With the crossbows Kimec and Barileth are crafting, we won't need to." The fire licked up, orange and red tongues of flame as Thurbag worked the bellows.

"Will bolts stop the undead?" Kragnak moved back into position as Thurbag pulled the iron out of the fire and brought it to the anvil. Dorian stepped back as well, letting them work. He ignored Kragnak's lingering gaze.

Kragnak spoke a few words of direction, and Thurbag held the flattened iron in place. They got to work, Kragnak hammering and Thurbag turning it between blows.

It was clear that Kragnak wasn't holding back, and that he expected Thurbag to react quickly. He did, turning the iron and setting it just in time for the hammer to fall.

In a few minutes they worked together to draw the flattened steel into the shape of a sword, before it cooled. Dorian looked on, pleased at the change. He had Emelda's and Kimec's reports from earlier. When Kragnak was satisfied he plunged the sword into the bucket of water.

"Get out three iron ingots. We'll be making a breastplate." Kragnak had worked up a sweat again, and he moved in close while Thurbag went to fetch the iron. "What aren't you telling us?" he whispered.

An interesting question.

He wasn't telling them many things.

He wasn't telling them that he knew the necromancer so well because he had been driven to it in the past.

He wasn't telling him that he had decided to take whatever this necromancer had, to use his power to finally be with his wife again.

Dorian opened his dry mouth, tasting the ash of the forge and the tang of the iron. "I expect them to breech the wall, or find a way around it."

Kragnak eyes widened, and he looked down at his hand. "So you expect a fight."

Shrugging, Dorian took a seat on a crate.

"Which is why we need the armor," Kragnak said. Dorian nodded. "And steel will protect better than iron."

"In every way it is better."

"Then we need the flux stone. I know how to make it, just give me the flux."

"We're still searching. The mountain is..." Dorian searched for the right words, then settled on, "resistant."

It was an understatement. The blasted thing was practically made of granite. That was well and good for the fortifications, but they were on an expedition to find ore.

"Who will fight?" Kragnak's question broke his concentration.

"Everyone. We've already arranged it, next week training will start for all dwarves."

Kragnak let out a breath. "Even me?"

"Yes."

"But I can't." He held up his wooden arm. Dorian reached out and touched his other arm.

"You won't have a choice. Better to be prepared with one hand than die with two."

Kragnak paled, but Thurbag returned.

"I've got them here." He held up the ingots.

"Put them in the fire." Kragnak glanced back to the crates they had to store their bars. "I will start on the pig iron, until you can bring me what I need."

"Good." Dorian stood and dusted off.

"I haven't made much armor."

"After what I've seen you do, I'm confident you'll do fine," Dorian said, clapping him on the back.

Dorian left them to their work to return to his own. So many things to do, and time was marching on like it always had. Kragnak depended on him.

The promise he made to Mughan, the risk he would be forced to take. All of it would come to pass if they didn't find it. All the dwarves depended on him.

His time was coming swiftly to an end.

12

In Flux

Thud.

Dorian shifted, stepped to the left, and pulled.

Thurbag's eyes opened wide as he fell forward and flat on his face.

"Better, but watch your center of gravity. Again."

Coughing dirt, Thurbag got to his feet. He wiped off his front and checked his wooden training axe.

The sounds of training surrounded them, grunts and blows, occasional yelps from a dwarf learning a valuable lesson.

Dorian hoped it was enough.

They reset, and Thurbag attacked. Dorian defended and Thurbag got a few more close calls.

"You're too fast," Thurbag said after another evasion from Dorian.

"I can see where you're attacking." They sparred more, Dorian showing him more pointers, until time was up. Dorian announced the end of training, to heavy sighs of relief.

"Come on, you bag of rocks," Barileth said, smacking his own training sword against his shield. "Giving up so quickly? Who wants to go another round?" He laughed wickedly.

No one took him up on the offer.

Instead, they put up their equipment and filed out and back to bed. Some of them would be very sore in the morning.

"We're in trouble if they don't send any fighters in the next group," Mughan said. Dorian had seen him linger, and he had been waiting for this day. "Unless you think we can perform a miracle."

"We don't need a miracle. We just need them to be competent enough to hold off a few skeletons." Luckily, skeletons weren't that competent themselves. Dorian shelved his own gear, inspecting the work of the others. "I know what you want to talk about."

"Come now, at least give us a chance to bond about it." A grin spread across Mughan's face.

"You know as well as I that we haven't found any." Despite them almost doubling the depth of the mine. "Confounded granite," Dorian muttered.

"Makes for great walls though," Mughan said, taking up a seat on a stool. "If we could work on them more than a few hours a day."

The weather had complicated things. Dorian was hoping for a few more weeks, but a winter blizzard had moved in and dumped more than a foot of snow.

"We'll finish the watchtower in a few weeks at most." *I hope.*

"I hope," Mughan said. "We can be sure of a little respite, though. There is no way you'd attack with an army right now."

"Agreed." Dorian crossed his arms, almost burning from the victorious glow emanating from Mughan.

"How are you doing?"

It caught him off guard. "Out with it, no more games."

"Have you been getting enough sleep?" Mughan watched him with that piercing stare. Dorian couldn't help but feel uncomfortable.

"What does my sleep have to do with it?" He bared his teeth.

"You're too paranoid Dorian. Yes, we need to talk about the cavern, but perhaps you've been pushing yourself too hard lately?"

"Perhaps I have."

"It's a season of rest and recovery. Why don't you rest while I carry some of your load?"

Dorian stared at him. "You're serious."

"Of course." Mughan held up his hands, an offering. "It's in both our interests."

This he understood. What he didn't know was how it was in Mughan's interest. *Unless he is planning to replace me.*

"I am planning on replacing you, if you're wondering." Mughan held up a finger before he could protest. "But only in due course. You won't be expedition leader forever, will you?"

"No."

"So if you share the load now, all the easier for me to take power when you leave."

"You've always been about yourself, haven't you?"

"Come now, is that any way to talk to a friend? Despite our differences, I thought you would know me better than that."

Dorian didn't like it, not one bit. He wasn't sure Mughan had the ability to lead.

Then again, he wasn't sure he did either.

Still, although he had come to their aid, Dorian wasn't sure where his loyalties lay. "I do call you friend."

"Then, as a friend," Mughan put a hand on his chest and made a mock bow, "I am obligated to say what needs to be said, however hard it may be for you to hear. You're slipping, Dorian, and you need rest just as bad as Yander does."

"You knew about that?"

He smiled sadly. "Everyone knows. They'd be fools not to."

It struck Dorian like a cave in. Thoughts flashed through his mind, carrying him away, until they brought the question. "What does everyone else think?"

"That he needs rest. That he thinks he's doing it because he has no other choice. My personal opinion," Mughan lowered his head, "that he's doing it to make up for what happened to Emelda."

"I tried to talk to him about it."

"I take it he didn't respond well?"

"No."

"My dear friend," he bit off the word, not unkindly, "this may be an area where I can help. I've dealt with dwarves for years."

Dorian narrowed his eyes. "And what, exactly, is your experience?"

"A bit of this, a bit of that."

"No. You know about my past, it's time to return the favor."

"Then where would my advantage be?" Mughan looked innocent, holding up his hands as if to defend himself. "Even after everything you've been through, you still haven't lost your faith that there is good in dwarves."

"You don't speak like a commoner, so who are you?"

"A wandering son, exploring the world and looking for my own little piece of it."

"And you've found it here?"

"Better here than elsewhere. There is good earth to be mined, and enough food for all." Mughan leaned in. "I can see a future filled with good things for use. Jewels, gold, luxuries beyond compare. That is the world I want to live in."

"That world is an illusion."

"Clouded by your past." Mughan leaned back and laced his fingers behind his head. "You fail to see what could be because of what has been. I know what you've been through--"

"You don't know," Dorian growled. "And you don't know why I'm doing this."

"So tell me then." Mughan waited, letting the silence stretch.

Should I tell him? Dorian stroked his beard, then came to a decision. "If I finish this contract successfully, I get to see my children."

"And you get to return to Zirad?"

"Yes."

Mughan shook his head. "I can't say I understand. I have no children of my own, but I see that it drives you. So let it drive you to where we need to go. We both know we need steel. We both know you aren't going to find it in time by digging."

"So that leaves the cavern?"

"Dorian, you saw them. Are they going to survive without strong armor to protect them? Thurbag couldn't land a blow on a blind vole, let alone a goblin." The torch flickered and spat.

"With teachers like you, I know they will." But the thought gnawed on him. What kind of excuse could he give? Winter would be over soon. The passes would clear and the enemies would march.

And the necromancer had his pick of the dead to choose from.

He was out there, searching, and Dorian knew it. And no matter how much he disliked it, Mughan was right, too.

The cavern was their best chance, as much as he hated it.

"I'll accept that we need to enter the cavern. My time has run out, it seems, and I won't go back on my word." Dorian didn't want to do it. He had tried to find any excuse, but each was more hollow than the last. "But if we're going to take this risk, I will be the one to lead it."

"Fair enough. Let me lead the mine in your absence."

"How long do you think I'll be gone?"

Mughan shrugged. "Long enough we might need someone in charge around here. We only caught a glimpse of that place, but I imagine it's just as big as it seems."

Dorian let out a sharp laugh. "We can hope it isn't. Large caverns tend to have their fair share of...undesirable creatures."

"Like the one you killed?"

"Yes."

Mughan picked up a training axe and spun it. "A cave spider like that wouldn't have liked competition, would it?"

"That doesn't make the cavern safe."

He swung it in a lazy arc. "But it does mean that there aren't any more of them."

"You don't understand what can be down here. Zirad has been tamed, made docile over the years of exploration and mining. Everywhere else out here," Dorian shook his head, "there's a reason I don't want to do it."

"I'm surprised you care so much about them."

The comment struck him as odd. Every day, sharing the same table, working and sweating alongside them.

In less than a year, it would be over.

They would disperse or stay. Each dwarf had to decide for themselves where to go and what riches they would have.

If they could find any.

"I might not be the same dwarf I was."

Mughan grinned. "So there is something underneath all that stone. We just had to dig deep enough to find it."

Dorian shrugged it off. "We won't be gone long, a few days at the most. I'd prefer to not be out over night, but I don't think we'd cover enough ground that way."

Setting the axe back, Mughan rubbed his hands. "So we get down to it now. Who will you take? Not me, of course."

"You don't want to go?"

"Someone needs to keep this place running while you're gone."

Scenes of what might happen when he was gone flashed through Dorian's mind. Would he turn the others against him? Lock up the way back?

Leaving Mughan behind might not be the best decision.

"Then we should have Dozotaine, Olgim, Glorithoid, and Barileth come with me. And I'm still not sure about leaving you in charge."

"What's the worst that could happen?"

Walling them into the cavern came to mind.

"You'll only be gone a few days," Mughan said. Dorian knew it was supposed to be reassuring, but somehow the bared teeth didn't make it feel that way.

Somehow he had to find a way to channel Mughan, to keep him useful and away from causing trouble. He had a tingling, not that he would do anything malicious, but some chaos could ensue.

For a moment, he considered what Mughan could do with knowledge. If he taught him, what would he do with it?

Would he even be able to lead an expedition like this? Or perhaps later on, when it was successful. Mines that grew may not have had the same problems, but they had problems nonetheless.

"Are you sure?" Dorian asked quietly.

"I'd assume so. Unless you found something quickly."

"No. Do you really want to lead the mine?"

Mughan considered his question and looked up. His eyes seemed distant, and Dorian felt a different sort of stirring. *He isn't impetuous.*

"Yes, I suppose I do."

In some ways, he could see Mughan doing well, but he still wasn't sure. He had managed to lead the migrants here well enough.

"Do you?" Mughan turned and met Dorian's gaze. Dorian looked deeper, watching his eyes for any flicker, any indication of self-doubt or hesitation.

"Yes." His voice was firm, and his eyes locked onto Dorian's. There was a fire there.

Something passed between them, something Dorian couldn't give a name to. It was that moment that convinced him.

"I'll keep that in mind." He stroked his beard, this time in thought. "In the meantime, we should discuss the upcoming journey. We'll need to prepare quickly."

"Why is that?"

It was Dorian's turn to smile. If they were going to do it, there was no sense in waiting. "We'll leave in a week."

13

UNEXPECTED

Distant shouting interrupted his swing. Dorian turned to listen, and the others did the same.

"What is it?" Thardegith asked.

Dozotaine cut him off with a quick wave of his hand. It sounded like Olgim, but he couldn't make out the words.

A few moments later, he could.

Like one, they turned and ran. They met him on the stairs, rushing down yelling, "They've come."

"What direction?" Dorian asked. Olgim stopped as he approached, but Dorian didn't.

"From the north."

"Come on." *This was too soon, we aren't ready.* "Are the others in place?"

"How many?" Dozotaine asked.

"I don't know. We were waiting for you. You don't need to run, though." Olgim had turned to scramble after them, but he was losing ground. "Mughan said he would meet them."

"Of course," Dorian muttered. Right on the eve of their departure, they were attacked. "Let's hope everyone else is ready. Olgim, where is your weapon?"

His heart was pounding, and the stairs weren't helping his endurance. *How could he forget again?*

"It's in the armory."

"What have we told you," Dozotaine growled. "Always have it in an attack, no matter what you're doing."

"Attack? There's no attack."

Dorian stopped short and turned. "What?" The others had done the same. Olgim was puffing a few stairs below, and stopped to lean on the wall.

"It's dwarves. Dwarves from the north."

"You made it sound like we were being attacked." Dozotaine glared at him.

Olgim stiffened. "I did no such thing."

Still breathing hard, Dorian turned back up the stairs. "No use arguing about it now. You came to get us, and you got us." He thought about sending the others back to keep working. "Since we've come this way all of you might as well come. Be more clear next time."

He was recovered by the time they reached the mine entrance. Mughan, of course, was at the main gate, ushering in a line of dwarves. The noon sun had passed, now starting its descent to the horizon.

They were staring at the now finished walls, mouths open. Metal clanged together, and something clucked from one of the migrant's packs. The sleeves of their coats were frayed and dangled in the still harsh wind of winter.

Dorian planted at the entrance, the other miners behind him. "Welcome. Where are you from?"

"Zirad," the first dwarf said. Dorian introduced himself as the remaining migrants clustered together against the cold.

"Come in, and welcome to Seventh Hall." Feet stamped and hands rubbed together as Dorian and the others pointed out the traps along the entrance.

"How did you come to be traveling so close to winter?" Dorian asked.

Saggamli, the eldest of the group, blew warm air into his hands. "Spring came early in the valley, and with the rivers swollen, we thought the mountains would be easier to traverse. We were eager to get here."

"Eager to get here? To the right." Dorian motioned down the hall.

"Yes, extra bonus for early arrival," Nofibela, his wife, said. She looked at her husband, and her smile faded. "Not that--"

"In here." Dorian held open the door for them. "There are many reasons we came, the quest for riches being the most common."

"I took the liberty of arranging some refreshments for our new arrivals while you were gone," Mughan said, bringing up the rear. "I hope you don't mind, but I'll go help them."

Dorian wasn't sure if he meant it to make him jealous, or that he was contrite, but he did feel a tinge of shame that he didn't think of it earlier. The mix up in the mines had thrown him off.

But by the time he even thought of a reply Mughan was halfway to the kitchens, and the migrants were waiting. They buzzed around the great hall, admiring Kimec and Lumdir's furniture and the height of the ceiling.

Dorian bade them sit and further introductions were made. In addition to the Duskminers, Saggamli and Nofibela and their daughter, Ondare, there was Hatheck Opalbrand, Bermic Kegforged, Vadgrala Runebreaker, Glarrore Woldforge, and Gofrac Ashelly.

Emelda led the welcoming party for the expedition, bringing in two roast chickens on a platter, followed by a flow of food and drink.

Faces perked up and smiles spread, and ale flowed. Yudoline ladled out steaming mugs of wine spiced with cherry, and the dwarves tore into the food.

Plates were passed and stories exchanged, and soon the frozen dwarves were thawed and laughing. Dorian felt some of his tension flow away as he laughed at some of the stories in turn.

"Tell me what you did in Zirad." Dorian turned to Nofibela and Saggamli to his right, then dipped some rockbread in the butter and took a bite.

"We work with stone," Saggamli said. Another stonemason, good. "I am but a humbled mason, but my wife has won praise for her engraving."

"Saggamli, please," Nofibela said, blushing.

"No, it's true. She's worked in the King Lightaxe's Palace." Saggamli was glowing, and Nofibela smiled.

"I had been admiring the work you've done here," she demurred. "Good, strong columns and granite is so lovely to work with."

"We could use some refinement here," Dorian said, lifting his mug and sweeping it around the room. "As you can see, we've been a bit busy and have left it...rough."

"You'll have plenty of work here," Saggamli said. The mention made Dorian think, and some of the air lost its merriment for him.

Another eight dwarves. Another eight mouths to feed.

And another eight more hands to put to work.

Dorian took a deep breath, ignoring the sweat that was trying to work its way through his skin. All in good time.

It was already difficult trying to keep the others put to use as is, particularly with the weather inhibiting construction of the upper wall and towers.

Now he was going to need to keep everyone employed.

The blood drained from his face. *And we leave tomorrow.*

"What is it, was it something I said?" Nofibela was frowning, eyebrows drawn tight. She had said something, but he hadn't paid attention.

"No, not at all. Just...distracted by something. Can you start in here? Smooth the stone first, of course, and do some engraving on the columns?" He took a deep swig of ale.

"Of course!"

"We could use the reminder of home. It will make everyone happy." To be in a well-constructed cave again, floors smooth as glass and walls adorned with engravings. Everywhere a marvel to see.

It would do more than good, and it took care of one of the dwarves. Now he had to figure out what to do with the rest.

"Wonderful." Nofibela clapped her hands and beamed. "There is much to discover and even more to work with."

"Good food, good drink, and now good work," Ondare said. "We were right in coming here, I know it." He put a hand around his wife's shoulders, hugging her close.

"And rooms to sleep in." They had enough. Thankfully, Kimec had made them new beds, studier and bigger, and they had stored the others in another set of apartments they had carved for the stone. "We have apartments for all of you, and once we've given you the tour, you can unpack."

He made a mental note to have Kimec make more furniture. What was in the apartments was fine, but it was older and Kimec's earlier work. Now that he had iron tools, his work had improved.

Plates were emptied and chairs pushed back. The last dregs of ale and wine were drained. Dorian stood and motioned. "Olgim, will you show our new arrivals around?"

"Happy to."

"I'll come down and see that you're settled, and talk to you about the expedition and the mine. Take the day off to rest and we'll put you to work in the morning."

Olgim led the migrants away, hauling off their belongings and echoing down the tunnels. Dorian directed the others back to work, but Mughan pulled him aside.

"What are your intentions about tomorrow?" They retreated to a corner, out of the way of the few dwarves left to clean up after the lunch.

He had forgotten in the excitement, or rather had pushed the thought away every time it had come up. Dorian chewed his lower lip. The supplies were ready, the expedition fitted out.

"We'll still go."

"What about our newest members, then? Do you want me to stay behind and make use of them?" Dorian wanted Mughan close, was going to leave Yudoline in charge while he was gone. He had even written a week's worth of assignments.

He might as well tear it all up now. "We don't even know what use they'll be."

"Less than half a day, will that be enough?" Mughan asked. There wasn't enough time to do it all. Plates scraped as Yutatir stacked them to haul off to be washed.

"What do you propose?"

"You know what I want. Leave me behind, let me run the mine. Or," he shrugged, "put me in charge of the expedition. How hard can it be to guide a few well-armed dwarves through an old cave?"

"Don't underestimate what can be out there." Dorian thought for a moment. "Let me talk to them. Meet me in my room in an hour." Mughan agreed and they separated. Dorian walked down to the apartments.

Why did they have to come now? Couldn't they have waited for spring like always? In some ways he was troubled. Why would the king's men let them do it? He walked through the new apartments, kicking a few stray rocks from the doors and brushing off a fine layer of dust from the beds.

They would need something to sleep on, and the goats wouldn't be able to keep up. *There are the mines.* Silk was light, cool. All they had to do was harvest it. The cave spiders wouldn't mind.

Much.

Dorian sat on the edge of a bed and waited. Inside, he fought. He should be doing *something*, but here he was sitting and waiting.

He took a deep breath, taking in the dry air of the cave and releasing it. He had seen Mughan lead dwarves into battle. He could trust him to fight, if nothing else.

Could he trust him to manage and administer? Finding the best task for the migrants was important, but was it more important than an expedition into the heart of the cavern?

The only way he could do both was to put it off until later, but what would that cost them? If they had the flux stone they could be making steel and were more likely to survive.

And if the dwarves could navigate the mountains, couldn't the necromancer?

No, his instinct was right. They had to do the expedition. As much as he hated it, he knew that he was better put to use here, despite his knowledge of the underground.

Footsteps echoed down the stairs and Olgim's voice carried. Dorian got up, stretched his legs, and met them at the entrance.

Apartments were claimed, belongings put down, and Dorian began to take stock of the dwarves.

He moved from room to room, questioning them on their past experience and what skills they had. As he went, his hope of soldiers was crushed. Only Hatheck had any military experience, and it was over a decade ago. Retired, he now worked as a jeweler.

In all, they had a merchant, farmer, animal caretaker, weaver, jeweler, mason, engraver, and apprentice blacksmith. Kragnak would be pleased to get more help, and he could shift Thurbag somewhere else.

It was going to take time, though.

"Have you ever worked with silk?" Dorian asked Ondare. She couldn't have been more than thirty years old. She nodded.

"I wouldn't be any good at it though, I mainly worked with wool." She looked down and wrung her hands.

"Far better than I could do. You'll be very helpful here." Dorian bade them to get some rest and left. The decision was clear, however difficult it might be.

Mughan was waiting for him, leaning up against his door.

"You'll lead the expedition." Mughan smiled. "But if you feel anything is wrong, get out of there as soon as you can."

14

BREAKING THE FAST

Chapter Fourteen

The locks rumbled as they drew back until they finally reached the end of their travel with a crunch. Dorian helped Mughan pull the door open, in awe of Lumdir's crafting ability.

It was light and could have been opened with a single dwarf, but solid stone. The dark cavern gazed back at them, uninviting.

His skin pricked, but there was no other way. He had to send them.

"You've got your supplies, make good use of them." Dorian surveyed the group, all in sets of iron armor with the best weapons they had, except Webcleaver, of course.

Five dwarfs would go into the cavern. He hoped five would come back. What danger awaited in the dark?

The black gaped at him, waiting to swallow them. Dorian took up his torch again and raised it, casting a small and pitiful arc of light that didn't even touch the tunnel beyond.

"We'll be back in a day or two, at most. Don't worry about us," Mughan said.

"Stick to the high places. Always be able to look down, but never take it for granted."

Mughan put an arm around his shoulder. "Don't worry so much. I'm sure we'll be fine. We've had a good teacher." He winked at Dorian.

"Best be off." His voice was gruffer than normal. The five dwarves lined up, two torches in hand and packs on. Dorian got out of their way.

They stepped through the door one at a time, Mughan first and Dozotaine bringing up the rear. Dorian had kept Yander away, even though he wanted to go. He needed him in the mines.

Dorian watched them march, listening to the creaking of their armor and the rattling of their supplies. *Did they have enough rope?*

It was too late now, they took everything else they had. That reminded him he could get Ondare to weave some more if she was up to it.

They reached the tunnel and turned. The light from their torches lingered, then darkened, then disappeared. They were gone.

Dorian drew in a breath, trying to stifle the fear and uncertainty. This might be like the Mine of Tramesh. He squeezed his eyes shut and tried to block the memory.

No, this would be different, successful. It wouldn't end in blood and death. It couldn't. Almost a quarter of the expedition was going out there, and they needed to succeed.

He had to remind himself of the mission, that his children waited on the other side. That his wife was waiting. She was cold, stuffed away in some vault like the others.

And he had to get her out.

His heart burned, longing for the bygone days. Days of happiness, of plenty. Days filled with light and love that had been taken from him in a moment.

Dorian licked his lips, tasting sweat and stone. A glimmer of doubt crept in. Was it truly the right thing to do?

They were gone now, swallowed up by the bowels of the earth. He could do nothing else for them other than worry and wish.

So Dorian did the only thing he could. He shut the door, spinning the handle to force the six locking mechanisms tight, and turning the key so that only it and the twin that Mughan carried could open it.

He wished he had said something else, shared some secret bit of knowledge that would prove critical down there. He had tried as much as possible over the last few days.

He just hoped it would be enough.

Dorian turned on his heel, leaving the place at a brisk walk. He had work to do, they all did.

It was time to return to it.

The other were eating breakfast by the time he finished the lists, or filled them as well as he could. He looked to the dwindling pile of paper they had and knew it wouldn't last.

Something was going to have to change now, and he wasn't sure how to handle it. In all the other expeditions he had been on someone else had managed this.

"Good morning," Yudoline said as he walked in.

"Morning," Dorian mumbled.

She squinted at him as he sat, appraising him. "Have you been getting enough sleep?"

"Plenty. Saw them off this morning."

"And now we wait?" Kimec asked.

Dorian nodded and sliced off a piece of cold rock bread. He slathered it with goat butter and listened to the conversations as he took a bite. It was good.

"It will be quiet with Mughan to pester us," Kragnak said, his words ringing hollow and his smile forced. "We won't be nearly as unproductive."

"That reminds me," Dorian said. "You'll have a new apprentice today." He speared a potato from the bottom of the pile. It was still steaming. "Gofrac has some experience as a smith and knows his way around a forge."

"I almost finished my apprenticeship, before I came here," he said, nodding his head and wringing his hands.

Kragnak's smile faded. It was not what Dorian was expecting. He glanced at Thurbag. "What will Thurbag be doing?"

"The wall."

"I like building," Thurbag said halfheartedly. He shifted in his chair and refused to meet Krangak's eyes.

Kragnak was silent, but his shoulders hunched.

Dorian set down his fork and sighed. "You have reservations?"

"Whatever the expedition needs," Kragnak said, lips tight. The others exchanged looks around the table. Most of them knew where they would be for the day, the same tasks they performed every day.

Gofrac frowned and dropped his hands beneath the table. His head drooped.

"With our new friends there will be changes," Dorian said, addressing everyone in the room. "You all signed up for a dangerous mining expedition in the far reaches of Zirad, and we need to complete the contracts you signed."

And I need to see my children again.

"Thurbag has been doing well, that's all. I mean you no offense Gofrac," Kragnak said. The young dwarf looked back up.

"None taken."

Dorian took the last fried eye, watching the room carefully. The others were done, and conversation grew again.

The tension didn't leave the air though. There was a layer of it, pervading the smiles that were too bright and the laughter too loud.

This isn't my strength.

He knew he had to change something, to unite them.

"We'll be attacked," Dorian said, casually mopping up the rest of his egg. All eyes looked to him, and the conversation stopped. "We don't know when. It could be today, it could be tomorrow."

"What?" Ondare paled, and moved closer to her mother.

"Don't scare them Dorian," Yudoline said.

"It isn't to scare you. You deserve to know." Dorian spread his arms. "This is the life you've stepped into, and one you can leave. We are preparing, but I can't guarantee your survival."

Silence. Gofrac's mouth had dropped open.

"But, with your help, we stand more than a good chance of survival." He smiled, thinking about the future battle and, despite the danger, the benefits it could bring. "We've already repulsed two, with enough preparation a third isn't out of the question."

"We need to know more." Saggamli's eyes had hardened.

"Of course." Dorian told them everything he knew, and everything they were going to do about it. He answered their questions, but after he finished, the feeling had shifted.

Yes, there was fear here, but the tension was gone and the false happiness banished. The dwarves were real again, and he was glad for it.

"Is that why the others left?" Hatheck asked quietly.

"They went to find stone," Yander said.

"We have plenty here."

"Flux stone. We need it to remove the impurities in the iron to make steel," Kragnak said.

"And to satisfy the requirements of your contracts. The ones you may choose to break and return to Zirad, if you so desire," Dorian said, letting the weight of his words fall on them.

Dwarves fidgeted, played with their utensils, avoided eye contact.

"We came out here for a reason, might as well stay," Saggamli said, breaking the silence. The others weren't fleeing for the door.

Satisfied, Dorian leaned forward. "Then let's get to work."

Assignments were given, and the breakfast cleared. Dorian took the group assigned to the wall up with him, Thurbag, Hukgras, Olgim, Bermic, and Vadgrala, and walked them through the process.

The wind still chilled him and nipped at his nose, so he advised them to take frequent breaks. They stood next to the farms, still covered with snow.

Bermic gazed at the wall. "Why a wall at all?"

"We need access to the outside. If we were to retreat into the mine we'd be cut off from merchants and reinforcements." Dorian smiled. "And how would you have been able to reach us if we were trapped in the mine?"

He shrugged. "Knock on the door?"

"We'll be able to fire at any approaching enemy, safe behind the wall." Dorian pointed to the top, with spaced crenelations for protection. He had to give them some sense of security if he wanted them to stay.

They were going to need their help to survive.

"Hukgras will answer any other questions you may have. She's been doing this for a few months."

She smiled. "You'll get used to the weight. I have."

Dorian watched them start, satisfied that they could finish the job, and then left.

Warmth washed over him as he entered the mine, and he stamped his feet to wake them up. His coat wasn't doing as well as it used to in keeping out the cold.

After checking on the other migrant arrivals, he went down to the mine and followed the sounds of mining. With most of the miners on the expedition there was no one left but him to help.

The steady clink of the pickaxe against the stone led him to Yander at the bottom of the mine. He had started another tunnel again, this one traveling horizontally into the deepest part of the mountain.

He had already gone more than a two dozen yards. *This tunnel hadn't been here last night.*

"Feel anything?" Dorian joined him, after touching the wall for a moment. There was something down at the far end, but he wasn't sure what.

"I think it's more iron." Chunks of rock fell on the already littered path. He stopped. "I wanted to go."

"I needed you here." Dorian grasped the warm handle of his own pickaxe, hefting it.

"Why not keep Thardegith then? He's just as fast as I am."

Dorian snorted.

"You know what I think?" Pick met stone. Stone showered down.

"No." He hoped Yander wasn't like this, he didn't have the energy to deal with it today. He hadn't been sleeping as well as he liked.

"I think you don't want me to find it."

Squeezing his eyes shut, Dorian set down his pickaxe long enough to rub his temples. His elbows creaked. "Yander, you know Thardegith is a fine miner but he isn't very fast. The dwarf just picked up a pickaxe a few months ago."

"Then what is it? I'm not good enough to find the ore out there so you keep me down here, caged in a cell of stone?" Yander's eyes were half shut, and his knuckles white on the handle of his pickaxe.

"You're needed here, for now."

"You treat me like a youngling. Like I can't make any decisions on my own."

Dorian's eyes opened wide. "Where is this coming from? When have I done that?"

"Go on, say it. I'm worthless to the expedition. All I can find is worthless iron and silver."

He had to take a deep breath. Yander wasn't making sense, and the anger was rising. Would he let it get the best of him this time?

The thought struck him like a lightning bolt. "This isn't about how I've treated you, is it?" Yander went quiet. "You feel like you aren't contributing, that you should be contributing more?"

Yander nodded. "We need that steel," he whispered.

"Yes, we do. But if we don't find it, we'll manage. We have good dwarves here. Like yourself." Yander's eyes shot to him, searching for mirth or mockery.

Dorian had none. "I know you want to be better. I know you want to protect Emelda." Like he should have protected Yolanda. "We might not have much time, but we do have some time." Yander looked to him, eyes pleading for something.

"You're doing a good job, and I can't live without you here in the mine." Dorian pointed down the tunnel. "I wouldn't have sensed that from the mineshaft, but you did. Your skills are growing and getting stronger."

"But I should be out there."

Dorian nodded. "I understand. For now, I need you here."

"For now?"

"I promise that once they've done some exploring, made sure it isn't too dangerous, you'll get to go into the cavern." Dorian clasped his hands. "We'll find what we need, together."

15

INTO THE DEEP

The tunnel snaked into the mountain, and Mughan couldn't help shake the feeling they were inside some sort of monster, swallowed whole.

Barileth whistled as he walked, the music echoing. "Have I ever told you about the time we slaughtered a nest of goblins?"

"I'm not sure now is the time..." Yutatir said, voice catching in his throat. A snap up ahead. "What was that?"

"That was my torch," Mughan said. "I know everyone is a little on edge, but we haven't even reached the main cavern. Please try and show a little decorum and act like dwarves with a spine."

Barileth laughed, the sound filling out around them. "That's the spirit." He clapped Yutatir on the back, almost sending him sprawling. "Nothing like a little insult to make dwarves forget their fears."

Mughan ignored him, leading the pack through another turn. If he remembered right, there was a branch.

It was there, up ahead. Two black holes like eyes.

"Left, or right?" Barileth asked.

"Right." They kept traveling, twisting and turning, until they reached it.

The tunnel dropped off, opening up above them and spitting them out into a vast expanse of cavern. Faint lights far below glowed miles away.

"Not bad," Barileth said.

"Getting down will be difficult," Dozotaine said. Their torches only lit up their immediate area, a steep drop in front that continued on to the right. "We weren't able to find a path last time."

"But we didn't have much time, either." Mughan shifted his pack, evening the load on his shoulders. "Shall we go down here?"

Barileth peered over the edge, torch outstretched. "I'd say we look along there." He pointed ahead of them. "It might soften."

The others didn't make a contrary motion. "On we go, then."

Mughan walked along the side of the drop. The path was wide enough for a few wagons side by side, but they walked in single file. Stalactites dripped their water onto the waiting stalagmites that grew along the undulating cavern ceiling.

Other than that and the sound of the dwarves, it was quiet. Mughan searched around them, but the biggest creatures they saw were the cave spiders in their webs.

Barileth was right, after a half hour or so the slope started leveling off. A short walk after that it was passable, if not uncomfortable. "Here we are."

"Good spot as any to go down," Barileth agreed.

Mughan started, the rich dark soil shifting under his boots. He slipped and regained his footing. "Careful here."

Inching his way forward, Mughan descended, followed by the others. Small rocks and dirt dislodged from their journey clattered down the slope.

After a while it evened out, allowing him a moment of rest and for the others to catch up. They still weren't at the base, which seemed far out of reach, but the torches caught something dark ahead of them.

"Mushrooms," Barileth said as Mughan stepped closer. He was right, a forest of them grew towering over them. They had to be twenty, thirty feet tall. "Kimec is going to be excited."

"And another food source too." Dozotaine walked over. Moss grew around the mushrooms, keeping the dirt tight. "This is good soil."

"Good enough to farm in." They already had good things to report. The others were going to be happy, and Mughan was going to get to tell them.

He knocked on the trunk of a mushroom. Solid through and through. Kimec might be able to work with it.

"How are we going to know how to get back?" Thardegith looked back up the slope. There was a trail from their footsteps, but it was faint. "I wouldn't know my way around this place without help."

"Our footsteps will stay. We'll follow them back." Barileth scuffed in the mossy dirt. "From here on out though..."

"Fell a few mushrooms?" Dozotaine suggested.

"That might attract attention."

"We'll leave a marking to lead us back." Mughan pulled out his sword, testing it against the trunk of the enormous mushroom. It cut through, a small trickle of fluid welling up in the gash. "You see it, and follow it back."

"What happens if we run out of mushrooms?" Thardegith asked. The forest of them was sparse, but up ahead it thickened.

"Then we'll adapt. Come on, enough wasting time. I'd like to double back along the slope, see where it takes us." He didn't wait for an answer, but turned to parallel where they'd come, only from the bottom of the slope.

Moss crushed under foot, sending up waves of aroma as they hiked. There was precious little talking, even as they stopped to rest and refresh for a meal. Mughan drove them on, cutting their time short, and soon the slope curved away, taking them farther into the left portion of the cavern.

The sloped steepened, and moss gave way to rock.

It was granite layered on more granite.

Barileth cursed the rock. "Won't give up anything. I say we go deeper into the cavern, farther down and see if the granite yields."

"Is it more likely?" Yutatir asked. Barileth shrugged.

"We'll go back to where we came down," Mughan said. "Unless there are any objections?" He didn't suppose there would be, and he was right.

So, they went back.

Yutatir lagged behind, dragging his feet. He was the last one back to their trail up the slope.

"Time for lunch." Mughan slipped off his pack, letting it plop and kick up a small plume of dust. He stretched, it felt good to get the weight off his shoulders, as the others followed suit.

"There's enough food down here to last a few weeks, if those mushrooms are good," Yutatir said, eying the mushroom trees.

"Ever been down this far?" Barileth unwrapped a hunk of cheese and bit off the end, chewing loudly.

"No."

"We aren't the only ones to find it attractive. Best be on your guard, lest you find yourself a meal for something else." He smiled wickedly, with a mouthful of cheese.

"He's only joking." Mughan shot him a glare.

"Only the unprepared dwarf finds themselves taken unaware."

"What kind of..." Thardegith swallowed hard, the rockbread in his hand untouched, "things live down here?"

"Spiders, trolls, creepy crawly things. You know, the stuff your mother told you to scare you into behaving," Barileth said.

"And great fortune, as well," Mughan said. "I've heard of dwarves stumbling into amethyst geodes, cracked open like an egg and waiting for the harvest."

Barileth snorted. "More likely to find a rat's nest down here."

Something squeaked above them. Thardegith's head whipped around. "What was that?"

It continued, along with a small flapping, and their torch caught glimpses of black far above.

"Bats." Barileth nodded. "Good sign. If they're out, then there aren't many predators around."

Yutatir let out a long breath, relaxing the grip on his axe. "So we're safe?"

"Finish up your meal, we'll be moving on soon," Mughan said. They washed down the food with ale and packed up without a sound.

They started down the slope again, this time making better speed.

"We should stop here," Barileth said.

Mughan looked back. That hadn't come that far. "Why?"

"To check the rock." Mughan nodded, noting that Yutatir was still lagging behind.

"Good idea, hold here."

Barileth dug into the moss, parting it to reveal a fine layer of rich, dark loam. It crumbled in his hands as he pulled it out of his growing hole.

Yutatir licked his lips, staring at it. "That's good earth. It would make for good crops."

"Once we clear everything out we'll come back," Mughan said. He pictured it now, row on row of moss and caveberry, as much as each dwarf could desire. They would be able to make everything the ever needed for food.

And the animals could graze on the moss too. The goats would eat it, and there were enough bugs crawling around that the chickens would get nice and plump.

His mouth watered at the thought of a nice, juicy roast chicken. It had been a while since they had one. Dorian refused to let any but the males be slaughtered for their meat. Claimed that the eggs would be better in the long run.

How long that would be, Mughan didn't know.

Hands scraped on rock, and Barileth motioned the torch closer. "Aye, good earth indeed." A few seconds later he shook his head. "Granite."

Yutatir had caught his breath, so Mughan urged them forward. Every few hundred yards they stopped to check. Every single time they found more granite.

The gentle slope took them nearer to the glowing patches of golden moss. An hour later they stumbled across the first one.

"Up ahead," Dozotaine said. "We should approach with caution."

"Kill the torches?" Barileth asked. "There are things down here that are attracted to the light."

"No, keep them lit," Mughan said. He didn't know why, but he imagined the darkness enveloping him. It wasn't a pleasant feeling.

"At least put out all but one." Mughan nodded, and Barileth extinguished his, leaving only Mughan's to cast a circle of light around them.

The mushrooms were thick here, obscuring the glowing patch up ahead, but Mughan nodded and they crept forward, weapons drawn and ready.

He didn't realize how far away they were until it took them minutes to work through the trees.

The moss stretched out for hundreds of yards in a sparsely mushroomed clearing, creeping beneath and up the trunks of the mushrooms and curling into tendrils of circles.

"That much could feed us for a winter, or more," Yutatir said. Barileth put his fingers to his lips and disappeared. Mughan searched the clearing for movement.

Even watching to the left where Barileth went, he saw nothing move.

So he scanned above them. Bats fluttered above, hunting, transiting, he didn't know.

Something glinted on the ceiling. Mughan moved the torch, and it did it again.

"Clear," Barileth said, materializing from behind them and making a few jump. "There's a stream up ahead."

Dozotaine marked the mushroom they had taken refuge under. "The day is lengthening. We either go on and camp for the night, or turn back for the mine."

"We should go back," Yutatir said.

"Then we would be wasting time." Mughan let his irritation show. "All the way back just to do it all over again. Besides, we have plenty of supplies to last us through the next few days."

"I say we go on too," Barileth said. He sheathed his sword, and others followed his lead.

"But think of our beds," Yutatir said. "So much better than the rocky ground."

"There's plenty of moss to cushion your head," Dozotaine said.

"And even more for your backside," Barileth said, then laughed.

Yutatir crossed his arms. "Laugh all you like. I had my fill of sleeping on the ground on the way out here."

"Used to an easier life?" Mughan asked. Yutatir's mouth tightened. "Down here you need to face the fact that life isn't going to be gold and rubies. Not until we find them, at least."

"And staying out will allow us more time to search." Barileth motioned farther out into the cavern. "Out there."

"Think of what waits us, the treasure just waiting to be picked up. It's even above us." Mughan pointed to the ceiling, waving the torch to get it to sparkle more. The effect was not lost on the others. "And if it's above us, how much more is beneath out feet just waiting to be picked up?"

Expression softened, Yutatir turned to Thardegith. "I suppose you want to go on too?"

"I wouldn't mind going back, but I think they have a point."

Yutatir sighed. "I can see we'll be going on. Well, no use waiting around then." He picked up his pack and slung it over his shoulder.

The others followed his lead, and Mughan led them around the outskirts of the moss, preserving it for a later harvest.

They left it behind, and Barileth showed them the direction of the stream. He heard it when they were stopped, far into the distance.

Mughan would have preferred sleeping in his own bed too, but if they went back, they would be spending even more time out here.

So they walked on, marking their path.

"It's quiet. Except for the water," Yutatir said. It tricked and gurgled, happy melodious sounds that were swallowed up far above, barely a whisper. The sound of the bats overhead had long since disappeared.

Thardegith screamed out in pain, punctuating the stillness of the cavern.

16

CAVERN SURPRISE

Mughan whirled.

His torch illuminated Thardegith, and something attached to his leg.

Less than a second later Barileth's sword cut through it, sending a spray of blood into the air.

"There's more of them," Dozotaine yelled. He was right. The space around them teemed with the pale white creatures, eyes glowing in the torchlight.

"Circle," Mughan said, jerking on his sword hilt. It wasn't coming out. An instant later, the mass attacked.

It was a blur, his heart nearly bursting through his chest. Somehow he wrenched free his sword, but not in time for one of the things to spear him in the chest with a bone white tipped stick.

Mughan waited for the pain, even as the spear scraped against his chest plate, but it never did.

Amazed, he looked down. There wasn't even a dent in the armor.

He slashed at the creature, but it ducked out of the way and jumped back. It counterattacked, but he managed to knock the spear away.

Clenching a mailed fist, Mughan punched out, hoping to catch it by surprise.

But he missed.

"What are these things?" Yutatir yelled, swinging his axe to Mughan's left. He managed a quick glance around while the creature retreated.

They were back-to-back, a press of bodies crowded around the torch he had dropped. It hissed in the moss, but kept burning.

"Flesh crawlers," Barileth said, then roared as he scored another hit on his opponent. "No telling how many of them there are."

"Damned thing cut my back," Thardegith said, swiping at another. They were massed in front of them, but behind them seemed clear.

Mughan didn't have much time to think about it, because two of them attacked him at the same time. The first he blocked, knocking away the spear with his sword, but the other dug in between two plates on his arm.

He grabbed the spear and smashed his helmet into the twisted creature's face with a satisfying crunch. Pain lanced from his left shoulder then, his mind catching up to his body, and he pushed the creature away.

The spear tip was bloody, and he threw it back into the crowd, hoping for a hit.

"Fall back, back to the entrance," Mughan said, ducking to avoid another swipe at him. More landed on his armor, but glanced off. It was doing its job.

They moved back, falling under the press of bodies that seemed unending. Thardegith took up his left side, and Barileth hacked away at his right.

Mughan barely kept up, blocking and parrying. His sword was heavy, and his reactions were slowing. The creatures were more reckless now, pressing their advantage, and the dwarves moved quicker back.

Barileth and Dozotaine were effective, leaving a trail of bodies and separated body parts behind them, but the creatures didn't seem to care.

"They won't leave us alone until we are dead or leave their territory." Barileth pulled out his sword from another one, letting it fall to the ground.

"How do we know when we've left?" Mughan asked. His lungs were on fire now, and his muscles not much better.

"When they stop attacking. Take Thardegith. Dozotaine, we'll provide cover." Mughan took Thardegith's arm over his shoulder, with Yutatir on the other side, and turned and ran.

Thardegith yelped in pain every time his foot hit the ground, and he was heavy.

"Drop the packs," Mughan said, sloughing off his own. Yutatir followed, and they smashed open behind them, scattering their supplies everywhere.

Dozotaine and Barileth held back the horde, slashing in the retreat and forcing them away from the other three's flank.

The mushrooms blurred, an occasional mark helping him make sure they were going in the right direction.

"I can't go on," Thardegith said, panting. "Leave me and save your-selves."

"Shut up," Mughan said, pulling his arm harder to keep him off the ground. He was rewarded with a grunt, but Thardegith didn't say anything.

Then, up ahead, the ground sloped up. They were almost there.

"They aren't stopping," Dozotaine said, his face covered in blood.

"It's a big group. I'm not sure we can get out of their territory." Barileth swiped at another creature, but it stepped out of the way and hissed at him.

Mughan wasn't sure if it was laughing, or warning them.

"Then we fight, and kill them." Mughan jerked his head up. "We take the high ground, force them to come to us."

The reprieve was over, the creatures had regathered and rushed in for the kill.

They were only a few more feet away, and Mughan knew that they could make it. All they had to do was get to that slope.

But his legs were weakening, buckling, under the weight of Thardegith and his pack. Yutatir was gasping for breath. They wouldn't be much use to the fight like this.

Mughan licked his dry lips. Salty, sweat and blood mixed together. He spat it out. Less than a few feet now.

Yutatir cried out. Mughan glanced over.

A spear caught him in the unprotected knee. It ripped out, gushing blood, and he cried out again.

But they were almost there. Mughan pushed Thardegith off him, letting him tumble with Yutatir to the ground with a groan.

"Go," he said, and turned back around. Barileth and Dozotaine sported dozens of wounds, but they had halved the number of attackers, or more.

But it didn't matter, they still kept coming.

He oozed sweat. Dirt was everywhere, and the smell of blood, both dwarven and a strange acidic smell of what had to be the creatures.

Without the torches he could barely make them out. "Light a torch when you get up there." He joined the other two, catching a spear in the chest before swatting it away and stabbing the evil thing that got him. "We hold here."

The fighting was easier on the up-slope, and with armored boots and legs he felt safer. Their spears reached for his head, but he had enough time to react now.

And they were gaining the upper hand.

"Picked the wrong day." Barileth crushed a face with a mailed fist and stabbed another.

Dozotaine, likewise, was decimating his opponents with the added height advantage. Bodies started piling up, and they retreated up.

Then, light flared up behind them, blinding their opponents.

"Now, charge. For Seventh Hall!" Mughan ignored his aching muscles, even though they felt like jelly, and ran forward. The creatures hissed in surprise, and were caught by his sword and armored body.

He crashed into one after the other, barreling through them in a hole, until he burst through their line to the other side.

Dozotaine and Barileth were right behind him, cutting their own path.

Now, the creatures scattered. "After them. We can't let them get away now, they'll go into hiding and recover," Barileth said.

Yutatir had joined them, despite his wound, hacking the stragglers with his axe.

But the fight was over, and the creatures weren't that fast. Mughan and the others stopped the fleeing creatures, ending their lives.

When the last one was dead he sat down hard, stars floating through his vision. He gulped in deep breaths of the fragrant air, the blood mingled with the crushed moss of the mushroom forest.

"Good work," he said. "Who's hurt?"

"My leg," Thardegith said. The others had their cuts and scrapes, but nothing more serious than Dozotaine's bleeding head wound.

"Albino flesh crawlers," Bairleht said, crouching down beside Mughan. Now that the fighting was over he was able to get a good look at them. Pale white, almost translucent, they were semi-humanoid and about the same size as the dwarves. The nasty teeth and elongated eyes, however, made them seem otherworldly. "Would have killed us if they had the chance. We should look after them."

Regretfully, Mughan got back to his feet, his shoulder throbbing now.

"Barileth, can you go get our supplies?" He remembered where they were and went to get them while the others tended to Thardegith.

"We have to take your armor off." Mughan knelt next to him. The leg didn't look straight. "It's going to hurt."

"I've still got ale," Dozotaine said, and uncapped his skin. He gave it to Thardegith, helping him hold it to his lips, while Mughan undid the straps.

"How is your leg?" Mughan asked.

"Better now," Yutatir said, patting the bandage he had rolled from Dozotaine's supplies.

"Good. Ready?" Thardegith nodded, clenching his teeth.

Mughan pulled the last buckle free and took off the plate in the same smooth movement, trying not to disturb the leg.

Thardegith moaned. It was bent over, broken.

"Thing...came out...of nowhere," Thardegith panted through the pain. Mughan shifted it, and his face clenched involuntarily.

"Hold on, we'll get you fixed up in no time," Mughan said. He glanced up impatiently. Still no Barileth. "Dozotaine, can you cut down that mushroom?"

Dozotaine pulled out an axe. "Splints?" Mughan nodded. While they kept Thardegith comfortable, as comfortable as possible, the sounds of Dozotaine's axe drifted off into the cavern.

"Not the first time I've broken something," Thardegith said, breathing deep. "Back in Zirad I fell out of a tree. Broke my arm. You can set it now, I'm ready."

"Dozotaine's almost done. We can wait." Mughan watched the mushroom line for movement. Nothing.

Finally, the mushroom toppled with a soft crunch and a kick of dust into the faint light of the torch. Dozotaine handed two sticks of hardened mushroom to Mughan.

"Anyone else done this before?" Mughan asked, looking hopefully to Dozotaine. He shook his head. "Ready?"

Thardegith took another swig of ale, then nodded.

With a swift motion Mughan grabbed his leg and pulled. Thardegith paled, every muscle in his face clenched, but he didn't cry out. Bone ground on bone, and then it was back in place.

"Done." Thardeight let out his breath, gasping.

"Here," Barielth said, over Mugahn's shoulder. He took the offered cloth and wrapped it around the leg and splints. "Sorry it took me so long, the stuff was spread from here halfway to Zirad."

Thardegith drew quick ragged breaths. "How does it feel?" Mughan asked.

"Like fire. I think I can walk though."

"Not happening. We've got the mushroom trunk so we'll make a crutch. Until then sit here and rest." Mughan wiped off his head and beard. Dirt mixed with sweat. "How is your leg?"

"I can walk on it," Yutatir said. He stood for confirmation.

"We should hunt them down, make sure their nest is wiped out," Barileth said. "If we don't, they'll escape and make trouble for us later."

Yutatir's eyes bulged. "We barely survived the first time." He gestured to his scratched and dented armor. "Or did you forget?"

"It won't take very long." Barileht looked out into the cavern and scratched his head. "Probably. We can split up, us three and you two, and be back before you know it."

"Is that the wisest idea?" Dozotaine asked, carving away at his makeshift crutch. Shavings of the trunk fell with every slice of his axe. He grimaced.

"We need to go back. Thardegith needs rest. We need rest." Yutatir pointed to his own leg. "Mughan, tell him."

"Let me think." Mughan tapped his chin. They had the door, they could lock it. On the other hand, it wouldn't be a nice surprise if these crawlers somehow found a way in.

"You can't be seriously considering it." Yutatir stared with eyes as big as the moon.

"Can you get him back on your own?" Mughan asked.

"No."

"It wouldn't be that hard," Barileth said. "Just a few feet up the mountain and back along the edge. You'd be back before dinner."

Yutatir pulled himself, all four feet of him. "I haven't been working the mines like you have. I'm afraid it wouldn't do."

Mughan considered, twirling his beard. "It can't be helped then. We'll go back together, rest up, and then regroup. Let's get the supplies in order first."

"What about if I go alone?" Barileth asked.

"No, too risky. We've survived, let's not push our luck now."

"Fine." They gathered their supplies, dividing the torn packs as best they could, and readied themselves. Before they did, Barileht went back to the battlefield. All eyes followed him as he knelt down beside the mass of crawlers.

"What are you doing?" Yutatir asked.

Barileth looked back and slung a crawler over each shoulder. "What does it look like?"

"Why?" Mughan asked.

A big grin split across his face. "They were so welcoming, trying to eat us and all. I figured I should invite them back for dinner."

17

DEEP CONVERSATION

"You were right, again." The hematite shone in the light of the candle, a great scar of it on the side of the tunnel. Dorian turned back to Yander.

He was frowning.

"You aren't pleased?"

"No."

Dorian broke off a big chunk, hefting it in his hand. "This will make a good load of iron or steel." It was cool in his hand, and rough.

"If we can get the flux."

"We'll find it. The others should be back soon with news of the cavern, a few days at most." The candle flickered, still sending up a small smoke trail that wavered and dissipated. "Come on, help me."

They dug it out, a few wheelbarrowfuls, and took it up to the mineshaft. They dumped it there, until they could get more help, and went back down.

"Tell me what you feel," Dorian said when they reached the lowest levels. He had thought about digging deeper to see if they could reach another rock layer, but hadn't decided yet.

Yander closed his eyes, breathing like Dorian had taught him, hands on the stone. His lips tightened. "More...iron ore. To our right."

"Deeper?"

Yander shook his head. "Up one level." He led and Dorian followed, up the stairs and into the exploratory tunnels. This one ended in a few feet, a quick dig that didn't yield results.

"It's pretty far up there." He pointed to the right. Dorian felt the wall. *Nothing.*

"Best get digging then." Dorian hefted his pickaxe and got to work. While he chipped away the wall Yander carted the stone away. They traded every few feet, getting some time to refresh and rest.

They made good time, eating into the mountain, and they worked in silence. Feet turned into yards.

Dorian thought about the explorers. What did they find? Did something else find them?

There was no way to prepare them, but he should have done better. Instead, he had wasted half the day trying to place the migrants into jobs that might or might not work.

What good was a weaver without enough yarn to spin? Should he have forced Kragnak to accept Gofrac? What if they didn't have time?

Time. It all came down to that.

Years wasted, years taken from him. All the time he could have spent with his wife, his children. Happy days, sad days, it was all gone.

And here he was, trying to fight for just a few more days, a few more weeks to see his children again.

And get back his love.

He had to get back to her. Take her back from the dwarf that stole her from him. He ground his teeth and funneled all his rage and anger into the pickaxe, sending chips flying.

One cut his cheek. He remembered her cheek, how soft and warm. The way it fit his hand. Her smile. Her touch. Her smell.

It took his breath away from him. He had to do it, he had to get her back.

But at the same time every fiber of his being raged at him, collected its voice and screamed at him.

No.

It wasn't right. It wasn't natural.

There is no other way.

He wouldn't let her go. His children needed their mother.

They certainly hadn't had a father. Another pang of sadness cut through his heart. All those years, his children were growing up without him. Becoming dwarves.

Another fear. Would they even remember him? After all this work, all this time?

Would they hate him? Blame him? Would they be turned against him, not even know who he was anymore?

The fear gnawed at him, and he tried to fill it with stone. The pickaxe rang, the stones fell, the tunnel advanced. He wrestled with his own thoughts, blood raging inside him.

He tried to hold it back, tried to think of some other way.

But he knew, like before, that there was only one way.

They dug deep into the mountain. As they did Dorian sensed the ore. Nonexistent, then faint, then loud enough he knew it was a big one.

"It's big," Yander said. Dorian grunted, swinging again. Chunks of rock fell.

"You heard that even though it was this far away?" Dorian asked.

"Yes." His face was drawn, almost gaunt beneath his beard. For a moment Dorian wished he had the old Yander back, even though that would mean a constant barrage of talk and questions.

It pained him to see him like this. He had to do something.

A rock shifted, revealing the ore behind. Now, it was more than a song. Dorian whistled. "This is going to take more than a few wheelbarrows."

He was smiling. They wouldn't be running out of iron anytime soon. Yander didn't share his excitement.

"It isn't gold. We don't have the flux to turn it to steel so what good is it?"

How can I break through to him?

Dorian took a deep breath, then shifted a chunk around until it was about the right height to sit on. He did another and sat.

"Sit here." He patted to the stone. Yander reluctantly joined him. His emotions still whirled, but he felt like he was in control of himself.

"You've had trouble before, but you're stronger now."

Yander looked down. They were both covered in stone dust. It had settled in the tunnel, leaving just a faint trace of its smell.

"I'm not sure how to say this." Dorian searched for the words, stroked his beard. "I have...had a wife, and I know what you're going through."

"Do you?"

"Yes. Since that night I've been thinking about it." He paused. "Usually every night."

"The truth is," Dorian continued. "We met on a mining expedition, just like you and Emelda. We were married, and finished our time there. I had earned enough to buy a place in Zirad, where it was safe."

"What was your wife's name?"

"Yolanda. She was sweet, and caring, and I didn't want anything to happen to her. Our first child was born in Zirad, and we raised him, but I grew bored and the money grew tight so I took another expedition."

The candle burned down and threatened to go out, so Dorian lit another. It flared up. "They came with me, but we were almost overrun with goblins. She almost died, and so did my son."

"Why are you telling me this?" Yander asked, turning back to face him. His eyes plead with him.

"So that you know you aren't alone." Dorian smiled a half smile. "I imagine that's why I took a liking to you, that I saw something of myself in you."

"I can't imagine that. You don't say anything." Yander's face cracked a little, and Dorian couldn't help but laugh.

"Not everything, just enough of a reminder. And I remember what it was like, to fear losing my wife and my son."

"So what did you do?"

"I protected her fiercely, and when that expedition was over we went back to Zirad. We had our second child, a girl, and were happy for a time."

Yander frowned. "But you went back, kept going on expeditions."

"Yes. Yolanda didn't want me to go, but I had to. Someone got it in their mind I was valuable. That every expedition I went on succeeded, where most failed. That I kept coming back with ore and riches.

"So we went, and we came back. Together, as a family. Until I was sent on an expedition far too dangerous for a family. Deep in the heart of goblin territory. Too far to protect, or even supply.

"My family stayed behind, like I asked. We started the expedition, succeeded, and were about to return. But they wanted me to stay.

"I did it on the condition that my family would come to be with me, that I could stay there with them." He didn't mean to go on like this, to reveal what he kept hidden for so long, but he couldn't help it.

The words poured out of him like molten metal out of the crucible, hot and fiery. How long had he tried to forget? Had he told anyone before?

"Yolanda left Zirad in the fall, long after the goblins should have been dormant. We thought it was safe. She left the children with her parents." His voice was even, monotone. Any hint of emotion would end him, and he knew it.

"What happened?"

"They killed them, to a dwarf." A long row of coffins. Marching down the street, guarded on every side. He guarded her in death, but not in life. "There were too many, and too few soldiers to defend her."

"I'm sorry." Yander stirred. He didn't know what to do, to say. Dorian knew that. He wouldn't either, if he was in his place.

"When I say I have some inkling of what you may be feeling, I know." Dorian stared hard at Yander. "You might feel alone, but you aren't. We've worked hard to make this place safe." *And I hope we've done enough.*

Yander shook his head. "I can't help feeling that we haven't done enough. That there is more."

How many times did he have to say it? Dorian forced his grief into anger and annoyance. "Good."

His head snapped up. "Good."

"If you felt adequate, you wouldn't be. It means you'll be driven to do more, to be better, every single day." Dorian locked eyes with Yander and leaned in close. "Never give up that feeling. Channel it. No matter how dark the night, no matter how hard the rock.

"There will always be more. More to do, more to say, more to be." He grabbed on to Yander, and held him. "So hold to it. Cling to it. Fear it. Love it."

"I don't know what to do."

"Prepare. Those who are prepared sometimes find that they have planned for the worst."

"But we're doing that already. You say I should feel this way, but it doesn't feel very good." Frustration played across his face, brows wrinkling, mouth tightening.

"I could have done more for my wife." Dorian took a deep, shuddering breath. "I could have asked for more guards. I should have asked for more guards. I should have been there with her, protecting her."

He squeezed his eyes shut. He didn't want to leave her behind, didn't want to go without them. And that bitter parting was the last memory he'd have of her.

All for a king that couldn't do it without him.

But he'd have her back again. "I won't lie to you, tell you it gets easier. It doesn't." Yander was looking at him with pleading eyes. Making him feel better wouldn't help any of them in the long run. "So bear the burden."

"Bear the burden," Yander repeated. His face softened, then hardened again.

"No matter what."

"Surrounded by enemies, bear the burden," Yander said. A half smile played on Dorian's lips.

"Yes, even then."

"I'll try to remember." He grabbed hold of his pickaxe and started to rise.

"See that you do. Oh, and Yander."

"Yes?"

"You won't need to bear it alone. You have me, and Emelda. Even Mughan might be able to lend a hand once in a while."

"I've been getting better, haven't I?"

"Only at fighting, and mining, and a few other things," Dorian said.

"It doesn't feel like it though." His grip tightened on his pickaxe.

"That might mean you have a ways to go, and that, even though you're getting better, you aren't there yet."

"Like a journey," Yander murmured.

"Like a journey."

"There isn't anything else you can teach me about the song, is there?"

Dorian smiled. "I've taught you everything you need to know." He pointed to his head. "Now you just have to take what's up here." He pointed to his chest. "To there."

"I--"

Faint ringing drifted down the tunnel. They exchanged glances. They ran for the stairs.

18

THE BELL TOLLS

Chapter Eighteen

Dorian and Yander ran, grabbing their axes resting a few yards up the tunnel, and rushed up the stairs.

"What is it?" Yander asked. "More migrants like last time?"

"No, I'm afraid not." *It's too early. Had they gotten through the pass already?* "Save your breath."

They had been at the bottom of the mine. Stairs stretched on for what seemed like forever, and Dorian was glad he was in the lead otherwise Yander would have left him behind long ago.

Despite his occupation, he had years on him and was feeling it now. Muscles burned, lungs burned. The only thing that didn't seem to burn was his mouth as he gulped down the cool, dry air.

The tunnels were empty when they reached the top, and they went to the barracks as decided long ago. The door was open and they burst into the room.

Everyone was there, weapons and armor at the ready.

And Mughan and the others were back.

"What's happened?" Yander asked as Dorian stopped to catch his breath. The cavern exploration group was covered in blood and battered like they had been hit by rocks.

And Thardegith was in the bed, bandages covering his leg.

"We were attacked," Mughan said calmly.

"Albino flesh crawlers," Barileth added, pointing to the bodies by the door. A wash of relief flooded through him as he realized all five were still here.

"You survived," Dorian said. "Good."

"We were raising the alarm to go back in," Mughan explained. "To take care of the rest of them, if we missed them."

Dorian confirmed their story with a quick glance. "Did you kill all that attacked you?"

"Yes."

"Then you've killed them all. They do everything as a pack." Dorian arched his eyebrow. "Why bring them back?"

"To eat, of course," Barileth said. Questions flew from the other dwarves, but Dorian waved his hand to stop them.

"Let them speak. Tell us about the cavern."

They went through the story, from the entrance to the battle.

"Mushroom trees?" Olgim said, eyes glimmering, when they recounted that part. "I have to see them."

Dorian listened closely, making mental notes, until they described the fight. He tried to hold his tongue.

"So we came back here to get help in hunting down the rest," Mughan said.

"That was foolish." Eyes swiveled to Dorian. "The entire pack took you by surprise." He shook his head. "You should have heard them coming, but you were making too much noise and had too much light."

Dozotaine didn't change expression. Barileth looked down, actually looked chastened.

Mughan's mouth tightened, and his eyes narrowed. "We managed all right in the end. But we need to hunt down the rest, if we're going to explore more of the cavern."

"You've killed them all."

"What?"

"They attack as a pack. If you killed them all, that's all there is." In some ways he should be thankful if that's the worst the cavern had to offer.

He still wasn't sure. "But if that's the way you're going to explore then we need to rethink going back in."

"We did the best we could." Mughan bristled, standing up. His hands were shaking.

Dorian didn't care about his ego. The stakes were higher than that. "We'll talk about it later."

"Mughan did a good job," Barileth said. "I'm not sure we would all be here if he didn't do what he did."

Strong praise, considering Barileth's opinion of the dwarf. He filed the thought away, even though he wasn't impressed. "They aren't silent creatures. Even if they were there had to be thirty, forty of them." He watched their eyes, and it confirmed his suspicion.

"So what are we going to do then?" Kimec asked.

"We need that flux," Kragnak said.

"He's right. The pass." Dorian shot Barileth a look. He shrugged in reply.

"We'll be finished with the defenses in a month, or less if we have every dwarf lend a hand." Dorian raised his hands as protests flowed toward him. "It seems like the most prudent path."

"Walls will only hold if they have good dwarves with good weapons defending them." Mughan stood up.

"We have enough crossbows to hold back an attack."

"And what if they break through?" Mughan asked. "We have to go back in the cavern. We need that steel."

"It looks like you all came out well with the iron armor." Dorian eyed the marks and scratches. None of them penetrated, whatever had made the marks. Bone weapons, he guessed.

"The steel isn't only for ourselves," Barileth said, voice low.

What if there was something else out there? Something bigger and more dangerous?

He kept going back to that night, the attack on the mine. He should have protected them then, and he needed to do it now.

But with the flesh crawlers gone, the chance of that happening was low.

For now.

"Let me go," Yander said. "I'll go get my armor and be ready in a few minutes."

"See to them," Dorian said. "You need to have your wounds looked at. Even you Barileth." He had the least amount of dwarven blood on him, but the most flesh crawler.

"They live in peaceful caves. Likely moved in a year ago after the spider attack." The others watched him as he helped take Mughan's armor off, layer by layer. "We'll have some time before the next group moves in, or something worse."

"How did they get there?" Hatheck asked, eyes wide.

"Either another cavern or from the surface." Metal rattled as the breastplate came off and they set it off to the side. He asked for a bucket of water and Emelda ran off. "We don't need to go back down today.

We'll regroup, resupply and go back in a few days after everyone's rested."

"Won't take more than a day," Barileth said. "The sooner, the better."

"More than a day might be warranted." Dorian watched as Yudoline examined the field dressing. Thardegith winced as she prodded and unwrapped. His leg was a dirty brown and red mess. Dozotaine's head didn't look much better. "In the meantime, can you fix these?"

Kragnak evaluated the offered breastplate, running his hand along the dent. "Not too deep. It won't take long." He dropped his voice, getting close to Dorian. "Steel wouldn't have been damaged at all."

"We'll find it." Dorian returned his attention to Mughan and Barileth, while Yudoline treated the others with the help of a few deputized dwarves, including Emelda. The bucket of clean water she had soon ran dark.

"I want you to rest. We'll form another party to search the cavern."

Mughan's eyes narrowed. "I want to go back in there."

"I'm not sure that's prudent. I sent you in there without preparing you."

"There wasn't anything to prepare for," Barileth said. "Other than a new food source."

"And I don't like the insinuation." Mughan crossed his arms, brows lowered.

"No fault is assigned other than to me, no offense is meant. But I can't afford to take another risk like that. Thardegith is useless now for the next few weeks. That's a burden we can't repeat."

"So you're going in without us?"

Dorian stroked his beard. "I don't know yet. But it sounds like we need a good dwarf here to keep things going. Are you up to the task?"

Mughan's face brightened, and his posture relaxed. "Could be, if you needed it."

"We have a lot to do here. Let me think on it while we get these taken care of." Dorian turned his attention to the flesh crawler bodies. "Barileth needs some help taking care of these, and I need everyone else to go back to work."

Olgim volunteered to help, with Mughan, as those not commandeered by Yudoline to help with the wounded went back to their respective tasks.

They dragged the corpses back to the kitchen. Barileth sharpened a knife and directed a stack to hang near the fire.

"It's going to get messy," he warned, eying the sharp blade. "Anyone with a queasy stomach should leave now."

"Let's get on with it," Dorian said, taking his own knife. The mine would have to wait, and any chance of finding flux stone with it. "On the bright side we'll eat well tonight."

He carved up the flesh crawler, dumping the blood and anything unfit to eat in a bucket for Olgim to empty outside. Barileth was faster and better at it, but no one other than him had the experience.

"These might be too tough to eat," Barileth said, whistling while he worked. "But it beats hunting. My prey has learned too well it's dangerous to be around here."

"We can't live on chickens," Dorian agreed. With only a few kids, the goats wouldn't be producing meat for a while either. "But the flesh crawlers are meat eaters. They must have had something around to help them."

Olgim hauled in the empty bucket, exchanging it for the one they had filled. "Did I hear something about meat?" He perked up, his rotund belly significantly smaller than when he arrived.

"I can't promise anything," Dorian said, cutting off a haunch and adding it to the pile. Barileth was already on his fourth crawler.

"I wish you could." Olgim sighed, then waved his hands at Barileth's look. "Not that I'm complaining. The rockbread is good, and there's always more than I can eat of it." He stared longingly at the pile of meat. "It's just been a while since I had a good pork chop."

A half-finished tub of rockbread dough sat by the fire, well away from their pile of meat. The thought of a good chop, covered in salt and drizzled in butter, made Dorian's mouth flood with saliva.

"This will last a few weeks, at least." They needed different types of food. The dwarves could only eat the same thing day in and day out for so long. Eventually one of them would snap, which could prove disastrous. "It sounds like there will be more food sources in the caverns."

"The mushrooms we saw would be a good addition," Barileth said. He wiped his hands off, finishing more than his portion of the butchering. Now the smell of blood and meat mixed with the smoke of the fire. "And there had to be more."

"I suspect there is." Dorian made his final cut. The work was harder than it looked. "Put those away and get them preserved." The others should have been done with the injured by now. "Olgim, would you check on Yudoline?"

Olgim went, and Dorian and Barileth took seats to rest on nearby barrels.

"How did Mughan do," Dorian said. "Really?"

"Not as bad as I feared." Barileth leaned back. "It was my fault. I should have heard them coming, or smelled them. The things give off an odor you could track a mile away."

Dorian leaned forward. He wasn't sure what to think. He was surprised he had said that earlier. Was he ready to leave Mughan in charge?

"It isn't wrong not to trust him," Barileth said.

"Hmm."

"I'm not too fond of him myself. Always puffing himself up too much. Thinks too highly of himself."

"That can be fixed."

Barileth grinned. "You want to bring him down, just enough?"

"I'm still deciding." Dorian shook his head. "We need every dwarf we can lay our hands on. The early migration was a boon, and one I won't forget, but we're too few for my comfort."

"And the ones here aren't make of firm enough stuff," Barileth said. He cocked his head. "Looks like they finally decided to show up and make some food. I'm starving." He reached over and plucked a potato from a sack.

Dorian heard the footsteps too. "Spring is almost over and soon summer will be here soon. I'll be surprised if we're not attacked by then."

"And if we aren't?" Barileth took a bite, crunching into the brown flesh. It dripped into his beard as he chewed.

"Then I expect we'll have a fight that might not be winnable." Dorian slapped his thighs and stood. "Either way, I'll make sure we're ready."

"You're going back in, aren't you?" Barileth tossed him a potato. Dorian caught it and rubbed off a chunk of dirt. The other dwarves streamed in the kitchen, with Yudoline in the front and Olgim taking up the rear.

"We're going back in Barileth. I'm taking you with me." *And Yander, too. I just hope he's ready for it.*

19

Into the Dark

Chapter Nineteen

How long has it been?

Dorian stared at his armor arrayed on his bed. Candlelight glinted off the reflective surface of the metal. He reached out a tentative hand.

Cool. All the warmth fled from his fingers. He pulled the breastplate off the bed and put it on, letting the weight settle on his shoulders. He knew he shouldn't take too much time, that the others would be waiting.

Two parts excitement, one part fear. It flowed through him like molten metal. The first entry had been done already, but the cavern was still fresh. Still unexplored.

Still wild.

The armor clanked as he put it on, one piece at a time, until all that remained was the helmet and his axe.

He flexed his fingers in the gloves, listening to the creak of the leather and scrape of the metal.

Lost in a moment, he remembered all the other caverns. All the other expeditions. The fights, the discoveries. What would this one hold?

Dorian stuck his axe in its loop and donned the helmet, cool against his head. The feeling disappeared halfway down the stairs as it warmed to his body.

Yander was already there, with Emelda, talking in hushed tones in the corner. Emelda touched his arm as she whispered. Yander turned slightly, not avoiding her but not accepting her either. He wore a frown but nodded to Dorian.

The door leered at him. He kept his distance from it and the lovers as he waited. The others trickled in, Barileth first. Mughan was right behind him, then Dozotaine and Fimroul. Hatheck lugged the packs and dumped it.

There was an air of anticipation, but no one spoke. Mughan checked his armor, cinching down a few straps and making some adjustments.

It felt better. "Thanks. Try not to burn the place down while I'm gone."

"By the time you're back you won't recognize the place. Give me a few extra dwarves and we'd have a palace to rival the Emerald Palace." His smile was tense.

"Everyone ready?"

Yander walked away from Emelda, not giving her a look back. She watched him go, a hand trying to grasp him and then sharply withdrawn.

As if she were hurt.

Faint lines sprouted around her eyes, but she hid it well. The other dwarves affirmed that they were ready and they all donned their pack.

"Out we go." Dorian nodded to Mughan and Hatheck, who spun the lock and opened the door.

His hand found comfort in his axe, and Dorian took a deep breath. His mind went blank as he stared at the darkness.

That day. The screams.

Death.

"Dorian," Barileth whispered, nudging him softly.

"Let's go." Dorian's voice was strong, for that he was grateful. He strode forward, not breathing as his foot crossed the threshold.

And then he was in.

But nothing happened.

Dorian kept walking, not bothering to look back at the others. Their footsteps followed, then were swallowed by the mossy floor.

"Barileth, take lead." Dorian fell back, letting him lead through the twisting tunnel, and fell in step with Yander.

"She didn't want you to go."

Yander looked away. "No." The tunnel opened up as they walk, the edge of the cliff dropping into the cavern beyond. Faint traces of golden moss.

"This is a big one," Dorian said. He estimated its size around three or four miles, maybe more.

"We'll follow this for a while," Barileth said, "Then go down."

"Awful long way down." Fimroul peered over the side, dangerously close to the edge. Dozotaine grabbed him and pulled him back.

"Not wise," Dozotaine said, as rocks clattered down the steep slope. Fimroul swallowed hard and nodded.

They went down the path, hugging the cavern wall.

"What do you feel down here?" Dorian asked. An opening this large was always disorienting, having been among the song of the earth so long just to hear it silent.

Yander frowned. "Not much. I don't think I can feel as well."

Dorian nodded. "That's usual."

He dragged his hand along the wall. "Still a lot of granite." Yander furrowed his brow. "Gems farther in. No ore."

"Feel through your feet too."

"You can do that?"

"Not as well. It takes more concentration."

Yander nodded, concentrating, and they kept walking.

They got to the slope where they had descended earlier. The ground was churned and kicked up.

"Down we go?" Dorian asked.

"How did you know?" Barileth feigned surprise and led the way down.

"Extinguish the torches. We go in the dark."

"Are you sure?" Fimroul asked.

Dorian nodded. "We'll take some time to acclimate." The torches hissed as they thrust them into the dirt, going out one by one.

The last plunged them into complete darkness. Around him the dwarves breathed. Short, tight breaths, Fimroul he guessed, everyone else a touch too fast.

His eyes adjusted, then allowed him to see outlines. There was enough golden moss in the cavern to allow them to see, even Fimroul.

"I'm starting to make out shapes," Fimroul said, relieved.

"How is everyone else doing?" Dorian asked. They could all see now, and Dorian started down the slope.

They followed, dirt and rock sliding ahead and around them, until it evened out.

"Careful, we didn't get all of them," Barileth said. Dorian was seeing better, and could move around the bodies. He warned the others and knelt down to check the ground.

"Barileth, over here." He joined him. "Can you track them?"

"Easy, for now. Once we get back to the ambush point, I'll need some light."

Dorian nodded. Flesh crawlers weren't known for flying so he expected Barileth would find them.

He was right, the tracks were easy enough for Dorian to track back to the ambush point.

"This is it." Barileth stopped and looked around.

"We'll rest here while Barileth picks up the tracks." Dorian walked over to the mushroom while the others dropped their packs and drank from their skins.

He touched the trunk, scraped some off and smelled it. Earthy, with a hint of decay. The crown rose up high enough to fit three of him under.

"What is it?" Yander asked.

"Black Oakshroom. Haven't seen a grove this mature in a while." He looked up, examining the gills underneath the cap. A memory tickled him, just out of reach.

"Over here," Barileth said. "They came this way." They gathered their things, regrouped, and followed him.

"I hear water," Yander said.

"There's a stream up ahead." Barileth led them, following the tracks.

"That's good, right?"

"Depends on what's in it." Dorian stepped over a chunk of moss. "It could be a good source of fish. Or it could just be a quagmire filled with danger."

"Let's hope it's the first one," Fimroul said. Dorian pictured his grimace, and couldn't help but smile.

"More likely than not."

"Where does it come from?" Yander asked. "We don't have a spring anywhere above us."

Dorian shook his head, then remembered they probably couldn't see that well. "We're deep enough it isn't the snow melt. Could be some sort of aquifer with too much pressure. Water tends to make its way where it wants, despite the obstacles."

"It would be from below us? How deep could it get?" Yander stopped, held up by Barileth who was checking the trail. The moss on the ground made it hard for Dorian to track the flesh crawlers.

He was glad Barileth could. "All depends on the aquifer. I've seen them come nearly to the surface, and some hundreds of feet down."

"This way." Barileth turned them to the right. The water was louder now, a trickle turned into a flow. It sounded like they were moving along with the stream now.

And the mushrooms were thinning out. Dorian let the conversation die out naturally. They needed to be quieter.

Or so he told himself.

Instead, he kept going back to his memories. Lost in thought and confronted by the past, it seemed like the worst came to mind.

His failings. His lashing out.

His sentence.

He was glad of the gentle crush of their footsteps upon the moss, thicker now that the mushrooms were behind them.

And now there was enough golden moss to give them light. The other dwarves were visible, their features tight and drawn.

Except Barileth, who looked eager. Dorian was surprised he wasn't rubbing his hands with anticipation.

And then he heard it.

"What was that?" Fimroul's voice wavered as he stuttered to a stop. Dorian smiled and exchanged a glance with Barileth.

"Shhh." Barileth put a finger to his lips. He crouched down, and Dorian followed his lead.

Fimroul swallowed loudly. They advanced, hunched over and cautious, toward the sound and a shape looming out of the darkness.

Shapes moved in the darkness up ahead, dancing and shifting. Dorian tingled with anticipation, trying not to laugh. There was another sound.

"It knows we're here," Barileth said, a look of horror on his face. Fimroul lagged. A deep, pungent smell wafted through his nose so heavy he tasted it.

"Wait." Yander stood up. "I know what that is." He squinted into the dark, then pointed. "They're over there."

"What is it?" Fimroul retreated.

"Cave cows." As if on cue, one mooed and grunted, the sound they had heard earlier. Barileth and Dorian burst out laughing.

"Light the torch." Dorian walked to the shape after he recovered, belly aching and threats of more laughing barely held back.

"I thought..." Yander trailed off.

"We're at their nest. Like I said, they killed them all." Dorian shrugged. "Otherwise they would have attacked."

Sparks flew, and the torch flared up. Dorian held a hand over his eyes, temporarily blinded by the light. He licked his sweaty lips as they adjusted, salty.

The eyes of the cave cows glowed yellow, reflecting the torch, as they surveyed the dwarves.

"What are we going to do with all those?" Fimroul asked, mouth agape.

"Eat them," Barileth said. "I hope."

"That's an idea. The flesh crawlers were going to." Dorian searched through the crude lean-to, hewn from the trunks of the Oakshrooms. Filth and mold wafted from under it.

"They keep them as pets?" Yander asked, staring over the mushroom fencing. He leaned against it to watch them.

"As a source of food." Dorian pushed aside a bunch of moss, revealing a depression. He knelt down and scooped up a bunch of the crumbly, wet substance. "They'll eat the oldest cows."

He took a bite. Rich and moldy. "This batch is almost ready too."

"What is it?" Yander and Fimroul wandered over.

"Cheese. They milk them, and ferment the excess in the ground." There were a few more covered holes, with batches at various stages. The others tried some.

"I'll be." Fimroul's eyes opened with delight as he chewed. "That's not half bad." Some crumbles dribbled in his beard.

"Steaks. This is a good day." Barileth smiled. "What else do we have?"

"Hold on, not quite yet." Dorian frowned. Something wasn't right, but he couldn't put his finger on it.

"What are these?" Yander held up an adolescent Oakshroom cap. He was standing next to a stack of them, covered in mold and dirty milk stains.

"Buckets. Flesh crawlers aren't the best toolmakers, but they do for milking." There were bed caves carved behind the lean-to, but no flesh crawlers. "We caught them before mating season. That's good."

"Mating season?" Yander peered into the caves.

"We need to go take a look at that stream." The water trickled from somewhere behind the cows, who by now had lost interest in the newcomers and were grazing on the moss. "I bet they were using it as a water source for the cows."

"Right. Let's go then, the sooner we get these cows home the better off we'll be." Barileth swung around.

Then, the thought that had been tickling him at the back of his mind came to the forefront. *What am I going to do about this?*

"We can't get them back to the mine." Dorian struck the hard, rough post of the lean-to. The entire thing shook a little, rained down bits of debris on the party. It had taken them hours to get this far.

It wasn't a light walk that a dwarf could just run down and back from.

Barileth swung around. "What? Why not?"

Dorian shook his head, then turned back to look where they came. "I don't know how we're going to get them up that slope."

20

QUARTER

Chapter Twenty

"We'll just drive them up," Barileth said. "It can't be that hard."

Dorian shook his head. "It was too steep. They'll never make it up." He eyed the herd. "They can survive where they're at, but someone will need to come down and milk them once a day, at least."

"Who's going to do that?" Yander asked.

The flesh crawlers had set up a large pasture, one side the stream just large enough to keep the cows from crossing. The moss snapped as they grazed on it, sending wafts of the musty smell all around them.

"That's a problem for later." He didn't want to tell them he didn't know how they were going to do that. "Since we're down here, we might as well do what we came to do."

"This is all granite here," Barileth said. The moss had been scraped off the rock by the previous occupants, and Dorian ran his hand along the cool, rough surface.

"Through and through." He looked up at Yander. "What do you hear?"

Yander closed his eyes, and concentrated. The rock sang under Dorian's hand, a few interesting chords here and there, but nothing of note. "Not much."

"So what do we do now?" Fimroul asked. Dorian's stomach grumbled.

"Take a break and eat." Dorian sloughed off his pack and took a seat on the ground.

"Can't say no to that." Barileth took a scoop of the cheese with a chunk of rockbread. Dorian liked the idea and tried it himself.

The crumbly cheese went well with the rockbread, softening it and adding a hint of tang. Dorian chewed his as the others struck up a conversation.

"Do you think that river leads to a waterfall?" Fimroul asked.

"Ha! That, a river?" Barileth shook his head. "It's barely a spring."

"Oh." Fimroul's eyes dropped to the floor. "I've always wanted to see a waterfall. Ever since I heard about the Great Falls of Seratath."

"I've never heard of that before," Yander said.

"They're the largest in Zirad," Dorian said. "Over three hundred feet tall, through the Seratath mountains. The mist alone rises up more than fifty feet in the air."

Fimroul's eyes shot up and gleamed. "You've been there?"

"Once." The rush of water so great he felt it in his heart, the fresh smell of mist. Even the taste of the water as it condensed on his lips. "They used to have contests to climb the rock face next to it. They would throw these hooks up to catch the outcroppings, climb a rope, then do it again."

"Sounds crazy." Barileth smiled. "I like it."

He would never forget that moment.

"Is it really as great as they say?"

"More." Dorian took a swig of his ale, letting the bubbles pop on his tongue.

"When was that?" Barileth asked. There was an undercurrent to his tone, and he didn't make eye contact. It was too smooth.

Dorian shot him a sharp look. "Long ago. What about you Barileth, have you done any traveling in your soldiering days?"

"Just like you, I suppose. A bit here, a bit there."

"Tell us about it."

"I'd rather not."

"Too many graves in the past?"

Barileth bit off a chunk of rockbread viciously. "Too few."

That ended the conversation. They finished their food, consolidated the supplies, and arose.

"We'll go farther in, down slope. We might get lucky." Dorian strapped on his pack, the weight once again crushing against his shoulders. He would be glad to leave the flesh crawler encampment and its underlying smell of death and filth.

"Follow the river?" Dozotaine asked.

Dorian nodded.

They set out, trampling the moss and lichen that grew in the dark. The air was still and cool. Other than the sound of the stream, it was quiet.

They walked for hours, stopping every so often to check the rock. The cavern went down at a steady rate, only dropping or leveling out in a few places.

The moss thinned, patches of golden moss lighting the way for them, and the rock turned to grains of sand.

At another stop Dorian dug through the shallow layer of sand and weak moss. He rubbed a few grains together between his fingers. It was rough, and fine.

"We might be getting close," he said, standing back up.

"I think we should go over there." Yander pointed away from the stream, which had widened thanks to a few more additions.

"What do you feel?"

"Nothing. It's just a hunch, I suppose."

Dorian looked around at the group. "Any objections?"

"What if we get lost?" Fimroul asked.

"We'll follow the noise back to the stream," Barileth said. "We aren't getting anywhere this way. At this rate we'll have to sleep down here."

"A few more hours of this and I'll want to," Fimroul said.

"Let's go. We can rest later." Dorian veered them away, into the darkness and away from their landmark.

They hadn't gone more than half an hour when the crunch of their footsteps turned to padding on stone and moss again.

"Hold on." Dorian stopped the group and turned to Yander. He nodded.

Yander stepped forward and dropped his pack. He carefully knelt down, hesitated, and scraped back the moss covering. "It's not granite."

The others let out a deep breath.

"What is it?" Fimroul asked.

"Light the torch." Dorian dropped down beside Yander, helping him to brush back the trailing moss from the slick surface.

Wafts of the green, damp aroma of moss rolled off it, particularly pungent. Dorian wiped the sweat from his brow as the click of the tinder flared up a torch.

He smiled.

"Is that...?"

"Yes." The surface was creamy white, with streaks of black and flecks of gray. Dorian sensed something else and put his hand on the rock's surface.

It was faint, but it was there. Tiny grains of it, more or less.

"It's beautiful," Yander said.

"What is it?" Fimroul asked.

"Marble," Barileth said. "And it looks like lots of it."

"Can you feel it?" Dorian asked.

Yander furrowed his brows, stroking his beard. He touched the rock again. "Yes...I can."

"That's gold." Dorian smiled, and his heart soared.

"Gold!" Fimroul's face broke out in a smile, and he started to dance, spluttering the torch he was holding everywhere. The others raised their voices. "Sorry."

"It's good news." Dozotaine stood with crossed arms, but even he looked happy.

"That's better than flux stone." Fimroul looked around as everyone laughed. "What's so funny?"

"Marble is flux stone." Barileth slapped him on the back, almost making him fall. "We've found more than what we've come for."

"Oh." His face broke back into a big smile.

"This is a good day." Dorian took his pickaxe out and started breaking chunks out with Yander as the others cleared the moss away.

There was more than enough, a field of it at least. Enough to warrant a proper excavation. Dorian stopped, wiping back his hair, the feeling of fine marble grit on his hand, and glowed.

"I've been listening to this." Yander pulled out a transport sized chunk, letting it fall to the ground. Puffs of dust scattered. "I think I have its sound now."

"Could you find it again?"

Yander looked concerned at first, then a grin spread across his face. "Yes. I feel it now."

Dorian smiled. "Good. With enough luck we'll have plenty more to go after when we get back to the mine."

"That's the thing. I think with our twists and turns we aren't that far from the mine. Or at least not so far we couldn't come back here from inside."

Not that far. Dorian stopped, stroking the rough whiskers of his beard. Most of their journey was spent picking their way through the landscape, and stopping more frequently than he wanted to check the rock beneath them.

Yander could be right. They might not be that far from the mine. It had been a few years since he had been this far out, and he had to conceded to himself that he was rusty.

Age and confinement had taken its toll. He was a young dwarf no longer.

"That would be good news if it is." He turned back to the others. "All right, everyone pick up as much as they can and take it back. A few good chunks will last the smithy."

"Carry it back?" Fimroul blanched.

"What do you think we were going to do with it? Throw it?" Barileth sidled up beside the dwarf.

"No, I suppose not." Barileth handed Fimroul a big chunk.

"Here, you start and we'll follow."

"You lead the way Barileth." Dorian shot him a warning glance, to which Barileth only grinned.

"Fine. Should have left our gear at the outpost."

That was a good idea. They wouldn't need as much now. Dorian breathed deep of the damp, musty cavern air. A weight was off his shoulders, and he would sleep better tonight than he had in months.

But then, that tickle at the back of his mind kicked in. He would get to see her. Once more, just to say goodbye.

"Dorian, everything all right?" Yander was beside him, and he shook some of the thoughts away.

"Move out, the faster we're back, the better." He slung his own chunk of smooth marble against his back, and the party set forth.

It was slow going, carrying as much stone as they were. Frequent breaks were necessary, but the spirits of the party never dampened.

There was even conversation, and a little laughter, as Barileth told a few war stories. His lips were looser than they used to be.

At the flesh crawler outpost they dropped their unneeded supplies and hurried the rest of the way back. It was late by the time they arrived, and only the dwarf assigned to watch would be awake.

So Dorian dropped his load and unlocked the door, swinging it open with a whisper.

"Good to be back home," Barileth said.

"Agreed." Home. I haven't had one of those in a while. Dorian realized it was true, and had been for some time. This is where he belonged, this was his family. The thought made him sad and happy at the same time. "Everyone inside."

"You think we want to stay out here?" Fimroul huffed across the threshold, kicking up stone dust that tickled his nose and almost made him sneeze. "I'm exhausted."

"Sleep after work, take it up to the forge and then we'll be done for the night," Dorian said. Fimroul groaned, but led the group back to the winch.

It took a few more minutes to get them all up to the forge, but after that they had five chunks of marble lined up in the red glow of the still warm coals.

"Ain't that a sight to see." Barileth's eyes shined in the light, reflecting the red and making him seem otherworldly. The smell of the forge fire smoke still lingered in the air, thick enough to taste. Without a word the dwarves went back to their beds, and slept.

Shouts woke Dorian the next morning. He smiled when he realized they were good. Blinking the sleep from his eyes, he dressed and went to the workshop.

Flames leapt from the forge, kicked up by a fervor of joy. Kragnak was urging Thurbag and Gofrac on at the bellows, blowing great gouts of air into the forge.

"Dorian, look!"

"I know." Others had gathered, eager to see what the commotion was.

"We'll have steel now. Think of it, real steel!" He had prepared a crucible, and almost knocked it over in his haste and wild flailing. He crushed the marble, throwing the mixture into the crucible, then turned his attention to the sand beside the forge.

In it he set depressions, bars that would soon house the cooling steel. He built a main trench that split and fed each of his forms, and then it was ready.

"Never seen him this wild," Kimec murmured at Dorian's elbow, meant only for him.

"Let him enjoy it. We all need something to look forward to." They talked, and Dorian joined them, as hungry as he was. He slipped out and brought back a tray of food to distribute.

While the smiths worked the others ate. Cold meats and goat cheese, with leftover rockbread that was hard but still soft and golden on the inside.

And Kragnak smelted. Iron and flux went in together, and the crucible was thrust into the fire. Licks of red and white and yellow pelted the crucible, and Kragnak urged it all on.

Soon the smell of melting metal mixed with the food, and interesting combination that still excited him. Dorian brushed away the crumbs of his breakfast on his scratchy tunic and rose.

The metal was liquid now, flowing and bubbling bright yellow. Kragnak scraped the top of it, pulling out chunks and tossing them aside as if they were trash.

"Slag," he explained to the others. Sweat ran down his head and neck from the heat of the forge, but he couldn't lose that smile.

"Save it. There's gold in it," Dorian said. Kragnak nodded and kept working. Gofrac fell off the bellows, gasping for air, and Dorian took his place. Up and down they went, until Kragnak told them it was ready.

He and Thurbag pulled the crucible out of the oven with big tongs, one on each end, and upended it onto the form.

Liquid steel poured from its mouth, flowing down the main runner and hissing. Steam from the damp sand billowed into his face and mouth, hot and moist on his lips, and the metal ran into the forms where they lost their color and started to cool.

Dorian looked on with satisfaction. With this they would fulfill their contract. With this they would make arms to protect themselves.

With this he would see his children.

21

THE CLOUDLESS SKY

Down into the mine Yander went, carrying light and pickaxe. The air was all the same temperature down here, cool.

Each step took him deeper into the mountain, farther from the sun and the air above, but he didn't mind. Something shone in him, anticipated this moment, and relished it.

The sound of gold.

He couldn't get it out of his head. Even as his feet scraped against the rock and his torch gave off flickers of light the song played in his mind.

Not knowing where to go, except for a vague sense of where the cavern was, Yander let himself be taken, wandering the tunnels and feeling the rough stone of the walls beneath his fingers.

He closed his eyes and let all his consciousness flow into the mountain around him, listening to the song of stone. The granite was the most prevalent voice, but even in that he could sense slight discontinuities with gems or precious stones.

Breath ran through him, fluttering his mustache. He reached deeper, he reached farther. There was more than just gems here.

A way and down to his left was a group of iron, a small vein, but there nonetheless. Something else, copper he thought, was off to his right, and up a level or to.

But it was the song of gold he searched for, listened for, ached for.

With gold he could buy safety for Emelda. He could leave this place and travel the world. He could settle down.

And when he found it they would have more steel. More armor, more weapons. Thick, and unyielding, but still light. It would repulse the rotten arms of the dead and protect them.

His legs still took him through the tunnels, even as his eyes shut. The sound of the rock let him see, let him avoid rocks in front of him.

Then, far ahead of him, he thought he heard it. Fainter than a butterfly's wings on the wind.

He tried listening again, stopping where he was.

It was gone.

Yander frowned, and opened his eyes. He lost it.

But what was it that Dorian had taught him? To give up? He shook his head.

No. How often he had come to that before, and just dug for the sake of it.

No.

He took a deep breath, calmed his mind, and tried again.

Let the song flow through you, Dorian had said. Yander planted his feet and did so, reaching out around him.

Through the granite and the ore the song came. There, he heard it again, somewhere up ahead and a little to the right. He was sure of it.

His eyes flashed open. The torch still sent it's smoke trail up, snaking around his head and tickling his nose with its smell.

Yander smiled and got to work.

The pickaxe rang against the stone. Chunks of it crashed to the floor, and he stepped over them to get to the next one.

His tunnel was rough, but it aimed right for the sound he had heard. Each day he dug as far as he could before stopping.

Dorian heard reports every morning before he returned to his work, catching him before he left. He came back too late to speak with anyone except Emelda.

As he got closer he got a better feel for it, and his muscles sang with use. Down he went, just a slight pitch, to get to it. Working on a few hours of sleep each night Yander advanced into the earth.

Days slipped by, then weeks, until his sense of it sharpened.

He knew then that he was getting close.

It was like pebbles scattered into the water, tiny sounds that merged and grew. But now the sound got louder with every foot he advanced into the rock.

He didn't know how long he dug, covered in stone dust and sweat. He dug until his arms ached and his legs protested, and kept digging.

Then, the song changed. The deep feeling of granite was lighter here, and he smiled.

A few feet more and the dark gray yielded to white. He stopped then, gasping to catch his breath into burning lungs.

Stone dust covered him everywhere, and he shook it off into the tunnel as he stumbled back and fell to a sitting position.

There it was. White and gray. Specks of gold were in it, mixed in but not visible. But he could hear them.

"This is it," he said. All of his pain and frustration surfaced, beaten by a sense of accomplishment. "We will survive."

A crow circled up above, screaming at them. Dorian shielded his eyes from the sun and watched it make lazy circles.

And in his stomach a ball of dread grew.

Only when it went east did he relax, turning his attention back to the horizon and the sinking sun.

The others were finishing up down below, laying the last of the rocks on the southern wall before turning to sleep.

He would keep watch tonight. The sunset was lackluster, a quick dip to below the horizon on a cloudless sky. With it went the warmth, the cool night breeze wicking away his warmth.

Dorian scanned the mountains, then walked to the other side of the watchtower. He leaned on the smooth stone window, looking down over their handiwork.

The wall was almost complete, all except the crenelations. Both towers were finished also, and only the roof of the pressing room was left.

Cherry trees grew in the ground now, planted months before when they had a chance to find young saplings to transplant farther down the valley.

Beside it grew the above ground crops, alive with green in the day and casting odd shadows in the night. A silvery moon gleamed on the twisting leaves as they rippled in the wind.

What else to do, other than wait? Dorian adjusted his grip on the crossbow, thinking about the necromancer out there in the world. Early autumn and he still hadn't come.

It was up to Kragnak, then, to finish the arms. He had provided the raw materials, and the others would have to finish it.

Dorian watched the stars, wondering if his children were watching them. Did they see the Hammer and Anvil, pride of the smiths? Or did they watch Artu the Goat crossing the Mountain like he was now?

They twinkled and blinked, millions of them, and the night stretched on. The chill grew colder, and Dorian wrapped his coat around himself, listening to the rustle of the trees down the valley and smelling the ripe smell of near harvest.

What would life be like in Zirad again? Would he stay in a place filled with so many memories?

Or would he leave with his family, travel east or north to friendly lands. Lands that welcomed dwarves and gave them a place to live and a meal to eat in exchange for another hand at the pickaxe.

How would he do that with his children?

With a start, he realized that they weren't younglings anymore. Xanther had to be thirty years old, or more, with Ruby right behind him.

They would have their own lives, and he wasn't part of it. They might even have their own families, their own children.

Dorian ran a hand down his beard, distressed at the realization. The time had fled him, and it was not on his side now.

Ruby wouldn't be the same small dwarf, bouncing on his knee next to the fire and giggling away. She would be tall, like her mother, and graceful.

And Xanther, no longer the dirt covered child with a light mist of stubble on his cheeks. So eager to join in the digging, and so poor a digger at first. Would he be doing something else?

He felt that all that was left of his life was locked away in the crypt with Yolanda. If he could get to her, bring her back, she would help him.

She would know what to do.

She always had. When a child was sick, she was there. When he came back from his expeditions, she was there. Always with a smile, always with a warm hand and a careful word.

He buried his hands in his head and slumped back. *Oh, how I miss her.* Grief washed over him in waves, threatening to overwhelm him.

So long without hope, there was one with power over the dead. One that threatened them.

But one that gave him an opportunity as well.

He could steal that power, and use it as his own. He would bring her back and make everything right.

He had to, not just for himself, but for his children. They needed a mother again. And he needed his wife.

Dorian lifted his head, watching the stars twinkle. She had loved them too, when she had a chance. "Like little fires in the sky," she had said "our own pebble lights."

Off in the distance an owl hooted, and wings flapped in the dying wind. Now the air was stale and dry, rough against his throat, the morning not far off.

Time had slipped away from him this night too.

He remembered his duty, scanning the terrain for signs of the enemy, or any other enemy that might threaten them.

Thurbag came up to relieve him. Dorian stretched his arms, feeling a stiffness in them and in his back.

"Morning," Thurbag said. "It's going to be a warm day, isn't it?"

"It is."

"Breakfast is good."

Dorian briefed him on the surroundings and left him to watch, his knees creaking as he descended the stairs.

The dining hall was mostly empty, just Emelda and Nofibela already at work smoothing. Dorian appreciated the work she had already done on the floors, now smooth and level. The tables didn't rock anymore.

He greeted them and tore into the eggs and mushrooms, spreading a thick layer of butter on a still warm loaf of rockbread.

"Quiet night?" Emelda whisked away the leftover dishes, leaving him the plates of food. He nodded. Her smile was tense, almost forced.

"As quiet as ever." In some sense he wished they were attacked, it would mean the end of waiting for it. All the preparation, all the work set to their defenses would come to a stop.

But then they could focus their work elsewhere, from safety to building industry, or more.

Dorian watched Nofibela work, chiseling with a smooth hand and a steady clink of the chisel on the rock. After there was enough rock chips she would brush it away.

Her aim was smooth, and she never went back over a section of rock she touched. It was almost glass smooth, a minor ripple or imperfection here or there if you really focused on it.

As he finished his meal she stopped to rest.

"Where did you learn that?"

She smiled. "Most of it was from doing under my teacher, Stigian Rockteller."

"He taught you well."

"I'll need to hear the stories you know." she continued when he looked at her. "For the engravings."

"I thought you would use the old legends."

"I could, but this place has its own stories. Shouldn't the stone speak to those?"

He pondered the question for a while. There were stories here, good and bad. "I would like that, very much."

"What about your story?" She crouched back down, focusing on her work. Her chisel blows were a steady ring of music, added to the crack of the fire in the fireplace.

"Not much to tell of me." When she didn't say anything he added "That others would care much."

"I've heard a few already."

A sharp bit of anger rose inside him, and it showed in his tone. "They talk about me behind my back?"

"No, but they do talk."

"And what stories do they tell?"

She rocked back to her knees, stopping her work and watching him. "Fear, and love mixed together. A dwarf who knows what he's doing. A dwarf who is lost."

Dorian snorted in derision. "I know where I am."

"Do you now?" She continued her work. "Talk is easy, but actions are harder."

Plate empty, Dorian realized he was lingering. He pushed back and collected the remains of breakfast. Half the dining hall was smoothed already, including the pillars.

More than half.

"I've got to go. Keep up the good work."

"And you as well," Nofibela said.

As he took his plate back to the kitchens to wash he couldn't help but feeling off balance. Was he lost?

He didn't think so, but he didn't know where he was going.

22

OVERSHADOWED

Chapter Twenty-Two

He started chanting, ancient and blood-soaked words. The wind blew cold, but Vasknar didn't feel it. The words floated on the air, twisting and spinning the magic.

It had taken him time to find this place. Too much time. A gibbous moon cast a pale-yellow glow on the barren field.

Light bent around Vasknar as his words continued. They crescendoed to a fever pitch, and the corruption seeped into the ground.

Power flowed through him. Tingling, exciting, deep.

Cracks and snaps as the spell took effect. Long dead hands struggled and erupted from the damp earth. Bodies followed.

Ruined, shattered, they shambled up from the field, still clutching spears and shields and heads. An entire sea of them, at least a hundred or more.

And then the power fled, leaving him weak. Vasknar stumbled and dropped to one knee, supported by the rotting goblin to his left.

"My lord?" it asked.

"Gather them," Vasknar wheezed, waving a hand proffered by another. He sucked in deep lungfuls of the night air. "We march."

The fire burned a cheery red, stoking Kragnak's happiness.

His hammer rang on the steel, sparks flying with every hit. His muscles strained, sweat poured out of him.

And he loved every second of it.

Gofrac turned the steel after every three hits, as directed, and Kragnak had to admit he was doing pretty well, if reluctantly.

Much better than Thurbag, who had drawn watch today.

The steel cooled too much to work anymore and Kragnak nodded, stopping to let Gofrac put it back into the fire to heat up.

"What are you making?" Gofrac asked, still watching the steel and shifting it in the coals. Kragnak took a turn on the bellows, pulling it with his left hand. It wasn't as hard as it used to be, both this and the forging.

"A replacement for this." he held up his hammer arm. It had done well, but now it was behind his skill. Barileth had given him some pointers on how he could improve it, and he had been eager to try them. "This is the last piece."

He eyed the shelf of parts, thinking. "And I think we can finish it today, with enough luck."

Smelting had gone faster with extra help, and a good pile of steel bars lay in the crates next to the forge.

Gofrac let him know the steel was ready, and together they worked the metal into a long, thin ribbon. Kragnak measured along its length, cutting it to the proper size.

Now, with everything ready, he worked to put it together.

Most of the leather straps were gone now, replaced by steel pinned with rivets, which would strengthen his swing.

Kragnak walked Gofrac through his plan, how he was to assemble it, and he listened patiently.

"Ready?"

"I have a question, if you don't mind." So far, Gofrac had been relatively quiet, answering questions when asked and not volunteering any information.

Some of this was from Kragnak's own anger and mistreatment, and he knew it. The first few days had gone about as well as his first few days with Thurbag.

But Gofrac had taken it with patience, doing everything Kragnak asked, and what's more, he stayed late to clean up the forge for the next day. Sweeping ashes, polishing tools, and arranging the sand had made work more pleasant the next day.

"Go ahead."

"Why not start with the straps and rivet them first?"

Kragnak cocked his head, looking at the pile of parts once more. He planned to start from the base and work up from there.

"I mean no offense," Gofrac added in his slow and plodding tone. "I thought it would be easier to keep them in place on one side."

"No," Kragnak stroked his beard. "That's a good idea. I hadn't thought about it. That's good Gofrac."

Gofrac dropped his head, but it looked like he was pleased. they got to work, stopping for lunch, and had it assembled before dinner, with the exception of the hammer.

Kimec came to fit the strapping, helping fit it to his arm like the first. They were late for dinner, but Kragnak walked in with a bright, shining new arm.

Whistles and words of congratulations greeted him, which made him blush.

"Someone needs to make a better hammer," Barileth remarked, pointing to a good dent on the end.

"I know, I know." Kragnak took his seat, and Dorian nodded to him with a small smile. He squirmed uncomfortably and looked down at his new arm.

Firelight glinted off the metal, which still smelled of rubbed oil. The hammer attached to the front was showing some rust and looked shabby in comparison.

That would be the next project, and through dinner he stewed on it, rolling it over in his mind.

"Dorian, may I speak with you?" Kragnak tugged at his elbow after dinner. "In private?"

Dorian nodded and followed him to the workshop. The other dwarves stayed behind to take a small bit of leisure after the long day and the long months. Dice rattled after them, along with cheers and groans.

"May I take a few gems?" Kragnak asked when they were alone, eyes on the floor.

"What for?" Dorian followed his gaze to the hammer. In the hands of a skilled jeweler those gems would be more than worth their weight in barter value.

On the other hand, they needed steel more. And right now Kragnak was the one dwarf who could provide it at the volume they needed. They could spare a few gems.

Dorian put a hand on his shoulder. "Take the rubies, as many as you need. And silver, if you need it."

Eyes met his, wearing an expression of thanks.

"I'll get Hatheck to cut them, however you need them."

"thank you. You won't regret this." Kragnak extended his left arm, and Dorian took it. Flesh met flesh, warm and full of life.

For a second Dorian regretted his plan to bring back his wife. She had died long ago, and yet he dwelt on what could not be. He pushed all thoughts of her out of his head and left as Kragnak worked feverishly behind him.

He hoped that Kragnak would find what he was looking for.

Through the smoke of the forge Kragnak gathered what he looked for. His hands felt rough and smooth alike, and he worked in a fever dream.

His head swam and his heart pounded, but his arms worked steadily. The best piece of steel went into the fire.

Alone, he worked long into the night, hammering and shaping, feeling the form of the metal. It seemed to take shape of its own will, stretching and bending into shape under the power of his arm.

He felt no fatigue. He couldn't stop. It pulled him, dragged him along. He wouldn't stop.

The metal formed into a hammer, straight and true. With a chisel he etched runes into its sides as the silver melted in the crucible.

When the engravings had completed themselves, pulled from somewhere deep in his memory, he poured the silver into them. It hissed and bubbled, and then he set the rubies on each side.

He polished and scrubbed, then quenched, setting them tight into their bindings and folding over straps of silver.

There was nothing else in the world. All other things fell away. The heat of the forge, the bubbling of the quench pot, the smell of smoke.

It blew away, overshadowed by the great thing that was being worked.

Finally, after how long he didn't know, he blinked. All at once he felt the exhaustion hit him, and his legs shook like jelly, but he couldn't tear his eyes away from what lay before him on the anvil.

"By the beard," he whispered. "Scaratoth." The word slipped out of his lips, imbuing the hammer with some sort of glow. Flame of the Red Dragon in the old tongue, the speech of the smiths that lay half forgotten.

The rubies glowed like eyes, runic dragons running along the head of the hammer. He dare not touch it at first, but he couldn't let his eyes off it.

With a trembling hand, he reached out and caressed it. The steel was cool and smooth, polished to a mirror shine.

All at once, he picked it up. It was as light as a feather, then his mind caught up to his hand, and felt its weight.

Kimec found him the next morning, fire of the forge dead and gone, holding it in his arms as he slept.

"Kragnak." He shook the dwarf awake. "Look what you've made," he said when his eyes had opened and blinked away the sleep.

"Beautiful, isn't it?"

"Beyond. How did you make such a thing?" Kragnak looked down, cradling it like a mother holds a new born.

"I don't know. Something spoke to me, guided my hand as I made it."

"Well done."

Kragnak looked up, eyes shining in the darkness. "It's time." He scrambled to his feet.

"You should get some rest." Kimec helped to steady him.

"No time. I have arms to make."

The harvest came. All the dwarves were caught up in it, picking and gathering, preserving and storing. Not a single hand was idle.

When Dorian had a chance to search the horizon he took it. Trees had long ago given up their green and now were almost at the point of giving up their leaves, too.

Gold and brown leaves fluttered in the breeze, and some ripped off and flew along the side of the valley into the mountainside.

It was an ill wind that blew, tugging at his beard and hair. His heart fluttered each time he looked to the south, but each time the horizon was empty.

Black smoke rose from the kitchen chimney. *Must be starting dinner.* He turned his attention back to the farm, digging up potatoes.

When he had unearthed a bundle of them, he knocked off the rich, dark earth. Some of it worked its way into his shoes, grinding against his worn socks every time he moved, and through the holes of them to scrape against his skin.

Each bunch was thrown into a bucket, and another plant dug up. He tossed the stems aside, a growing green pile of them larger than it had been this morning.

"Knock off more of that dirt," Dorian said. Ondare took out the last few she had put into the bucket and wiped off the dirt.

"Better?" she asked. He nodded.

"For whoever peels it. Or whoever eats it." He shook another bunch, scattering the dirt like pebbles on the ground. It made an almost rain-like sound.

Ondare struggled with the task, digging with hands too soft for this kind of work. She went half the speed he did.

So he worked with her, pointing out what she was doing wrong. When she looked at him with wrinkled nose, he feared he had spoken too harshly.

"What is it? Something I said?"

"No, not you at all. Do you smell that?" As she said it, he did. Smoke, but not the smoke of the wood fire or of the forge. There was something else burning. Flesh, and plant matter.

The forge fire was trailing its small white plume, flared every so often as they stoked the fire.

But when he turned behind him, a fear gripped him. Big, black plumes belched forth from the earth. It felt like a snake constricted around his heart, and he dropped his potatoes and sprinted to the mine entrance.

"Where are you going?" she yelled after him.

"Sound the alarm, get everyone out as soon as possible.

He cupped his hands and yelled to Barileth in the watch tower. Peals of the bell rang out, clear and with warning.

Smoke was seeping out of the entrance door when he got to it, and when he forced it open, it billowed out, stinging his eyes and nose with an overpowering stench.

Dorian covered his nose with his sleeve, batting away what he could, and charged into the tunnel.

Inside, dwarves yelled and sounds bounced around the tunnel in confusion. The light of the torches barely burned through the smoke, and he had to crouch down to avoid it.

Something came his way as he picked through the traps and he grabbed at the dwarf's arm.

It was Olgim, terrified and face smeared with soot and ash. He was coughing.

"What happened?"

"Kitchen," he coughed. "Something caught fire in the kitchen. We couldn't," he was overcome with retching.

"Go outside. Tell the others to get water." They had moved some of the food stores out of the kitchen, but there were months' worth of food and all the good meat.

He rounded the corners, reeling back from the heat.

Orange flames licked out of the kitchen, threatening to consume him.

23

AFTERMATH

Chapter Twenty-Three

Ashes, black and thick, that smelled burnt. Dorian kicked his way through the remains of the fire.

"It happened so fast," Olgim said. "We couldn't--"

Dorian saw something, kicked away some ash, and pulled a frying pan out. It was black, but still intact. The fire hadn't burned hot enough to melt it. "It was no use. We had to let it burn itself out."

As much as it pained him.

"Olgim, get some rest. Mughan, Fimroul, Hatheck, start cleaning this up. Throw out everything that has been ruined. I'll go see Emelda."

The dwarves nodded and moved in with hastily assembled brooms of stick and valley grass and shovels. He made a note to have Kimec make more wooden shovels and let them to their work.

Emelda was sitting on the bed when he came by, Yander by her side. Bandages covered her hands, and the right side of her hair was shorter, almost all her facial hair singed off.

"How are you?" he asked. Her red, puffy eyes found his, and he saw the pain in them.

Not only physical.

"I'm sorry." Her voice trembled. "I wasn't looking, I--"

"No." He held up a hand. "No need to be sorry."

"She's had a hard time," Yudoline said. "I've treated her burns with the salves I know, but it won't ease her pain."

"You have to believe me. I didn't mean to." Emelda struggled to get up.

"We've plenty of food in storage, and we've got a few cows to slaughter now." He didn't want to let her know how much of the harvest had been lost, and most of the ale and wine. "All we need you to do is rest up and get better as fast as you can. I want no excuses, either."

Emelda nodded, and Yander whispered in her ear, rubbing her back. His hand sought hers, but then pulled back when she flinched from the pain.

"And you stay with her," Dorian said. "Whatever she needs."

"The mine--" he started to say.

"Will still be there when Emelda's better." A few more hands lost, and at such a crucial time. He wasn't sure they would be able to collect all the harvest now. Some might rot in the field or underground.

But that wasn't giving him the uneasy feeling he had in his gut. That was coming from something else, something to the south.

Far south, he hoped. But he knew he couldn't take a chance on that.

He turned to Yudoline, who was by now the de facto healer of the expedition. "Let me know if you need anything else."

Almost everything in the kitchens was ruined, save a few metal implements that had escaped major damage or that Kragnak could repair.

With the damage cleaned and dumped outside, the kitchen felt large and cold. Dorian inspected the chimney for damage, but it was usable.

But dinner was long overdue, so they dined on cold, salted meat and uncooked vegetables. Dorian ate his and brooded, withdrawn from the conversation around him. They didn't have time for this, the defenses weren't yet ready.

Just when things were starting to turn around.

He missed her. His heart ached for Yolanda, for her comforting words and her constant companionship.

Dorian closed his eyes and remembered her for a moment amid the noise surrounding him. The way she smiled as he came in the door, dusting off her hands on her apron. Her steadiness, always being there for him.

And he hadn't been there for her when she needed him most. Dorian dragged a hand across his face. *I'll make up for it.*

He retreated to his room, weighing the options, when Mughan knocked and entered.

"Half the harvest, gone." He sat down opposite Dorian.

"I know."

"What are we going to do about it?"

"The food I'm not worried about."

Mughan's eyes betrayed his knowledge. "They are long overdue, aren't they?"

Dorian nodded.

"Which means what? Whoever it is out there is preparing, getting stronger." Mughan sat back and chewed on his lower lip. "Which means a bad time for us."

"It troubles me, waiting this long. The necromancer was powerful at the first attack. What power does he have now?" Dorian pretended to scratch out some words on the records open before him, but there was no ink in his pen and the words were invisible.

"We've enough steel to outfit everyone in armor, and it shouldn't take that long now that Kragnak's finished the weapons."

"I'm afraid it won't help. We're four and twenty, what good will that do against a horde of undead?"

"Not much," Mughan conceded. "So, what are you going to do about it?"

"I don't know." Dorian stared at the blank page. His room smelled like dwarf and leather. For once Mughan seemed to be speechless.

Dorian licked his lips, dried from the thought that popped into his head. "We could leave."

"Leave? And go where?"

"Somewhere else. Somewhere where we could survive." He buried his head in his hands. It was going to repeat again, he knew it. Just like it did before.

"We'd be fugitives. No one breaks a contract with the King, you know that. It's more than a death sentence."

I've already met my death sentence. Mughan pulled on his shoulder, swinging him around.

"You can't give up on us, not now. Not after we've come this far." His eyes were blazing with red hot fury.

"You could be the expedition leader."

"And clean up your mess? I think not." But there was a flash of something else in his eyes, dampening the rage and anger. "Of all the hopeless situations you've been in, is this really the worst?"

Dorian considered the question. "No." he brushed away Mughan's hands.

"Then get angry, and do something about it."

"I want to."

"Prepare for war Dorian. Ready this mine against the forces that come, and ignore everything that tells you not to."

What was his own heart saying? There were dwarves here that relied on him. Dwarves he cared about.

His children were waiting for him. Could he really bear never seeing them again?

And Yolanda waited for him. Sleeping in the tombs of her forefathers, but waiting nonetheless.

"Yes." Dorian got up and paced the room. "We prepare for war. We make our stand where we can and let them come."

Mughan smiled, grabbing hold of his arm again, infused with excitement. "We shall meet them. To a dwarf we will fight, and we will win."

"We have days, maybe less. Winter is coming and he won't risk an early snow to keep him away from us."

"The walls are built, the crossbows and arms ready. Now all we have to do is plan," Mughan said, taking his seat again.

"We will plan. I can't help but wonder what good it will do." Dorian returned to pacing.

"If we don't stop them at the wall, we fall back and let them come into the entrance tunnel." Mughan looked up thoughtfully.

Dorian stopped. "Lure them in? I'm not sure our traps will help much against the undead."

"Not all, but Barileth thought of some nasty surprises. And with the holes we can boil oil and water, rain it down on the attackers and let them taste heat."

"I'm not sure fire will do much against them." Dorian considered his own research. "Unless..."

"What is it?"

"We can use it as a distraction. Weaken them enough to fight hand to hand." It might work, if there were not too many. "We'll slaughter some cave cows." He brushed his hand through his beard. "We need the meat anyway, and we'll render the fat into oil."

"The kitchen is ruined, we can't use that."

"We'll use the fire in the hall, use it for a kitchen in the meantime." Dorian shook his head. All that food, just gone. "We could pour it on them, light it on fire." *Did fire kill the undead?* He didn't recall hearing that, but hoped it was true.

"And if we were desperate enough, we can use the escape tunnels to come in behind them and attack them from the rear." Mughan was smiling again, this one that stretched to his eyes.

Dorian shook his head. "It's too much of a risk. If we open them, then they have a clear path inside. And then we would have no hope."

"Unless we sealed them as we left."

"That would doom the dwarves who went outside." Dorian shook his head. "I won't do it."

"I can lead them. Bring them back alive, you'll see."

Dorian thought about it. "We can survive Dorian, just let us."

"I'll think about it," he said at last. "But we have preparations to make."

The crisp chill of autumn wind carried him up the stairs. At the top Dorian stopped to catch his breath.

"Storm's coming in," Yander said. Dark clouds played on the horizon, and the smell of rain was thick in the air.

"Let's hope it holds." Dorian clutched at his axe, grateful for the weight and feel of it. It was hard and solid, and kept him rooted in place. It wasn't long now.

The sound of wood on wood and shouting rose from the courtyard. Barileth led the sparring match, a nightly event after dinner for weeks now.

Dorian watched from his perch as Yander joined them, picking up a training axe and squaring off against Dozotaine. Besides Barileth, he was the most skilled fighter.

After a brief circling, the fighters attacked. Yander cut from high, but Dozotaine blocked it and returned it with a vicious cut to the knees.

He barely moved back in time, and Dorian winced, almost feeling the wind as the training sword swept by.

Yander retreated, more cautious this time. Dozotaine shifted his stance and went on the offensive, testing him with strikes and sweeps.

He didn't bite, but kept his head and waited like Dorian taught him. A clap of swords from fighters behind them distracted Dozotaine for a moment, and Yander seized on it.

Dropping his shoulder, Yander rushed in before Dozotaine could strike, and clipped him. Dozotaine staggered back, but recovered in time to parry an axe blow.

But Yander had him on the defensive now, bursts of speed from his long hours of practice with a weightier axe helping him.

Despite Dozotaine's experience, Yander overwhelmed him with pure ferocity, until he was driven to his knees to yield.

Pride flooded him, and also a small touch of awe. From a youngling that couldn't even pick up an axe, now to this.

He had hope that Yander wouldn't need it.

The fighters finished their sparring and went through a few forms that Barileth taught them. Most left, going back to get some sleep, but some lingered.

Yander and Barileth were the last to go, facing off against one another in unarmed combat.

It wasn't a fair fight, and Barileth tossed him every time, but always Yander got back to his feet to go again.

The evening was quiet. Nothing stirred on the horizon except a few birds flying south and squirrels at their frantic gathering.

Finally, Yander and Barileth went back inside, leaving him alone to watch the day recede and lightning flash. The sky darkened with the storm, and twilight followed close behind.

Peels of thunder kept him company, and the wind whipped up and whistled through the watchtower as he kept a lonely vigil.

Movement on the southwestern horizon caught his attention, and he peered closer, hoping that it was a figment of his imagination.

But his hope was in vain.

We need more time. We aren't ready yet. The trees stirred at the coming, then parted. Two hulking shapes came out of the tree line, shambling past stumps and felled trees.

His heart caught in his throat as behind the two dead bears, a rider in black came out of the shadows.

Even from this distance, their eyes locked. Pale, cold eyes that sucked the life from his own with a cruel malevolence.

He had come.

His army streamed out from the woods. Skeletons and dead goblins poured out, and it looked like they wouldn't ever stop.

Dorian rang the bell.

24

ASSAULT

Deep within the bowels of the mine, the alarm sounded, triggered by his touch.

Dorian stood on the watchtower as the army advanced toward him, icy fear gripping him.

There were more than just a few, there were dozens, if not hundreds, of undead.

Foul odors blew in advance, a mixture of sorcery and the rotting flesh of the half-decayed goblins. They mixed with the skeletons of long-dead warriors, from where Dorian had no idea.

So he gripped his crossbow tighter and went down to above the gate, waiting for reinforcements and checking over his armor one last time.

The necromancer stopped his forces outside the woods, gathering them into formation. Dorian was grateful for the respite.

A pack of wolves made up the rearguard of the enemy, not long dead and revived by black necromancy.

The skeletal horse of the necromancer stood still, eyes blazing red as it kept its master.

The eyes of the necromancer bore into his, not wavering. Assessing.

Behind Dorian, dwarves were coming. Their armor clattered and Barileth urged them on with shouts.

Up the wall they came, joining him in his vigil.

Barileth cursed, made a sign, then took up his place next to him. They were all there, and they fitted bolt to crossbow in preparation.

The necromancer was too far out of range, even though Dorian wanted to let loose at him. The cleared ground still had to be crossed, and he hoped that the advantage would be theirs.

His heart fluttered and twisted, beating in his body so hard he could feel it. Dorian drew a deep breath of the foul air, but even underneath it was the change of autumn.

"How many, do you think?" Mughan asked, taking up Dorian's other side.

"Too many."

"That'll make it easier to hit," Barileth said, hefting his crossbow and resting it on the edge of the wall. "And more body count to earn."

There was an odd sound in the distance, more than a rustling of trees. He didn't know what it was and couldn't put his finger on it. A crack of thunder rumbled from far away.

"Rain too? This isn't our night." Mughan fitted his own bolt, as were the rest of them.

All dwarves were here on the wall, each taking their preassigned place. Yander looked to him with grim determination, with Emelda at his side, and Dorian nodded.

"Save your bolts. Aim for the head. I'm not sure anywhere else will work." He couldn't break the necromancer's gaze.

Does he have it with him? There must be some account of his power, like all great works of magic. In and under the fear Dorian felt a shiver of hope, and something else.

Desire.

To wield such power, to take it as his own. It would be magnificent in his hands. Not used for evil, but for good.

To bring Yolanda back. To protect his children from the grave that eats all. To keep that everlasting mouth at arm's length.

The display of it was awesome, even now as the full forces of the necromancer arranged before them.

Bones rattled and shook, great sounds of the undead underpinning the army. A sort of mist welled up around the necromancer, tendrils of it snaking along the stumps of the dead trees.

Then, the necromancer pulled back its hood, revealing the pale man beneath.

"That's him? Doesn't look so bad to me," Barileth said, but his voice held an edge of fear to it he could not hide.

The necromancer lifted his hand and said something. His voice traveled across the gap like he was standing right next to them.

"Give up now, dwarves, and I may let you live. Fight against me and I will kill you all."

The wall was silent.

"I will not give you another chance." The voice was raspy, long unused.

"You may come," Dorian said, lifting up his voice unmagnified by magic, "but we will fight."

The chill of the air showed his breath. "Hold fast. They will attack with all their might, but we shall stand. No matter how dark this night gets, we will see the light of day on the other side." He lowered his voice so that it only carried to the other dwarves.

Hands shifted grips, someone's teeth chattered. Dorian didn't know if it was from the cold or from fear, but he hoped that they would be strong.

There were so many of them.

The mist swirled around the jeering, leering forms of undead. Eyes glowed, burning through it. The stench reeked of pure evil.

And then the necromancer gave one hand motion, and they came.

The skeletons and goblins went first, the other animals parting to let them through. The necromancer sat on his still horse, watching Dorian.

"Let them come closer," Barileth said. "Another few hundred feet or so. We don't want to waste any bolts if we can help it."

Dorian checked the barrel next to him, a supply staged like others along the walls. He wished he had more practice, but it was too late for that.

The foe shambled forward, then was in range.

A bolt flew from Barileth's crossbow, whistling through the air, but he was already cranking on it before it fell.

It struck a skeleton in the eye. With a rattle of bones it collapsed.

The dwarves let out a cheer that echoed in the valley. Hope surged in Dorian, until the skeleton's place was taken by another, a seemingly unending supply of them.

"Loose," he ordered, squeezing the cold trigger of his own crossbow. The string twanged, brushing his cheek with air as it flew, and hit a skeleton.

But it did nothing. Dorian blinked, expecting some effect, but the skeleton walked on with a bolt in its shoulder.

As he cranked his crossbow back, he watched with dismay as the others likewise had the same result. A flurry of bolts flew in that first volley, but little found a killing mark.

Most missed, and most of those that hit had no effect.

Dorian shot again and loaded again. The army had crossed over half the distance to the wall now, and kept coming.

The animals were joining in now, following on the heels of the others. Dorian aimed for the goblins, hoping that he would do better.

His hands ached from the cranking and the cold.

"It isn't working," Mughan said, firing another bolt. "They aren't dying."

"Speak for yourself," Barileth said, loosing another killing shot that landed right in a goblin's eye. The creature dropped without a sound. "If you can hit it in the head, it will."

"How am I supposed to do that when they're moving?" Another twang of crossbows.

"What are they going to do when they get here?" Fimroul asked, panting.

"Keep firing," Dorian said. He sighted, taking a deep breath like Barileth taught, and aimed right for the eye.

This time the bolt struck the goblin in the neck, but it was good enough to take it down.

But they kept coming.

"You don't want to know what they can do," Barileth said.

"He has a point." Mughan reached for another bolt. "What are they going to do when they get to the wall? It's three feet thick in the thinnest place."

"We'll just have to chuck rocks at them." Barileth killed another skeleton. "I'm up to four."

Four. Besides another handful that was all they had managed to stop. Four, out of hundreds. Daylight had fled, only a glimmer of the sun's light remained in the twilight.

And the necromancer would be even stronger.

Dorian saw it in their eyes. They glowed brighter, with more evil it seemed.

Then, they were at the wall.

"Shoot them down." Dorian peeked out over the edge, despite there having been no arrows fired so far.

The skeletons and goblins were trying to climb it. Dead fingers searched the stone, looking for a notch or crack to enter.

It was easier to hit them this close, and the dwarves were having better success. Bones and bodies littered the slope to the wall.

Dorian prayed that the wall would hold, that they had done their job.

"No you don't." Barileth shot at a goblin that had managed to find a hold, and was a few feet up the wall.

It fell back into the army, crushing a skeleton before jerking on the ground.

"Help, over here!" Yudoline waved frantically with her crossbow. Beneath her a few skeletons were scrambling up, boosted by the bodies of their brethren.

Dorian took aim, but before he could a few more bolts hit the skeletons.

"I thought the wall was smoother than that," Dorian said.

"We didn't have much time now, did we?" Mughan cranked at his crossbow furiously. The ammo barrels were getting lower, and the enemy still was at full strength.

The wolves rushed in, leaping over their skeleton companions and jumping as far up as they could.

Bolts were redirected and tried to stop them. A few wolves got dangerously close to the edge, and landed on their feet to get another run.

"Give up. You cannot win." The voice of the necromancer boomed out at them.

"Need more bolts here," Kimec yelled.

"Barileth, do you think you can hit him?" Dorian asked.

Barileth turned back and aimed. "I can try."

"Do it."

He shot as high as he could. The bolt whistled, then came back down in a graceful arc before planting a few feet in front of the necromancer.

He didn't even twitch.

"There's your answer," Dorian yelled. He fired another shot, this one hitting a wolf in the leg. he hoped it would stop it.

How can I take it? Dorian shook he head. He wasn't even sure they would survive this.

"Go get rocks," he said to Kimec. "Use them to take out the skeletons."

They were at the gate, doing something. Sounds rang out, like they were smashing it with their swords. Dorian didn't see anything large enough to act as a battering ram, and was sure the stone gate would hold against them.

He wasn't worried about what these skeletons and goblins could do to it. They weren't strong enough.

Kimec and others on the farther edges of their line came back, huffing and carrying leftover bits of rock from the wall construction. Dorian was glad he didn't make them take them away now.

He took one, dropping his crossbow for the moment, and raised it up over his head.

Another undead goblin had found a perch and was searching with rotten hands for another way up.

Dorian aimed and loosed his rock. It hit with a nasty crunch, sending the goblin back to the ground.

This one didn't even move.

But once again, another took its place. Their bolts ran low, and he gave the order to consolidate the remainder for Barileth's use.

The clouds parted for a moment, letting some light from the night sky in. It had seemed like hours had passed, but a quick glance up showed that the evening star had just come out. It had to be less than an hour, and they were almost out of ammunition.

The dwarves formed a chain now, hauling rocks to the wall. Lumdir chipped them apart, made them easier to carry.

They couldn't hold out like this, not all night. And they wouldn't be able to kill all the skeletons.

At the base of the wall the skeletons fell back whenever any of the dwarves came close. They were learning, and few attempted the climb now.

"We're winning. We've beaten them back." Fimroul hurled another rock down.

If not for the vast numbers of remaining undead, Dorian would have agreed with him. Another crash of thunder rolled over them.

The thunder continued, growing louder. Dorian hurled another rock onto a skeleton, tearing off an arm, then realized the thunder was too steady.

He peered through the trees at the edge of the forest, but the clouds gathered, cutting off all light and plunging them into darkness.

It doesn't matter. Whatever comes, we'll face it.

25

CHALLENGER

"Why aren't they climbing?" Mughan asked. A flash of lightning lit up his face, showing the field of battle as if it were day.

Masses of undead roiled beneath them, and the necromancer stood silently watching.

Is this draining his power? Or does he have an untapped reserve, waiting for a moment of weakness?

"And why didn't they bring ladders? Surely they could have made them." Mughan took a rock from Yudoline, and turned to throw it.

"They're too stupid to think about that." Barileth laughed as he chucked his own, crushing two skeletons at once.

"No, he's not stupid." Dorian stared at the necromancer, watching his cloak flutter in the wind. "He's planned something else, I know it."

But what?

Dorian turned back to the yard. "Lumdir, how does the gate fare?"

The dwarf ceased splitting rock and ran over to it. The undead continued to attack it, and the army was spreading out, following the undead wolves around the walls.

Searching for a weakness, probing wherever they could.

And there weren't enough of them to cover the wall. "Spread out, Barileth take the west wall, Mughan the east." He split off a few dwarves to each group, and they thinned.

"The gate still holds," Lumdir said from below him. "It will hold through whatever they do to it."

The crashing thunder was getting louder, distracting him. Skeletons and goblins were getting hand holds now, carving at the wall with rusted sword and axe. How long they had been in the grave he didn't know, but these skeletons looked like fighters.

Dorian kept up the barrage of stones, but the time between supply runs was getting longer. Fimroul was supplying him and the others on the south wall, but since they spread out there weren't enough haulers to keep up.

He threw down another rock, kicking himself for not thinking of this possibility. The bolts had proved ineffective compared to the rocks, which crushed undead. He should have had piles of them ready.

At some point they would have to abandon the wall. There weren't enough of them to stop all the undead.

It was only a matter of time.

His arms ached, he hated the smell of death that surrounded them. He wished he was warm and dry, mining deep in the earth covered in dirt and earth.

But until they repelled these attackers, that would never be.

So, despite his aching arms and his burning lungs, Dorian kept throwing.

"Look." Yander pointed to the forest, which Dorian realized was where the thunder was coming from.

It wasn't thunder.

Trees swung and tilted. Something was coming through them. Something big, something powerful.

His stomach dropped and fear welled up inside. But he had to be strong, he had to look strong.

And his legs almost gave out when it came through.

Branches and leaves burst apart. A huge skeleton hand brushed them aside like gnats. And his mouth gaped.

"What..." Fimroul dropped his rock, and it fell on his foot. He cursed, but gazed at the horror.

"Dorian," Yander said.

He licked his lips, trying to wet them. His throat was dry. "I see it."

And still, the necromancer didn't move. Staring at them, staring at him, he was still.

How are we going to survive against that?

"Barileth, to me." It was slow, maybe they would be able to get in a lucky shot before it reached them.

"By the beard!" Barileth let out a long series of curses and sprinted to the south wall. "Had to bring a giant, did he?"

"Can you hit it?"

"I can try." He hefted his crossbow and loaded it. "It needs to be closer."

"How big of a target do you need?" Movement caught Dorian's eye. "Over there!"

Yander threw a rock at a skeleton that had nearly mounted the wall. It knocked it over, but the others had seen the path. They were grouped up, ready to follow.

There were too many, they had to retreat.

Unless Barileth was able to kill it. He steadied his aim on the wall, sighting down. Dorian willed his bolt to fly steady and true.

The crossbow clicked as Barileth pulled the trigger, loosing the bolt. Dorian watched on with anticipation as it went for the giant.

All it had to do was hit the eye, Dorian was sure of it. But the necromancer had raised a hand. The bolt flashed in the sky, then a dark form streaked.

Dorian blinked. It was gone.

"What was that?" He threw down another rock, with less power now that his arms were tired. It still killed a goblin.

Something dark circled the giant. Dorian squinted, watching wings flap.

"I don't think I'm going to be able to hit it." Barileth cranked, pulling back the string. Another bolt loosed, another bolt was struck from the sky by the winged protector.

And the giant crossed the distance with alarming speed, each step crushing the earth beneath it.

The undead army scattered before it, giving it a wide berth.

"It's coming for the gate." *Of course, the weakest point in the wall.* The club in its bony grip wasn't even a true weapon, just a trunk of a tree stripped of most branches, stout and hearty.

Dorian wasn't sure if the gate could handle it.

"We can't kill it," Dorian said. The rock pile behind them was almost spent already. He raised his voice, watching the necromancer for a reaction. "Everyone back inside. Retreat."

The words came out of his mouth bitter. The first line of defense had lasted all of an hour. The strongest stone, made from the earth. The head of the giant reached over the wall. What good would the rest of them be?

"Give me a distraction, I can still kill it." Barileth raised his crossbow. The barrel of bolts was almost empty, and Dorian scrounged.

His own crossbow wasn't ready, and he cranked furiously. He glanced behind him to make sure the dwarves were retreating.

"Ready?" he asked, raising his crossbow.

"Now." They loosed their bolts, the giant barely a few yards away now.

Barileth's flew true, Dorian's off to the side. The giant's strides were bringing it to the wall, there would be no further shots.

One bolt was knocked away, the other glanced off the giant's cheekbone. It didn't even flinch, but kept marching on with thunderous footsteps.

Barileth cursed the bird out loud. Dorian threw one last look at the necromancer before turning to run. He looked smug.

Inwardly, Dorian cursed the necromancer also. "Get back inside," he yelled at Fimroul, who was at the rock pile for some reason, off to their left.

Down the steps Dorian took them two at a time, each landing jarring his entire body. His teeth chattered and he tasted blood from his cheek.

And then he was on the ground, right behind Barileth, sprinting for all he was worth. Fimroul had dropped his rocks and was running too. He was going to be first, just a few feet ahead of them.

Behind him was a loud boom and a massive cracking. Stones flew past him, then something knocked him on the side of his head.

He woke up on the ground, head swimming. His body wouldn't respond, which he found odd at first.

Then, fear flooded him, and sensation returned. His head was wet and he struggled to his feet. He turned.

Skeletons and goblins were pouring through the ruined wall, which lay in a pile of rubble. As he watched a section of the wall slipped free and crashed down, striking a goblin.

He coughed, dirt and dust thick and clogging his mouth and throat. The ringing in his ears lessened.

Someone was yelling at him.

Turning, he saw the mine entrance open, Barileth screaming at him with a limp left arm.

Off to the side Fimroul lay in a puddle of his own blood, eyes forever open and staring, surrounded by rock.

With forced, halting steps he ran for safety.

"Get inside," Barileth was yelling. "Dorian, run."

He urged him on, Yander peeking out behind him.

With a rush it seemed like the world returned to him. His head ached, and his feet barely supported him.

But if he didn't make it to the door he wouldn't live long.

And he would never see his family again.

Driven on, he forced his feet to respond. There were less than a few feet left now.

He dare not look back.

Fear was in Barileth's eyes.

He was going too slow.

No, I have to make it. A few more steps.

One foot in front of the other, he continued.

Hands reached out, grabbing him.

They pulled him inside. Yander slammed shut the door behind him with a crack, but he didn't stop.

"We've got to get deeper," Dorian panted.

"Barely made it," Barileth said.

Yander pulled him with a hand around his hip, and Dorian was grateful for the help.

Dorian wanted to look behind him, but feared to. They had locked it, and now there was banging on the stone.

"It won't last long against that giant." His head wasn't the only part of his body struck, and his leg injury was flaring up again. Pain throbbed and lanced in various places.

"How are we going to survive?" Yander asked, fear plain in his voice.

"We'll survive," Barileth said.

We have to.

But it was difficult to see how. "They can't bring the mine down, so I think they'll use the giant to make an opening and come in that way." He reasoned out loud, feeling the trembling of the earth under the skeleton giant's feet.

"They're going to destroy my traps." Barileth cursed, brushing past them. A long gash ran down his arm, trailing blood.

Blood poured down Dorian's head too, filling his nose with the smell. The undead had no blood, drained of it in death.

They were almost halfway down the entrance tunnel when the earth shook with a percussive boom.

Supports rattled and dirt rained down from above. Luckily, the supports held.

"We aren't going to survive much more of that," Barileth said, looking back. Dorian risked his own.

The great stone door, fortified with all of Lumdir's skill after the goblin attack, had almost shifted in the earth. A ray of night came in the upper left, lit by a flash of lightning.

"Faster." His heart leaped and pumped, the door at the far end of the tunnel coming into sharp focus.

Despite his pain, Dorian ran.

They made it to the door when the second hit came, smashing the entrance door and wrenching it, with its frame, from the mountain.

Skeletons poured in, but Dorian only had a moment before they were gone, locked into the entrance tunnel with a quick swing and click of the rock.

"What happened out there?" Yudoline asked, rushing over with her bandages. Emelda and Olgim saw to Yander and Dorian while she examined Barileth.

The tunnel was crowded with dwarves, pressed in and breathing in the small space. A torch illuminated them.

"That giant is going to be a problem," Mughan said. So far, it looked like everyone else had made it.

"Fimroul's dead," he said. A hush fell over them. He knew they wouldn't be able to make it without some death, but the dwarf had deserved better.

Another boom, another tremor that rattled the torch in its sconce. Olgim wrapped his head with a bandage, stemming the flow.

"Everyone to the fortifications," Dorian said, breaking the silence. "Light the fires, man the crossbows. They aren't going to stop. Not now, not ever. Not until everyone of us is dead and enthralled in unlife. Go, like your life depends on it."

Wordlessly, the dwarves went to their assigned stations. Fimroul was up above, with the murder holes. That was one less dwarf to fight, one less dwarf to defend.

And one too many dead.

Olgim finished bandaging him, he thanked him and set off to his own station down the left-hand side of the fortifications.

The end of the tunnel was in ruins, crushed by the giant's club. The other dwarves had taken up their crossbows, firing them into the corridor.

With a grim face, Dorian took his too.

There wasn't much light in the entrance tunnel, and when his eyes adjusted his spirits raised.

Cage traps were filled with the undead army, at least ten of them, struggling and reaching out of the bars. As he watched another trap went off, crushing at least two more.

Twangs proceeded bolts striking the undead, more than a few of them striking home.

He raised his own, taking down a goblin in the neck. A few more moments later rocks started coming down from the murder holes.

For a moment, he hazarded a hope.

Then, he saw a sight that drained the blood from his face.

26

DESPERATION

Dorian's stomach churned. In with the sickness he felt was a feeling of awe, which repulsed him that he could even think that.

Fimroul's skull had been crushed, exposing the brain. The one remaining dead eye glowed.

Was this his fate? Was this the fate of all of them?

"They keep coming," Mughan said, shooting through the arrow slit.

"Then we'll keep killing them until they stop," Dorian said.

"What if they never stop?" Hatheck asked. "We can't keep fighting them forever, not with that giant."

As if to punctuate his thoughts, another shudder ran through his feet. Dorian finished loading another bolt and found Fimroul in his sights.

He hesitated.

The dwarf had been kind in life, not too bright but eager to help wherever he could.

But he wasn't alive anymore, was he?

In his indecision, a blade slid through the arrow slit, stabbing into his shoulder.

Dorian stepped back, the sword scraping on his armor and sending small sparks that revealed a skeleton at the other end of it.

His hand went immediately to Webcleaver, drawing it and swinging it in a smooth arc. The sword knocked away, but his axe couldn't reach through the small slit.

So Dorian picked up his crossbow and shot the skeleton.

The sword dropped, caught in the slit by the hilt. Somewhere on the other side of the hall someone screamed in pain.

Mechanisms whirred in the entrance hall, the last set of traps triggered. Dorian hoped the spinning blades were cutting them up, breaking them into bits, but the sound soon jarred and stopped with a scraping metal sound.

Something smelled like it was burning, wafting through the small slit. His shoulder was bleeding, the sword had caught a weak spot in the armor.

Then, Gofrac grunted to his right, and gurgled. Dorian looked over to see him fall over, blood gushing from his neck. Dorian rushed over to cradle him, putting pressure on the wound.

His hands slipped, and Gofrac looked into his eyes, mouth opening and shutting. Blood came out, not words.

He didn't stand a chance. A few seconds later, he was dead, his life spilled onto the floor. Wide eyes stared at him, which Dorian shut with blood-soaked fingers that trembled in sadness and anger.

His ears rang, and his vision blurred for a second. Dorian squeezed his eyes shut to get the image out of his mind, but the fall played over and over again in his mind.

We aren't going to make it.

All the energy seemed to go out of him then. Gofrac was just a youngling, on the morning of his life. And he was under Dorian's care, tasked with protecting him and keeping him alive.

And he had failed, like he had failed before.

All the dead danced through his mind then, pleading with him to save them. Ridiculing him for being so weak, for allowing it to happen in the first place.

They would all be alive now, if it wasn't for him. Happy, living out lives of productivity and happiness. Having children, raising them. Enjoying the fruits of their labor.

Instead, they were dead and cold in the ground.

Like all of them would be soon.

No, I can't think like that. As long as we fight we still have a chance, no matter how dark the night.

Dorian set Gofrac down, the warmth already being taken from him. "Sleep deep, Gofrac." He gave one last look before turning back to the danger.

"Watch the holes, they've found a way through," Dorian yelled. The others on his side were already back farther in the hall, warned by either the screams around them or the experience themselves.

Deep thudding was coming from the door, the undead already at it. Some of the traps were still working, but not many.

"They keep coming," Glarrore said, voice shaking. She held the crossbow in her arms just as shaky, but still fired.

"Fire until we use up all the bolts." Thunder rolled in through the opening, the smell of rain thick as it hissed outside. Dorian wiped off his head, his fingers still smelled of blood, and he tried to ignore it.

How long would they hold? Another boom outside, followed by the sound of splintering and falling rocks.

Dorian choked back all his fears, fueling it with anger.

They had killed Fimroul. They had killed Gofrac. These undead would kill them all, and the anger burned within him.

Bolt by bolt, Dorian found his mark. Now that the tunnel was thick with them there was little room for them to evade.

"Like fishing with bolts," Barileth yelled from somewhere, laughing as he did. "Let's teach them what happens when you attack Seventh Hall."

The undead had filled the entrance tunnel now, the traps spent and broken. Dozens of them shuffled around, clawing at the arrow slits and pounding on the locked door.

Pushing away the evil thoughts in his head, Dorian cranked on the crossbow, loaded it, and shot a skeleton in the eye.

It crumpled with a rattle. Whether it was from the undead's bones collapsing or a death rattle, Dorian couldn't tell.

And then he heard the necromancer's chant, and his blood ran cold. The light in the tunnel seemed to flicker and fade, drawn in at the power of the necromancer.

It was beyond what he had known. Far beyond.

The chant was in a foreign, powerful tongue. Crossbows halted, and hesitated, his own among them.

Curiosity overcame anger then, for a moment, and Dorian peeked through the arrow slit to get a quick look.

The necromancer stood at the entrance to the tunnel, hands in the air and robes flowing black in the wind. His hood was flared back, revealing a pale face contorted in effort.

Darkness swirled around him, the chanting growing louder than he could have guessed. The foul smell came back, worse now, and Dorian recoiled automatically in horror.

He was bringing his dead warriors back from death.

And there was nothing Dorian could do about it.

He was too far out of range of his crossbow, not near enough to the murder holes.

The voice crashed on the wind, reached its zenith, then cracked with an explosion that made Dorian clap his hands to his ears.

Opening his jaw, Dorian struggled to hear, but had to look.

In the corridor the undead pressed forward, but their dead lay on the ground or trapped in the traps.

Still lifeless.

Puzzled, Dorian wondered at this.

Then, there was a sound behind him.

The scrape of metal on stone. The sound of armor moving.

Dorian's mouth went dry, and his heart rate spiked.

He turned, fear realized, as Gofrac rose from the dead.

Turned to the enemy, his eyes opened and glowed, searching. they found Dorian.

Hands reached out, alive mere moments before, now cold and gone.

He was close, and in his stunned state, Dorian failed to react in time.

Gofrac grabbed him. With the strength of a smith he squeezed at his arms, then threw him up against the wall.

It knocked the wind out of Dorian, who keeled over and tried to cough, but the air wouldn't come.

He rolled away from those undead hands, hearing the shouts around him. Gofrac wasn't the only one who had been raised.

Dorian tried to push back, and succeeded, but Gofrac's undead body regained a foothold and came on again. The lifeless eyes watched without seeing. Nothing of Gofrac remained, not that quiet strength, not that small smile.

Nothing.

He was robbed of everything.

It wouldn't stop. Unless he killed it, it wouldn't stop.

The thing was searching for a weapon now, and saw Webcleaver next to it.

Dorian tried to regain his breath as he crawled for it first, sucking in stone dust and dirt.

They got there at the same time. Dorian tried to wrench Webcleaver free of the undead grip, but it was too strong.

So Dorian yelled a yell of rage, channeling all his strength, and spun Gofrac, smashing it up against the wall.

It shuddered, but kept gripping it.

Dorian did it again, and again. It seemed to have an effect, but his rage could only fuel him so long.

And then, he realized, he would have to kill it.

To kill Gofrac.

After just seeing him die in his arms.

Without having the chance to say goodbye, without ever apologizing to him.

He would be killing him with his own hands. A dwarf he had vowed to protect, had even told him.

All this flashed in his mind in an instant, because the thing that once was Gofrac released one hand and closed it around his throat.

With a grip like iron it cut off Dorian's air. His body, already running low on air, screamed at him, and he almost panicked.

Gurgling came out of his mouth, unbidden, like the death of Gofrac.

Dorian pushed with all his remaining strength, twisting Webcleaver toward its thumb. The grip broke, and the axe cut into what once was Gofrac's arm.

No blood spilled.

It was an odd observation to make, but Dorian twisted Webcleaver in his hand, spinning the axe and severing an arm.

As it dropped to the ground, he breathed deep of the sweet, vile air. Strength returned to his body, and he pushed the once-Gofrac back, stepping away to give him enough room to swing.

It came at him again, but this time Dorian was armed and prepared, axe at the ready. He swung, beheading the once-Gofrac, and the body crumpled like a sack of potatoes.

His head lay in the rock, the light from his eyes gone now, and gone forever.

Dorian staggered back, slumped against the cold rock wall behind him.

He was so tired. The air still felt sweet on his mouth as he gulped in deep mouthfuls.

How many more would die? And how many by his own hand?

They were all of his hand, one way or another.

Dorian dropped Webcleaver with a clatter, then put his head in his hands.

What was I thinking, that I was going to get a second chance?

He had failed to kill the necromancer when it was weak, failed to obtain his power. And he never would.

They would all be slain here. Yander, the dwarf he had hated with a passion, at first. Emelda, barely a girl with so much love in her heart.

They would lie here, headless, staring at him. Accusing him.

A weight fell on him, then. *This is the end now.*

He closed his eyes, laid his head against the wall. There was nothing more to do but die with the others.

How long he sat there he didn't know. Despair filled his soul. He wouldn't see his children again, but that was for the best.

What kind of father would do the things he'd done?

"Dorian, get up." His eyes opened slowly. Yander was kneeling beside him, bloody and covered in dirt.

He shook his head. "No."

"You promised me that you would see this to the end. That you would protect Emelda."

"I can't. Look how he accuses me."

"Gofrac is dead. We are not. Get up." The eyes still stared, as they would ever stare.

"The night is not over." There was anguish on Yander's face. Dorian was puzzled, he didn't know why. "And we need you. Now, more than ever. We need you."

Yander stood and held out his hand.

He's serious. Dorian blinked, then stirred in a fog. Sounds came to him, the sounds of fighting. The others were still fighting.

The others.

Ruby, Xanther. They might not know him, but he was still their father. They would have no other.

And Yander. So much stronger than before, a true dwarf. *He dared come find me in all this, dared to tell me the truth.*

Dorian stared into those eyes. He couldn't let him down now, he couldn't let the others die.

At least, not without a fight.

And they had stopped the necromancer twice before. They could do it again.

We will do it again.

Hope chased away his despair, banishing it to the far reaches of his mind. Dorian reached up and grasped hands.

Yander's hand was warm, and strong from his years of mining. He helped him to his feet, even as the sounds of battle surrounded them.

Dorian set his jaw. This was his home. These dwarves were his family.

And he wasn't going to let them die.

27

HUNTED PREY

Chapter Twenty-Seven

"It's good to have you back," Yander said. "I thought we lost you."

"You did, for a time." Dorian reached down and picked up Webcleaver. The percussive blast of the giant rang through the tunnels. "But I'm here now, and I intend to stay."

Yander smiled and clapped him on the back. Dorian couldn't help but return it.

"Kragnak," Dorian bellowed, heading back to the main corridor.

The dwarf appeared. "Yes?"

"We need to take down that giant, and we don't have anything to do it with. How about you fix that?"

"What did you have in mind?"

"Bolts won't do anything against it, or rocks." Dorian stroked his beard.

"We're out of bolts," Bermic said.

"Running low on this side too," Barileth said, from the other tunnel.

"It looks like the giant is trying to bring the mine down on us all." Mughan walked up to join Dorian, Kragnak, and Yander. "If they crack the mine, we'll get a waterfall of rain in with the undead."

Something tickled his memory, then gave him an idea. "We have rope still, don't we?" Dorian asked. *It could work...*

"Yes, plenty."

"What if we pull the giant down?" The others looked at each other.

"How?"

"Hooks." Dorian turned to Kragnak. "Can you hammer out some hooks, like a fishhook? Then make some way to attach it?"

Kragnak nodded. "I've seen something like it before, if you give me enough time. The forge should be ready, and I have some bar that I can use."

"Go, do it." The door shifted next to them, raining down dust, from a particularly heavy blow. They all turned to watch, but it held.

Kragnak ran to the workshop, while Kimec went to get the rope.

"We're out." Barileth threw down his crossbow and joined them. "And the rocks aren't doing much either."

There was a crunch, as a rock from a murder hole found a mark, or Dorian hoped that was the case.

It could have been the door too.

"We don't have much time, and we still have to deal with the undead." He laid out his plan as quickly as he could, and the others nodded in agreement.

"Mughan, can you lead the raid?" He couldn't be in two places at once.

Mughan smiled. "I'll be there." He cracked his fingers. "It's going to be a good giant hunt, and I get to keep the skull when we take it down."

Dorian and the others laughed. "I'll give you the whole thing if you can." They divided the remaining dwarves into groups.

"So how do we stop them?" The door shook with another hit.

"Stoke the fires, I want them raging." Dorian had a glimmering of an idea and hoped it would work. "We'll feed them something they won't soon forget."

The dwarves scattered, assigned to tasks. It was quiet in the tunnels, and Dorian hazarded a look into the entrance tunnel.

He was there, surrounded by his army. Dorian's heart leaped. Fimroul was beside him, like a dog at its master's feet. The necromancer towered over him.

Their eyes met.

"Why do you resist the inevitable?" His voice rasped, high and papery. "You will die, like the others. And I will raise you, to serve me."

Dorian stared at him, wondering what kind of man this was. He wouldn't give him the satisfaction he wanted.

So the man stretched out his hand, pointing to door. "Open this door. I might let some of you live."

"I don't believe you." Dorian felt the man's power pulsing around him in a dark shroud. His knowledge might be limited, but it did exist.

"The female dwarfs, is that why you resist?"

"I fight for all of us."

There was an odd sound, a high-pitched laugh. "How noble you are, locked away behind that strong door. Tell me, how was it you came to abandon your dead to me?"

He stroked Fimroul's hair with a pale, thin hand.

"Get your hands off him," Dorian snapped. The stroking paused, for a moment, then continued.

He raged at it, wanted to tear the necromancer limb from limb. But all he could do was watch behind his walls of rock.

"What are you going to do about it?" He mocked. "Come, leave your hole and fight me here."

"I'll meet you." Dorian bared his teeth. "But it will be on my terms, not yours." Fear still filled him, but it was overwhelmed by the desire to fight and live. Giving up wouldn't help any.

"Your King won't save you, you know." Dorian let the necromancer talk. Every minute they survived was one more they prepared. He just had to hold him off long enough. "He isn't coming. He's abandoned you."

"I never cared," Dorian said.

The necromancer paused. "Ah. I see. You style yourself a King yourself, don't you? Here to lord over the others, get them to do your bidding." Pounding continued on the door, so far in vain. Dorian glanced over at it, but couldn't see it from his vantage point.

The necromancer strolled over to a cage, examining it. "You'll set up a kingdom here, it seems."

"What do you want with us?"

"I want you to die so that I can experiment on you, raise you to life again." The dark eyes flashed back to him. "I can give you an immortality, of a kind."

Dorian must have reacted, because the necromancer smiled. It was sickly, and filled him with more dread than he expected. "But I see you've been acquainted to my type of magic already. You've been touched by it."

Dorian drew in a sharp breath and froze. "A dwarven practitioner of the great arts. How unusual."

With a quick glance Dorian saw he was alone. "You don't know what you're talking about."

"I see it." Those eyes pierced his soul.

A scrape of metal on stone alerted Dorian to the danger, and he pulled back just as a sword pierced the place his head had just been a moment before.

He stumbled and fell back to the necromancer's laughter. "Very quick. You've avoided death this time, but how long can you last?"

Dorian sat up. The sword was waving around, trying to get to him. *He means to lock us in here until he can get to us.*

He shivered, then scrambled to his feet. With his axe he knocked the sword down, breaking it off. It tumbled and clattered to the ground, while the skeleton holding it shrieked an unearthly sound.

"I'll give you a chance to leave, but one only." Dorian stood on shaky legs, but his voice was firm. The necromancer watched him through the arrow slit.

"You dare give me commands?" he hissed, eyes narrowing. A rage flared up in them.

"Leave now, and we won't come after you."

"You'll be the last. I'll butcher everyone in front of you. Flay them alive, torture them without mercy. But you, I'll save you for something else." The necromancer's voice had gone quiet, and dark. Dorian believed he meant every word.

"Remember, I gave you your chance." Dorian retreated down the tunnel, panting with a racing heart.

Curses and whispers followed him, but he still belonged to the living. The necromancer's art had no hold on him.

But that little thought jabbed him. As long as he was living. Were he to die...

28

HOOKED

Hammering from the workshop roused him from his dark thoughts and warmed his soul. The icy feeling he had talking to the necromancer slipped away by the time he reached the workshop.

The forge was blazing, three dwarves working the bellows. Kragnak worked at the anvil, hammering with his improved hammer bending a sword over.

Next to him a pile of strange looking creations lay. The remains of the old iron swords, Kragnak had fashioned them into hooks and attached them together.

"To help catch anything they reach," Kimec said, as Dorian looked at them. "Kragnak's idea."

The heat from the fire felt welcome on his skin. Kragnak, satisfied with his work, quenched another. Kimec was taking the finished hooks and attaching ropes.

"You think this will work?" Mughan asked quietly, coming up to his side.

"I'm not the one going out there," Dorian said.

"I don't like your confidence..."

"It will work. Otherwise we aren't going to have a good time in here."

"I'm less concerned about your good time and more about my life," Mughan said dryly, with one eyebrow raised.

How different this day had turned out to be, and how different Mughan had become.

Or was it he that had changed? Either way, he had no reservations about sending him out as the leader of a critical attack.

"Whatever the case, make sure you come back. I need someone to take over when I leave here."

"I can't guarantee anything other than greatness."

"Greatness." Dorian shook his head. "If only we had the time."

"We're given what we have. We can't ask for more." The fires raged, and anger and power raged inside Dorian. Mughan fell silent, and they watched Kragnak work with lightning speed.

As one was finished and quenched, another started. He was moving faster than Kimec, who was merely tying a rope to the end.

Less than a few minutes later they had everything they needed. The hooks were distributed, ropes coiled around arms and farewells given.

Dorian clasped Mughan's hand tight. "Go, for Seventh Hall. Wait for the signal."

"For Seventh Hall." Mughan nodded and turned back. "Alright you slowbodies, get your gear and get moving."

He took Dozotaine, wounded by a fight with Saggamli who had been risen from the dead, Thurbag, Yutatir, and Kimec.

Yander asked to go, but Dorian shook his head.

"Why not?" He brimmed with rage and energy.

"I need you here," Dorian said. "And you'll better be able to protect Emelda."

Yander considered this for a moment, and the anger seemed to cool. He nodded and followed Dorian back into the corridor.

From here the smell of cooking fat and oil spread through the mine. The door was moving more now with every hit from the enemy outside it, and more and more dust rained down.

"How long will it hold?" Yander looked at it nervously. Dorian felt the same way, and they were running out of time.

They were always running out of time.

"It will hold," he said, with more conviction than he felt. If it didn't they would all be dead.

Fire raged in the fireplace of the great hall too, mixing the smell of ash and soot with the bubbling oil in pots hanging above it.

The room was in chaos, dwarves running everywhere and sounds making it hard to think, let alone hear anything of importance.

Dorian stood there for a moment more, than bellowed in his loudest voice "Calm down!"

Heads turned his way, as his voice echoed around the great hall. His voice died away. "Everyone stay calm. We need to get these up to the murder holes as soon as possible."

"It isn't ready yet," Yudoline said, adding more fat into a pot. "We've got everything we can cooking, but it takes time."

Dorian nodded, then sat at the table. He folded his hands and leaned back, feigning ease.

The others returned to their work, this time more orderly. They still spoke, but at an appropriate volume. Yander joined him, fidgeting.

He turned his attention to the wall, and was surprised.

How long had the carvings been there? Dorian blinked, as if seeing them for the first time.

A dwarf holding an axe carved into the wall gave him hope. It was wielding it against a great spider, terrible in form and towering over the dwarf.

"Someone's been blabbing, I see." Dorian touched the wall, remembered the day. They had lost good dwarves, but in the end they had won.

The stone was smooth and cool, almost glass-like to the touch.

Yander shrugged. "She found a way to learn it. We weren't going to tell her not to carve it. Besides, that's been there for a few days."

Days. Dorian shook his head. What had he been doing all that time? He barely remembered Nofibela finishing the floors, now free of rogue stone that would catch the foot.

"It's ready," Yudoline said, leaning over the biggest pot with a spoon. "Take it."

Dorian sprung to his feet, joining with Olgim in carrying the pot. Great waves of steam washed over him, thick with the smell of fat.

They took it past the remains of the butchering, out the hall and up the stairs to the chamber carved out above the entrance tunnel.

The giant had done its work here too, the far side of the room was smashed and caved in, but there was plenty of room to do their work.

"Careful now, to the far hole." They carried it, still steaming, and set it down next to the hole.

Dorian took a quick look, then drew back. There were plenty of undead back here, but no sign of the necromancer.

No matter, they needed to kill the army, anyway.

They grasped the sides of the pot and tipped it, splashing the burning hot liquid down onto the heads of the skeletons and goblins below.

At first nothing happened, then they looked up. Some of Dorian's hope faded. He had hoped that the heat would do something, but glowing eyes stared at him unfazed and unharmed.

"What happened?"

"Nothing." He couldn't hide the bitterness in his voice. Olgim drooped at the words.

"Do you mean to invite us to dinner?" Dorian froze, the necromancer's voice coming from right down below them. He looked over the edge.

There he was, unharmed and staring back at him. "It was supposed to kill you, but I'll settle for inconvenience."

Another group appeared and sent down their bubbling oil. It hissed as it hit the floor below, splashing up onto the army.

"I tire of your impudence. Come out and die like the vermin you are."

"Get the torch," Dorian whispered. He raised his voice. "If you tire of us then you should leave."

"If you will not die, perhaps you will learn?" The necromancer's tone changed, softening. "I could make you a great dwarf, one that wields unlimited power over death. Even to suspend death itself."

Olgim was shuffling as fast as he could, heading for the torch at the end of the room.

"The powers of the old works are strong, and they fill the dead with life once more. Something once led you down that path, but I can show you the whole way."

Dorian saw Olgim and the others, but couldn't watch. His heart was drumming, his mind was racing.

The very thing that he desired most in life offered up before him!

"You can raise anything. A loved one, an enemy, yourself."

It was like a shot of lightning through his veins.

But no, he couldn't. Or could he? Would the necromancer hold true to his word? Dorian desperately wanted to believe him, that he could see Yolanda once more.

Touch her living face, hold her living body. It was all too much.

"Come down and join me."

"Dorian." Olgim was beside him, a look of concern in his eyes. Dorian shook from the dream, discarded the vision of his long-dead wife.

Tears were at his eyes, and he blinked them away.

The torch flickered, sending off smoke. Olgim held it out to him. All it would take was one spark to start the fire below.

And yet...

He ground his hands into fists on the rough, cold stone, gasping for air as the pressure surrounded him.

All at once he realized it was some sort of spell, some sorcery of another kind, and in the knowing he was able to overcome it.

"Dorian, do it." Yander urged him on as he dumped another pot of fat into the hole. "For the sake of Seventh Hall, do your duty."

Dorian took the torch, and held it above the hole, but stopped.

If he let this torch go that would be the end of his dreams. The end of her.

He would never see her again.

Yander met his eyes.

Dorian let go.

29

OUT

Flames licked up and heat washed over him as the fire spread with a fury.

Dorian stumbled back, raising his arms to protect his face, but it was over a few moments later.

Smoke billowed up the holes, and he crouched down, coughing to expel the thick, oily smoke from his mouth and lungs.

It clung to his throat, with a mild taste of beef fat, and he spat it out.

"Is anyone hurt?" Dorian asked. The others answered him, all saying they were fine. "Then to the door."

He unsheathed Webcleaver and ran.

"How will we know what the sign is?" Yutatir whispered. The others hushed him, and Mughan ignored him.

Instead, he watched the entrance to the mine and the surrounding troops. The giant skeleton was taking a break from smashing the mine for some reason, and stood among the waiting skeletons and undead goblins.

Rain poured down, running into the hatch they had hidden among the other rocks in the courtyard.

All they had to do was cross a few feet, grapple the thing and pull it to the ground. Mughan glanced back, counting their numbers again.

He couldn't see how this was going to work in practice, but they had some of the stronger dwarves to help.

Flames leapt from the entrance to the mine, flashing off rusted halberds and swords and running up into the rain.

Mughan smiled. "That's it. We go now." He pushed the hatch up, flinging it behind and letting it clatter. There was so much confusion in the courtyard they wouldn't notice.

Indeed, all the dwarves were out in seconds, spreading out into the formation Mughan had planned before, hooks in hand and ready to deploy.

The skeleton giant milled about, peering into the hole he helped create that was once the door to the mine.

"Aim for the shoulders," Mughan whispered as loud as he dared. Rain ran into his mouth, fresh and clean and cold.

It soaked into his shoulders, running down his neck and into his shirt. Mughan hardly noticed.

"Now!" He swung his roped grapple in a few arcs, then released it. It flew as lightning flashed, along with others.

And it hit the skeleton giant in the head with a crack. Mughan let out a yell of triumph and yanked hard. The rope went taut, then caught a neck bone.

Other hooks caught, and a few failed. "Pull, with all your strength!" They had attracted the attention of the rear skeletons, who by now had realized that something was amiss.

They were near the feet of the giant, who was surprised by the attack. It turned, crushing a goblin beneath giant feet, and tried to face them.

Mughan held on, even as the rope in his hands was yanked from him, burning into his palms. Clenching down he grabbed harder and stopped the rope.

"Pull, pull, pull." Mughan kept up a steady rhythm, not letting the giant's tottering make him falter. Each time the dwarves pulled the giant was put more off balance until it finally seemed to be able to stand no more.

"Now, put your backs into it!" Mughan pulled with all his strength, muscles straining and vision turning red. His planted feet shifted, and he pulled harder.

The giant fell.

Skeletons scattered as it crashed down, whipping the giant tree club in an arc that sent most of them flying into the wall.

Mughan ducked out of the way, narrowly avoiding a leg bone, and drew his sword.

It was still moving, tangled in the ropes. He couldn't let it get up and rushed in, ducking past a skeleton and up to the giant's head.

An undead giant eye made him pull up short, but then without hesitation he plunged his sword into it.

There was resistance, then a sucking sound. Bile spewed out, covering him and making him choke with its stench.

The giant let out a bellow that shook him to the core, pressing against his lungs, and then died.

Mughan, panting in the rain, looked up to find himself surrounded.

"Unlock it," Dorian said. Even through the door and the walls, the sound of crackling flames reached him, licking its chops to devour.

"We're so few," Yander said, tugging at his beard.

"I know. There's only one way to end this, and it won't happen if we lock ourselves away behind a wall." Dorian shifted the grip on his axe, smelling the oil of the steel and the leather of the grip over and above the death that surrounded them.

He took comfort in its weight, checking the hone on the blade. Only a few nicks, otherwise it was sharp.

While Yander and Emelda worked on opening the door, the torchlight flickering, Dorian took and stamped out the fear still residing at the nape of his neck.

Breathing in and out in a steady rhythm, Dorian controlled himself. His vision focused, coming into a tunnel with one thing at the end of it.

"It's ready." Yander stood, both hands on the handle, ready but nervous.

There was no going back now. He steeled himself. "Open it."

Yander pulled, straining against the door that had shifted with the assaults from the giants and undead. It ground and protested, puffs of stone rising, but it went.

Heat flushed at him, the smell of burned bone coming with it, as the door showed him the rest of the entrance tunnel.

Ruined and smoking, flames licked at the edges of the tunnel where the fat still coated the walls in an ever-thinning layer.

Skeletons moved, blackened by the fire, clawing at the ground or trying to advance into the mine.

And at the end of it stood the necromancer, robe singed and burned in places, face covered in burns. His hair was gone, and patches of his head burned red and oozing.

But his eyes found Dorian, and there was nothing but pure hate.

He stretched out one burned hand, pointing to them. "Kill," he said, voice rasping and filled with smoke.

30

CONFRONTATION

"Seventh Hall," Dorian yelled, charging forward. He swept down at a skeleton trying to rise, lopping its head off in a second, barely losing momentum.

The others followed behind him, and Dorian left the bulk of the undead to them, carving a path to the one person who controlled them.

He raised the undead, tearing them from whatever awaited in the afterlife. There would be no peace for them.

Splitting another skull with his axe, Dorian realized the horror that would have awaited Yolanda, and nearly wept.

A goblin stood in front of him, almost all bone, mouth agape and jaw hanging by one side. There was no life in its eyes, the burned and scarred face held no hint of anything but evil.

That was what he was going to do to his wife.

Bile rose in his throat, bitter to accompany the vision of seeing her rise from the dead, not as she once was, but a horror like these very undead he now fought.

The goblin parried his first attack, reaching out with a bony hand to try and hold him, but he shoved it away and brought an elbow to its face.

It didn't seem affected, and swung its sword up and into his torso, ringing against his armor and sparking.

"To your left," Yander said. Dorian turned and ducked as a skeleton swung a rusty sword where he had once been. He dispatched it with an overhead chop and felt a lancing pain in his right leg.

The goblin withdrew its sword, bringing it up for a killing blow to Dorian's head.

Bellowing in anger and pain, which disappeared in the blood lust of the fight, Dorian swept off its head with a mighty chop.

The necromancer strode to him, eyes blazing. "You take from me the one I need the most. I will have your head as an example." He drew a blade, which whispered from the scabbard.

It seemed to pull in the light. Behind him the rain pounded outside, and more sounds of fighting came with it.

"You shall have my steel to eat," Dorian said, fighting off the exhaustion of the night, and blocking the attack of another skeleton to his right.

But then the necromancer was upon him. His sword flashed and whispered, enchanted by some dark magic. But the necromancer's attacks were clumsy and stilted.

Dorian should have been able to fight back easily, but the necromancer fought with rage and power that overwhelmed him, forcing him back into the entrance tunnel.

"Die you filth," the necromancer said. His blows sent shivers into Dorian's arms, and some found their mark.

Step by step, Dorian yielded ground. The necromancer advanced, then held back, sending his undead to fight for him.

All the while looking on with hatred and rage in his eyes.

This is it. This is how I die. Dorian's parries were getting sluggish, and he no longer had the strength left to attack.

All his concentration went into keeping alive, but there were too many. One after another the undead came, and when he had blocked one or avoided another, it seemed like the necromancer was there, adding another cut beneath the protection of his armor.

Without it he would have been dead long ago, but it absorbed the bulk of the attacks.

It was all Dorian could do to keep his vital areas protected.

"For Seventh Hall!" That was Yander, from somewhere behind him. Had the others fallen back too? Another skeleton forced him to abandon that thought, and he felt his left hand take another blow.

"Seventh Hall!" Confused, Dorian took a feeble swipe at the goblin in front of him. Didn't that come from ahead of him?

And then Yander was at his side. The dwarf fought like a hero of old, sweeping back the undead from around him.

Dorian gathered his wits, and his strength. Skeleton attacked, and Yander slew. One after the other, he pressed forward.

"Get up, Dorian." Emelda was at his side. He was kneeling. Her eyes shined. "You promised to protect him."

No, that couldn't be why he was doing it. Dorian looked back to the dwarf. He had engaged the necromancer, trading blow for blow. He had the advantage in terms of strength and skill, but the necromancer was weaving some form of magic and had pure anger and fury on his side.

Emelda helped him to his feet, then waded up with her spear flashing.

That they would leave him behind, where he should be ahead, infuriated him. What good was he back here?

Anger flooded back into him, and a desire deeper than his desire to live, deeper than his desire to see his wife again.

He knew that there would be a time, there would be a day he would see her in the afterlife.

But not Yander. He couldn't let him die.

His focus changed to the necromancer. A dozen emotions flashed through him, pity, anger, envy, jealousy, hatred, fear.

And then he saw something he never expected. Mughan was wading through the undead at the other end of the tunnel, laughing and stabbing with Barileth and the others at his side.

"Seventh Hall." The words bubbled up from inside him, just a small whisper. He let them flow through him, the love and desire to protect them refreshing him and returning the strength that was taken from him.

The spell of the necromancer lifted like a weight. Yander was lagging with his fight, overcome by the magic like he had.

"Seventh Hall!" Dorian bellowed and charged forward, rushing to protect Yander as the necromancer's foul blade came down.

He brought Webcleaver to bear, slamming upward.

The necromancer's blade rang back, and he stumbled, eyes widened in surprise.

Dorian spit blood from his mouth and wiped his beard. "Death is final in this place."

Then Dorian attacked. The necromancer parried, then tried to fall back, but it was too late.

His power was gone, no longer holding Dorian.

One more swing sent his blade spinning out of his hands, another took off the arm raised to protect himself.

Then Dorian raised Webcleaver.

"No," the necromancer said, fury in his eyes and hatred in his voice. "I can teach you!"

The axe came down, whistling, and ended the necromancer's life.

31

MOURNING

Dorian watched his only hope of ever seeing his wife again drain away. Darkness enveloped him, so deep he couldn't even see his own hands.

Ice covered him, his life draining away, but he resisted.

Then, it was over. Light crept back into the world, heat into his limbs. Webcleaver was scorched, but gleamed in the light of the night.

Dorian realized the noise of rain was gone, as was the rain itself.

Around him, skeletons toppled and clacked. Drained of the power of the necromancer, they returned to the dead.

Great sorrow filled him, and he fell to his knees beside the dead necromancer.

"It's over." His throat choked, filled with thick, foul-tasting smoke and dust, but that wasn't what made him stop.

Blood was leaking down his leg, the old wound joined with a new one. All at once his muscles gave out, his legs shaking and his arms falling open, letting Webcleaver fall.

And Dorian wept.

He let her go. Let her fall away. Let her die.

She would never come back to him, in this life. He would never see his wife again.

A hand on his shoulder, gentle.

Dorian looked up. Yander smiled, tears in his eyes also. The other dwarves surrounded him, beaten, wounded, bleeding, but alive.

They were alive.

I'm alive.

My children are alive.

"You know who I am now. He spoke the truth," Dorian said. "In my grief, I too touched the dark power."

"You aren't him," Yander said.

"I wanted his power."

"And yet, here you are," Mughan said. "Victor and the one who survived. You didn't fall for his lies."

There was a hole in his heart, one that would always be empty. But now he knew the extent of it. He was at peace with it.

"Look at me, blubbering like a baby." Dorian wiped the tears from his face. "You must think me weak."

Emelda leaned down and smiled at him. "Let's get you taken care of. No dwarf thinks less of you."

Murmurs of agreement ran through them.

He looked out the door, ruined and shattered. Stars twinkled in the sky through the lessening clouds, wispy and layered.

His children might be looking on those stars tonight. Dorian stood, legs still shaking, and let himself be lead deeper into the mine.

Wetness dripped down his leg. His vision blurred, and everything went a little hazy. Tripping, he was caught by hands that lifted him, pulling his arms over their shoulder.

The world went dark, and Dorian slept.

He awoke and groaned, all the scars of the battle bearing down on him in force. His head throbbed with a lancing pain between his eyes, but his shoulder and leg were far worse.

He tested his toes, wiggling them in the cool air of the mine. They swirled the air, testing it.

It tasted fresh, but underneath it was a thin layer of blood and something else.

Death.

He was in the hospital room, now filled with other dwarves.

"Welcome back to the land of the living." Barileth grinned at him under a heavy bandage on his head and over his left eye.

"How long?"

"Not more than a day, by my reckoning. Said your leg almost drained you, if Yudoline hadn't gotten there in time." Barileth laced his fingers behind his head and leaned back, closing his eye. "Figured you were too hard to die from a little wound like that though, and I was right."

Dorian swung his legs over the side of the bed, and Barileth's eye popped open. "What do you think you're doing?"

Dorian paused at the edge of the bed, letting his head regain its blood and willing the tiny spindles of light creeping in from the sides of his vision back to where they came.

"Where do you think I'm going?" He tested his legs, and they held his weight.

"Bring me something back to eat," Barileth yelled after him, chuckling as he left.

Using the rough walls of the tunnel to help him, Dorian scraped and crept along the corridor.

He had to stop every so often to catch his breath, but then he made it. The other dwarves sprang to their feet as he walked into the dining hall.

"Where are they?" Dorian leaned on the edge of the door, glad of its support.

"You get back in bed this instant!" Yudoline wielded a spoon in his direction, still dripping with the soup or whatever liquid it was she had just used it for.

The aroma of the food enticed him, but he had something else to do first.

"I'll take him," Yander said. They didn't look good, covered in bandages and wraps, but there were more of them than he expected.

But there were less than he hoped.

He leaned on Yander the rest of the way down to the mine until they got to the temporary holding chamber.

There they were, under sheets out of respect.

"So many," Dorian said.

"Could be worse. It would have been, if we weren't ready."

He counted them. Five. Five dead. Against an army of the undead that would have been good to most, but not him.

"I'll leave you to say goodbye." Yander let him go. "Call me when you're finished."

Dorian sat among the dead for a long while, remembering. He said no words. It didn't feel right.

Then, one by one he revealed them and said goodbye.

Too many. Far too many.

In the midst of the granite, Dorian mourned.

Epilogue

Bars shone in the candlelight, reflecting the orange and yellow flame and casting it into a hundred shimmering facets.

Tufolin scrutinized one, turning it over in his hands with a keen eye.

"Pure as some of the best I've seen." He smiled and looked up. "Your smelter has done well."

"Well enough," Dorian said. A storm was coming, a spring rain that blew up sometimes in the afternoons as the clouds went up and over the Tremble Mountains.

The counting started, then finished. Tufolin shook his head. "I don't know how you did it. You must have found a thick vein of gold."

"Biggest I've seen. Whoever let the king know about this place should be rewarded."

"And all this in a few months?" He eyed the other boxes of steel bars, dozens of them.

"We delved deep, like you said." Dorian wore a smirk.

"You certainly did." Tufolin shuffled his papers. "Take me down to the cavern you mentioned."

He was secure in his knowledge that they had met the terms laid forth in the contracts, consensual for the others and forced for himself.

With small talk to keep him company, they descended through the mine, through the door and the tunnel, and down the well-worn path along the edge of the cavern.

"You can see it there." Dorian pointed to the glowing light, and the shifting forms that walked among them. Dots were blacked out every few feet, canopies of the great mushrooms.

"Any more signs of them?" Tufolin peered out into the cavern, surveying the view. Dorian could almost see him doing the calculations in his mind.

"None yet. Or of the other kind." Dorian led him to the slope, and down into the outpost. Vadgrala was there, watering the cows, and Dorian greeted him, introducing him to Tufolin.

They went over the makeshift ranch and farms, stretching far out into the land reclaimed by the dwarves.

"As you see, plenty of land to support more than a contingent of dwarves." Dorian rested his hand against the Oakshroomwood fence, slick with moisture from the breath of the cows.

"You've done well, all things considered." Dorian marveled at the compliment, knowing that Tufolin didn't give them out lightly.

"So will the king honor his word?"

"The King will honor his word," Tufolin said with a small bow.

Zirad loomed on the horizon, a great city that shimmered with the heat wave of early spring.

They were still a way off, but Dorian was too nervous to think about it.

How many years had it been?

What would they say?

He breathed out, then in. Waves of smells flowed over him, the rich aroma of the flowers undergirded by the thinner smell of the meadow grass. There was smoke in the air, even as far as here, from the monstrous smelters that spewed great plumes of it that he saw miles away from the city.

"Relax, Dorian." Tufolin walked beside him, ahead of the rest of the convoy of merchants. The fortune they had discovered was attached to the oxen, weighed down by the gold and steel.

"I can't," Dorian growled, tucking his chin down and peering out from beneath his hat.

"Your son and daughter are safe, waiting for you." Tufolin's gait was steady, like the dwarf.

Dorian didn't answer, and made the rest of the journey in silence. His stomach twisted in knots.

Only when they crossed the great Iron Gate did he think of it. "I'd like to see my wife first."

Tufolin shot him a troubled look. "I don't think that would be a good idea."

"I don't care what you think about it." Dorian returned his look with a steely gaze.

"That can be arranged," he said, at last, with a sigh.

They went through the city, and Dorian couldn't help but be overwhelmed by the sheer numbers of dwarves.

They were everywhere, selling wares, working, hauling, marching.

The crowd thinned as they went until they were near the palace. After stopping and separating from the goods, which were bound elsewhere, Tufolin disappeared.

He returned later, after an uncomfortable wait beneath the shadow of the palace, and led him down a side alley.

Through twists and turns, down into the belly of Zirad, Tufolin led him to his wife's final resting place.

A calm came over him when Tufolin turned. "We're here." The catacombs were still and quiet, a hush for the dead. Tufolin's words were quickly swallowed up by the thick layer of dust around them. "Through there."

Dorian went into the room, heart pounding. The air was stale and tasteless.

Rows of tombs ran down both sides of the room. He read the inscriptions, of those he could.

They were ordinary dwarves. No kings or princes here in this place. Somehow, that comforted him.

His heart caught as he read her name. Dorian closed his eyes and put his hand on the inscription, tracing the rough indentions.

He was there for a while, he didn't know how long, kneeling beside his wife.

His knees complained when he rose again. She would stay here until the end of time he supposed.

After one, final, ragged breath, Dorian turned, ready to see his children and join the land of the living once again.

"No use denying it." Barileth swung his pack on. "Life's gotten boring around here. Too much so for me." He grinned. "Besides, how am I going to spend all this money around here?"

"We'll be sorry to see you leave," Mughan said. Then, after a pause, "But not too sorry."

With a sharp bark, Barileth continued his goodbyes, finally arriving at the Helmsplitters. He clasped Yander's hand, gave Emelda a firm hug, then put a hand on both their shoulders.

"Keep this colony going, no matter what Mughan says."

"We'll do our best," Yander said. The boy was firmer now than he had been, but had lost that haunted look in his eyes. Barileth was glad for it.

He turned to the open entrance door, and the long road ahead. "Barileth." He turned. "If you see him..." Yander choked up.

"I'll tell him." With a half smile, Barileth left the colony, knowing it would prosper. The last wave of migrants had seen to that.

Pausing at the gate, he looked out over the valley. The apple trees had put out their flowers, great fat, pink bursts among the greens of the forest top. Bees arced their lazy paths around him, drunk on pollen and fat on honey. A gentle spring wind caressed his face, and the high sun soaked into his body.

Barileth cinched up his pack, strode out into the world, and started his journey without a care in the world, a whistle on his lips and a spring in his step.

Eclectic Stories

Thank you for spending your precious time reading this book.

If stories make you salivate, learn more about lore, take an exclusive sneak peek behind the scenes, and get writing updates in my newsletter, Eric's Eclectic Stories.

As a bonus you'll get *Stories from the Deep*, a Patmos Sea Fantasy Adventure anthology that gives a glimpses of lore, extra prologues and epilogues, and character backstories.

If you aren't satisfied, unsubscribe at any time.

Join at erickercher.com.

-Eric Kercher

Also By Eric Kercher

Patmos Sea Fantasy Adventure Series

*Fathomless Pursuit - Architect's Prize - Ironbound Path
Sunken Prey – Unanswered Prophecy – Hardened Pilgrim – Final
Peace*

Seventh Hall Chronicles

Seventh Hall - Ode to the Survivors - Bastion of the Deep

Epic of Hornblood Castle

*Siege of the Unfinished Keep – Winter at Hornblood – Branch of the
Everlong*

Castlebound Adventures

Rats in the Cellar!- Save the Cat!

Collections

ERIC KERCHER

Red Eagle Anthology – Searchlight Anthology

Stand Alone

Planet Reaping – Dukedom Rumble – Savage Space Salvage

About Author

Eric Kercher was born and raised in a small town on the Great Plains on good books. After attending a small state school on the east coast he joined the US Navy to serve his country and explore the world. He worked on submarines, and the world beneath the waves captivated him with all its mysteries and wonders. After spending time in larger cities, he's settled down in a quiet town with his wife and children. When not on an adventure in a good book the author enjoys creating dust woodworking, architecture, and spending time with loved ones.

Find out more at www.erickercher.com.